CW01304599

SURVIVING THE FALL

Book 1 of The Fall Series

Stephen Cross

Surviving The Fall

Copyright © 2016 by Stephen Cross

All rights reserved. No part of this publication may be reproduced, distributed, or transmitted in any form or by any means, including photocopying, recording, or other electronic or mechanical methods, without the prior written permission of the publisher, except in the case of brief quotations embodied in critical reviews and certain other noncommercial uses permitted by copyright law.

Cover image attribution: Kiselev Andrey Valerevich / Shutterstock.com

Also by Stephen Cross

SURVIVING THE FALL
Book 1 of The Fall Series

STEPHEN CROSS

AFTER THE FALL

The world belongs to the dead

Surviving The Fall

Also by Stephen Cross

THE FENCE WALKER
Book 3 of The Fall Series

Stephen Cross

Also by Stephen Cross

DARK ISLAND

Surviving The Fall

Table of Contents

Holiday Apocalypse 10

The Inn at the End of the World 54

Zone Lima Delta 98

The Dead Lands 156

Train to Hell.. 220

Tower Block of the Dead... 286

Plane Dead 362

The Facility 430

Holiday Apocalypse

Chapter 1

Saturday 20th May, early evening, Cornwall

Jimmy sighed and glanced in the rearview mirror to the back of the minibus. The old cow was still moaning about her 'bite'.

"Alright, Violet, alright, we'll be back soon enough, and nurse can sort you out." He turned off the A-road onto a country lane. It was six in the evening, it would be another thirty minutes until they got back to the rest home, and then another half hour until he could sign off. He couldn't wait, what a bloody day.

Stan leaned forward, "Really, Jimmy, you should have called the police and an ambulance. Violet needs immediate medical assistance. I'll be sure to report you."

There were mumbles of agreement from the rest of the van's occupants. Jimmy rolled his eyes. Calling the police would have been a nightmare; an hour waiting for them, more time making a statement, another few hours in the hospital. He would have been stuck there until midnight, and there goes his date with Britney.

"I have a headache," he heard Violet moan from the back of the van.

"She has a headache!" parroted the rest of the olds.

Jimmy dug around in the glovebox and pulled out some ibuprofen.

"Here you go," he passed the tablets to Stan. "Get her to take two of these."

Stan looked at the tablets. "She can't take these! Not with her other medicine. We need to get her to a hospital."

Jimmy shook his head, "We're closer to the care home now than we are to any hospital." He glanced at Violet again. She was sweating and pale. Clammy like a fish. Maybe that old drunk who bit her had some sort of disease. Jimmy started driving faster, just in case. Best to get back to the care home sooner rather than later. Keep himself out of trouble.

What sort of a nutter bites people anyway? The trip had gone smoothly right up to the end of the day. Lovely afternoon in Newquay, the old buggers walking by the sea with their ice creams, then as they were about to set out home, some loon - a horrible tramp who appeared from nowhere - attacked Violet, just as they were getting in the minibus.

Jimmy was quick, he was pleased with that. Kickboxing was paying off. Jimmy had punched the tramp hard, and he had gone down like a sack of shit. The tramp had got straight up again though, to give him his dues. Luckily, by then, all the other olds had got Violet and themselves in the minibus, shit-scared the lot of them. So Jimmy knocked the tramp down again and got in the van himself. Not worth fighting drunks, they kept going until you knocked them out, and then you're in danger of the pigs doing you for assault! Crazy world alright.

Jimmy thought that would be the end of it until Violet started moaning about the bite. On her neck, apparently. Just a nick, but enough for her to make a fuss all the way home. They loved a fuss.

"Jimmy!" shouted Stan, "She's passed out!"

"What?" He looked in the mirror. Her head lolled to the left.

Stan leaned forward, "You silly young fool, I told you she needed medical assistance, she must have a dangerous infection!"

"Look, just shut it and look after her, we'll be there in twenty minutes."

Jimmy drove faster, ignoring the shouts and moans aimed at him. He was for it now, there'd be all sorts of inquiries. Might even lose his job.

He raced the van through the narrow Cornish lanes, taking chances on the blind bends. The olds started shouting about his driving. Couldn't bloody win, could he?

There was a scream from behind him. "I've had enough of this," he said to himself before shouting, "What's going on now?"

More screams, louder, and a strange moaning sound. Stan was trying to crawl into the front seat, "Stop! Let me out, let me out!"

"What the bloody hell are you doing?" shouted Jimmy. "Get back!" He pushed Stan's face, but the old bugger kept coming. Jimmy gave up and let Stan fall headfirst into the front seat.

Jimmy took a turn too fast and nearly ended up hitting a wall. He righted himself and put his foot on the accelerator. Satisfied he was going in a straight line, he turned to see the source of all the chaos from behind, and his face was immediately sprayed with blood.

Violet clamped her teeth down on Deborah's cheek and ripped the flesh off in one thick slab, all the way down to her shoulder. Blood spurted across the roof of the van as Deborah screamed, the bones and muscle of her jaw visible, the flesh under her eye socket flapping as she tried to pull herself away from Violet.

"Fucking hell!" shouted Jimmy. Transfixed on the scene of horror unfolding in the back of the van, he let go of the steering wheel.

The van swerved and hit a telegraph pole. Jimmy sprung forward, and his head hit the steering wheel. He blacked out immediately, which was just as well...

Chapter 2

Monday 15th May - Leeds

Jack sat at his desk and switched on his computer. The familiar hum broke the silence of the empty office. He was always first in, and last to leave. He cursed to himself as he tidied a pile of papers that had been untidied by the cleaners. They were paid to clean, not touch people's stuff.

For half an hour, Jack worked in silence preparing for the day, organising his tasks. Meetings, and a few hours to work on the council budget.

Lights across the office hummed into life as his colleagues arrived. Conversation sprung up around the different cubicles. Phones began to ring. Printers started to chug into life. Jack's peace over.

Stewart, all smiles and shining brown brogues, approached Jack's desk. He perched himself on its edge, moving Jack's pen to make space for himself. Jack eyed the pen.

"Hey Jack, how you doing?"

"Good, thanks." Jack looked up only long enough to make brief eye contact, then returned to browsing the day's news on his monitor.

"I've just been in a meeting with Peter. He said he asked you to redo your report using my new spreadsheet."

Jack nodded, although not really listening. An article about Brazil caught his eye.

"Hey look, sorry about that," continued Stewart. "Must be a pain to have to redo your report?"

Jack moved closer to the screen, focusing on the article. "What?" Jack glanced at Stewart. "Yeah, don't worry about it. It won't take me long."

"You sure you don't mind? I can have another word with Peter if you like?"

Jack stared at the screen, his body tightening in anger. The news from Brazil was bad. He remembered Stewart and smiled, "Look, really it's ok. Honestly. I don't mind."

Stewart nodded, "Knew you'd be cool with it. Cheers pal." Stewart jumped off the desk and made to walk away, then paused. "Oh, by the way, you're going on holiday next week aren't you, to Brazil? You should check out the news. Some weird shit going on down there." He walked away.

Jack called his wife.

"Amy, have you seen what those bloody idiots are doing in Brazil? They've closed the airports!"

"What?"

"Something's going on, riots or something. Our insurance had better cover us for this…"

Jack realised his voice was rising above the standard office din and drawing attention. He walked quickly to the corridor.

"I've been looking forward to this holiday for six bloody months, it's the only thing that's kept me going."

"You said riots, Jack?"

"Riots, so-called terrorist threat. Usual bollocks."

"It may be over by next week," said Amy. "Why don't you contact the airline? I'll phone the hotel and see what we can find out."

Jack let out a slow breath. "Ok. Good idea". He looked out over the gray and miserable skyline of Leeds. Heavy clouds sat motionless above the city, dripping slow rain onto the roads and people.

"And Jack…"

"Yes, I know. I'll be calm."

Reuters Special Report 15/05/2016

Brasilia, Rio De Janeiro, Sau Paulo and Curitiba are among many Brazilian cities to have closed their airports under order of the Brazilian government.

A Whitehouse leak claims Washington is about to call for an all-ports closure of not just Brazil, but many surrounding countries, including Bolivia, Paraguay, Columbia, and Venezuela.

The nature of the crisis is still uncertain, and restrictions put in place by the military are making it difficult for the press to collate information further than that provided by government agencies. Reporters are under strict military curfews, currently not allowed to leave hotels. We have obtained the following from our reporter, Sam Thomas, in Rio De Janeiro.

"The view from my balcony is like something from a horror movie. The city is on fire. Gunshots and screams are the soundtrack. Violent clashes between protesters, the police, and the military have escalated to unprecedented levels throughout the night.

"It is unclear when the riots began, and even what the rioters are protesting. I have interviewed a chef in my hotel, who started his shift just before we were interned. He told me the violence started late last night in one of Rio's largest favelas.

"To add to further speculation and fear is an apparent internet shut down. People are unable to access Twitter, Facebook, and

many other social network and news sites. I have had to file this report using my satellite phone on the balcony, as the hotel internet connection is inaccessible.

"It seems the Brazilian government is very keen to stop the world from finding out exactly what has happened."

Jack sat in the office canteen waiting to speak to the airline, his phone held to his ear.

He took a sip of his coffee. The canteen was dotted with the same people sat in the same chairs, talking about the same things to the same people. He shook his head and looked to the ceiling where the strip lights beamed.

He listened to the on-hold music for five minutes before there was finally an answer.

"I've read that all flights into Brazil have been canceled?" said Jack. "Can you tell me what's happening?"

"That's correct, Mr. Barnes, we have been told there is a government decree closing all travel into and out of Brazil, passed early this morning."

"Ok, why is that?"

"Erm…" There was a pause. "We have been told this is due to civil unrest. We don't have any further information at the moment. I'm very sorry, Mr. Barnes."

"So what about our flight next week? We're due to fly to Sao Paulo on Tuesday."

"We have no news on any flights for next week, Mr. Barnes."

"Great, so I just have to sit and wait?"

"I'm sorry, but there's nothing more I can tell you."

Jack hung up the call. He sighed and sat back in his chair, staring at his coffee. The one thing he had been looking forward to all year. The break he needed. The break from this place. Gone.

Chapter 3

Tuesday 16th May, Leeds

The mood at home was somber.

"It says here," said Amy looking up from her laptop, "that thousands are dead already. What do you think has happened?"

Jack shook his head. "I don't think anyone knows what's going on. I'm reading here some nonsense about people eating people. It's ridiculous."

"People eating people?" said Amy. "Why would you do that in a riot?"

Jack rolled his eyes. "That's what I mean. It sounds like no one knows what's going on. Annie," said Jack to his six-year-old daughter who was climbing over the couch, "can't you go and play in the dining room?"

"No! I want to play here. What's a riot?"

Jack ignored her and continued to scan the internet.

"Come over here, darling, your Daddy's busy," said Amy.

Annie reluctantly sat next to Amy on the other couch.

"Hang on… Here's a video on the BBC." Jack followed the link.

'Steven, how are things in Sao Paulo now?'

'Well Sue, this is a city in a state of absolute panic. Buildings and cars are on fire, people are in the streets in force; some in groups, some alone, some trying to escape, and others looting freely.

'The Military and police are trying to keep control, but it seems even their numbers are dwindling as the rumours of a terrifying virus are starting to spread. Whether or not these rumours are true is hard to tell as there is no official response from anyone in authority, other than to stay indoors.'

'Can you tell us more about these virus rumours, Steven?'

'Well, I spoke to a man earlier who said he was trying to leave the city with his family. He told me he had seen some of his neighbours covered in blood, that some of their skin and flesh was actually hanging off, and these neighbours were trying to eat people.

'I also managed to speak to a fireman, who told me that his crew was deserting. He said he had seen people covered in blood eating each other. The fireman called it 'Devil's work.'

'These reports are only rumoured, Steven, we must emphasise that?'

'Yes, as I have said, there has been no official response, and we are dealing with gossip and hearsay at the moment. However, the actions of the government have done nothing to quell these rumours. All air and seaports have been closed, and it appears that the military is controlling all roads into and out of the city.'

'Thank you, Steven, for that report. That was Steven Blacksmith, our reporter in Sao Paulo.

'To recap, there is no official stance from the Brazilian government on the riots occurring across the country. These riots have now spread to neighbouring South American states. News

blackouts seem to be trying to contain what is happening, but information is leaking out through remaining internet channels and through exclusive reports such as ours.'

"Wow," said Amy.

"What's a virus?" said Annie.

"It's like a cold," said Jack.

"That sounds pretty bad?" Amy said. "I don't think I want to go anymore, even if we could."

"If that's what's actually happening, of course."

"What, you think they might be lying? Why would they do that?"

"I don't know. This news blackout though…" Jack stood up abruptly. "Anyway, it looks like our bloody holiday is off, no matter what's going on."

"Jack…"

Without saying anything, Jack left the room.

He made his way upstairs to his music room. A small box room with a chair, his hundreds of records stacked up on shelves across one of the walls, their many colours and textures taking on the appearance of abstract art. His immaculate Gibson SG guitar and Marshall stack sat in the corner of the room. Next to his chair sat an expensive record player.

He moved his finger along the spines of the records, looking for Led Zepplin IV. He took it out and carefully removed the vinyl from its sleeve. Being careful to hold it only on the edges he blew across its surface and, with precise movements, placed the record on the turntable.

He turned on the amp and sat in the chair, guitar resting on his round belly. With a practiced motion he dropped the stylus onto the record and quickly repositioned himself, so as soon as the music started, he was able to hit the matching notes on this guitar.

Jack closed his eyes and played along, note for note.

As he did for the next song and the one after that.

When the first side of the album finished, he sat in silence and looked at the framed picture on the wall, from a newspaper cutting taken fifteen years ago. A local newspaper had written a glowing review on one of his band's gigs, noting that the lead guitarist played with a natural verve and ferocity that 'guaranteed' he would soon be moving on from small local venues, that the 'bright lights' beckoned.

The door opened, it was Annie.

"Annie, what did Mummy tell you, you don't come into the music room."

"But Daddy, I have nothing to play with."

Jack rested his head against the back of his chair. "Ok," he said. "Let's go to your room. We can play there. You might break something in here."

Annie smiled.

Chapter 4

Wednesday 17th May, Leeds

Jack had no enthusiasm for the day. He wanted out of the office, to go to sleep and forget all about Brazil. Having resigned himself to the holiday being canceled, he had heard enough about Brazil and its bloody virus.

"Hey Jack, how are you?", Stewart appeared and took his normal place on the edge of Jack's desk, this time on top of one of Jack's reports. "Pretty bad news about Brazil, eh?"

Jack nodded.

"Look, bad break about your holiday. You need a bloody holiday from this place, who doesn't?"

Jack smiled and glanced at Stewart again, "Six months we've had it booked."

"Sure, but listen," he repositioned himself closer to Jack. "I was talking with my girlfriend last night, and the thing is, we have a holiday chalet in Tulloch Bay, down in Cornwall. Beautiful, mate, absolutely beautiful place. It's no Brazil, but..."

Jack turned from his screen to give Stewart his full attention.

"The thing is, it's empty for the next few weeks. We usually hire it out, but we've had to redecorate, pipes were leaking. So the bathroom isn't pretty, but everything works. You and the family will love it! What do you think?"

"Really?"

"Sure. It's perfect for your little girl. There's a pool, you're right by the beach. It's all gated, so safe for her to run around. As I say, it's no Brazil, but..."

Jack couldn't help but smile. This sounded like a break. "Stewart, that sounds great. Just great. Only thought is, how much will it cost? With Brazil and everything we're a bit light on the cash front."

Stewart held up his hands, "Jack! Don't worry about it, seriously." He shook his head at Jack's protestations. "It's on the house, I won't have it any other way. You guys will love it."

Jack stood up and shook Stewart's hand. "Thanks. Really, you don't know what this means. What, with everything happening, it felt like, well, things weren't great. Thanks so much, Stewart, I owe you."

Stewart laughed. "No worries, as I said, it's not a problem. I'll get you the keys tomorrow. Here's the website," Stewart scribbled a URL on a piece of paper. "Check it out, show your wife."

"Thanks again, Stewart. You're a... You're a good mate."

Chapter 5

Friday 19th May, Leeds

Amy pulled the latest load from the washing machine. Now they were leaving for holiday tomorrow, she only had today to get everything finished. She hung the wet clothes on radiators; hopefully, they would be dry by tomorrow. The dryer had broken five months ago, and they hadn't got it fixed - they had needed money for Brazil.

Jack's clothes would mostly be in the basket, apart from his hoodies - they would be in the music room. She opened the door and entered carefully. She stepped over a guitar lead and reached for the two hoodies that sat on his seat.

She paused and looked at the newspaper cutting on the wall. She had always liked the way Jack looked in that picture. He was slim with long hair, and his eyes had a look she hadn't seen for a long time; belief in himself.

She packed the hoodies into the wash basket and moved into the bedroom. She needed to find the beach towels. Although only May, the weather was promising to be kind next week, and she was looking forward to some beach time with Annie.

She reached in behind the back of the wardrobe, behind her many dresses and pulled out the beach towels. A light blue piece of clothing from between the linen fell to the floor.

It was her old nurse's uniform. She'd only worn it for a week before resigning to go on tour with Jack.

She stared at the uniform for a moment.

I really must throw it out, she thought.

But not today.

She picked it up and tucked it in the corner of the wardrobe.

Amy continued with the housework. She finished with twenty minutes to spare before having to pick Annie up from school. She sat down for a rest in the lounge and turned on the television.

The news was on. Amy quickly fumbled with the remote to pick another channel, but still heard, "…UK government have joined several other European countries and the US to close their borders as of immediate effect…"

Jack sat in the office with his headphones on, watching the latest from the BBC.

'The Prime Minister has assured the nation that the UK is well protected from the virus, with our island status offering an excellent natural defence. He reminded us that no case of the as-yet-unidentified pathogen has been recorded in the UK.

'The opposition has criticised what many see as a draconian response from the government, which has seen ships turned away from many of the UK's ports, planes being denied permission to land, and even a channel tunnel train being stopped from entering the British terminal. Others have commended the Prime Minister for his decisive and brave action.'

Jack rubbed his temples. He hoped that Amy wasn't watching any of this, she was worried enough as it was. The sooner they got off on holiday, the better. They could just ride it all out in Cornwall, relax for a few weeks and then get back home just in time for everything returning to normal.

He tried again to log onto the Brazilian forum that had been releasing news about the outbreak, but it was still dead. Even some American sites were starting to drop. The United States had their first case two days ago.

He looked at his watch, three hours until home time.

Annie listened carefully as Daddy read to her. She lay in bed with her favourite Teddy, Mr. Fred, and she pulled him tight as Daddy got to the exciting bit of the story. She had heard this one many times, and it was her favourite, especially the part when the giant climbed down the beanstalk after Jack, and she knew that Daddy's other name was Jack, and she liked to think that this story was about Daddy.

Daddy was in a good mood. She liked Daddy better when he was happy. It made her happy too.

He finished the story and put down the book. He smiled at Annie and grabbed the covers, "Here comes the snuggle monster!" He leaned in wrapping the sheets tightly around Annie as he gave her a big hug, making the snuggle monster noises. Annie laughed with delight.

Daddy said, "You don't look very tired young girl? Do you not feel tired?"

Annie shook her head. She had a funny feeling in her tummy and couldn't stop thinking about two things - one was the holiday, which made her feel good, and the other was what Thomas had said at school today, which made her feel bad.

"Daddy?"

"What is it?"

"When we go on holiday, is there monsters?"

Daddy didn't look happy anymore, and Annie wondered if she had said something bad.

"What do you mean, monsters?"

Annie took a deep breath, "Thomas at school today said that his Daddy said they need to go away because the zommies were coming and everyone was going to die, and I asked what zommies are and Thomas said they're monsters that eat people and they have come from Brassil. Are the monsters going to be where our holiday is?"

Daddy didn't say anything for a moment, and Annie was sure she had said something wrong.

"Sorry, Daddy."

"What are you sorry for? Sweetie, you don't have to be sorry about anything." Daddy leaned in and gave her a nice big hug. Daddy felt like the biggest thing in the world when he hugged her.

"I'm scared of the monsters…"

Daddy smiled and said, "Listen, ok, this Thomas, I've heard you talk about him before, and you've said he's a silly boy. Is he a silly boy?"

Annie thought for a moment. Yes, he was silly. She nodded.

"Silly boys say silly things. Things that aren't true. They like to say them because it makes everyone listen to them. There are no monsters."

"Really? But the TV man also said that the infective was coming in the country."

"You mean infected, and you don't have to worry, Annie, that just means some people are sick. We aren't going to see any of the sick people, and there are no monsters."

Annie thought about this for a moment. Daddy was usually right about most things. "So you mean there are no monsters? I don't have to be scared?"

Daddy smiled and held her hand tight, "No darling, you don't have to be scared. Even if there were monsters, do you think I'd let any of them hurt you?"

Annie knew he wouldn't. Even when he had a sad face, he was always nice to her. "No, you wouldn't let them." She smiled, feeling better.

"I'll never let anything hurt you, Annie, I'll always be here to protect you, ok? You remember that. Daddy will always be here to protect you because I love you more than anything in the world. Ok?"

Annie felt the bad stuff leaving her stomach. She knew that Daddy would look after her, and wouldn't let anyone hurt her, even if they were monsters or the infective.

She could go to sleep now and look forward to the holiday. She hugged Mr. Fred tight and kissed Daddy as he leaned in to say goodnight.

He would be happy tomorrow - Mummy and Daddy were always happy on the holiday days.

Chapter 6

Saturday 20th May, morning, Leeds to Cornwall

The next morning, the sun was shining. The blanket clouds that had poured so much rain for the past week were nowhere to be seen. Maybe things were turning around, thought Jack. Some beautiful weather, some time by the beach. He picked up his acoustic guitar and carried it downstairs to add to the pile for the car.

"Jack," called Amy from the lounge.

"Coming," he dodged past Annie, ruffling her hair as she ran passed him upstairs.

"Getting Mr. Fred!" shouted Annie.

Amy was sitting in the lounge, the news on. He frowned. Although not explicitly mentioned, there had been a somewhat unspoken news embargo in the house for the past few days. Why break it today?

"Have you seen this?" said Amy. Her skin was pale, and her voice meek.

Jack looked at the TV - images of military vehicles driving through towns and along the motorways. Empty airport lounges and grounded planes.

Amy said, "They say we should stay in our homes."

Jack motioned for Amy to be quiet, "Let me listen."

"Cases of infected have appeared overnight in London, with reports of fighting, riots, and panic. The military has been called in, as emergency services struggle to cope with the tens of thousands of people trying to leave the capital. The Prime Minister has called for calm, asking people to stay in their homes until further notice. No travel, unless an absolute emergency, should be undertaken until this crisis is resolved."

Jack shook his head slowly. This is what happens when no-one tells anyone what's happening. Panic, he thought. Panic and violence, all because the government doesn't trust the people with the truth.

Amy stared at him. "Well?" she said.

"What do you mean?"

"I guess we stay here?"

"No," said Jack immediately. "We are going on this holiday. You saw what the news said, it's only London, and they're containing it."

"But Jack, the Prime Minister said that…"

"Who cares what he says? Do you really think they're telling people this because it's the best thing for them?"

"Well, yes…"

"It's not." Jack picked up the remote control and turned off the TV. "Look, think about it. If this virus is dangerous, where do you think we'll be safest? Here, Leeds? I'll bet there are people already on trains and cars with this illness, heading north as we speak."

He sat down next to Amy and rested his hand on her knee. "We will be much safer out in the middle of nowhere for a few weeks, than in a built-up area with millions of people. The fewer people, the less chance of us getting ill."

Amy breathed out, and her shoulders dropped. "That does make sense, surprisingly," she said smiling.

Jack hugged her. "Good. Then let's go soon before those idiots shut down the motorways."

"You think they'll do that?"

"Maybe. Probably not." He paused and looked at his wife - there was still uncertainty in her eyes. "You, me, and Annie, by the beach, while all this nonsense passes. It'll be the safest place to be."

Amy nodded, taking another deep breath. "Ok. Let's do it."

"That's my girl." Jack kissed her. He felt excited; this wasn't just a holiday, it was an adventure, like the ones they used to have.

Annie ran in with Mr. Fred and beamed to see her parents in an embrace. She joined in the hug. "Mr. Fred is ready! Let's go!"

They made good time, and within an hour Yorkshire was well behind them. Jack had worried that everyone would be fleeing the cities, but no, not Leeds. The Yorkshire folk seemed happy to ride out whatever was happening right where they were.

The traffic snarled up around Birmingham, however. Jack wasn't surprised, this is where the M40 joined the M6. Traffic from London trying to get north would meet traffic from Birmingham. Traffic trying to escape the threat of a raging virus, for example.

As the lines of cars crawled slowly, Jack, Amy, and Annie played a few games of I Spy, then some cards, then Annie got bored and restless.

Jack's hands tightened on the wheel. Looking at the odometer, he quickly calculated it had taken an hour to travel 4 miles.

"Maybe we should get off the motorway?" suggested Amy.

Jack nodded and turned off the next junction, which took another thirty minutes to reach.

Traveling through the smaller roads past Cirencester, Swindon, and heading towards Bath, they made slow time but managed to avoid any large traffic jams. It was apparent, however, as the day passed from early afternoon to early evening that they would not reach Cornwall until late in the night.

"We need to stop, find a B&B or something," said Amy.

Jack nodded. Annie had had an hour's sleep, but since waking up thirty minutes ago, her mood had quickly deteriorated.

They stopped a mile or two past a town called Frome, finding a pub on a country road called The Fox and Hounds. They booked in, and after dropping off the essentials in their room, went back downstairs for dinner. The pub was old, rickety, and low-ceilinged with comforting wooden beams. An open fire burned in the corner and a few regulars sat at the bar. No one else was eating.

A portly landlord offered a smile as wide as his waistline.

"Are you guys from London then? Sounds like you got out just in time."

Jack shook his head. "No, we're from Leeds. On our way to Cornwall, for a holiday."

The landlord laughed. "Fine time to take a holiday. Mind you, probably best to be away from the cities. Things seem to be going to hell pretty quickly."

"What do you mean?" asked Amy, glancing at Annie, pleased to see her engaged with her colouring book.

"Have you not heard? All over the news. London is 'Closed'. The military has declared it a quarantine zone. No one in, and no one out." The landlord shook his head. "People are going nuts. If there wasn't panic before, there is now."

Jack and Amy looked at each other, worry creasing both brows.

"How can you close London?" asked Jack. "Surely there must be some laws or something? You can't just stop people from leaving a city. Bloody hell, this isn't China." Jack's skin flushed.

"National emergency, they say. They can do anything in a national emergency."

"Unbelievable. So what is it, tanks on the street?"

The landlord nodded. "So it seems. All the roads barricaded. The news stopped reporting on it a few hours ago, but it was all over the internet for a while. BBC site is down now, though. Lots of sites are down."

"The same as Brazil," murmured Amy.

The landlord continued. "They are talking about extending the zone, shutting of county borders. I've even heard talk of safe camps."

"Safe camps?" echoed Jack.

"Aye. Somewhere to put everyone until the virus is contained."

"An internment camp, in other words." Jack shook his head.

"Things are going crazy alright," said the landlord. "If I were you, I'd get off nice and early tomorrow. Get yourselves to Cornwall. You're best as far out of it as you can get." The landlord stared at the fire for a moment. "Wish me and the missus could do the same."

Jack became conscious that Amy was squeezing his hand tight. He saw the unspoken plea in her eyes.

"Ok, look, we'll have our meal, then I think we might get going," said Jack. "Forget about the room. Sorry, but after what you've said…"

The landlord nodded. "I understand. I'll get you a full refund."

Jack held up his hand, "Don't worry about it."

"No, you'll get your money back. Just get your little one out of it." He smiled at Annie, who was colouring in a horse with a purple crayon, oblivious. "Now, let's get you your food. I'm Mac, by the way. Pleased to meet you."

Chapter 7

Saturday 20th May, night, Cornwall

The 4x4's lights carved a path through the darkness. It was approaching midnight, and Stewart's directions had brought them to the far reaches of Cornwall, threading their way through narrow lanes walled high on each side by fields. Jack drove slowly to navigate the sharp bends, struggling against the tiredness tugging at his eyes. There was no question of stopping for a rest, however; ever since the landlord's tales of rapidly escalating violence across the country, Jack had been overcome with a sense of urgency. He had no wish to be prisoned in a 'safe-zone,' whatever the hell that was. They would get to the holiday park and sit it out for the next few weeks, or, well, as many weeks as it took.

Jack relaxed as the road opened up to two lanes. The first lights he had seen in a while zoomed passed in the opposite direction, going much faster than they should.

He noticed Amy checking on Annie, who had fallen asleep a few hours ago.

Amy whispered, "Jack, I think I'm a bit scared."

Jack took his eyes off the road for a second to give his wife a reassuring smile. "I know. It'll be ok. Look, whatever is happening, I'm sure it'll be resolved in a few days. You know the government, always prone to overplay things, to overreact. We're doing the right thing."

Amy nodded. "I suppose. It's best to be away from it, I guess."

"Far away. Is she still sleeping?"

"Yes, I think she... Jack!"

Jack didn't need the shout, he had seen it. He slammed on the breaks and managed to swerve past the minibus that blocked half the road. The car slid from left to right, and the sound and smell of burning rubber filled the still night air as the wheels tried to grip the road. Eventually, they came to a stop.

Silence.

"Are you ok?" Jack managed to say to Amy, his heart beating fast.

Amy was breathing heavily, her face ashen, her hands gripping the side of her seat. She didn't respond to Jack but quickly looked into the rear seat.

Amazingly, Annie was still asleep, her arms around Mr. Fred.

"Well look at that," said Jack. Relief turned into cautious laughter.

"Oh, thank God. Well done, Jack, well done." She reached over, and they hugged for a moment.

"Look," said Jack. "You stay here with Annie, I'd best go and check out that minibus. People may be hurt."

He opened the car door but paused as Amy grabbed his arm. "Jack..." She looked straight into his eyes. "Jack, maybe we should just go."

They should. But he needed to check the van, someone could need help. It was the right thing to do.

"I'll only be a minute, ok? Just a minute. I promise. I'll go and look, and any problems, I'll phone someone, and we can go."

Amy's hand dropped from his arm. "Be quick."

The night was warm and still, and silent. Jack wondered briefly at the lack of sound, what was missing?

Insects.

There were no insects. Maybe the wrong time of year, Jack thought as he took out his phone and turned on its torch. There were no street lights here, and the darkness was complete.

The minibus was about twenty or so meters from their car, and Jack approached carefully, shining his light across the white vehicle.

The front of the vehicle was wrapped around a heavily splintered telegraph pole that was close to collapse. The front and side doors were both open, and a strange red paint job marked the side of the minibus. It was empty.

Jack moved closer, and his heart skipped a beat as he realised he was not looking at a strange paint job, but a thick streak of blood.

That was enough. Jack turned on his heels and ran to the car.

It was too late.

A scream cut through the air. Amy.

"Amy!" He ran faster. Holding up the torch, he saw two figures around his car, one of them reaching in through the driver's door.

He pushed the nearest figure out of the way, as hard as he could. He grabbed the second, the one leaning into the car.

The first person, now on the floor, grabbed Jack's leg. He, or she, was pulling themselves closer, and in the split second that Jack had to take in the scene, he was sure he saw teeth gnashing fast, the person's jaw aiming for his leg. His thoughts paused - news reports, rumours, people eating people, the infected.

He tried to pull his leg away, overtaken with panic, pushing his body against the car.

The other figure still lay half in the vehicle.

"Amy!" he shouted.

"Here!" she screamed in reply, and a shocked Jack could only watch in complete surprise as Amy appeared, her arm wielding some sort of weapon that she hammered down upon the writhing body on the floor.

Its skull exploded onto the road, and Jack stared at his wife as she straightened up, out of breath from the effort, blood splattered over her face and dress. "On the forum I read, they said you have to get them in the head. I got the one in the car too." She held a lug wrench in her hand, pieces of flesh draped across the metal, blood dripping to the floor.

He smiled at his wife, "Amazing."

His smile was short lived.

Amy screamed as a hand appeared from the darkness and grabbed her around the head. It pulled her into a gaping mouth that sank its teeth into her neck. Amy's eyes opened wide with a look of incomprehension and fear. She dropped the wrench and it clattered on the ground. Blood spurted from her neck, falling warm droplets landing on Jack's skin.

Another scream, this one louder, of a higher pitch; it was Annie. Jack spun around to see his daughter up against the window, her eyes wide in terror as she witnessed her mother being attacked.

He picked up the wrench and, struggling in the darkness to see where the attacker ended and his wife began, he raised his arm and brought it down with speed upon the skull of the figure. Both Amy and her attacker fell to the ground, and Jack reached for his wife, but he was too late.

Hands grabbed Amy's ankles and pulled her away from Jack. More shadows - people it seemed, covered in blood - emerged from the dark, falling upon Amy's spasming body. Their heads bobbed up and down, taking bites out of his wife.

Her screams filled the air, she called his name, "Jack," over and over.

Then there was another scream, as chilling as his wife's, this one shouted, 'Daddy!'

Pulling his eyes away from his dying wife (she's dying, my God, she's going), he saw another body crawling through the passenger door, trying to get to his daughter.

For a few seconds, Jack stood motionless, his brain unable to make a decision.

"Annie!" Amy's yell disappeared into cries of pain, mixed with the satisfied grunts of the creatures feeding on her and the sound of ripping flesh and cracking bones.

Jack ran to the car and pulled on the legs of the creature trying to get in. It turned around swiftly, and under the car's interior light Jack saw the face of an old woman, one-half of her cheek hanging off to reveal part of her jaw.

Jack brought down the lug wrench upon her head, and it sank into her skull. The body of the old woman went limp. "It's ok, Annie, Daddy's here," he shouted through gasping breaths, unsure as to whether he was going to scream or cry.

He pulled out the body and tried to pull the wrench out of the old woman's head.

It was stuck fast.

"Daddy!" his daughter screamed.

Jack turned; he was surrounded. Five, six, he didn't know, he couldn't count, all he knew was his vision was full of blood covered old people shambling towards him.

Beyond them lay his wife (she's gone, beautiful Amy, she's dead, I let her go.)

They came closer, moaning, their arms held out, their jaws snapping.

He couldn't get past them, he couldn't get to Amy.

One of them, the only young one in the group, lurched forward and Jack only just stepped to the side in time. The young one fell to the ground and started to scramble madly towards Jack's legs, click-clack-click went its jaws.

Jack scurried into the car and pulled the door shut. He grabbed Annie, pulling her into the front of the vehicle. She shook and sobbed and yelled. He put his arms around her and squeezed her tight - "Annie, Annie, are you ok?"

Thump, bang, on the windows. The zombies (was that what they were?) had reached the car and pressed up against the doors in dumb persistence, like flies. Blood from their fresh wounds smeared against the glass.

"Daddy! Where's Mummy? The monsters!" Annie could hardly form the words, each syllable punctuated with a cry or a scream.

Jack looked out into the darkness again, trying to see Amy, but he knew... He gripped the steering wheel and let out a cry, a primal yell. He turned on the ignition and rammed his foot down hard on the accelerator.

The engine roared, and they were moving, and the monsters were gone.

"We have to get Mummy! Mummy!" yelled Amy. She leaped into the back seat and stuck her face up against the rear window, the noise of her crying filling the car.

Jack's tears flowed freely and made it hard to see. He struggled to keep driving, to keep going, but he had to. He had no choice. He had promised Annie he wouldn't let the monsters get her.

Jack breathed deep and fast as he steered through the narrow roads towards their destination.

His hands shook, and he felt fear at a level he hadn't known possible. He reasoned he must be in shock, otherwise, how was he able to function after what had just happened?

(She's dead, torn apart.)

He glanced at the back seat to see Annie, his little Annie, lying curled up in the fetal position, her body shaking with sobs that grew into full-grown cries in horrible waves.

"Annie, Daddy's here, I won't let anything happen."

Amy told me not to go, thought Jack, and I ignored her. She'd be alive if I'd listened.

He pulled over to the side of the road and quickly dialled 999. He held the phone up to his ear, nothing. He looked at this phone again, no signal.

He fought the urge to throw the phone against the floor, to punch the dashboard, to headbutt the wheel of the car until he was dead.

Jack flinched as he saw movement in the headlights of the car. It was only a fox, trotting happily through the night.

He started driving again.

The lights of the holiday park shone brightly ahead. Jack pulled up to the gates where a few men stood around a barrier. They quickly surrounded his car and motioned him to wind down his windows. Under the lights of the nearby port-a-cabin, Jack saw a stern look on each of the men's faces. They each carried a weapon of some sort; a baseball bat, a spade, a large knife, a metal bar.

Jack wound down his window. One large man approached but stopped short by a few meters, eyeing Jack carefully.

"Where do you come from?" he said.

"Leeds," Jack said, and then, unable to stop himself, "They got my wife. I don't know what they are, I have a daughter…" He felt the tears running down his cheeks, and he stared at the man.

The man said, "Your card?"

Jack looked at him with the comprehension of a dumb rabbit.

"Your membership card? Are you a member here?"

Jack realised what the man was talking about. The security card for the park. He fumbled in the glove box and pulled it out.

The man took the card and ran it under a scanner by the barrier. There was a beep. He nodded to one of his colleagues in the darkness. The man leaned into the car, "You're lucky, we're about to lock this place down. Thought we would wait and catch some stragglers. Get to your chalet… You look in a bad way."

The barrier rose.

"We need the police, my wife is gone," said Jack

The man shook his head, "You need to get to your chalet, no-one is coming, not anymore." He rested his hand on Jack's shoulder. "I'll come and see you tomorrow."

Jack saw sorrow in the man's eyes, one that matched his own. "Ok, thank you."

Jack drove through the barrier.

"You ok, Annie? We're safe now."

"Can we get Mummy?" The words hit Jack like a hammer. He had no answer.

Jack found the chalet and parked up. He sat with the engine idling, feeling dumb, feeling impotent. What was there to do? Why get out of the car? Why?

He jumped as a figure appeared beside the car. He reached for the wrench but relaxed as he heard a soft voice, an old man's voice.

"Easy pal, easy... You ok?"

Jack looked up to see an elderly man in a checked shirt standing beside him, with a torch in one hand and a spade in the other. "No," said Jack.

The man nodded. "Ok. I understand. I'm Mike."

Mike peered into the back seat and saw Annie. He turned and called into the chalet next door, "Marge, there's a man and a little girl here. They don't look so good." He turned back to Jack. "Come on, we need to get you inside. It's not safe out here."

Jack nodded and got out of the car. He opened the back door and picked up Annie.

The old man took his arm and guided them into his large chalet. A woman, Marge, assumed Jack, was standing by the door. Her face dropped in sadness when she saw Annie. "Oh my, poor girl."

"They got her mummy. Amy. My wife."

"You poor people..." Marge guided Jack to the couch, where he sat down, Annie on his knee.

Mike closed the door and locked it. He turned off the light, and they were left with the glow of only a small lamp. "They can get attracted to light." He turned on the kettle. "We don't know what they are. They first appeared in the afternoon. We tried to call the police, but there was no answer, the phones are all dead, the internet dead. So we've just tried to keep 'em out."

Marge wiped a tear from her eye. "You must sleep here tonight. You poor people, your poor little girl…"

Chapter 8

Sunday 21st May, morning, Cornwall

When Jack woke the next morning he had a few blissful moments of amnesia. His mind hovered in the state between dreams and reality, then the dam holding the awakened world burst and all the memories from the previous day returned.

He swallowed hard to stop himself from crying out. He felt the weight of Annie next to him, he turned to see her asleep, her peaceful face in denial of the horror that would greet her on waking.

How she had got to sleep, he didn't know.

There were voices outside. Careful not to disturb Annie he slipped out of the bedroom and made his way outside.

Four men stood by the chalet. Mike and the big man who had let them in last night were amongst them. On seeing Jack, they stopped talking.

Mike said, "Are you ok?"

Jack nodded.

"Good. This is James," he motioned to the big man. "He's the manager of the park."

James said, "Hope you slept well?"

"As well as can be expected."

There was silence. The sky was clear and deep blue, birds sang, and the sun shined. Jack felt the early warmth upon his skin.

He said, "What's going on?"

James replied, "I don't know. We managed to lock the park down overnight, everyone helped. We killed over thirty of them. They're still coming."

"Can I help?"

Mike said, "Everyone can help. Just being here is a help. What would you like to do?"

"Keep my daughter safe."

James walked over to Jack. "They got my son, yesterday afternoon." He turned and looked out towards the sea, visible from the porch of the chalet. "But we can make it safe, here. I believe we can. There are only two roads in, we have blocked them with mini-buses, and we have a healthy amount of barbed wire - used to keep out the little troublemakers from the village. The danger is the beach, the fences there are weak, but so far only a handful have come from there. We're getting a group to work on it."

"What's happened to the rest of the world?"

"Who knows? Radio dead, TV dead, no internet. Hell, this holiday park is the rest of the world, for all I know. You want to help with the fences?" asked James.

Jack said, "I'll come along when Annie wakes up. I need to be there when Annie wakes up."

James nodded and took Jack's hand, which he shook. "We'll see you soon. Good to have you here, Jack. Good to have you."

Jack turned and headed back to the bedroom.

Jack held Annie as she sobbed. He rubbed her head softly.

"You said there was no monsters," she said.

"I know. I'm sorry, I was wrong, honey. Daddy was wrong." He cradled his daughter and rocked back and forth slowly.

There was a knock on the door of the bedroom.

"Hello?" said Jack.

Marge pushed the door open a little, "Hello, I was wondering if you wanted anything?"

Annie looked up at Marge. "Who are you?"

Marge gave her a broad smile. "I'm Marge, and I believe you're Annie?"

Annie didn't return the smile. She buried her head back in Jack's arms.

"I don't know what to do," said Jack quietly to Marge.

"Just what you're doing. I'll get you a cup of tea."

It was early afternoon. Jack joined a group standing on top of a sand dune, looking over the beach. There were five men and two women, James and Mike among them.

"Hi Jack," said James, "Everyone, this is Jack." James introduced him to the rest of the party, but Jack forgot the names immediately. The events of the previous night were still looping through his mind. There wasn't room for anything else, especially the names of strangers.

The air and the sea were still. The sand dunes lay between the holiday park and the beach, which stretched for about half a mile in each direction before meeting the headlands.

A few figures wandered on the beach; disparate, apart, aimless. Infected, guessed Jack.

"The fence by the beach isn't strong, we haven't really been looking after it for the past year or two," said James. "The posts need to be hammered in further, and we need to wrap an extra layer of barbed wire around the perimeter."

"You think that'll keep them out?" said an elderly man with a beard and a T-shirt that said 'Real Ale Club.'

"I don't know," replied James. "But it will be better than we've got now. We can do more serious improvements later."

James looked over the group. "We'll walk the length in pairs. See you've all got your weapons handy. One of each pair takes a sledgehammer for the fence posts. Look out for each other." A woman and the elderly man sheepishly picked up a sledgehammer. Jack reached forward and took one.

"Make sure the posts are in tight," said James. "We'll do the barbed wire this afternoon."

Jack was paired with Ian, an accountant from London who appeared to be in his fifties. Jack pounded in the first post they came across as Ian held it tight, both of them continually checking for nearby infected. The ones on the beach roamed to the sea and back towards the sand dunes, before turning to the sea again. Every now and then, though, one would disappear into the boundary of the sand dunes.

"It's scary, isn't it?" said Ian. "Knowing they are close, knowing that we are hunted."

"Hunted?" said Jack, taking a rest.

"Yes, being hunted." Ian took off his glasses and wiped them with his shirt tail. He was a thin man with pointed fingers and a long face. "This virus, it's going to challenge the human race, let us show what we're made of."

"You think?"

"Yes. We haven't been hunted for a long time, not since we lived on the savannah. We're prey again."

Jack hoisted the sledgehammer above his head, "Or maybe the army will just kill them all, or they'll find a cure and in a month we'll all be back to normal." He drove the hammer down hard on the pole. The dull thud got carried away by the wind. The post had been loose when they found it and had wobbled easily under light pressure. It was now tight in the sand, but low. Jack wondered if this would work.

"Ah, here we go," said Ian, looking past Jack. "Just a teenager, very sad."

Jack turned to see what at first glance appeared to be a young, drunk girl. Swaying and stumbling across the sand, barely keeping balance. She was wearing a blood-stained blue uniform, some sort of nurse. She nearly tripped over a clump of grass, and her head turned to reveal a massive gash in the back of her neck, with what appeared to be brain matter hanging down on her shoulder, the uniform stained black.

Jack's heart raced, and the memory of last night flashed into his head - his daughter screaming as he plunged the wrench into the old man's head; his wife disappearing through screams into the darkness of confused limbs and bodies.

"I'll let you do the honours, Jack," said Ian, smiling.

Jack stared, but couldn't move. Sweat formed on his palms, on his brow. His breathing became heavy and fast.

"Jack?" said Ian.

Was his wife now one of these things? Stumbling through a field, looking to kill someone. Maybe she had killed someone else already.

"For Pete's sake Jack, you'll have to be quicker than this." Ian walked forward and raised this baseball bat. He waited until the girl reached the fence then raised his bat, and with a speed and strength that belied his thin frame, he smashed the bat hard into the girl's head. The skull caved in quickly, blood and brain tissue spilling out to land on the sand with a plop.

Ian turned around, "Now, that's how we need to... Jack!"

Jack spun around, feeling hands on his neck. He stumbled back and fell onto the sand, a heavy weight landing on top of him. Hands grabbed his face and pulled at his skin, nails dug into his cheeks.

A face, an old man, covered in blood, teeth covered in blood, only a few inches away, snapped at him.

Jack pulled his arms up and pushed at the head of the man. The opposing force was great, and Jack struggled to push him away, his hands slipping on the fresh blood on the man's forehead.

Panic overcame him, and he screamed as he scrambled against the monster.

There was a crack, and the man was gone. A few more blows and Jack felt warm blood splatter on his face. He turned towards the sound and saw the face of the old man; impacted, squashed into the sand, a mix of flesh, skull, and blood. Its jaws gnashed once, slowly, then stopped. Ian stood above the mess, blood covered baseball bat in hand.

He pulled Jack up. "Are you ok?"

Jack nodded, not sure if he was.

"Bloody hell," said Ian. "We need to be sharper, or we're finished, Jack. That one came from nowhere."

"He was on our side of the fence," said Jack quietly.

"What?" said Ian, breathing heavily.

"He was on our side of the fence," said Jack louder, his eyes opening wide. He grabbed Ian by the shoulders. "He was in the barriers!"

Ian stared at Jack. "That means…"

A loud shout rang out from behind, in the direction of the holiday camp. Another cry, more urgent.

"They're inside," said Jack. "Annie…" He picked up the sledgehammer and ran back towards the camp, followed by Ian.

Charging down from the sand dunes into the park, Jack was met by chaos. He stared in dismay at the horde of dead marauding through the park; on the roads, over the grass, in and out of chalets. Amongst them ran people, at least Jack thought they were people; the ones who were shouting for help, who weren't covered in blood.

Annie was in Mike and Marge's chalet, a few hundred meters away.

Jack and Ian looked at each other, nodded and ran off in different directions. Jack held the sledgehammer up ahead of him, and ran into the nearest infected, using the sledgehammer as a battering ram. The target's head crushed on contact with the weight of the hammer. Jack pushed the body over.

He sensed movement to his left and swung the hammer on instinct. It connected with the head of an old man covered in blood, his right arm hanging off. The old man collapsed as his skull shattered.

Jack ran forward a few yards and again found himself surrounded by more of the infected. He smashed and swung his way through, blood splattering over his face. He was already out of breath, but he couldn't stop.

He managed to make good ground, running fast, ducking in and out of outstretched hands. He didn't have the time or energy to tackle them all. He had to get back to the chalet, to Annie.

Then he fell.

As he tried to run around an old disfigured woman, he swerved too far and caught the curb, flying forward until he hit the floor hard. He rolled, and the sledgehammer slipped out of his hand. There was a pain in his knee, but he forced himself up immediately. Two hands grabbed his shoulder, but he pushed them away, running backward, looking for the sledgehammer. It was a few feet away from him. An old man stumbled in between Jack and his weapon, but Jack charged forward, shoulder barging the thin frame out of the way, the old man letting out a moan as he fell to the ground. Jack ducked down and grabbed the hammer, which he brought round and down onto the old man's head.

Jack saw the chalet. He ran again, fighting the pain in his chest as his out of shape lungs fought for air. He ignored the stabbing pain in his knee; his only thought, Annie.

He ran on automatic, swinging the sledgehammer, barging bodies out of his way, dodging grasping hands and snapping jaws.

And then he was there.

The chalet was clear, he ran up to the door with a quick look behind. He was being followed. Jack opened the door with one hand, his other holding the hammer up, facing the body as it approached.

"You in there Annie?"

"Daddy!" Small arms clasped around Jack's waist.

"Go back inside, Annie," he shouted, "Go back inside!"

Annie screamed as she saw the approaching corpse, covered in blood.

"Back inside!" shouted Jack again. He felt her arms being pulled from him, and he glanced inside the chalet to see Marge yanking Annie away from the door.

The infected, an old woman with a gaping hole in her chest, her heart visible, was only a few feet away. Perfect distance, thought Jack, as he brought the sledgehammer down hard. Its head collapsed like a cardboard box. He pushed the dead carcass away and jumped inside the chalet, closing the door behind him.

Chapter 9

Saturday 21st May, evening, Cornwall

After comforting Annie, Jack joined the cleanup patrols.

"They got in through the woods," said James as they walked around the perimeter of the fence, the sun setting. "Must have been nearly a hundred of them. We think they were from the old people's home. It's about two miles away. So many of them I guess our fence just gave way."

"We'll need something stronger," said Jack.

"We're getting some cars and caravans out there now, use them as barriers until we can think of something more permanent."

They stopped by the edge of the woods. The evening was peaceful, a dark red sky reflected in the sea. Almost as if the blood from the park had drained into the water.

"How is Annie?" said James.

Jack shook his head. "She's not good. I should be with her."

"You should. You should go now. You've done enough to help today."

"Have I?" asked Jack. "Will anything be enough?"

His knee was numb with pain, every muscle in his body ached, and his hands were red raw to the touch, covered in burst blisters from wielding the sledgehammer.

"Who knows what the hell is going on, Jack. Or how long it will last. We need to keep strong, pull together. Until help comes."

"If it comes."

James rested his hand on Jack's shoulder. "You need some rest, we all do. That nursing home thing has got to be a one-off. We'll get the stragglers, lock this place down. I've worked here most of my life, I know it like the back of my hand. I'll be up tonight, making sure we get that fence in the woods sealed."

Jack saw the blackness and rings under James' eyes. "You need rest too."

"I can't," replied James. "If I do, I start thinking of my son."

Images of Annie flashed through Jack's mind. Her smiling face at last year's birthday as she opened her presents. Then her screams as she watched her mother dying.

"I'm going to go back. I'll come find you at first light."

"Thank you," said James. He turned to look into the woods, where the rumble of engines could be heard.

Jack walked back to the chalet, where his daughter was waiting.

He saw Annie's face looking out of the window of the chalet. She smiled when she saw him and rushed to the front door. Jack ran to meet her.

He lifted her up and held her tight.

Holiday Apocalypse

The Inn at the End of the World

Chapter 1

Mac, the landlord of the Fox and Hounds, pulled another pint for old Johnny. Bitter, as always.

"I tell you, Mac, you ought to close, get things locked up. This virus…" said Johnny, his voice loud in the near empty pub.

"Not before we finish our pints, though," said Gaz from the end of the bar.

Mac chuckled to himself, a deep rumbling sound as the laugh resonated through his thick frame. "Don't worry fellas, I ain't closing this place anytime soon. Even if you got a virus, you still need a pint."

He looked up to the muted TV and saw the now familiar images of the military barricading the motorways, flames in London, and the Prime Minister's face, no doubt calling for calm. Funny he wasn't standing in Downing Street. The white wall behind him suggested he was far from his official residence, miles away in a bunker probably.

"Oi, Mac, another pint please!"

Mac nodded to Gaz, "Coming up."

Gaz and Johnny were his only customers. Two diehards that made their way to the pub no matter the weather, nor the state of their health or finances. A young couple with a daughter had been in earlier, on their way to Cornwall, but they left straight after dinner. It was a quiet night alright.

"Hey Mac, mind if I light up?" said Johnny.

It was nearing eleven. Mac couldn't imagine any new customers appearing to cause a fuss over an old fella having a smoke. Not on a night like this, not given everything that was happening.

"Sure, Johnny, knock yourself out."

Johnny nodded his thanks and lit up his thin and bent hand-rolled cigarette.

Gaz sipped on his pint, looking thoughtful. "This virus, then, Mac. Sounds like one of them flesh eaters. What do you think?"

"I don't know, Gaz, I'm no doctor."

"Nah, sure, but from what they say on the news, and them pictures on the internet…"

"Can't ever be sure what you see on the internet. Could be kids with a makeup kit for all I know. Probably is." Mac poured himself a small whiskey.

"Ok, but if it is one of them flesh eaters," continued the young man, "it must be eating the brain too, driving everyone crazy. I mean, I've seen it on the news, and it looks real enough - they had that one video where you saw that fella biting another fella."

Johnny nodded, "Aye. Haven't seen that video again, though, have we?" Smoke billowed around his head as he spoke.

"It's being covered up, I reckon." Gaz took a sip from his pint. "You have to be pretty mad to eat someone, don't you?"

Mac nodded his head, "Definitely something wrong with you if you have to eat someone." He noted the fire was down to embers, it was getting late. Probably a good time to check on Angie. "You fellas alright for a minute? Give a shout if anyone comes in."

He went over and poked the fire, then made his way upstairs. He walked past the B&B rooms and to his bedroom at the end of the dimly lit corridor. His wife was in bed, watching TV.

"It's getting worse," said Angie.

The TV news showed police and soldiers pushing back crowds of people in the darkness of London.

"I thought I said it's best not to watch that."

Angie waved him away. "What's it matter. What happens, happens."

Mac sighed. "Ok, love. Anyway, I thought you'd be up, I wondered if you wanted some water or anything?"

She smiled at Mac, "That would be nice."

He fetched a glass of water from the sink in the en-suite bathroom and put it down on her bedside table. He moved her walking sticks out of the way and rested on the side of the bed, giving her a quick hug.

"Oh, get off me, you big softy!" But she held on to him, tight. "Do you think we'll be alright?"

"I don't know, love," he said. "We always have in the past."

"But this is different, Mac. Oh!" Angie let out a gasp.

He followed her gaze to the television. The picture had gone, replaced with static.

"Mac…" Angie's voice was high, filled with fear.

"Probably just the signal…" He changed the channels, but nothing, static on each one.

"Mac, what's happening?"

He shook his head and stared at the screen, "I don't know."

"Who's downstairs?" asked Angie.

"Just Gaz and Johnny."

"Can we close up?"

He squeezed his wife's hand and gave her a smile. "No problem. I'll lock up. They can leave when they leave."

"Ok. Thanks."

He kissed her on the forehead and got up to go, "And turn that tele off."

Downstairs he found Gaz standing underneath the giant TV that hung over the fireplace. He was pressing button after button on the remote control.

"Looks like your TV is dead, Mac. Must be the aerial."

Mac knew it wasn't the aerial - he had cable.

"I'm going to lock up fellas. You're welcome to stay the night of course." Both Gaz and Johnny lived alone.

"Cheers Mac," said Gaz. "But I fancy the walk. I'll just finish my pint, and I'll be on my way, I don't want to be any trouble."

Mac walked to the front door and turned the deadlock, then bolted it. He tested it with a rough shake. "Don't be daft, lad. Get your head down in one of the rooms upstairs."

Gaz started to protest again, but Johnny interrupted. "Listen to what he says, Gaz. Mac knows his business. Don't you, Mac?"

Mac nodded at Johnny, before pulling on the handle of one of the windows.

"Mac thinks something funny is going to happen tonight, that's right, ain't it?" He lit another skinny cigarette. "Reckons we might be best not walking the streets."

Gaz sat down and finished his pint, a confused look on his face. "What you mean?"

"The virus," said Mac.

"Oh."

"Here lad, have another drink. On the house." Mac pulled Gaz a pint of lager, and they sat in near silence for a while, with only the sound of the fire crackling softly. Mac thought how peaceful it all was, without the TV. It reminded him of back in the seventies when he first opened the pub, just a young lad, him and Angie, his beautiful bride. No TV in pubs back then, no fruit machines. Just the noise of conversation, of laughter, of life.

Gaz broke the silence, "So you think the TV going off is to do with the virus?"

Johnny answered, "I think that when there's riots, and when the police and army are shutting down whole cities, and when there's a virus infecting all from America to China, that maybe it's just best to stay put. Amongst friends like."

"Ok," said Gaz, his face suddenly pale. Gaz lifted his pint, a slight shake in his hand, and took several large gulps a little too quickly. "Since it's on the house then, best make use of it..." He gave a weak smile.

"Careful son," said Mac, "you don't want to be passed out anytime. Anyway, you two, I'm going to go up and see to the missus," said Mac. "She ain't sleeping well. As I said, you fellas can help yourselves to the booze but don't go daft. No-one's staying in any of the rooms upstairs, so take your pick."

"Cheers Mac, I'll see to it that we get sorted," said Johnny, his voice croaking as the late night and cigarettes began to take their toll.

"Night, Mac, and thanks," said Gaz. "Reckon they'll have the TV fixed tomorrow."

"Reckon they will," said Mac. He stopped at the bottom of the stairs, "Oh, and don't let anyone in."

Chapter 2

"Ok Angie, that's them two sorted. Are you right? Do you need help with your night business?"

Angie shook her head. "I'm fine love, my leg isn't too bad tonight. Managed to get to the bathroom and stand for a good few minutes."

Mac changed into his pyjamas, "Well that's good to hear, life in you yet!"

Angie laughed and threw a pillow at him, "Enough life in me to give you trouble, Bill Macintyre!"

Mac caught the pillow and threw it back beside her, smiling as he did so. "I don't doubt there is my dear."

He quickly went to the toilet and cleaned his teeth, then climbed into bed. He pulled his wife close to him, getting comfortable. Then he frowned. "Dammit. I forgot something."

"What is it?"

"Never mind, I'll just be a minute."

Mac made his way downstairs again, turning sharp right at the bottom of the stairs to the cellar door. He opened it and descended the stairs, turned on the dim light and fought his way past beer kegs and pipes to find what he was looking for. Tucked away in the corner of the room was an old crowbar.

He gripped it tightly with two hands and felt the weight before making a practice swing. It felt stiff and heavy in his arms. He swung it a few more times until he got used to the action.

Mac took the crowbar with him back upstairs, the mumbled conversation of the two drunks at the bar drifting up behind him.

"What do you need that for?" asked Angie when he got back to the bedroom.

"Just to be on the safe side. You know what people are like when their TVs aren't working." The joke fell flat. He could see the worry in Angie's eyes.

"You really think things here might go, well, like in London?" she said.

Mac shook his head. "Not at all love, but you know me, still an old boy scout, best be prepared, dib dib dob."

"I'll dib dob you…" She cuddled in next to Mac. He turned off the light and lay still, his worry keeping him awake. He couldn't let Angie see him worried or scared, but he was. He felt his heart beating fast and strong under his pyjamas. He reached his left hand down beside the bed and felt the cold metal of the crowbar. Within reach. Good.

Mac awoke with a start. A bang on his door, and Gaz's voice, high with panic calling his name. Mac grabbed the crowbar and jumped out of bed.

"What is it?" shouted Angie.

"It's Gaz, don't worry love, I'll sort it out. Silly beggar's probably just wet himself."

Mac opened the door and slipped out into the corridor, closing his bedroom door behind him. Gaz stood in boxer shorts and a t-shirt, his thin frame even more apparent without his usual baggy layers.

"What the hell are you doing? It's three in the bloody morning," hissed Mac after a quick glance at his watch.

Even in the darkness of the corridor, Gaz looked scared. "You have to come downstairs - someone's trying to get in."

"What?" Mac didn't wait for any further explanation and charged downstairs.

Johnny, still dressed, was leaning up against the front door. The only light was that of the optics from behind the bar. A half-empty whiskey bottle sat next to the till - it looked like Johnny had been having himself a late night party.

The front door rattled against the bolts, and a muffled voice came from outside.

"Who is it?" whispered Mac as he sneaked up beside Johnny.

"Don't know. I was having a few more drinks, and suddenly the door started banging. I ran up, woke Gaz, told him to get you - thought I should get back down here and guard the door, like. Sounds like a man and woman."

As if to confirm this, a woman's voice from the other side of the door shouted, "Please, someone, open the door, my husband is injured, he's been attacked." The voice was that of a youngish woman, but it was shrill with fear and punctuated by sobs. It was soon accompanied by loud bangs as she began to hammer on the door.

Mac motioned to Johnny and Gaz to stay by the door. He trod lightly to the bay of seats on the left of the door where the window would allow him a view outside.

He opened a tiny gap in the curtain, being careful to allow no light to escape. He peered out.

The Fox and Hounds pub stood on a country road a few miles from the town of Frome, with no buildings or streetlights nearby. Outside was completely dark.

As Mac's eyes adjusted to the darkness, he saw two shapes. The larger figure, the man, sat against the wall of the pub, not moving, holding his neck. The woman was up against the door.

Shouting, still banging on the door. She looked frantic, like a rabbit, her head turning in all directions as if being hunted.

Mac returned to the two by the door.

"Do we let them in?" said Johnny.

The banging on the door became louder, "Please! Let us in, he's going to die!"

Mac shook his head. "We let no one in. He's been attacked, you know what that means?"

Johnny nodded, and Gaz said, "What you mean?"

"The virus, you idiot," said Mac.

The woman banged again, her shouting now more like sobs.

Gaz looked at the door, then at Mac and Johnny, "Maybe he don't have it, maybe it was a big dog or something?"

Mac didn't respond, but held his ear against the door, listening.

Johnny looked at Gaz and held up his finger to his lips.

The banging stopped, but the crying continued.

"Sounds like she's giving up," said Johnny.

"Aye," whispered Mac. He sneaked round to the window again and peeked out to see the woman kneeling by the man, her arms around him, her body rocking with sobs. "They're on their way out of here, I reckon."

Suddenly the lights came on. Mac squinted in the sudden brightness as he pulled the curtain shut, but he knew it was too late, the woman's head had snapped up at the light.

"Bill Macintyre, you let those poor people in," said Angie, who was stood at the bottom of the stairs. She was in her nightgown, holding on to the door frame, breathing heavily, sweat on her brow. Her left hand held on tight to her walking stick, shaking.

"Bloody hell woman, what the hell are you doing down here! You'll bloody kill yourself coming down those stairs," he ran to her and took her by the arm. She shrugged him off and pushed him away, nearly falling over as she did so.

"You let them in, Mac! We don't turn away people who need help!"

Mac, surprised at the sudden ferocity in his wife took a step back. He looked back to the door of the pub, where the banging and shouting had returned with increased vigour. Johnny and Gaz stood still, knowing this was not their argument.

"Mac, let them in."

Mac shook his head and held out his hands. "We can't, Angie, you don't understand, they might have that virus, we let them in, and we'll all get it."

Angie steadied herself on the frame of the door and took a few steps forward to prop herself up on the side of the bar. She let go of her hold and took a few tentative steps. Her legs shook.

"We ain't never turned anyone away from here that needed help."

Mac stood rooted to the spot as his wife struggled towards him. As much as he wanted to help her, he knew she wouldn't let him.

"And I didn't marry no coward," she breathed as she got within a few steps of Mac, the pain apparent on her face. "Now, you open those doors, and you help those people."

She fell the last few feet into Mac's arms and let out a small moan.

Mac grabbed her tight and quickly lifted up her slight body. He turned to the two by the door. "Let them in. Be careful. Any funny business…" He nodded to the crowbar he'd left propped up by the door.

Mac carried his wife upstairs. "You silly old bat," he said. "You know how to push my buttons alright."

He laid her down on the bed. She forced her eyes open and smiled at Mac. "Told you I still had it in me."

Mac kissed her on the forehead. "I'd best get back down to make sure those two turnips don't do something daft…"

The injured man was laid out on one of the tables, the woman holding his hand and sobbing, her head down. Johnny stood by the man, his fingers pressing against the man's neck, feeling for a pulse. A trail of blood led from the door to the table, its source obvious - the man had a large gash in his neck, a large square of flesh hung free to expose the man's tendons. Blood pooled slowly on the table.

Johnny shook his head at Mac.

"He's dead?" whispered Mac, being careful that the woman should not hear. Johnny shrugged. Mac came over and felt for a pulse. Nothing. The slowly trickling blood suggested he had bled out. There was nothing left to give.

"Have you phoned an ambulance?"

Johnny held up his mobile phone, "Dead. Landline dead too."

Mac felt the man's chest, no rise or fall, no beat.

Maybe if he had opened the door earlier...

He sat down next to the woman. "Hello love, my name's Mac, this is my pub."

She looked up at him. Young, maybe in her late twenties, brunette, her cheeks stained with mascara and eyes red with crying. "He's dead isn't he?"

Mac nodded. "I think so."

She sat back on the chair and let out a sob, a hopeless, empty sound. Mac looked down to her two hands, holding her pregnant belly. Mac closed his eyes and cursed quietly. He wished Angie was still here, she'd know what to say.

He took her hand. "Why don't you come upstairs, we can get you a room. You can rest up for the night." He nearly said that things would seem better in the morning, but he suspected that things would get worse.

She snatched her hand away from him and let out an angry cry. "That bastard! He just jumped at us, from nowhere, just grabbed Ed and bit him on the neck, like an animal. Ed pushed him, and then we ran. He killed him."

"They'll catch him," said Mac.

"But they won't will they? It's the virus. That virus we've been seeing all over the world, it's here isn't it?"

Mac nodded. "It might be."

She wiped the tears from her face. "Get me a drink. A whiskey."

Mac motioned to Ellie's belly, "Are you sure you should be…"

"Get me a fucking drink!"

Mac nodded to Johnny who was already on his way to the bar. He poured a generous glass for everyone.

"I'm sorry," she said. "I just don't… I just don't feel that any of this is real. It all feels like I'm not here somehow, things like this shouldn't happen. Am I in shock?"

"You might be. Thanks, Johnny." Mac took a sip of his whiskey and passed a glass to the woman.

Gaz sat down on the other side of the woman, "What's your name?"

"Ellie," she said.

"I'm Gaz. This is Johnny."

She didn't respond.

Gaz said, "We're all staying here tonight. Mac and his wife are real stand up, you won't find better. They'll look after you, especially Angie. She's in bed, but you can meet her tomorrow."

"We have to call someone," said Ellie, ignoring Gaz and turning to Mac. "Don't they need to know if someone is dead? The police, the ambulance?"

"Phones is dead," said Johnny.

Mac said in a soft voice, "You should stay here. I'll sort you out a room. I can walk down to the town tomorrow and get the right thing done for your Ed."

Her eyes met Mac's, and he looked into a vacant sadness. "It's not safe to go out, is it?" she said.

"No, it's not."

"Ok. I'll stay here. Thank you."

Chapter 3

The next morning Mac opened the curtains to a beautiful, bright, and sunny day. Rolling farmland stretched to the town of Frome, where plumes of smoke rose like fluffy stalagmites.

"Shall I go see her?" said Angie, sitting up in the bed.

Mac yawned, he had hardly slept after the arrival of Ellie and Ed. "It may be best if you do. I felt all clumsy last night, didn't know what to say. Couldn't give her a hug, could I? Big lump like me. Last thing she'd have wanted."

Angie eased herself out of bed and got her walking sticks. "I'm sure you did right." She pushed on the sticks and stood up. "Pregnant you say? So sad. That little one without a Dad now." Mac saw tears in her eyes.

"I'll go make a few cups of tea for you both," said Mac.

"Aye, you do that."

The kitchen was downstairs, behind the pub lounge. He set the kettle boiling and went to check on the pub.

Ed's body was no longer on the table.

The bloody sheet that had covered him was on the floor a few meters away, rolled up as if dragged.

"Shit," said Mac. His first thought was that Johnny or Gaz had moved the body, but why would they do that? They had all gone up to bed together, why would one of them come down to move the body?

Maybe Ed hadn't been dead… "Hello?" he said softly, scared. His pub had never seemed so silent.

The kettle started to whistle, and Mac jumped. "Stupid bugger," he said to himself.

Angie knocked gently on Ellie's door. A muffled voice said, "Come in."

"Hello, I'm Angie… How are you?"

Ellie lay on the bed on her side, staring straight ahead, her eyes red and puffy. She made no answer.

"Do you mind if I sit down?" Ellie continued to stare unblinking, not acknowledging Angie, who eased herself down on the bed.

"You poor girl," said Angie as she rested her hand on Ellie's shoulder. "It's been a terrible time for you. I can't even imagine how you must be feeling."

Ellis sniffed. "No, you can't," she whispered.

"It must feel like the end of the world." Angie moved a little closer to Ellie, "But you must know that there's a way through this."

Ellie made a snorting sound. "My husband was killed by something biting his neck apart, and I'm seven months pregnant. How the hell do you think I'm going to get through this?"

"Can I tell you something?"

Ellie made no movement.

"I've been married to Mac now for nearly forty years. We've been in this pub for almost all those years. I've seen all sorts of tragedies, and I've seen people get through them. We even got through our own tragedy, many years ago. Do you mind if I tell you?"

Ellie glanced at Angie and shook her head slightly.

"Well, me and Mac got married when we were young. We got a little bit of money when Mac's parent's died and put it into this pub. We were only in our twenties, maybe the same age as you, and it was tough at first, but it all worked out.

"With things going well, we decided to start a family. It was the only thing I ever wanted, to be a Mum, have a little baby to look after. Mac was keen too, so soon enough I got pregnant, and we had a little boy, David.

"Having David was the most wonderful thing in the world. He was the most beautiful, happy baby I'd ever seen. Everyone loved him, always laughing, always happy. Just you wait, Ellie, the love you feel for your child is bigger than anything you'll ever feel in your life."

Angie paused for a moment, staring into space, a faint smile on her face.

Ellie sat up a little, looking at Angie now.

"David was nine months old when we went to Scarborough, it was the first break we had had in years. We were so looking forward to it, the car was packed up with all David's things," she laughed to herself, "it's incredible how much a little baby needs, but you'll find out all about that.

"So there we were driving along the front of North Bay. The sun was shining, much like it is today, and we were so happy - me, Mac, and David.

"And then the van happened. Not a big van, just one of those smaller ones, but it swerved across the road and clipped us. Mac tried to avoid it, but he wasn't able to do anything. We ended up hitting the barrier and going straight into the sea. It was high tide, so the water was right up against the wall.

A few tears formed in Angie's eyes.

"It wasn't that deep, about eight feet or so, but enough for us to sink. I managed to get free, as did Mac, but I couldn't move my legs, I found out later that a nerve in my back had been damaged. I floated in the water calling for help, trying my best to keep my head above water. 'My baby,' I shouted. I remember I screamed that over and over. Eventually, some hands grabbed me and swam with me to the shore.

"Someone had rescued me, and someone else had rescued Mac. He was nearly dead - he had almost killed himself trying to get David out of the car. But it was too late."

Tears flowed freely down Angie's face. "I saw his little body, lying on the promenade as a man tried to resuscitate him. But he was gone, my poor little angel."

"The worst of it is, he never had a chance at life. I keep myself alive by thinking how he must have loved those few short months he did have."

"How do you get over something like that?" said Ellie.

Angie wiped the tears from her face. "Oh, you don't really, not properly. But we learned to cope, and we learned what is really important in life, and we focus on that. On being kind, on helping people. Like you." Angie smiled at Ellie.

Chapter 4

Mac cursed himself; he had left the crowbar upstairs in the bedroom. He would feel safer with the heavy piece of metal in his hands. He looked around the pub now with eyes of suspicion, each shadow, each noise a potential danger.

Sneaking up the stairs, he made his way to his room and opened the door slowly. The crowbar still lay on the floor. He took it and walked back into the corridor.

That's when he heard the scream.

"What was that?!" cried Ellie.
"I don't know…" said Angie.
The door flung open, it was Mac. "You two ok?" he said.
They nodded.
"Good, stay here, that sounded like Gaz."
Mac backed out of the room and walked round the bend in the corridor, to where Gaz and Johnny had stayed.

He saw Johnny first, and then behind him, he made out two figures struggling.

"Get out of the way!" shouted Mac, running past Johnny.

Gaz was backing up towards the end of the corridor. Ed, the seemingly alive but dead Ed, shuffled after Gaz, a guttural moaning coming from his throat, filtered through the hole in his neck.

"Back off pal!" shouted Mac. Ed paid no attention and continued to advance on Gaz.

Mac approached quickly and pulled on Ed's shoulder. Ed spun around and hissed at Mac, then reached for him, his jaws snapping open and shut.

Mac swung the crowbar high and fast, and it connected with Ed's skull. It shattered immediately, blood and white fragments of bone flying through the air. Ed wobbled, and Mac smashed another heavy blow down hard. Ed fell to the ground with a dull thump.

Mac, breathing heavily, looked at Gaz, who said, "What the fuck?"

Mac shook his head. "No idea, son. But I think we can assume that things are fucked."

Johnny's voice came from behind, "The bugger bit me."

Mac turned to face him.

"I came out of my room, and the bugger was walking up and down this corridor, moaning. I was sure he was dead, you saw it last night, right, and I freaked out a little. He started coming towards me, and I tripped up." He held up his arm where there was a large gash, the blood flowing freely. "That's when he fell on me and bit my arm."

"I got him off Johnny," said Gaz. "And then he came for me." Gaz was pale, his pupils full, his hands shaking.

Mac eyed the bite on Johnny's arm. "Let's get that seen to, I'll get Angie. And leave the talking to me. Last thing that poor girl wants to know is that her fella came back alive and started trying to eat people." Mac shook his head. "Christ on a bike…"

Gaz and Johnny headed down to the bar, and Mac went to Ellie's room. He found the two women sitting up on the bed, holding each other's hands, their eyes open and expectant.

"What's happened?" said Angie.

Mac opened his mouth but didn't know what to say.

"Mac, what is it?"

"I don't know. Well, I do, but it's all wrong. Everything is… Johnny's been bitten. He needs some help cleaning the wound."

"Bitten?" said Angie, "what by? Some sort of animal?"

Mac didn't answer but glanced at Ellie. His eyes told her everything.

Ellie's face fell, "It was Ed, wasn't it? He's become one of those things! Oh my God, he's become one of those things!"

Angie wrapped her arms around Ellie and said, "Mac?"

Mac nodded.

"I'll stay here with Ellie."

"Ok… no wait…" He ducked out of the room and looked up and down the corridor. Empty. "Take her to our room, and wait there. The door is stronger. Lock it. Don't let anyone in unless they speak to you. You got that? Make sure whoever is at the door speaks to you."

Angie nodded and stood up with the help of her canes. She held out a hand to Ellie, who followed Angie blindly, taken over by a second grief.

Downstairs, Johnny was sitting on one of the soft-back chairs that lined the walls of the pub. His injured arm rested on a table; a pint of bitter in front of him.

"Reckon I'll need something stronger than that soon, this thing hurts like a bugger," said Johnny. Gaz had wrapped a white cloth around the bite. The blood was quickly turning the bandage red.

"Apply more pressure, Gaz," said Mac as he pulled a bottle of Whiskey down from one of the optics. "First, pour a load of this over the wound."

Johnny laughed, "Best place for that will be down my throat!" His laugh turned into a cough. He grimaced and clenched his teeth. "I tell you, this arm though, it bloody hurts. He took a fair bite. Think I might need a doc, Mac."

Gaz nodded enthusiastically, "He's right Mac, think you can get a doc?"

Mac motioned to Gaz to follow him as he walked around the other side of the bar, out of sight of Johnny.

"Look, Gaz, keep an eye on him. There's any funny business, use that," he pointed down to the fire extinguisher.

"Mac? What do you mean?"

"I mean, whack him round the head with it."

Gaz looked at Mac, his eyes wide open. "You think he might turn into one of those things like that fella did?"

Mac nodded. "I do. Now listen. I'm going to go down Marshall's farm, it's only a mile or so, so should be back within the hour, if not sooner. My missus and that girl are locked in my room. Keep it that way.

"Watch Johnny like a hawk. He's probably got that virus now. So if he starts acting funny, keep your distance, and get round here, get that fire extinguisher and knock him out."

Gaz stared at Johnny.

"Do you understand, Gaz? It's very important."

"Ok… yes. I do. Watch Johnny, any funny business, then hit him on the head."

"Good lad. Now," Mac pulled out an ice bucket from under the bar and filled it from the fridge. "Bring this out, so Johnny don't ask what we been up to."

They walked back out to the bar.

"I'll see you two in a bit. Careful with that whiskey, Johnny, that's the expensive stuff." He winked at Johnny. "Lock the door behind me Gaz, don't let anyone in except me."

Chapter 5

Once outside the pub and walking quickly down the country road that led to the Marshall's farm, Mac felt exposed. He looked at his mobile phone, still no signal. He didn't think the phone line would be working at the farm, but it was worth a try. If he couldn't get help soon, then Johnny was a goner, he was sure of that.

He could see the farm on the crest of the hill, and he quickened his pace. He was nervous, scanning his surroundings as he walked. Every tree, every lamp post, every hedge was now a potential hiding place for one of those things. Maybe the one that got Ed was still hanging around.

He jumped as a pheasant took off from a nearby hedgerow. It powered low across the field, its wings making an eerie whistling sound.

He started into a quick jog and was soon breathing heavily and sweating. He couldn't remember the last time he had run anywhere. He was just past sixty, and he owned a pub, why would he need to run anywhere?

Smoke still rose from Frome, a few plumes as before, one very black. Well, if there's no fire brigade around, thought Mac, maybe there's no police around, or army, or anyone. Maybe this is it.

Mac forced his thoughts to stop. You'll go mad, son, thinking like that. Get yourself together, get to the farm and get some help.

Soon enough, Mac reached the driveway of the farm. A few hundred yards down the path and he'd be at the house. He took one last look around. The main road into and out of town, visible from the farm's position atop the hill, looked like a huge car park. Hundreds of cars in a higgledy-piggledy line like a child's game. A car horn blared in the distance, its deep constant sound cutting through the country air.

Mac reached the front door of the farmhouse, it was open.

"Hello?" he called in, surprised as his voice jumped an octave. He cleared his throat and said again, "Hello?"

Nothing. He stepped in carefully. Before him, a large hallway led to the kitchen, with open doors to the left and right. A staircase led upstairs.

Mac peered to his sides and quickly walked past the open doors, into the kitchen. On the large table in the middle of the room sat a picnic basket, full of tins and bottles of water. Another box sat next to it - tablets, bandages, medicines.

More tins of food lay across the floor, and in the corner was a smashed bottle, its white contents spread across the floor. The fridge door was open.

Mac gripped his crowbar, holding it with both hands, ready to strike.

He stepped into the hallway and went through the doorway on the right into the lounge. The curtains were closed, but Mac could make out the familiar shape of the fireplace and the furnishings. He had spent many a night in here with farmer Andy, sharing their love of whiskey and talking drunken nonsense. Good times.

Mac backed out of the room and checked across the hall, the dining room. Nothing out of place in there either.

The staircase became an ominous beast, and Mac wondered if the best thing to do was just get back to the pub.

But he wasn't going to be a coward. Andy and his wife, Caroline, might need help.

He walked up the stairs slowly, wincing as the odd stair creaked loudly, announcing his presence. And as if in answer, a large thump came from one of the top rooms.

Mac stopped still at the top of the stairs - a short landing with three doors leading off, which he knew to be the bathroom, the office, and the bedroom. The hallway curtains were half open, and a thin beam of light shone in, particles of dust flitting in and out of the rays.

There was another thump from the bedroom.

Mac eased forward, moving as quietly as he could. Even so, there was another creak as a floorboard shifted under his weight. Another bang, this one louder, and with it the bedroom door shook.

Mac felt sweat forming on his back and across his brow. His breathing seemed louder than the floorboard's creaking. He swapped the crowbar from hand to hand, wiping his palms on his jeans.

He reached forward to the door handle. He pulled the door open and jumped back with one motion; a motion that saved his life.

Farmer Andy fell through the open doorway, his hands stretched out. He let out a moan and fell to the ground by Mac's feet. He immediately pulled himself towards Mac, managing to grab onto his ankle.

Mac moved backward and came to a stop against the bathroom door. Andy pulled himself closer to Mac and raised his head at an unnatural angle, almost right back against his neck. His forehead was covered in gashes, and one of his eyes hung out of its socket.

Mac brought the crowbar down with all his might on Andy's head. He felt the metal smash the bone and sink into the brain material underneath. Warm black blood squirted out and spread over the wall and Mac.

There was another moan, this one more high pitched and Mac looked up to see Caroline stumble out of the bedroom, her nightgown covered in blood. Her chin was red and what appeared to be a piece of stringy pink flesh hung from her open mouth. She advanced on Mac.

He pulled on the crowbar, still in Andy's head, but it held fast - stuck. Caroline was only a few feet away.

He pulled again, harder this time, feeling something go in his back, but it did the trick. The crowbar yanked free, taking with it a large part of Andy's brain, hanging off the end of the metal. Mac swung the crowbar at Caroline, and it connected with her head. She lost her balance and fell down the stairs. She tumbled to the floor and landed on her head, an audible crack signifying a broken neck.

"Christ on a bike…" said Mac, out of breath, and out of belief.

He made his way down the stairs and stared at Caroline's dead body. Was she really dead? He carefully stepped past her and went into the kitchen. He took the picnic basket and medical bag.

About to leave, he paused. A phone sat on a small desk by the door. He picked it up, no ringtone. Dead.

Mac left and got back to the pub as fast as he could move.

Angie was in her bedroom with Ellie. There was a seat in the corner that Ellie took, and Angie sat on the bed. She flicked the remote control from one channel to another, seeing nothing but the same blackness, or static, depending on the channel.

"Do you have a radio?" asked Ellie.

Angie nodded. "Yes, but it's downstairs. Maybe we can try it when Mac gets back."

"How long do you think he'll be?"

"He shouldn't be too long. The Marshall's is just down the road. They're good friends of ours, I'm sure they'll be able to help in some way. Even if it's just to have some friends around. Things are so strange, it will be nice to have some familiarity."

"If they're ok," said Ellie, staring out the window to the farmland beyond the pub.

Angie didn't reply. They sat in silence for a few minutes.

"What happened to you and Ed, how did you end up here?"

Ellie shook her head. "I told him we should have stayed in the car. But he is…" she paused, " was, so pig-headed." She wiped away a quickly forming tear.

"What happened, did you break down?"

Ellie shook her head. "No, we were on our way to Bristol from London. We had left before the military closed it. We got out just in time."

"What was London like?"

Ellie looked at Angie with tired red eyes. "It was awful. It was like a war zone. People were running around on the streets, fighting, stealing stuff, trying to get into people's cars. And then there were the others, the ones with the virus. Police were useless, army were just shooting anyone that moved."

Angie shuddered to think how terrified Ellie and her boyfriend must have been.

"Ed wanted to leave earlier, I should have listened to him. Maybe he'd be alive… In the end, it was obvious there was no choice, we had to go. Things were just crazy."

Ellie sat back and took a few deep breaths. She blinked hard a few times as if trying to wipe away the memories.

Angie gave her the time she needed.

"I have family in Bristol, you see, so that's where we headed. We spoke to them on the phone when we left, didn't manage to get in touch after that. The phones went, internet went. But we kept going. Traffic was a nightmare, worst ever. We tried turning off onto smaller and smaller roads, and it seemed to help a bit, we eventually got onto some little road and made good time, until we found ourselves stuck on an A-road, by Frome. That's the town near here isn't it?"

Angie nodded.

"So we got stuck. Just didn't move. It got dark, and people started fighting, horns blowing, everyone getting mad. Ed told us we had to ditch the car and get somewhere for the night, anywhere, away from all the people. I think he was scared that things were going to get real bad. I wanted to stay in the car. I told him that I shouldn't be going anywhere with the baby and that."

Ellie paused again and shook her head angrily. "I should've listened. Things were out of control. What did I think was going to happen?"

"When did you get out of the car?"

"It was past eleven. Some car up the road just blew up. At least I think it did. Big bang, and then flames and smoke. Loads of people left their cars then. Loads stayed. God knows happened to them.

"We got out, took our backpacks and set out on the fields." Ellie's voice took a faraway quality. "We stayed away from other people, Ed said it was dangerous. We tramped through fields for hours. Had to stop often as I can't walk very fast, get tired, what do you expect? He did the best he could, even tried carrying me at one point, but it was no good. Eventually, we saw some lights, and headed towards them."

She stopped speaking. Her head went down into her hands, and she sobbed quietly.

Angie waited, herself staring out the window. It was such a beautiful day. She couldn't remember seeing a sky so clear and so blue, and then she realised why - there were no vapour trails, no fading streaks of white cloud left behind by many jets flying to and from London.

Ellie started speaking again, her head still down. "That was when it came. It was so dark, we didn't see it - the man, the thing, the virus thing, it came through a hole in the hedge. We were on a path, you know, between fields, and it was just there, suddenly. It came for Ed and grabbed him straight away. Ed fought with it and eventually he got it on the ground and smashed its head with a rock. You have to get them on the head, that's what people in London were saying. Ed got it. But it had got Ed too.

"We sort of knew he was probably going to get the virus, but we thought that if we got help, we could fix it. Maybe the doctors knew. If we could get to hospital… We found your place soon after."

Angie continued to stare out the window, tears blurring her vision. So much pain, so much loss. How much more? This seemed like just the beginning.

Chapter 6

Mac jogged to the pub; his clothes stuck to him with sweat and his straining lungs crushed against his rib cage. His shins ached with every step he took.

That's what the easy life does for you, he thought.

Suddenly there was a huge noise above him. He looked up to see three fighter jets screech across the sky, low and fast.

He couldn't help but smile. The air force was in action, which meant someone was fighting this.

Maybe the army would eventually get all the infected, thought Mac. If they could just stay safe until then.

That's it, we can lock down the pub.

He ran up to the door and knocked softly, nervous looks over his shoulder.

"Gaz, Gaz, it's me, Mac, let me in."

Nothing.

"For Pete's sakes, Gaz, open the bloody door," he said a little louder.

He was about to hammer on the door, his temper up, when he realised what the silence could mean… And if the worst had happened, he didn't want his banging to get his wife coming downstairs to open the door.

He peered in the window through a gap in the curtains. The table where he had left Johnny and Gaz was empty.

The door was bolted from the inside; he would have to find another way in.

He made his way around the back of the car park. Against one of the walls of the pub, sat a large wheelie skip. Thankfully it was mostly empty, so not too heavy, and he was able to shift it with little effort.

Underneath was the cellar chute.

He took off the key ring that he'd attached to this belt that morning - a habit forty years in the making. He smiled, Angie always called him a creature of habit, like an old bear, she said, that never left its cave and did the same things every day.

He unlocked the cellar chute and eased up the door with one hand, holding the crowbar loosely in the other. His grip was tired, but he didn't want to be caught by surprise.

He peered in; nothing but shadows. Gently walking down the stairs, he waited for his eyes to become accustomed to the light.

There was movement in the corner of the cellar.

He stiffened and grabbed the crowbar, holding it high, ready to strike.

"Mac, wait, it's me, it's Gaz."

Mac sighed. "You bloody idiot. I nearly brained you!" Gaz had been crouched down behind one of the casks. "What you doing down here? Where's Johnny?"

Gaz spoke, through tears. "Sorry Mac, I couldn't."

"Couldn't what?"

"I couldn't do him. Like you said. I couldn't do him."

"You mean he turned?"

Gaz nodded. "Aye, about ten minutes ago. He sort of passed out, went really pale like. I got the fire extinguisher like you said to. He was all sweaty, and his veins were sticking out. I didn't know if that was funny business or not…"

"Just tell me what happened son."

"He opened his eyes, I thought he was just waking up, but they were all black, like none of the coloured bits. He suddenly went for me across the table - look!"

Gaz held his arm forward, and Mac could make out a deep scratch across Gaz's arm.

"Have I got it now?" The lad's voice shook, breaking in pitch every few words.

"Not if he didn't bite you." Although Mac didn't know for sure. He grabbed Gaz by the shoulders, "What happened, where's Johnny?"

"I ran. I don't know, I'm sorry Mac, I fucked up. I just came down here and hid. Bloody hell, I'm sorry Mac."

"Gah," said Mac, letting go. He looked around for a weapon - a chair leg lay in the corner. "Here," he said thrusting it at Gaz, "Take this and follow me. And stop your bloody crying. Pull yourself together, lad."

They made their way up the stairs with Mac in front. The cellar door led to the bottom of the stairs. To the right was the pub lounge, and to the left, a short corridor led to the kitchen. All looked quiet.

They took a few steps forward, then Mac heard a clang to his left. He held up his hand, "Listen…" he pointed into the kitchen.

There was a sudden tumultuous crash, the sound of metal hitting the floor, and then a low moan.

"Bugger's in the kitchen," whispered Mac.

They moved slowly to the kitchen door, and Mac peered around the corner to see Johnny, or at least what used to be Johnny, stumbling about the kitchen. There was a table in the middle, and Johnny, confused, walked back and forth between the wall and table.

Mac eased back into the corridor. "He's in there alright. Against the back of the wall. You go round one side of the table, I'll go the other."

Gaz nodded quickly, sweat forming on his forehead.

"You alright with this?"

Gaz nodded again, "Yeah, sure. I got it."

As soon as Johnny saw Mac and Gaz enter the room, he let out a loud moan. His movements became frenzied as he pushed against the table, trying to get to them. He bent over the table in a futile attempt to reach them both, moving slightly from side to side, but no definite direction taken.

"We move at the same time," said Mac. He moved to the right, and Gaz moved to the left.

Johnny moaned again, now confused as to which way to go. His arms moved out in both directions.

Gaz and Mac moved slowly along the sides of the table. "Keep your eyes on him… No sudden movements…" Mac held his crowbar up ready to strike, as did Gaz with the chair leg.

"That's it Gaz, nice and… Gaz!"

Gaz tumbled, and he let out a yell as he fell to the floor.

Johnny spun around fast; he rounded the corner and dived on Gaz. A series of yells, each getting louder than the last.

Mac darted round to Gaz's side of the table and reached for Gaz to pull him out of Johnny's reach, but then Mac felt his feet slipping from under him. He landed hard on the floor; the tiles were wet and slippery. Soup. That was the crash earlier - Johnny had knocked a pot of soup onto the floor.

Mac skidded around, trying to get up. He felt a hand grab his ankle and he kicked it away. He scurried back against the far wall.

"Mac! Mac!" shouted Gaz.

Blood spurted out of Gaz'z mouth as he shouted. Johnny was pulling himself along Gaz's body, biting, tugging at the flesh. He ripped at Gaz's stomach, and with the help of his hands, began to pull out a long chain of intestines that went straight into his mouth. Gaz looked down in horror for a few seconds, his cries escalating to an unbearable volume before he passed out.

Mac pulled himself up, and nearly landed on his arse again. There was a sharp pain in his ankle. "Bollocks," he shouted.

Johnny looked up from his feast and hissed at Mac. Johnny stood up and began to make his way towards him.

Mac, in shock and pain, backed out of the kitchen, reeling in fear and disgust. He turned and hobbled down the corridor, then realised he hadn't shut the kitchen door behind him. He turned and saw Johnny emerging, a new speed and fervour in his motion. Mac practiced a swing, but he was unable to get any strength into it, his ankle shouting in pain, threatening to give way.

He turned and made his way up the stairs, pulling himself up the banister. When at the top, he ducked behind the wall and carefully looked down to the bottom of the stairs. Johnny soon appeared but stopped at the first step. He looked around, without looking up. He sniffed, his attention seemingly caught by something back in the direction of the kitchen - Gaz's corpse no doubt.

Mac sighed in relief as Johnny turned and headed back the way he had come. Mac made his way back to the bedroom - no doubt his wife had heard all the noise.

He knocked gently on his bedroom door, "Angie, it's me, Mac."

It only took a few seconds before the door was opened by Ellie.

Mac went in quickly and shut the door behind him. He bolted it. "Help me move this dresser here, against the door."

"Mac, what happened? We heard all sorts of noise from downstairs, some terrible screams," said Angie as Mac and Ellie moved the dresser. "Where's Gaz and Johnny?"

Mac limped over to Angie, "They're both done for." He hugged his wife, easing himself down beside her on the bed.

"They're infected?"

Mac nodded. The strain on his face showing as the pain in his ankle intensified.

"What happened? Are you ok?" said a worried Angie, as she looked him up and down. "You're covered in blood!"

"Were you bit?" said Ellie, her urgency forcing the question into a shout.

Mac shook his head. "Just pulled my ankle. The blood's not mine. We tried to get Johnny, but Gaz slipped, and that was that. I tried to help him but fell over too. That bloody soup. Johnny had knocked it on the floor."

"Oh Mac," Angie hugged her husband again, burying her head in his neck.

"Where are they now?" asked Ellie, calming down.

"I think they're in the kitchen. It's not pretty in there… Christ on a bike. Here Angie, have a look at my ankle will you?"

Angie eased up Mac's trouser leg to reveal a very red and swollen ankle. She gently felt around the joint and moved his foot slowly as Mac grimaced.

"Can you move it?"

Mac's foot moved slowly up and down.

"Good. I don't think it's broken, maybe you just sprained it."

"It bloody hurts. You got any of them tablets?"

Angie nodded, "Ellie, can you get some ibuprofen out of the dresser, top drawer."

Mac took the tablets and lay back on the bed. "Bloody hell. What is happening…"

Ellie sat down on the chair by the window. "There are six now."

"Six what?" said Angie.

"Six plumes of smoke. There were only four earlier this morning. And I can see a helicopter, but it's not stopping anywhere."

Mac sat up, "A helicopter?" He limped over to the window. "I saw a few jets going over when I got back from the farm. That helicopter looks like a Chinook, military." He turned to the women, "Looks like we're getting ourselves sorted. Knew our boys would get in action soon enough."

"You think the army is going to sort this out?" asked Ellie.

"That's what they're there for."

"But that didn't happen in the other countries."

Mac dismissed her with a wave of his hand and a smile. "They don't have the British army though, do they? This is what we're good at. Against the odds, Battle of Britain and all that. Did you know that in 1943…"

"What happened at the farm?" said Angie.

"It wasn't good." He felt a pang of sadness. "Andy and Caroline… well, they didn't make it."

"Oh no," said Angie, tears welling up her eyes again. "This is so awful, just so awful."

Mac put his arm around her.

"So what do we do?" said Ellie.

"We wait for the army. I reckon they will be sorting out the cities first."

"So we just sit here? In this room?" said Ellie.

Mac felt a shade of doubt. There was no telling how long the army would be. London, Bristol… might take some time before they headed to the smaller towns.

"We can lock down the pub, there's plenty of canned food in the kitchen, should last us for a good while. Only problem I see is…"

"Our resident infected," said Ellie.

"Aye, Johnny and Gaz. Although I guess they ain't Johnny and Gaz anymore."

"Ellie's right," said Angie. "We can't just stay in this room, we have to find a way to, well, get rid of them," said Angie, the last part of her sentence whispered.

Mac rubbed his brow, deep in thought. "Ok, so here's the situation. I can hardly walk, God knows how long 'til it gets better, You can't walk," he looked at Angie, "and you are very pregnant," he said To Ellie. "Those buggers are tricky, that can move fast when they want to."

They sat in silence for a while.

"Seven," said Ellie as a new plume rose from the town.

"You're in about best shape, Ellie," said Mac. "How would you feel about braining some of those, what you call them, infected?"

Ellie said, "It would be a pleasure."

Chapter 7

Ellie held the crowbar in her hand, felt the weight and took a few practice swings. It felt good to have something to do other than sit around and think. She didn't want to think anymore. She wanted revenge.

Mac talked through the plan once more.

"Ok Ellie, you go into your bedroom, close the door, make sure they can't see you. Me and Angie will open our bedroom door a gap, keep the dresser up against it and start making a hell of a racket, get them up here.

"Once they're busy trying to get at us through the gap, you come out of your room and finish them off from behind. Easier that way."

Ellie nodded. There were butterflies in her stomach, but her mind was calm and clear. Gaz and Johnny weren't the ones that had got Ed, but they would do. It was the same virus, and getting rid of these two would kill a little bit of it.

"Remember Ellie, super quiet. They can move on a penny, nearly got me this morning. Got poor Gaz no problem. He was only on the floor for a second.

"Now, let me see that swing again."

She pulled back the crowbar and swung once, twice, with the flat end of the crowbar. Mac had warned her against using the bent end - "It'll get stuck in the brain."

Her back hurt a little when she swung, but then it had hurt for the past few months. No difference there.

"Let's get started," said Ellie.

Mac pushed against the dresser and moved it a foot. He prised the door open slowly and poked his head through the gap. He looked up and down the corridor.

"All clear. You sure you want to do this?"

Ellie nodded.

Mac pushed the dresser back a further foot so that Ellie could squeeze out.

"Good luck," said Angie quietly.

"Remember, they won't see you coming."

Ellie pushed her way into the corridor. She heard the dresser being pushed back into position and the door was jammed shut, so only a small gap was showing.

"Ok," came Mac's hushed voice.

Ellie walked the few yards to the next room, on the opposite side of the corridor. She opened the door carefully and peered into the room before entering. It was empty.

She went in and pulled the door to, leaving a slight gap so she could see out to Mac and Angie's room.

It was so quiet. Ellie heard her heartbeat and the ringing in her ears. Was this what the world would be like from now on, silent? Had everything stopped?

"Ok Mac," she threw her whisper across the corridor.

There was a few more moment's silence, and then Mac and Angie started to bang against their door, and yell. "Hey! Hey! Up here, come on! Hey!"

Their voices, Mac's low timbre, and Angie's high falsetto worked in unison to create a racket. All Ellie had to do was wait, surely the infected would be along soon.

Her heart started to beat in double time, and she held her belly. Doubt raced across her mind, what the hell was she doing?

The only thing I can do, she thought. Killing these two and then locking down in the pub was the best way she could protect her baby. Tears began to flow. Thoughts of everything that could, and should, have been with her and Ed flashed through her mind, taking on a vivid reality, so real they felt almost like memories. But there never would be any memories of her, Ed, and their child.

The sadness became anger. Just in time.

A heavy moan droned from the bottom of the corridor. Ellie peeked through the tiny gap in the door, holding her breath, scared they would hear her, or maybe smell her.

Two figures slowly made their way around the corner at the bottom of the corridor, shuffling almost silently through the heavy carpet.

Mac increased the noise he was making, but there was no more sound from Angie.

Both the figures were covered in blood, and the one at the back seemed to be trailing some pink tubes from its stomach. Ellie realised the tubes were the young man's guts, hanging freely from an open wound in his abdomen. Ellie pulled back from the gap and held her hand to her mouth, stopping herself from throwing up.

She sat up against the wall, breathing fast, her heart like a piston in her chest. Sweat formed on her brow, and on her hands. She gripped the crowbar tighter.

I can do this, she told herself. She placed her hands on her belly. I have to do this.

The moaning became louder, and Ellie willed herself back to the crack in the door to see the two infected by Mac and Angie's door.

"Ellie! Come on Ellie!" shouted Mac.

Ellie went to pull the door open but froze. She couldn't do it, her arms wouldn't move.

She breathed deeply. She closed her eyes and thought of Ed, of the times they would never have together. And it was the virus that had done this, the virus that stood a few feet away.

"I love you, I miss you," she whispered.

She pulled the door open slowly and stepped gently towards the two corpses battling to get into Mac's room. She tried to ignore the trailing guts that hung and stank from the stomach of the nearest ex-man. He was going to get it first.

She raised the crowbar and, just as Mac had shown her, swung it down with all her might. Too much might.

The metal made sharp contact with the skull of the infected, and she heard a crack as the bone shattered, but she lost her balance and followed the crowbar, falling against Gaz. Warm blood splattered across her face.

She screamed as Gaz spun round to face her, but he was already dead for the second time. The crowbar slipped out of her hand as the body fell, and she fell with it.

Her only thought was of her baby, and she pushed her arms out to protect her belly from the fall. Her hands sank into Gaz's stomach and became entwined in the warmth of his intestines and bowel. She slipped further forward, and her right hand squelched up further into the torso, becoming wrapped in bones and warm fleshy organs.

She landed on her side, expecting Johnny to be on her, all gnashing jaws and teeth. She pulled her hands, wrapped in intestines and other unidentified fleshy lumps, out of Gaz's torso.

"Kill it!" Mac shouted from beyond the door.

Mac had pushed both hands through the gap in the door and gripped the skull of Johnny's corpse. Johnny was facing Ellie, his arms reaching for her, his jaws snapping viciously.

"I can't hold him much longer!"

Ellie pushed herself up, ignoring the pain in her back and belly and grabbed the crowbar from the floor. She gripped it tight, trying not to let it go, the sloppy blood on her hands making it hard to hold on.

She stood up straight and stared at the infected shell before her. She stared deep into its eyes and saw nothing.

"Ok Mac, let it go!"

Mac's hands disappeared, and the creature lurched forward, its arms locking around Ellie's shoulders. It got no further.

Ellie slammed the crowbar hard through the eye socket, deep into the thing's skull. There was satisfying crack. She closed her eyes against the spraying blood, and when she opened them again, the corpse was on the floor, dead again.

It let out one last long slow moaning breath, and then it was still. Everything was still.

"Ellie? You ok, Ellie?" Mac's head appeared at the gap in the door. She nodded. She was covered in blood and human insides. She had just smashed a crowbar into two skulls. But she nodded. She was ok. Her hand rested on her belly.

Mac pushed the dresser out of the way and opened the door. She ran into the room and burst into tears.

Angie and Mac both took her and hugged her, blood and guts and all.

Chapter 8

Mac nailed the final plank into place over the window. One more window to go, but he would be done by sundown, only an hour or so away. He picked up the pile of planks and hobbled over to it.

Placing the plank over the last window, he began hammering.

"Time for a break, Mac," said Ellie. She placed a cup of tea down on the table.

"Thanks, love, that's just great. How's Angie?"

"She's upstairs, sleeping." Ellie sat down and sipped from her cup of tea. "How long do you think it will be before the army get here?"

"I don't know, could be any time. I think we'll hear on the radio first. Important to keep scanning it. I imagine they'll put out some sort of broadcast once they've restored order in London."

"I hope you're right."

Mac blew gently on his tea and took a sip. "I do too."

They sat in silence for a few minutes. The events of yesterday seemed but a dream. He kept thinking, what if I just drive into town, what if everything is normal and it all just happened in my head?

But the fire plumes kept rising. The jets kept flying. The customers stayed away. And one of the infected had been scratching and moaning by the front door earlier that morning. He had watched through a gap in the curtains until it went away, stumbling blindly back onto the road and disappearing from view. He hadn't told the women. He'd have to tighten up defences. No telling how long they'd be in the pub.

"How much food have we got?" asked Ellie.

"Enough," he said. "We have tins of stuff that'll stay good for months. Water should be ok, as long as it keeps raining. I've got a water butt out back."

"Don't you worry, Ellie, you'll be safe here, and I'd guess you'll be giving birth in a few months in some military hospital somewhere."

"Not what I had in mind." She laughed quietly.

"No, life does throw the odd curveball. That's for sure." He remembered his son. So many years ago, but still so much pain.

A loud click sounded, and they were in darkness. The lights had gone out.

"Mac…' whispered Ellie.

He sighed. "I guess the power has gone."

Angie shouted from upstairs.

"Come on, let's go and see to Angie."

Angie lay in the darkness and looked up in relief when Mac and Ellie came into the room.

"What's happened, Mac? Is it a fuse?"

"You ok?"

She nodded.

"I'll go check the fuses." He was back a few minutes later, torch in hand.

"Not a fuse, it looks like the power has gone."

Angie began to cry. Mac leaned in and wrapped his arms around her. "Hey, don't worry. It'll be ok, like one big camping trip."

"Don't be stupid. Of course it won't." She found herself smiling anyway. "But thanks."

"Right, I'll go and get our camping gear, the candles and that, and I have a little stove somewhere," said Mac. "I'll rustle up some dinner."

Ellie said, "I'll help. Tell me where things are and I'll go get them, your leg…"

"Don't worry about me, I'll-"

"No Mac," said Ellie. "I don't mean to sound harsh, but it's not so much out of concern for your leg, but more than that, we need you to get better. We need us all at our full strength."

Ellie stood up, her frame casting a large shadow in the torchlight. "Things are different now."

Mac nodded. "Right you are…" He picked up the crowbar from beside the bed and passed it to Ellie. "Right you are."

Zone Lima Delta

Chapter 1

Sergeant Donald Allen stared straight ahead as Second Lieutenant Dalby read the mission orders to the platoon. Allen sensed the nervousness in Dalby, only out of training from Sandhurst three months ago. This was Dalby's first real-world situation.

It was 3:30 am, and raining hard; water dripped down the back of Allen's neck. Three troop carriers idled nearby.

"Ok men," said Dalby, "We are to proceed to Junction 16a of the M25 and assist with the containment of the London Perimeter. On no account are any civilian or hostile persons to be allowed to break the perimeter. All hostiles are to be met with lethal force.

"The civilians are to be corralled into extraction zones, ready for transport to safe zones.

"Any civilians trying to escape the perimeter ahead of extraction are to be considered hostile and dealt with accordingly.

"Any questions?"

There was shuffling throughout the ranks. One of the privates, Walton, called out, "What the fuck is the London Perimeter?"

"Watch it, Walton," said Allen. He cast him a stern look.

"It's ok, Sergeant." Dalby looked at Walton. "London is being closed. As far as I know, and as far as we need to know, the virus is running out of control in London, and a full evac has been ordered. To further contain the virus, the evac is to be managed."

Mumbling from the troops. Allen stood forward, "Ok, you lot, shut it. Listen to your officer." He noticed a few sharp glances in his direction, but the troops returned to order. Standing tight, staring ahead.

Dalby said, "That's as much as I know."

Walton spoke again, "So when does a civilian become a hostile?"

Dalby ignored the question and turned to Allen. "Sergeant. Reprimand that man." He turned on his heel and marched to the first troop carrier.

"Ok, Let's go," shouted Allen, his deep voice cutting through the wind and rain. "One section per truck, Charlie section in the first, Echo in the second and Indigo the third. Walton, you're with me."

The troops filed into the trucks. The rain fell harder. Boots stomped through wet mud.

The troop carrier rumbled along the main road. The wind blew through the tarpaulin sides, and the men sat tight together to preserve heat; Allen sat in the darkness in the far corner.

"Is this for real, Sarge?" asked Corporal Lewis.

"Don't know son. What do you think?"

"I think it's some fancy exercise," said Walton. Some of the other men laughed, and a few nodded in agreement. There was nervousness in the truck. Hardly any of these men, kids really, had seen real action yet.

"Enough with the wisecracks. Get some shut-eye," said Allen. "Exercise or not, no telling when you'll next be getting some rest."

Allen peered out of the side of the tarpaulin. The lane on the other side of the road was jammed with traffic. Some of the cars were empty. Even though it was 4 am, people were walking along the road; couples, families, small children. They all eyed the troop carriers, and some of the people waved, their eyes suddenly filled with hope. A dad pointed out the army vehicles to his small son, who beamed a smile and waved.

Allen closed the tarpaulin, he'd seen enough to know this was no exercise.

Thirty minutes later, as they neared the motorway, they heard the first unmistakable cracks of gunfire in the early morning air. Single shots, one after another.

The men in the back of the carrier shuffled uneasily.

"This is for real, isn't it?" asked Singh, a young private.

Allen spoke quickly before conversation buzzed up - "Ok men, keep your weapons on safety until we get on site. Stay in the trucks until the Lieutenant has our orders. Keep calm, look out for each other. From what I've seen, this virus does funny things to people."

"How do we know who has the virus?" said Walton.

"I don't know. We'll find out."

Allen looked over the troops in his section. The oldest was Corporal Lewis, only twenty-two. Allen had twenty years on him.

One by one, as the shooting became louder, each of the young men looked up to the Sergeant. He kept his expression motionless, not meeting anyone's gaze. He felt familiar anxiety fill his stomach. He quelled it quickly, stone cold; it was the way it had to be.

They went over a roundabout and down an exit onto the motorway, the gunfire now loud and continuous. Other military vehicles lined the road. The truck pulled into the side of the exit ramp and stopped. Shouting could be heard behind the gunfire. Screaming, too.

"Steady!" said Allen. The men held their weapons tight, sharing their glances between the back of the truck and the Sarge.

Dalby appeared at the back of the truck, "Allen, come with me."

"Stay here men," said Allen, "listen to Lewis." He nodded at the young corporal who nodded back as Allen jumped onto the tarmac.

At the bottom of the exit some military vehicles, combined with makeshift fences made of bollards and barbed wire, blocked the motorway entirely. The fences continued up and over the top of the steep embankments that lined both sides of the road.

And then the cars. Hundreds of cars filled the road on the way to London, as far as Allen could see. On the horizon, numerous plumes of smoke rose into the early morning blue tinted sky, telling of the many raging fires in the country's capital city.

Allen worked hard to stay calm in the face of the terrible sight and sounds before him. Screaming pierced the gunfire; a sharp falsetto of fear from the hundreds of people squeezed in between the cars, standing on the cars, squashed up against the fences, trying to climb the fences.

Soldiers were shooting into the crowd, the potent smell of gunpowder in the air.

Whether they were shooting the people or hostiles, Allen couldn't tell. He didn't know what hostiles looked like yet.

"Sergeant!" Dalby said. Allen pulled himself away from the hypnotic chaos of the fence and followed Dalby to a small encampment under the bridge, a few hundred feet behind the front line, where a hastily constructed base of operations stood - many tables where men typed on laptops and spoke into headsets. A large ordinance survey map of the motorway junction and surrounding countryside had been erected. A Major stood by the map, talking with other officers. He was a tall man, his hands on his hips, nodding at something another officer was saying.

"Sir!" said Dalby standing to attention and saluting. Allen followed suit.

"Dalby?" said the Major.

"Sir."

"Good, we need some relief on the northbound carriageway - that's this one - it's turned into a real shit show and the men holding are exhausted. We've lost four of them, can you believe it?"

"No, sir."

The major stared out to the barrier - "They've been coming all night. Can't blame the poor buggers, the virus is in there, and they want out, but we can't let it spread, can we?"

"No, sir."

"You're familiar with the orders?"

"Sir."

"Good. Get your men up on the trucks, and along the fence on the embankment, you'll have a good view of the whole scene. We are filtering people through two gates." He motioned to an area where civilians were being allowed through the fence and taken to waiting trucks. "We get the trucks filled, and off they go to the safe zones. Simple as that. Except any infected are possible zeds, so we take them to the holding pen, over there." He pointed across the crash barrier to the other side of the motorway, where a large number of people were contained in a makeshift cage. "They get taken to a field hospital in those trucks." A different line of trucks waited.

"You said 'zeds,' sir?"

"The Infected. Zeds. Z for Zombies. If it walks like a duck, Lieutenant."

Allen and Dalby glanced at each other.

The Major continued. "Anyone with a wound, bite marks, bleeding of any sort, is considered a possible zed. You see anyone on the other side of the barrier who is bleeding, who has any flesh wounds, who is attacking anyone else; they are to be considered hostile and executed with extreme prejudice. Is that clear Dalby?"

"Sir."

The Major cast a careful gaze over the Lieutenant. "This is not a pretty situation. Your men are going to have particular challenges today. Do you understand?"

"I think so, sir."

The Major looked Dalby up and down. "When was your commission?"

"Three months ago. Sir."

"Christ." The Major looked at Allen for the first time. "You seem like you have seen some action, Sergeant?"

Allen stood to attention. "Sir, two tours in Afghanistan, three in Iraq."

"Thank God for that," said the Major, seemingly satisfied.

Dalby threw a quick and sharp glance at Allen.

The Major pointed up the sides of the embankment. "The fence tracks up there and across a field for a good few hundred meters, before we hit a rock wall. The people are trying to sneak past the fence up there. Tell the men that if people get past the barrier, give them one verbal warning, then one warning shot, and if they don't turn back, they are to be considered hostile." The Major stared at Dalby. "Are we clear?"

"Yes, sir."

"Good, now get to it. And Lieutenant, Sergeant, I have a feeling that what we are doing here is going to be very important. Good luck." He turned to walk away, then paused. "One more thing gentlemen - you need to shoot them in the head."

Dalby and Allen nodded.

As they walked back to the trucks, the Lieutenant said to Allen, "Take Charlie section up the embankment, Sergeant, relieve the men up there. I'll manage things down here."

Allen knew he should be down here, in the thick of it, but he nodded.

"Ok, sir."

Chapter 2

Allen jogged to the truck holding Charlie section. At least Corporal Lewis was amongst Charlie, he had spent time in Afghanistan. Not much action, but it was a deployment at least.

"Ok boys, we're up the embankment, let's have you!" The men filed out, and Allen repeated the orders. He noticed a chilling in the ranks at the implications of what they were being asked to do.

"How can Brits be hostile, Sarge?" asked Private O'Reilly, a young scouser.

Allen wondered the same thing, but said, "We're not talking about Mr and Mrs bloody Smith from next door, lad. We're talking about the virus. Turns people into savages."

"But what about the ones who break the fence, are we really going to…"

"Pack it in!" shouted Allen. "You have our orders. Now get up the bloody hill."

The men climbed up the side of the embankment, where a number of tired looking soldiers were already stationed. Allen tapped one them on the shoulder, "Where's your section head?"

The young soldier said nothing and pointed up the hill, his eyes red and, so it seemed to Allen, empty.

Allen ran up the hill to where he saw another sergeant. "5th company, Sergeant Allen. Here to relieve you lot."

The Sergeant nodded at Allen. "You're welcome to it. This place is fucked." He was standing at the top of the embankment. A tall fence carried on for about a hundred yards across a flat farm field, where the land rose quickly to meet a high rock face of about fifty foot. Allen could see soldiers down at the far end. The present company's sergeant shouted down the line - "Ok lads, let's get the fuck out of here!"

He turned to Allen. "I've lost two men this morning. One got bit, the other shot himself."

"Shot himself?"

"That's right." He looked up the line and motioned to his men to hurry up. Three men arrived and continued down the embankment with their sergeant.

Allen quickly stationed his men. He put four along the fencing in the field and stationed the other four down the embankment.

The crowd of civilians on the other side of the fence was edging forward, taking advantage of the change of the guard.

Allen walked to the bottom of the embankment, inspecting his men's positions, making sure the cover was good.

"Ok! Single shots, mark your targets. Try and keep this lot back with a few shots at their feet. We can't have them swamping the fence."

His men started firing a few feet in front of the advancing crowd, who responded with yells, and a reluctant retreat. Allen stared at the crowd; ordinary men, women, children. He swallowed, his mouth and throat suddenly dry.

"This ain't right sir!" shouted Walton.

"They get past this fence, and you'll have to shoot them all. That what you want, son?" Walton put his head down, frowning. "Then keep your fucking trap shut and do your job."

There was a buzz on the commlink in his ear. "Come in."

"Serge, it's Lewis. You have to get up here."

"Roger. On my way. Walton, keep them back. I'm going up over the ridge."

Allen ran up the hill. The other side of the fence was teeming with people, all trying to find a way out of the hell they had suddenly found themselves in. Allen rested his finger on his machine gun trigger.

Allen paused. He saw a young man in a white t-shirt stained with blood. His mouth also covered in blood. He was stumbling mindlessly without purpose - not trying to scale the embankment, but wandering from left to right and back, his arms grabbing at people running past him.

That's what a zed looks like, thought Allen. He raised his gun and fired off a single shot. It hit the man in the chest, and he fell to the ground. Allen lowered his weapon and watched as the man got up again, oblivious to the new hole in his heart.

Allen swallowed hard. He raised his gun and this time hit the man with a clean headshot, blood and brain matter exploding from the back of his skull.

The man fell to the ground, and this time didn't get up. Allen nodded his head slowly, he had seen it for himself now. It didn't matter if it was irrational, if it was against everything he had ever believed - it was the reality. Let the politicians and the philosophers work out the whys and hows. Sergeant Donald Allen would deal with mopping up the mess.

He continued his sprint up the embankment, keeping a sharp eye for any more hostiles. As he reached the field, he saw why he had been called up. Hoards of people lined the area, the mass of them twenty feet or so away from the fence, an unstable invisible boundary holding them back.

His men reinforced the boundary with regular shots to the ground when anyone tried to break the ranks.

Allen quickly found Lewis, up near the end of the fence where the field lay against the impassable rocky rise. Still, people were trying to climb it, and mostly failing.

"Sit-rep Lewis," said Allen.

"You can see for yourself, sir, we can't hold this lot back anymore. They swamp, and we're done for."

Allen could see no way to disagree with his corporal. He pointed to the bullhorn on the ground next to Lewis - "You tried that?"

Lewis shook his head. Allen lifted the bullhorn. "Go down the embankment, you will be processed and taken to safety. I repeat, go down the embankment."

Angry jeers came from the crowd. Through the shouts, Allen heard certain words, clear as day - 'traitor,' 'fascist,' 'heartless,' 'robot,' 'murderers.'

Lewis lay down more suppressing fire, and the crowd sank back a few feet.

"Dammit," said Allen. He tapped his comm link. "Lieutenant," he shouted over the gunfire and shouts of the crowd. "We got some serious shit up here, this crowd is getting angry. We need to get them through the gate quicker."

"Sergeant," buzzed the reply, "we have also got serious shit down here. Do your job and contain the crowd."

"We need more men."

"All men are engaged at the gates, there are no men to spare. Contain the crowd."

"Sir, I don't think you understand the situation up here, we are unable to-"

"I understand the situation Sergeant, do as I say and contain the crowd. There are no men to spare."

Lewis, fear in his eyes, looked at Allen.

Allen breathed hard and swallowed. "Sir, I repeat, I don't think you understand the situation up here, we are unable to contain the crowd, one surge and this fence is down. We need more men, we need to fall back and re-establish a new defensive post."

A pause. Then the reply exploded through the comm link.

"Goddammit Allen! You'd better be right, I'm coming up there, and if I don't find a completely fucked situation, there's going to be trouble, is that understood?"

"Sir. Out." He signed off and shook his head, sighing.

Lewis allowed relief to show on his face, "Thanks, Sarge."

"Watch your bloody line," replied the Sergeant. He took a position in between Lewis and O'Reilly, about thirty feet away from each, and scanned the crowd for hostiles. Happy not to see any, he lay down more suppressing fire, forcing the crowd back again.

Allen knew the crowd wouldn't hold for long. There was fear in their eyes, and at some point, the fear of what lay behind them would outweigh the fear of his men and their guns. He had seen this behaviour in Iraq, many times. They didn't have much time.

The Lieutenant approached, walking, his handgun held by his hip. He had Collins with him. Allen took a few moments to calm himself. He could tell the Lieutenant was scared, too; scared men made dangerous decisions and took rash acts.

Dalby halted abruptly beside Allen, his hands on his hips, anger on his face, trying to hide the fear in his eyes.

"What is this, Allen, this does not look like a lost situation to me?"

Allen stood to attention, "Sir! I have seen situations like this before, sir. The crowd will not hold."

"Then lay down suppressing fire. I expected to see a situation out of control, and I see nothing but a bunch of civilians shouting obscenities, is this what you call out of control?"

"Sir, with all due respect, I've seen this before and-"

"Seen this before? In bloody Afghanistan no doubt?"

"In Iraq, sir."

"Do you think I don't know what I'm looking at?"

"That's not what I said sir, I-"

Dalby brought his face right up to Allen. "Do you think I don't know how to handle this situation?" he said.

"No, sir. I think that the officer is in complete control of the situation, sir."

"Damn right Sergeant. The officer believes there is no situation and you do not need extra men. Lay down suppressing fire and hold this crowd."

The Lieutenant turned on his heel and walked quickly towards the embankment.

Allen looked to the crowd - it had seen their captors arguing. The dumb intelligence that lived in crowds could smell weakness.

There was a wave of growing noise, and the mob began to undulate and move as one, becoming one, becoming a living being. This was the point of turning when the hundreds became one.

"Sir!" shouted a nervous Lewis from behind him.

"Hold!" shouted Allen, he turned to O'Reilly and shouted the same. "Hold!"

Dalby hadn't reached the embankment. He had stopped walking and was watching the mass of people on the other side of the fence, the ground by their feet churned into thick mud. People fell forward and became lost in the tramping feet as the crowd began an inexorable march forward, towards the fence.

Allen raised his gun and fired into the mud. Lewis and O'Reilly followed suit, as did Dalby and Collins. The shots were lost in the noise of the march. Dalby ran back towards Allen. "Hold them, Allen, hold them! They touch that fence, they're hostile!"

Allen froze, staring at the crowd, at the people. There was a moment's silence, and then suddenly it came.

The surge.

Within seconds they were on the fence, hands reaching through the wire, a cacophony of shouts and screams, anger and fear. The fence rattled violently along its length, the containing poles bouncing back and forth wildly.

"Fall back!" shouted Allen, and the company fell back about twenty feet or so, before taking firing positions.

Dalby, sheer panic in his eyes, shouted, "Open fire Sergeant, we can't let the fence go! We can't let them through! Open fire, dammit!"

Allen was frozen. For the first time as a soldier, he failed to execute an order immediately.

"Allen! Order your men to open fire."

He turned to look at O'Reilly and Lewis, both staring at him with wide eyes, scared and confused.

The Lieutenant marched up to Allen and grabbed him by the lapels. "A direct order, Allen, are you refusing a direct order?"

The throng pulsed against the fenced, wave after wave of pressure shaking the supports, pushing them nearer to collapse. Faces pushed up against the wire; young, old, men, women, children, shouting, screaming. Small hands extended through the gaps in the fence, reaching to him.

He felt himself being shaken again, "Damn you, Allen."

Dalby released Allen's lapels, spun around and pointed his gun at Lewis.

"Lewis, if you fail to follow my direct order I'll shoot you for treason where you stand."

Lewis, looking near to tears, shook his head slowly and raised his gun to the crowd, his hands shaking, his aim wild.

Sergeant Allen stood up and pointed his rifle at the fence. "It's ok, men," he bellowed above the noise of the mass. Regaining his composure, he spoke evenly, "Just a few shots lads, they'll break up. Just a few."

Allen scanned the crowd and saw an old man, his arms and neck twisted from the pressure of the people behind him. He took aim and fired, the side of the old man's head opened up as the bullet entered his skull. The man gasped, his eyes closed, but his body stayed still, the weight of the people behind him holding him up. The woman next to the dead man, now covered in blood, screamed.

Shots echoed from either side of Allen as O'Reilly and Lewis both opened fire.

Allen picked his next target, a man in his late fifties.

A woman that looked in her sixties.

A man in a checked shirt, in his seventies.

And so it went, one, then another. Mechanical, like a metronome, one shot, another one dead.

Bodies piled up.

Finally, it happened; realisation of the carnage at the fence. The crowd lost its consciousness, and the people turned and ran.

"Over their heads!" shouted Allen, "keep 'em running, let them hear the shots."

He glanced to his left and saw O'Reilly, his face red and with a wild look in his eyes, rapidly fire his gun into the air.

Twenty-three people lay dead by the fence. Allen thought it had been more, it had seemed like more.

About fifty foot from the fence and the people stopped running back; they instead swirled from side to side like an eddy in a whirlpool.

Zeds.

Afraid to go towards the fence, afraid to back away, they were suddenly caught in a terrible limbo with death promised either side.

"The zeds, Sergeant, shoot the zeds," shouted the Lieutenant. He stood watching with his hands and his gun held tight behind his back.

Allen cursed Dalby quietly under his breath, then shouted, "O'Reilly, Lewis, mark the zeds - we want clean headshots remember."

"We're protecting them now then?" spat O'Reilly.

Allen ignored the comment and picked out a zed, and fired.

The Lieutenant turned and walked down the embankment.

The three soldiers moved forward to the fence, took up positions and opened fire on the small number of zeds, not taking long to eliminate them.

With the zeds gone, and with a clear path to relative safety in the jungle of vehicles on the motorway, the people ran down the hill leaving the embankment empty.

Allen lowered his gun and lowered his head. He breathed deeply for a few seconds, then quickly stood up.

"Well done men."

Lewis shook his head. O'Reilly stared ahead, his grip on his rifle tight, forcing his hands into an unnatural whiteness.

"Keep your eye on the top of the embankment, mark your targets. Any zeds, take them out. Any civilians and we'll use this first," he motioned with the bullhorn, "and if they don't listen, set off a few warning shots."

"And we all know how well that worked," said Lewis.

"I know, son, it's not been a pretty day so far. But hold yourself up, we're not done yet."

He fought the feeling of nausea in his stomach and give Lewis a firm nod. He had to show Lewis that he was still in control, at least of himself if nothing else.

A shot rang out from his left, and a zed, stumbling over the top of the embankment, fell back, it's head exploding from a well placed shot by O'Reilly.

"That's it, keep it going."

"Sir," replied O'Reilly.

They bedded in, there was no telling when relief would come.

Chapter 3

Allen sat on his bunk and pulled off his t-shirt, stained with sweat and dirt. He needed a shower and some sleep, neither of which he would get.

The rest of his platoon was also bedding down in the hastily erected tent, part of a hastily erected base a few miles from the London Barrier. Night fell before they had been relieved and they had sat in darkness on the way back. No-one had spoken. Two men had been lost from the platoon - both victims of bites from people who had been okayed at the checkout. From what Allen had learned it was hard to tell if someone was infected, the only method was to look for bites, but if the soon-to-be-zed hid the bite, well, there was no way to know.

About three thousand people had been passed through the gate and moved to safe zones - a drop in the ocean guessed Allen.

The members of his platoon sat in silence. Lewis lay on the bed next to Allen's, staring at the roof of the tent, his hand behind his head. O'Reilly had his face in the pillow, hiding his tears.

The soldiers seemed to be trying to avoid each other's gaze, or maybe it was just Allen - every time he caught another man's eye, they hastily looked away. Allen didn't blame them - he knew what a first engagement felt like, but he couldn't imagine what it was like for these young men. At least he had been in the desert for his first, miles away from home, fighting a well-defined enemy. These boys had spent the day shooting at innocent civilians from their own country, and at strange infected half monsters - zombies, if the major was to be believed.

"Any idea where we are tomorrow, Sarge?" asked Walton, who had spent the day down by the gate.

"No," said Allen, glad that someone was talking. "I don't get told anything, you should know that by now. Best thing we can do is get some sleep. Wherever we are, you can bet it will be another long one."

Singh spoke from the corner of the room, "Don't think I can take another day like today. What the fuck is going on? Fuckin' madness this. It's not natural."

Allen pulled his kit bag up onto the bed. "It's best not to think about it, Singh. Just keep your head down, follow your orders and keep yourself alive. We've got a better chance of getting through this than those poor bastards behind the barrier."

Singh didn't answer, and silence fell upon the company again.

Allen took out a picture of his son, Adam, from the pocket on the front of his kit bag. He only saw his son every other weekend, his mother having shacked up with some estate agent a few years ago when he was on his last tour.

The photo was taken last summer while he was on leave. He always took Adam to the beach, down in Cornwall, a place called Tulloch's Bay; a friend let them use of their holiday chalet. Allen smiled as he remembered Adam charging into the breakers - he was his son alright, tough as nails for a lad of ten.

Allen pulled out his mobile phone, still no signal. He felt a stab of anxiety in his stomach as he allowed himself to think of his son and their mother - they lived in Fulham. He wondered if they had got out. It was all he could do to keep the tears from filling his eyes. It wouldn't be right for the lads to see him bawling like some little girl.

He placed the photo under his pillow and lay on top of it. He slowed his breathing down and counted backward from a hundred - it was a method the army psych had given him to calm himself, and it had seen him through many a long and lonely night.

He cleared his mind of any thought of his son, the only way he could ever sleep.

"Hey Sarge," said Lewis quietly in the darkness.

"Yes, lad?"

"Was it ever this bad in Iraq?"

"It was bad, but in different ways." He paused for a moment. "Never this bad though. At least then you knew who your enemy was."

They lay in silence for a minute or so.

"That Lieutenant's a prick," said Lewis.

"He doesn't know what he's doing, and he's scared shitless," said Allen. "But yeah, he's a prick."

Allen sat up and looked around the tent. A few men were asleep, a few pottering on their bunks.

He walked to the front of the tent, "Ok, lights out. Get some kip." He pulled the switch, and the tent fell into darkness.

The Sarge had them up at five the next morning, the lucky ones had got a full six hour's sleep.

"Ok, you lot, rise and shine. I want you kitted up and ready to move out in twenty minutes."

The men jumped up, groggy, their movements heavy. They showered, got dressed and were in the back of the trucks by five thirty, where breakfast was handed out.

Allen stood by the trucks, waiting for Dalby. The Lieutenant walked up to Allen.

"Sergeant," said Dalby.

Allen saluted, "Sir."

"We're going to Safe Zone Lima Delta. We are to report to the Captain there and assist in civilian processing and security. Wait on my command when we arrive. The situation is contained, but no telling how quickly that can change."

Allen nodded. He knew what 'contained' meant - no one was trying to escape yet, no zeds had got through the perimeter. Allen felt anxiety take hold again - he didn't know if he could face another civilian turkey shoot.

He signalled to the trucks to move out and jumped in the back of the carrier with Charlie section.

The men all looked at him, their eyes already empty - the sort of eyes that Allen was used to seeing at the end of a campaign, not one day in.

The trucks rumbled slowly out of the camp and onto the M4, heading away from London and towards Zone Lima Delta, eight miles away.

Progress was slow as the small convey weaved in and out of abandoned cars on the motorway. They had to stop several times, the men disembarking to help move a vehicle out of the way.

After thirty minutes and only two miles, Dalby called it - "We get out and march the distance. Road travel is impossible."

The platoon, twenty-eight men strong, plus the Lieutenant and the three drivers, hitched their kit on their backs and set off on foot along the motorway towards the safe zone, now just under six miles away.

Sergeant Allen took the lead, with Dalby walking a few paces behind, the men following. Allen and Dalby had shared no words other than the passing of orders since the event on the embankment. Allen was happy to keep it that way.

Allen wondered why the motorway had suddenly snarled at this point - all the lanes, including the emergency lane, were full from here for as far as he could see. Cars had even piled up on the sides of the embankment, some having rolled down onto the traffic below.

The men moved fast, acutely aware they were in the open, away from safety. "Keep an eye out, lads," shouted Allen. "Any movement, mark it straight away - but don't shoot 'til you're sure. There'll still be people out here."

At times they had to climb over vehicles as four or five cars, locked in some ferocious embrace, blocked the way entirely. The metal creaked loudly in the silent early morning air. Allen wondered if the zeds could hear and if they were attracted by sound.

"Sir," he said to Dalby, "I wonder if we should tell the men not to shout, to try and keep the noise down?"

"If you want, Sergeant," said Dalby, his gaze straight ahead, his pace consistent.

Allen gave the Lieutenant a concerned look as he walked back to the head of the column, "Keep the noise down in case they're attracted by sound." The lads nodded, a few said muted 'Sirs.'

It promised to be a beautiful day. The rising sun cast long shadows in the early blue light, and the temperature was already rising.

Allen eyed the cars. Most of them were empty, but some contained bodies.

"What do you think about these cars, Lewis? The bodies are giving me the creeps."

"Agreed, sir," said Lewis. "Any one of them could be a zed."

"We get stuck here, and we're in trouble. I'm going to speak to Dalby."

Allen caught up with Dalby.

"Sir, these cars - some of them have bodies."

"Yes, they do Sergeant." Dalby didn't look at Allen but stared straight ahead as he marched.

"Do you not think that we're putting ourselves at risk here? Some of those cars could contain zeds. This pile-up, there is no space to manoeuvre."

"What's your point, Sergeant?" said Dalby.

"I think we should get off the motorway."

Dalby immediately shook his head. "Negative, Sergeant. This is the quickest route to the safe zone."

"But sir, I think-"

"Your place is not to think, Sergeant." Dalby still hadn't looked at Allen.

"Sir," said Allen, trying not to let the frustration seep into his voice. He fell back to march with the leading group of the platoon, Lewis, O'Reilly, and Walton.

"Ok lads, I'm not liking our proximity to these vehicles…"

He paused as they squeezed through two large and crumpled four by four's.

Walton said, "I don't like the look of it either sir. Maybe we should get off the motorway."

Allen shook his head. "Not an option."

O'Reilly gave the Lieutenant, a good twenty feet ahead of them now, a sharp look. "He's going to get us killed. He's a bloody nutter."

"That's your commanding officer, soldier."

"Sorry Sarge, but you must admit…"

"It is what it is. Keep sharp, safeties off. Lewis, Walton, tell the rest of the men."

Lewis said, "Yes sir," then added, "You think there's zeds up ahead?"

"I'm not thinking anything, son. Just thinking we should be careful, no harm in that. Now go tell the rest."

Walton, O'Reilly, and Lewis told the rest of the men. Allen heard the cocking of weapons, safety catches being clicked off, and then a different kind of silence as they marched - a new watchful, alert silence.

After another ten minutes of marching, the traffic became packed even tighter, their progress impeded as they were forced to climb over numerous vehicles. The empty metal shells were all now strangely entwined with each other like a massive, terrible sculpture.

The road had a slight incline, making it impossible for the sergeant to see any distance ahead. He climbed up onto a nearby Range Rover. The cars spread out before him, a massive pileup that stretched for a few hundred yards before reaching the peak of the hill. Three of four large articulated lorries lay across both lanes of the motorway, the central reservation obliterated by their mass.

"What do you see, Sergeant?" shouted Dalby.

Allen winced at the volume of Dalby's shout and only shook his head in reply.

Dalby raised a hand and beckoned them on towards the peak of the hill and the wrecked juggernauts.

Allen was about to jump from the vehicle when he paused, he heard something. A faint, low undulating rumble, a wave of baritone. Low, depressing notes, like the sound of despair, thought Allen.

He climbed down onto the tarmac and jogged up to march beside Dalby.

"Sir?"

"What is it, Sergeant?"

"I am concerned about this snarl-up. It's getting too tight, and I can't see beyond the peak of the hill - I'm worried there's something after those juggernauts."

"I never had you down as a clairvoyant, Sergeant," said Dalby, his pace even and fast, his eyes straight ahead.

"Sir, I think we should maybe take it slowly, scout out what's behind those trucks."

Dalby turned to look at Allen. "You have a lot of suggestions recently, Allen. One would almost think you don't have much confidence in my decision making."

Allen didn't have time for this. "Sir, that is absolutely not the case. I have full confidence in your decision making, sir."

"Well, I'm glad to hear it."

"But, sir, I can hear something."

Dalby stopped abruptly and stared at Allen, his eyes narrowing with no attempt to hide his growing anger with Allen.

Even so, Dalby called the men to him.

"Scout out across those trucks in groups of four," said Dalby. "I want three men on top of the trucks, two either side of the motorway, and one down the middle where we can see that small gap." He eyed his platoon. "Keep it tight, and keep it quick. Just see what's on the other side, and report back here.

"Two minutes gents, we are late enough as it is."

Dalby turned and stared at the juggernauts, only one hundred feet ahead now. He put his hands behind his back and stood perfectly still.

Allen split up the men - Lewis, O'Reilly, and Walton led their own group of four each, and Allen went with three of the younger lads. "Well take the far side. Singh, take up the rear. I'll take point, Jones and Angus watch our sides."

They weaved their way through the wrecks to the other side of the motorway, climbing over the central reservation, gnarled and twisted where it had been hit by God knows how many cars during the pile-up.

"Keep an eye on those vehicles, lads. Call any movement straight away."

They were soon at the other side of the motorway, using the cars as cover, keeping an eye on the steeply climbing embankment that was their destination.

"What the hell is that?" said Singh. The noise that Allen had heard was now loud, filling the atmosphere with its mournful timbre.

"A good reason to keep sharp," said Allen.

They were at the far side of the motorway, their path blocked by a large articulated lorry lying on its side. It had slid into the steep embankment, obviously at some speed, as it was partly buried in the Earth. For Allen to get past it to see the other side, he would either have to either climb the embankment or over the truck. He preferred the truck.

"Give me a bunk up, Angus."

Angus, a stocky lad from Manchester, helped the sarge up. Allen got a grip on the top of the cab and pulled himself onto the doors of the truck, which were now the roof. The cab was tilted forward, and Allen spread himself flat so as not to slide down.

Keeping himself tight against the metal, he centred himself and took a look out over the other side of the motorway.

"Shit…" He put his head down as flat against the cab as he could, and willed his body to freeze - he had to fight the urge to throw himself back off the top of the truck.

There were no cars on the other side, just empty road and zeds. Hundred's of them, maybe thousands, moaning disparately, the source of the strange sound that had haunted the soldier's approach. Allen held his breath as he worked hard to stay calm and perform an effective reconnaissance.

The zed's roamed back and forth across the motorway, in and out of the woods that lined the road. The closest was only a few feet away, wandering to the trucks, wandering away, standing still.

A voice buzzed in Allen's ear, it was Lewis. "Fuck me, how many are there, Jesus…"

"No more talking. Mark your distances, counts, any possible side routes, and get back to Dalby."

A particularly loud moan echoed from just below Allen. He edged closer to look down and saw a man in a suit, the skin on the front of his face hanging off, one eyeball swinging against the exposed muscle of his cheek. The zed was standing right next to the cab, only a few feet below Allen. It was still, moaning loudly, and appeared to be searching, looking half up, almost sniffing the air.

Allen pushed back slowly from the cab, he had seen enough.

There was a loud bang as Allen's back foot hit a loose wing mirror, which fell off and slid down the slightly inclined truck onto the motorway, right at the foot of the zed in the suit. It immediately looked up and on seeing Allen, let out a different type of moan; more desperate, more targeted.

Allen watched in horror as one zed after another tuned into this sound and locked their heads in his direction. They turned one by one in a spreading wave that fanned out from the original zed. Within seconds, the ground below the cab was thick with zeds, all pushing against the truck, their arms in the air trying to get at Allen.

"Fall back," he shouted, silence no longer required, "fall back!"

He jumped off the cab.

"Zeds, thousands of them. They spotted me. Fall back!"

Allen and his men sprinted through the wrecks, back to their rendezvous point, where Dalby still stood with his hands behind his back, staring at the juggernauts.

"We have to fall back, sir," gasped a fast breathing Allen. "Thousands of hostiles, just past the trucks. No way we can get through."

The rest of the recon crews were arriving.

"What happened, sergeant?" said Dalby.

"I got spotted. I made a noise, and one of them saw me. He let out a shout, a signal or something, and... Well, you can hear it, sir."

The sound of moaning from the other side of the trucks had reached a deafening crescendo.

Dalby snapped his head round to stare at Allen. "Careless, Sergeant, very careless. You have put all our lives in danger." He looked at the trucks and the sides of the embankment. "Any way round?"

"Negative sir. We have to fall back."

A tear appeared in the side of the tarpaulin of one of the central juggernauts, and a zed fell through. A few more appeared, stumbled over the fallen zed and staggered into the wrecked jungle of cars. The tear widened as more and more zeds pushed their way through.

Dalby raised his handgun, aimed and fired. One of the zeds fell, its head splattering the tarpaulin red.

"Sergeant, fall back five hundred yards and circle into the woods. Let's have a team laying some cover fire."

Allen pointed to Walton, Angus, and Jones, "Stay with me men, we'll mark the retreat. Lewis, the wood on the side of the motorway we passed, about five hundred yards back? Take the rest of the men there, that's where we'll rendezvous."

Lewis started barking orders.

Allen and his team took up cover behind a van and aimed at the tear in the tarpaulin, now spread across the whole length of the truck. Zeds piled through, and within a short minute, at least thirty were now threading their way through the pile-up.

Dalby joined Allen's team, taking up position behind a car next to their van. "Thin them out, we'll pull back a hundred yards, then take up positions again."

"You heard the officer, lads, open fire!"

"This is more like it," said Walton.

The air erupted in gunfire, and zeds fell one after another. The tarpaulin was soon red, dripping in blood and flesh.

Within a minute, all the zeds had been cleared.

"Fall back, men! One hundred yards. We'll take up positions by that red truck," shouted Allen.

The men ran back through the wrecks and fell in behind a red works van. They took up firing positions between it and a neighbouring white Range Rover.

During their retreat, more zeds piled through and spread through the pile-up, following the soldiers with stubborn single mindlessness that saw them pass through the wrecks with disregard for personal damage; arms were left behind, gashes opened in legs, heads torn.

"Open fire!" shouted Allen, and again the air filled with the crack of gunfire.

The zeds fell, but with less regularity as more shots went wide, the targets being obscured by the tangle of broken cars and trucks.

A voice buzzed in Allen's ear, it was Lewis, "We're clear sir, in the woods. No hostiles."

"Ok Lewis, sit tight, we'll be there soon." The nearest zeds were only thirty feet or so away - with hundreds now following up from behind.

"Sir," said Allen to Dalby, "Lewis has them in position."

Dalby nodded. "Ok, Allen, let's get out of here."

"Ok lads, fall back, straight to the woods. Follow my lead."

The men stopped firing and began to weave their way back through the wrecks.

Dalby found himself at the back of the retreat with Angus.

"Where now sir?" shouted Angus above the rapport of his rifle as he felled two zeds.

Dalby looked up and realised he had lost sight of Allen and the other men. He heard their shouts and their gunfire, but couldn't see them.

Two paths through the pileup lay ahead - one to the right past a crumpled mini and another around the side of a truck.

"This way," he said, setting off to the left, past the truck. He glanced behind to see zeds closing in from numerous directions, their moaning a constant backdrop to the staccato percussion of gunfire.

Twenty feet in and he realised he had made a mistake. The path around the back of the truck was blocked. Two cars had piled on top of each other - it was a dead end.

Behind him, zeds shambled along the path they had just taken - they were trapped.

Angus opened fire, shooting his rifle on automatic, spraying the zeds with bullets.

"Single shots dammit. Aim for the head," shouted Dalby, but Angus ignored him, firing another short burst of automatic fire.

Dalby checked the ammo for his handgun, only half a clip left. He eyed the two piled up vehicles blocking his path.

While Angus was keeping the zeds busy, Dalby pulled himself up by the bonnet of the top car. His feet flailed in mid-air for a few seconds, but he was soon high enough to use his feet against the bumper of the lower car. He gave one final push and was on top.

The gunfire stopped, "Shit," said Angus, his gun empty. Zeds piled towards him through the gap. He spun round to see Dalby on top of the vehicles.

Dalby reached down and held out his hand, "Come on Angus, I'll get you up."

Angus grabbed the Lieutenant's hand and was pulled up a few feet. He was almost able to get his arms onto the top car's bonnet when he was grabbed from below by a pair of hands.

He let out a yell. Dalby felt Angus being jolted down. He tried to pull him back up but slid along the bonnet of the top car.

Another pair of hands grabbed Angus, "Help me! Sir! Get me up, get me up!" shouted Angus.

There was another, more powerful jolt and the top half of Dalby's chest was pulled over the bonnet of the car. One more pull and he would be over.

"Shoot them!" yelled Angus, his eyes wide with fear.

The Lieutenant only had a few bullets left, bullets he may need. It was a simple matter of priorities - his life was more important than Angus'. If Dalby didn't get back, then the platoon would be leaderless.

He let go of Angus' hand.

Angus only had a look of surprise for half a second, before a zed sunk its teeth into Angus' skull and peeled off the skin from his head, clean. His yells were cut short as a hand plunged into the back of his neck and yanked at his spinal cord, giving him a quick and merciful death.

Dalby jumped off the car and landed on the tarmac. He looked around quickly to make sure no one was near and punched the vehicle nearest to him several times. He inspected the cuts on his knuckles, red and bruised. He scraped his forehead against a shard of broken glass from a nearby car door. Blood trickled down his face.

Satisfied, he ran towards the woods.

Chapter 4

Allen joined the rest of the platoon sitting low in a deep impression in the woods, about fifty feet in from the motorway. Sentries were posted around the makeshift base.

"Everyone ok?" asked Allen.

"Affirmative sir," said Lewis.

Allen nodded and joined the men, dropping his kit onto the floor. There was immediate relief in his shoulders. He sat down against a tree and opened his backpack.

There was the crack of branches from behind them, and the men as one raised their weapons. They lowered them as Dalby emerged from the trees.

"Five minutes, men, then we march." He stood with his hands on his hips overlooking the platoon. "Angus didn't make it." The Lieutenant wiped the still flowing blood from his head. "I fell and got into a skirmish with one of the zeds. He saved my life. We've lost a good man."

There were curses and moans from the men. Angus had been popular.

"Let me fix that up for you, sir," said Walton, pulling out his medikit.

The Lieutenant nodded and sat down as Walton inspected the wound.

"This is real clean sir, what happened, glass?"

Dalby nodded. "Yes. Think I caught it as I fell."

Walton shook his head, "Fuck these zeds."

Allen took a drink from his canteen and pulled out the photo of his son from his kitbag. He shouldn't have looked at it, he knew that. But the pain was worth seeing his face again. He hoped Adam was in one of the safe camps.

"Ok, let's move out," said Dalby.

Allen picked up his kit again and they began to march.

They kept a wide perimeter around the motorway, and it was fifteen minutes before they saw their first zed.

"There, through the trees," said Allen, crouched behind a fallen tree. The platoon came to a halt and waited for instructions.

Dalby said, "Lewis, take him with your knife, let's keep it quiet."

Lewis nodded and set out quietly towards the zed. He successfully sneaked up behind and sunk his knife into its skull.

Over the next two hours, they saw no more than two or three at the same time, and they were dispatched quietly and efficiently. They made good progress, only stopping to check their position.

"Shall I take a team sir, scout up ahead?" asked Allen.

Without looking at Allen, Dalby held up his hand to halt the march of the platoon. "Yes, Allen, take three men."

He took Lewis, O'Reilly, and Singh. They used the trees as cover as they approached the location of Zone Lima Delta. The same despairing moaning noise as they had heard on the motorway filtered through the woods as they got closer to their destination.

The wood ended, and they crouched behind bushes that formed a boundary before a broad field that surrounded Zone Lima Delta, hastily erected on the site of an old airfield. Allen took out his binoculars and scanned the safe zone. A hundred yards ahead was a large fence at least twenty feet tall, lined with barbed wire. Zeds amassed around the airfield fence, two or three deep in some places.

Allen reported his position over his comm-link to Dalby, and the rest of the platoon joined them a few minutes later.

"There must be a clear entrance, sir, around the zeds. Maybe an access road?" asked Allen.

Dalby nodded and pulled out a large scale ordinance map that he spread across the floor.

"Singh," said Dalby, "report our position to HQ and find out how we can get in Lima Delta."

Singh pulled the radio out of his kit bag. "This is Charlie Romeo Fiver company," he repeated a few times, before receiving an answer.

Dalby took the radio from Singh. "This is Lieutenant Dalby, where is the entry point to Zone Lima Delta."

There was a pause, some static, and Dalby repeated his question.

"Negative, sir. There is to be no entry," came the reply. "You are to report to extraction point X-ray. It is imperative that you reach extraction point by 1200 hours."

The men looked at each other, confused.

"Repeat that," said Dalby.

The voice on the other side of the radio repeated the same instructions.

Dalby shook his head. "What about the people in the airfield? The whole place is surrounded by zeds."

Nothing but static.

"Dammit man, we've busted a nut getting here. X-ray is another two miles away. What the hell is going on?"

"Sorry sir," came the reply. "You have been ordered to report to extraction zone X-ray by 1200 hours. I must repeat that it is of the utmost importance that you reach the extraction point by then."

Dalby looked confused. "Why is it imperative?"

"Sir, you need to get away from Zone Lima Delta."

Dalby's eye's opened wide in realisation, nodding slowly. "Operation Horsefly..." He whispered. Then, louder, "Is Operation Horsefly in effect?"

He waited for a full ten seconds for the reply. "Sir, I repeat you must evacuate the safe zone area, and proceed to extraction point X-ray immediately."

"Ten-four. Roger, out."

Dalby passed the radio back to Singh.

"Ok men, we're moving out, here." He pointed to an old quarry about two miles away. It was only nine a.m.; they would get there with time to spare.

The men kitted up, exchanging confused looks.

"What's Horsefly?" asked Allen.

Dalby only gave him a fleeting glance as he pulled on his kit bag. "You don't need to know. All you need to know is that we are leaving." Dalby started walking, "Ok, men, move out!"

Most of the men followed Dalby, but a handful paused, looking at Allen who stood still.

"There are people in there, sir," said Allen, pointing behind himself to the airfield.

Dalby stopped and turned to face Allen. "It doesn't matter if the Queen of England is in there. We have our orders, Allen."

"What's Operation Horsefly? Why is it imperative that we get away from here?"

The platoon had stopped moving. Everyone stood silent, still, watching the exchange between their Sergeant and Lieutenant.

Dalby took a few steps towards Allen. "Sergeant, I suggest you get in line immediately."

"Horsefly... It's a slash and burn isn't it?"

Dalby paused a moment too long. Allen knew.

"It's a God-dammed slash and burn. That safe zone is compromised, and instead of rescuing the people, we're going to blow the airfield, is that it?" said Allen.

The soldiers looked at Dalby, waiting for his response. A few of the men stood up straight, their brows furrowed, the grip on their guns tight.

Dalby said, "The base is compromised. It must be neutralised. In three hours, anything within a mile of this location will be a ball of flames."

"Dammit, Dalby, there are innocent people in there - we put them in there!" shouted Allen. My son could be one of them, he thought.

Subtly, the men moved, some towards Allen, most towards Dalby.

"Allen, I think you forget who you are," Dalby shouted in return. "I'm the officer here, I have my orders, and we will follow them, is that clear?"

"We can't just leave them there - I'm tired of killing our own people." There were a few murmurs of angry agreement.

"Follow your orders, Sergeant!"

Allen snapped to attention, his arms by his side, staring straight ahead. "Sir, I respectfully decline to follow your orders. I request we mount a rescue mission of Zone Lima Delta."

Dalby rubbed his brow and looked at the men. Four men stood with Allen, but the majority were standing behind him.

"This is not a fucking bike club, Allen, you can't request anything. I am asking you once more to get your men in line."

Allen stood still. "Sir, I respectfully decline your-"

He stopped speaking as Dalby raised his pistol and pointed it at Allen, "This is direct insubordination in a hostile situation, Allen, I will not ask you again."

Lewis raised his machine-gun and pointed it at Dalby. This started a chain reaction, and within seconds, several members of the platoon had raised their guns, two sides, Dalby's and Allen's, opposing each other.

Silence fell upon the company, the men breathed heavily, one of the soldiers was shaking, the muzzle of his gun vibrating.

"We have a situation, sir," said Allen, who remained still, his arms by his side, staring ahead.

Dalby looked behind him to confirm once again the number of guns on his side. "You are outnumbered, Allen." He raised his voice to address the men standing behind the Sergeant. "If you all put your guns down now, we can forget about this, I will only report Allen. The rest of you, it's as if it didn't happen."

No one moved.

A loud rustle in the bushes by Dalby's men caught everyone's attention. There was a scream as one of Dalby's men fell forward, a zed attached to his neck. Blood spurted in a crimson ribbon high into the trees. One of Dalby's soldiers turned and fired. Another shot as a second zed emerged from the trees. Then a third, and a fourth. Within seconds the air was thick with gunfire as the soldiers on Dalby's side worked to contain the sudden swarm of zeds whose excited moans filled the air.

Allen looked about him - Lewis, Walton, O'Reilly, and Singh stood nearby, all watching for command. "Now!"

They ran from the clearing into the surrounding trees, in the opposite direction of the zeds. A bullet bounced off a tree by Allen's head, their escape not having gone unnoticed.

They ran deeper into the woods, keeping their heads down and dodging through the trees as shots fired around them. Quickly the shouts from Dalby and his men became faint - they were too busy with the zeds to give proper chase.

Allen pulled his comm-link from his ear, his mobile from his pocket, and a few other items of electronica from his kit bag as he ran. He threw them to the ground.

"Lose anything they can track us with," he shouted.

They ran for fifteen minutes or so, putting some distance between themselves and Dalby. Allen called the men to stop, and they dived behind trees and shrub, scanning the woods behind them. No movement.

Allen looked at each of the four men in the eye, one at a time, nodding to each.

Through heavy breaths, Lewis said, "What now, sir?"

Allen looked at his watch. "We have just under three hours until they burn the place. So that's plenty of time to rescue any civilians in there and get them a mile out. Last chance, anyone wants out, go now and get extraction with Dalby."

They all shook their heads.

O'Reilly said, "If I don't save someone soon, I'm gonna top myself."

"Ok, good." Allen felt a swelling of pride in the four men that stood by him, his faith that there were still good people in the world restored.

"Ok Lewis, when was the last time you climbed a tree?"

Lewis smiled. "I must have been about twelve, sir."

"Well, you'd best get remembering, I want you up that oak over there, right to the top. Take these," he passed the binoculars to Lewis. "I want a full recon, tell me what you see. The rest of us, disappear into the woods, keep an eye on all approaches."

The men scattered quickly and took up guard positions around the giant oak.

After a few false starts, Lewis made quick progress up the old tree. He got over his initial nerves and was soon near the top, its boughs swaying gently in the wind but holding him well.

Satisfied he was high enough for a good view, he wedged himself in tight against the trunk and took out the binoculars.

He focussed in on the perimeter fence of the airfield, about a hundred meters away. A thin circle of zeds surrounded the fence. Some were trying to push through, but most just wandered aimlessly around the perimeter, as if they knew there was something in there they wanted, but not sure what.

The inside of the airfield was scattered with bodies and debris; it looked like the remains of a battle. The carcasses mostly had bullet holes in their heads. What concerned Lewis, however, was the mass of zeds on the airfield.

The zeds were in both civilian and military uniform, suggesting the army hadn't been able to protect anyone, even themselves.

The airfield had two runways running parallel to each other, upon which lay a few burning vehicles. In between the runways were some buildings - three hangars, the control tower and a few nondescript brick buildings. Three planes, the size of small commercial jets, sat at the far end of the furthest hanger.

Zed's swarmed around the buildings, the control tower in particular. He focused in on the distinct bulbous top of the tower and found the reason why. People, in civilian clothes, were on the roof. They were free of blood and the damaged flesh of zeds - they were alive. A large white sheet hung off the side of the roof.

It said - 'SOS'.

He took a moment to wipe his eyes and focused in again. He estimated around twenty people on the roof, with a few children amongst them. Some of the people standing in the centre seemed to be focusing on the floor of the roof.

Lewis lowered his binoculars and realised they weren't looking at the roof's floor, but through what must have been a trap-door into the control tower below, which was thick with zeds climbing over each other, reaching for the roof, for the fresh meat.

Lewis quickly scurried down the tree - they didn't have much time.

Allen listened carefully to the Corporal's report.

"They must have retreated to the control tower, and at some point were comprised, but managed to make an escape to the roof. They're trapped there now, no way down, at least not without some heavy firepower, which I don't think they have."

"Any other signs of life?"

Lewis shook his head. "Rest of the place is a zed free-for-all. Whoever was there, they took a hell of a kicking."

Allen nodded and addressed his small company. "Ok, men, that's the situation. We have around two hours to get in there, get those people out, and get at least two miles away."

He felt some trepidation amongst them - it was a tough mission. They only had five machine guns, one grenade launcher, and two handguns. Almost seemed impossible. So he spoke quickly before they had time to second-guess themselves.

"We need a distraction big enough that will pull the majority of the zeds away from the control tower, so we can get those people out."

"What about firing some shots outside the fence," said Singh. "Draw the zeds over, then a few of us go in and get the people out."

Allen shook his head. "Won't work - after five minutes or so, we'll have every zed in those woods on us."

"I know what'll work," said Walton, a glint in his eye. "If those planes have fuel in them - a few well-placed grenades and they'll go up like Christmas."

"But what about getting to the planes?" said Lewis. "That place is crawling with zeds - we don't have the ammo to take them all out."

"Ok Singh," said Allen. "That's where your fence shooting idea might work. Me, Lewis and Singh will get to the far end of the airfield, fire some shots, draw the zeds over. Then O'Reilly and Walton can go in and take care of the planes. Be quick though - like I said, we won't have long before we're swamped."

"Sure thing Sarge," said Walton.

"Once those planes are burning," continued Allen, "that'll hopefully keep the zeds busy for as long as we need. We'll get in the control tower, clear it out, and get the people out. While we do that, Walton and O'Reilly can requisition us a vehicle, there must be something working in there."

"No problem," said O'Reilly.

"We'll rendezvous outside the control tower," said Allen, "and off we go into the sunset."

"Sounds simple," said Lewis, a wry smile on his face.

"What's plan B?" said Singh.

It was Allen's turn to smile, "We shoot the fuck out of anything that moves."

Chapter 5

Allen checked his watch. O'Reilly and Walton would be in position soon. As everyone had dumped their comm-links, this was to be a clockwork operation.

Just like the old days, thought Allen.

Lewis took up position with his back to the fence, he was the covering fire to take care of any zeds that wandered in from the woods.

Singh and Allen crouched facing the fence. The control tower was in the distance, the white SOS sheet visible, flapping in the gentle breeze. The end of the second runway that lay to the north of the tower was about 50 feet from their position. A handful of zeds were nearby.

"Remember, Singh, one shot each, in turn, thirty seconds apart. Let's not burn the ammo."

Singh nodded.

Allen stared at his watch for a minute. "Ok, it's time. Commence," said Allen.

Singh fired a shot into the air. Immediately the zeds turned and walked towards the fence.

"Dumb as cheese," said Allen.

Walton heard the first shot and nodded to O'Reilly - they were to go on the third. Hopefully, by then, most of the zeds would be following the gunfire over to the far side of the airfield.

As the shot's echo faded, Walton felt the silence for the first time. There was no insect noise, no bird noise.

The second shot. Walton looked at his watch, right on time.

He felt the adrenaline pumping through his veins - this was why he had signed up to the army. Not that turkey shoot yesterday - that was fucked up in all kinds of ways. Civilians behind cages, mixed in with zeds. Whoever came up with that idea had been a 5-star asshole.

The third shot. "Go!" he said. Walton jumped forward through the trees into the clearing. He glanced to his right to see O'Reilly running beside him.

Ahead, twenty or so zeds lined the fence, trying to walk through it and into the airfield, across to the sound of the shots.

Walton pulled out his knife and ran down the line of zeds, stabbing each in the back of the head. They were stupid, really stupid, it was easy. They didn't even know what was coming until Walton was on top of them.

He met O'Reilly in the middle of a long line of dead Zeds. "Good?"

"Good."

A clear view of the fence and the plan seemed to be working - only a few zeds were visible in the airfield, staggering in the direction of the gunfire.

Walton and O'Reilly pulled out their wire cutters and quickly made a hole in the fence, just big enough to let them through, and low enough to stop any zeds following.

Walton made the final cuts and held open the fence for O'Reilly to crouch through. Walton followed.

Straight ahead was the south runway. The group stood perpendicular to it, probably about a quarter way along its length. A few hundred yards away from the runway was their target: the three planes, standing by the last in a trio of hangers. Diagonally to the soldier's left, again about two or three hundred yards away, was the control tower.

"Let's go." They set out at pace up a gentle embankment towards the runway. Walton quickly scanned the centre - a few bodies, debris - from an exploded helicopter? And at the far end, a smoking jeep.

No zeds.

They ran across and down the embankment at the other side. Another shot rang out in the still air.

They ducked in behind a large signal box, and Walton peered around the side. They had a clear run to the first of the planes, which looked liked small commercial jets, but painted white with no windows.

"How do you blow up a plane with grenades then?" asked O'Reilly, breathing heavily from their quick sprint.

"They have the fuel in the wings, right? Let's shoot 'em up, and when the fuel's leaking hit them with the grenade launchers. Think it'll work?"

O'Reilly shrugged. "Can't think of anything better."

Allen nodded in satisfaction at the swarm of zeds congregating on the other side of the fence. The shots had drawn them in just as planned.

They moaned and pushed against the fence, like a rippling wave of dumb and angry animals. Each one seemed to have suffered a different form of violence. Some covered in blood, some with pieces of flesh and body parts hanging off. The odd missing limb. A gorged stomach with intestines getting twisted around the fence.

"Look, sir, on the control tower," said Singh.

The people were waving. Allen waved his right arm back, slowly. Then brought his hand down, looked at his watch, and fired another shot into the air.

Walton killed six of the zeds stuck in the hanger - they had been walking into the wall, trying to get to the sound of the shots by the most direct route. O'Reilly took out the other eight.

There was another shot.

"How many more shots?" whispered O'Reilly as they crouched by the door of the hanger.

"One, I think. Let's be quick."

The closest plane was about a hundred feet away, well within the range of their AG-36 grenade launchers.

O'Reilly grabbed Walton's shoulder, "Look, through that door, is that a truck?"

At the back of a hanger was an open door leading to another section of the hanger.

"Shall I go see?"

Walton nodded. "Check it out. I'll take care of these planes."

Lewis took aim and fired. The zed fell. He fired four more times in quick succession as zeds began to emerge from the trees.

"Sir, we're starting to get a lot of attention here."

"Singh, join Lewis. Let's just keep this lot at bay now," said Allen.

Singh took position next to Lewis and began taking out any zeds that stumbled from the woods.

The fence swayed in and out as the number of bodies on the other side swelled. The plan was working, but maybe too well.

A large group of zeds burst through the trees at once. Lewis and Singh let go some rapid fire, dispatching them quickly.

"There's a lot more coming, sir. Those two had better hurry up."

O'Reilly carefully entered the room at the back of the hanger, which turned out to be a garage. Tools and engine parts sat on tables that lined the room. A truck - a troop carrier - sat in the middle.

Three or four zeds bounced to attention as he entered the room and started their slow slog towards him. He took out his knife, ran around the other side of the truck, so he came at them from behind, and quickly knifed them in their skulls, spraying blood across the tarpaulin of the truck.

Once he had killed the zeds, he ran over to the wall where a row of hooks held some keys. He searched for a key that matched the license plate of the truck and grabbed it. He climbed into the cab and put the key into the ignition. He held his breath and turned it. The engine fired into life, no problem. Very healthy sounding.

He turned it off, took out the key, and ran back to join Walton.

"That was quick," said Walton, who was aiming for the wing of the nearest plane. "Any luck?"

"Lots, we got a truck," said O'Reilly.

"Great stuff. Ok, hold tight." Walton waited for O'Reilly to take cover.

Walton, let go a short burst of fire into the plane's wing. A clear liquid dripped freely onto the tarmac from the bullet-holes.

"Nice shot," said O'Reilly.

"That's nothing," said Walton as he pumped the under-slung grenade launcher. He fired. There was a dull thump as a grenade took off towards the wing.

Walton held his breath for a second, and then it hit. A powerful flash opened up the air milliseconds before a thunderous bang, and Walton and O'Reilly were thrown back by a wind shock.

They took cover behind the hangar door, the heat from the burning plane already making them uncomfortable.

Walton peered around the door to see the plane engulfed in a bulbous, billowing yellow flame, belching out waves of acrid heavy black smoke. The tower of smoke rose high into the air, like a thick, gnarled oak tree.

"Look at that!" shouted Walton.

O'Reilly let out a huge whoop.

The wing of the second plane caught alight.

"Get back," Walton and O'Reilly ducked back behind the hangar door, just as the next plane erupted with the same enthusiasm and noise as the first.

"It worked," shouted O'Reilly over the sound of the burning planes. "Fuck me, it worked."

They high fived each other.

"Damn right," said Walton. "Now let's get out of here. Don't think we're going to be alone for long."

They ran to the truck, the ground shaking as the third plane exploded behind them.

Allen, Lewis, and Singh turned round as one, as the sky erupted in an almighty bang. Within seconds, a thick plume of smoke rose from beyond the control tower.

"Yes!" said Lewis.

"They've done it," said Singh.

"Come on, let's move," said Allen. "No more firing - save the ammo. The plan ain't worked yet."

They followed Allen's lead as they ran along the perimeter away from the zeds emerging from the woods.

The zeds in the airfield, however, had lost interest in Allen and his men. The explosion took all their attention, and Allen had an inward sigh of relief as the zeds turned from the fence to make a slow migration towards the centre of the airfield, towards the fire.

"Ok, here will do." They stopped running, and Allen crouched down, taking out his wire cutters, making a low incision. He was quickly joined by the others, and they were soon through. They ran across the airfield, keeping a healthy distance behind the hoard of zeds.

They dodged the debris of the fight which must have occurred only a few hours ago, moving from cover to cover behind car wrecks and burned out tents. The zeds edged further and further away.

Allen checked his watch. They had one and half hours left to get to safety. Plenty of time, as long as Walton and O'Reilly had secured a vehicle.

About halfway to the control tower and the group of people on the top noticed them. They started to point, shout, jump up and down and make a hell of a racket.

"They need to shut up," said Lewis as they ducked down behind the shell of a jeep.

Allen watched in dismay as some zeds broke off from the leading group and headed towards the bottom of the tower.

"No worries, lads. Just makes our job a bit tougher. Most are still heading to the planes. Let's hurry up."

The group ran forward and were soon within a few hundred feet of the tower. About twenty zeds were walking around the bottom. When they saw the company, they shuffled towards them.

"They're thinning themselves out. Use your knives if you can."

They meet the oncoming group with their knives drawn, and quickly killed them with well-placed knife plunges and swipes, splitting the skulls and killing the brains dead.

Allen continuously motioned to the crowd on the top of the control tower to be quiet, but he was ignored, and more zeds were being drawn from the main horde.

The control tower was a tall, anonymous structure, seemingly built out of a single block of concrete. There was a small door at the base, which lay open.

"I'll take point. Singh, you watch our six. Lewis, you path clear with me."

They burst through the door, and Allen fired twice, clean headshots, to kill two zeds standing on the stairs. They cautiously made their way up the steps, illuminated by only the dull orange glow of the emergency lighting. Their heavy boots echoed in the concrete silence, every footfall and scrape amplified by the solid walls.

The top of the stairs ended in a featureless landing with a closed door in front of them.

"This looks like the door to the control tower," said Allen "Assume many hostiles. Lewis, you got the stairs?"

"Sure thing, Sir."

"Ok, Singh, you ready?"

Singh nodded.

Allen reached forward with one hand, his other holding his gun. He pulled the door open.

The truck squealed out of the hanger, O'Reilly hanging on tight as Walton rammed his foot down on the accelerator.

"Easy pal, we're not going far," said O'Reilly.

Walton smiled, obviously enjoying himself. He pulled the truck onto the feeder road that led to the north runway. From there it was a few hundred feet to reach the control tower.

Walton pulled the truck to the left and right to avoid debris strewn across the runway.

"Must have been a hell of a fight that went down here," said Walton.

O'Reilly nodded, his eyes on the road.

The control tower rolled up on their left, Walton brought the truck to a stop. No door - just a blank concrete wall.

"Door must be round the other side," said Walton.

"The Sarge said door to door, so let's get around the other side then."

Walton nodded, put the truck into gear and his foot on the accelerator. They only went forward a few feet, before the truck came to a stop, a painful screeching sound coming from under the cab.

Walton drove the truck back and forwards a few times, but still no movement, and the same high pitched sound.

"Bollocks," said Walton. "Must be stuck on something."

"I'll go check."

"Be careful."

O'Reilly jumped out of the truck. Many zeds were approaching from the control tower and the runway but were still some distance. He would have to be quick. He ran to the front of the truck and got on his hands and knees, looking underneath.

There was a significant depression in the tarmac, maybe the result of some ordinance. Stuck in it was a jeep door, which in turn was jammed against the truck's axle.

He popped his head up so Walton could see him. "Don't move the truck. We're stuck on a jeep door, I'll dislodge it."

"Ok, hurry up," shouted Walton, eyeing the approaching group of zeds from the control tower.

O'Reilly ducked back under the truck and yanked at the jeep door; a dip in its frame had caught on the truck's axle.

He jumped slightly as he heard shots from above. Looking to his right, some zeds fell to the floor - Walton was covering him. O'Reilly yanked at the door with more vigour, and it finally came loose with a screech.

In doing so, he cut his hand, and a large gash opened up. "Shit," he said, feeling the pain.

As he ran back to the passenger side door, he squeezed his hand to try and stem the blood flow - and missed the zed walking up the side of the truck.

O'Reilly began to hoist himself up into the cab. "Ripped my bloody hand open, didn't I-" He let out a loud shout in pain. A zed had his jaws clamped around his calf. The pain was immense, it felt as if someone had hit his leg with a sledgehammer, and was peeling the muscle off his very bone.

Walton yanked O'Reilly to the side and put a bullet in the zed's skull. It fell back onto the tarmac.

"Get in!" yelled Walton, pulling O'Reilly. He climbed in, and before the door was shut, Walton accelerated the truck, and they squealed away from the growing group of zeds.

"Fuck!" shouted O'Reilly, "I'm done for, I've got it haven't I? I'm done for!"

Allen and Singh stood still and calmly fired, shot after shot, into the crowd of zeds piling through the control tower door. One after another the zeds fell, forming a pile of bodies in the landing and doorway. The background of hisses and moans lessened as the number of zeds decreased.

"Reloading," said Singh.

"Aye," said Allen, as Singh took a few seconds to put in a new magazine.

"Last magazine," said Singh, shooting again.

Allen's gun also clicked to signify his mag was empty. He pulled the last magazine from his belt and clicked it into his weapon.

Lewis sat still behind the other two, staring down the dull glow of the staircase. He heard noises from below in between the shots. There was movement in the darkness at the base of the tower, most probably zeds, but nothing on the stairs.

Allen fired twice more, then stopped. No movement from the control tower.

"That's it! You got them!" said a voice from inside the control tower. It was someone from the roof. More shouts followed; Allen couldn't discern what was being said.

He signalled for Singh to cover him, as Allen swept the control tower. He cast a careful eye over each of the corpses, ignoring the shouts from above. He wanted to be sure first.

"Ok, Singh, looks good. Lewis?"

"Sir, movement below, but stairs all clear," came the reply from the staircase.

"Let me know if that changes."

Allen finally looked up above. There was a hole in the roof, a smashed through glass section. Around it were faces: civilian faces, scared, hopeful, happy. Old, young, men, women. A few couldn't stop talking, others stared with emotionless eyes.

He couldn't see his boy amongst them.

"Ok Singh, let's get this lot down. How's your ammo?"

"Low," said Singh. "About twenty rounds."

Walton pulled the truck up near to the door of the control tower, as close as he could get - a thick crowd of zeds surrounded the entrance.

O'Reilly was breathing fast and heavy, his teeth gritted, spittle coming out of his mouth. "It hurts Walton, really fucking hurts. What do I do?"

"I don't know, mate. I'm sorry, I don't know." And he didn't. Walton wanted to help, but what could he do? If he'd had a machete he would have cut O'Reilly's leg off - it might have helped.

But he didn't have a machete.

"Can you walk?" he asked.

O'Reilly nodded. "I think so. Yeah, I think so."

"Ok," said Walton, watching the zeds approaching the truck. "We need to clear the door. How much ammo have you got?"

"Not enough," said O'Reilly. "Not for that lot."

"Me neither…"

O'Reilly stared at the zeds. Walton was speaking, but he didn't hear him. O'Reilly closed his eyes and swallowed hard. The pain in his leg was spreading through him. He could feel the virus crawling through his veins, gripping his cells and taking him over.

"I can do it," he said.

"What?"

"I can do it. I can clear them. When Allen and the others come down from the tower, I'll shoot, and run. I'll clear them." He turned to face Walton. He was pale, sweating, in pain. "I'm finished anyhow."

"You sure?"

He nodded. "Don't try and change my mind."

"I wasn't going to." Lewis briefly rested his hand on O'Reilly's shoulder. "Pretty brave, mate."

O'Reilly checked his weapon.

Lewis took point down the stairs, Singh behind him, followed by the twenty-three people from the roof. Allen brought the rear.

Lewis held up his hand to stop the procession and Singh made sure they stopped. Zeds crowded the base of the tower. On seeing the descending humans, they crammed into the bottom of the staircase, trying to get up to the fresh meat.

Lewis opened fire. The shots rang out loudly in the confined concrete staircase.

"Nearly out of ammo," shouted Lewis up the stairs.

Allen ran down the stairs, past the huddled group of people. He joined Singh and Lewis who were firing to contain the zeds. As soon as one was shot, another appeared in the doorway.

Singh's was the first gun to click empty, followed quickly by Lewis. Allen took single shots into the undulating mob.

"We can't hold them much longer," said Lewis.

"Hear that?" said Walton, the shots from inside the control tower ringing out.

O'Reilly nodded.

"You still sure?"

O'Reilly nodded again. "Shitty way to go. What a fuck up. What a fucking fuck up." He put his hand on the door handle.

Walton grabbed his shoulder. "Hell of a good man, O'Reilly."

O'Reilly smiled, "Shut it, you think I'm a twat." He opened the door and jumped out of the truck, his leg almost giving way. He started to hobble away from the truck, away from the control tower, towards the runway. A few zeds on the edge of the group followed him immediately, but most stayed focused on the control tower.

O'Reilly started to shout, "Hey! Hey!" He fired his gun into the mass.

Walton watched, a smile spreading over his face as one by one, the zeds turned to follow O'Reilly.

"Well done," he whispered.

A few zeds made their way onto the bottom of the stairs, only a few steps below Allen and the company. Allen took careful shots, making sure he didn't miss, only shooting the closest.

"Get your knives ready, might have to melee our way out of this."

Light appeared at the door to the control tower as the zeds stopped pushing to get in, and instead turned and walked away.

"They're pulling out!" shouted Lewis.

Allen took a few more shots, then his gun clicked empty. He pulled out his knife. "Come on." He charged down the stairs, followed closely by Lewis and Singh. Eight zeds were left in the control tower; they were quickly killed by the soldiers.

"Where've they gone?" said Singh.

"Who cares," said Lewis, "let's get out of here."

Allen led the group out into the courtyard, where the truck sat, idling. Walton waved out of the window.

"In the truck," said Allen. He motioned the people towards the back of the carrier. He looked past the truck to the south runway. A large number of zeds were walking away from the control tower.

"Look after this lot, Singh, get them in the back, I'm gonna check in with Walton and O'Reilly."

He ran up to the open door of the truck and saw the empty seat. "Where's O'Reilly?"

Walton shook his head. "He got bit. See that lot?" he motioned towards the retreating group of zeds, "that's him."

"Christ…"

"They're in," shouted Singh from the back of the truck.

"Ok!" said Allen, "Get in the front Lewis. Singh, get in the back with me. Let's get these people out of here!"

Lewis jumped in the front of the cab and pulled the door shut. "You heard him, Walton, drive."

Walton put his foot on the accelerator, and the truck rumbled into motion.

"Where we going?"

"No idea, just get out of here. Think the exit's that way." Lewis pointed vaguely to the left.

Walton smiled and turned down the north runway, heading towards the fence. He pulled the heavy truck to the left and right. "Hope they're holding on tight back there!"

The odd zed gaped at the speeding truck, reaching out uselessly, before turning to listlessly follow.

Walton picked up speed as they reached the fence. "Let's hope this fence has been built in typical army fashion…"

Lewis held on tight as the thin wire barrier approached, "Walton, you sure you want to-"

The truck hit with a large metallic clang, and the fence doors flung open, the lock having snapped easily under the weight and speed of the truck.

Allen lifted the tarpaulin, watching Zone Lima Delta fade into the distance. He looked at his watch - fifteen minutes to get clear. Should be good as long as they didn't hit any traffic snarl-ups.

The civilians sat around the seats in the dark. Some were crying, some were silent, some were laughing, congratulating the soldiers.

The truck rumbled through the countryside, slowing at times as Walton navigated around a stationary vehicle. Soon they were clear of the woods and driving through farmer's fields. The land rose gently, giving Allen a good view of the airfield.

"What's going on, Sergeant?" asked one of the men in the back of the truck.

"I wish someone would tell me," said Allen. He gave a half smile and looked at his watch, only a minute to go.

Another man spoke up, "You lot left us! First, you don't let us leave London, then you pile us in a truck, imprison us, and then leave us there with those things!"

There were a few murmurs of agreement from one or two others, dark frowns on their faces.

The man, buoyed by the support, continued, "How can we trust you again? How do we know you aren't taking us somewhere else to lock us up?"

Allen looked at the man. He was in his mid-fifties, a large man with broad shoulders, wearing a tatty brown sweater.

Twenty seconds to go.

"I think we need to stop this truck," continued the man, "and find out exactly where we are going. Pick a leader, I mean, I know you are army and everything, but in this sort of crisis, who's to say you know best…"

Allen ignored the man and pulled back the tarpaulin entirely. He and Singh exchanged looks. The large man sounded more indignant, aware he was being ignored.

Three jets streaked across the sky, fast and low, the noise drowning out all other sounds. A few small bursts of light erupted under each of the planes, and a white vapour trail traced from the jet down into the woods. The airplanes pulled up and disappeared from view.

A few seconds later, the woods erupted in fire. Silence for a few seconds, and then a raging whoosh of wind and heat, like the sky itself had caught alight. A massive wall of thick black smoke rose rapidly as if being sucked into space.

Some of the people in the truck screamed as it rocked from left to right.

"Don't worry," said Allen, "it's only a few napalm bombs." He turned to the group in the back. "The rules have changed, you see that? There ain't no fucking committees anymore. I'm in charge." He pointed at the flaming airfield and woods. "That's what the government have in store. They're scared, and they're dangerous."

A woman looked at Allen, gripping tight a small child who stared with wide open eyes. "The army tried to kill us. How do we know you won't? Another order and-"

Allen interrupted her. "We ain't the government's army anymore." He looked at Singh, who nodded. "We make our own orders."

The truck slowed down.

Allen continued, "Best we can do is keep moving, keep our heads down. Trust us if you want to stay alive. Me and my men will keep you safe."

"Why are you so bothered about us?" asked the large man in the tatty jumper, his voice now soft and wavering, like a child's.

Allen smirked. "Maybe we're looking for redemption." He met Singh's eyes. "For our sins."

The truck stopped. The sound of a door opening and closing, footsteps, then Lewis and Walton appeared.

"Napalm?! They've lost their fucking minds," said Lewis. The fire burnt strongly, the tower of smoke painting the sky a dirty dark gray.

Walton said, "What now, sir?"

Allen looked around the back of the troop carrier, expectant faces waiting for his command, waiting for him to keep them safe. Eleven men, nine women, and three children.

"We go west. To Cornwall. I know Cornwall. There's plenty of places to keep low, away from people."

"People?" asked the woman with the child. "Why keep away from people, it's those things we need to be scared of."

"You think the zeds are bad? Wait until you see people when everything is taken from them. No electricity, no water, no food. The zeds will seem like teddy bears." Allen turned to Walton. "Get us to Cornwall."

Walton nodded. "On our way." He and Lewis disappeared around the side of the truck. The engine started up, and they were moving again.

Allen looked at the napalm cloud. Lucky he wasn't looking at a mushroom cloud. He wouldn't put it past them to use nukes, though. Had they hit the cities, he wondered?

He pulled out the picture of his son, his hand shaking gently.

"Sir," said Singh, pointing to the sky.

A large helicopter was in the distance, heading south.

"Dalby?" said Singh.

"Could be," said Allen. He put the photo back in his bag, sat back, and closed his eyes. He saw his son, smiling, holding his arms out to him.

Zone Lima Delta

The Dead Lands

Chapter 1

Harriet was stuck in traffic.

She had left London three hours ago after phoning her mum - 'Things in Manchester are normal,' said her mum. A hastily packed bag, a race out of the City before rush hour, but here Harriet still was, on the M25 and not moving.

Horns sounded. People shouted. Three cars ahead, two men argued, pushing each other. Harriet shrunk back in her seat. One man punched the other, and a fight ensued.

Harriet cursed herself for leaving London. Maybe things weren't so bad. It was all only rumours, wasn't it? She hadn't actually seen any of the infected, or zombies, as people had been calling them.

She turned on the radio and scanned through the channels, most still broadcasting the weird announcement - 'stay in your homes, don't travel, wait for the authorities to restore order.' This latest report had something new: warnings that civil disobedience was now a matter of national security, to be dealt with in the harshest terms.

The fighting men finished fighting. One of them lay still on the ground with a pool of blood around his head. Harriet breathed in sharply, scared.

A few cars ahead and a young family left their vehicle. A couple, a baby, and a toddler. The woman locked the door of the car, and they walked away through the columns of stationary vehicles.

Harriet jumped at a loud bang from behind her. She turned around. A thick pillar of smoke, about a hundred yards away, tumbled silently into the air. Its foreboding darkness contrasted sharply with the mellow orange of the early evening.

As she watched the smoke, transfixed, she became aware of a deep rumble. Harriet gripped the back of her seat, her knuckles white, her eyes wide. A crowd ran towards her; it squeezed between cars, it climbed over cars.

She fumbled for her phone - no signal. She cursed loudly and threw it to the floor. Shaking her head, she picked it up again and put it in her pocket. She reached into the back seat and grabbed her bag.

The crowd was on her. The car reverberated loudly with bangs as people bumped past. Men, women, young and old, some crying, some shouting at others to keep up.

Some bleeding.

Harriet's breath accelerated, and she felt afraid. She gripped her bag tight and stared ahead, the backs of the people turning into silhouettes against the setting sun. A young girl fell over, and Harriet sat up, grabbing the door handle of her car. A woman appeared against the flow of the crowd and picked up the little girl. They joined the rushing exodus and disappeared from view.

Harriet still gripped the door handle. Why did she feel such a compulsion to join the crowd? She saw the fear in their eyes and heard it in their voices.

Her breath became fast and shallow, she struggled to catch air. She was having a panic attack.

Breath deeply, stay calm, close your eyes...

There was a huge thump, and Harriet opened her eyes. Outside, a man with his face covered in blood pulled at her door handle, shouting.

Harriet screamed and backed into the passenger seat.

A second figure appeared, a woman, a policewoman. Harriet felt relief.

Authority.

Then the policewoman grabbed the man's head and sunk her teeth into his skull. She pulled back and the man's scalp peeled away revealing white and shining bone. She pushed the man against the neighbouring car and, spitting out the scalp, sunk her teeth into the man's neck. Blood squirted high into the air and covered Harriet's window.

Harriet screamed. She hurriedly opened the passenger door and scrambled to get out. She fell onto the tarmac. Someone running past stood painfully on her head, shouting - "Get out of the fucking way!"

Harriet struggled to her feet and joined the running crowd, no idea where she was going; she let the fleeing mob be her guide.

Another explosion erupted behind her, and multiple car horns honked like a herd of beasts.

Harriet wiped at her tears as she ran, fighting to get the breath she needed to keep going. She tripped over something, a person, maybe, but she pulled herself up and ran, ignoring a sharp pain in her knee.

The memory of the man's scalp being peeled off by a policewoman replayed through her head, accompanied by the thought 'that was a zombie, that was a zombie, that was a zombie.'

A car door opened and she ran straight into it. She fell painfully, winded. An arm pulled her up, and a woman's voice said, "This way, we need to get off the road."

Harriet followed the woman up the embankment of the motorway onto a farm field. A young boy ran with them. He glanced up at her, his face stern. "You have to keep up," he said.

Harriet kept up.

The field buzzed with fleeing people. It was getting difficult to see exactly how many as the light faded, the evening becoming the night.

They reached the edge of the field. It was bordered by a large hedge shielding a shallow ditch. They ducked into the ditch.

Everyone breathed heavily.

"I'm June," said the woman. She looked somewhere in her late forties, a lot older than Harriet. The young boy, she had no idea of his age; how can you tell one child from another?

"I'm Harriet," she said.

"Nice to meet you. This is my son Adam."

The young boy gave Harriet a sheepish wave.

"What's happening?" said Harriet.

June shrugged her shoulders. "I don't know. Those things are everywhere. Everyone's going nuts."

Adam said, "My dad says that in a crisis, people are the most dangerous thing."

June rolled her eyes, "Your dad doesn't know anything about zombies."

"He knows more than us," said Adam, unperturbed. He turned to Harriet. "He's in the army, a sergeant. If we can find him, he'll keep us safe."

This sounded hopeful, thought Harriet.

June saw the look in Harriet's eyes and shook her head. "I haven't seen him in over a month. We're divorced."

"He'll find us," said Adam with certainty.

June peered out of the ditch. "It's getting dark. I think we need to find somewhere to stay."

"I think I saw a housing estate, about two fields over," said Harriet.

Adam shook his head, "My dad says that in a crisis, the best-"

"That will do," said June. "Sounds good. I'm sure someone will help us."

Adam frowned at his mum as she grabbed his hand.

"Come on," said June.

The trio set off across the field, stumbling in the darkness. Ahead, the dull sodium orange of the estate's street lights led the way.

They walked down an empty street. The estate was a new development, a warren of small but modern three bedroom houses for young families. Seemingly endless roads and cul-de-sacs looking the same as the last.

Only a few had lights on; many of the driveways were empty.

They knocked on several doors, and the responses varied from silence, to lights out, to angry warnings to leave.

"This is useless," said June, "everyone is shitting themselves because of this virus."

"Language," said Adam.

June ignored him, "You'd think they would help two women with a child."

The next house with any lights on was on a corner. The grass was overgrown, and there was an old 4x4 pickup truck sitting in the driveway. The garden was scattered with motor parts and a rusted motorbike.

"Let's try this one," said June. They stood at the end of the drive.

"Looks dodgy," said Harriet.

"Look it's getting late, we can't be picky."

Harriet saw the curtain twitch, and a few seconds later, the door opened. A young man, thin, and wearing green combat trousers and t-shirt stood at the door. He motioned for them to come in. "Come on, hurry." He looked up and down the street.

The women looked at each other.

"Look," he said, "no one else is going to let you in. Half of them have legged it, the others are like bloody rabbits, holed up, scared."

"What do you think June?" whispered Harriet, not sure she liked the young man, but certainly not enjoying being outside in the dark.

"I don't know, he looks funny, but, he's right about there being nowhere else." June shrugged.

"Dad would say we should camp out," said Adam, "or find an empty building."

That seemed to make up June's mind. She took Adam's hand. "Well, Mum says we shouldn't turn down a warm house."

Harriet took one last look up and down the strangely quiet street. Empty houses, empty driveways. She couldn't see it, but she could feel it; something had changed.

"I'm Jake," said the man as he welcomed them in. Once in the hallway, he closed the door and locked it, thoroughly - there were four deadlocks on the door.

The house smelt funny, thought Harriet. Nothing nasty, just like Jake didn't clean as often as he should. The carpet was an old brown, and a pile of magazines sat on the porch - *Survival Warrior*. A samurai sword hung in the hallway.

"Come on, let's get you both a cuppa." Jake smiled widely as he led them into the cluttered and chaotic kitchen. He dug out a few cups from the cupboard and set the kettle to boil.

He was a small man, young, maybe in his mid-twenties.

He leaned down and smiled at Adam, ruffling his hair. "Alright young man? You want an orange juice?"

Adam smiled back and nodded. June moved in behind Adam, resting her hands on his shoulders.

"Are you in the army?" asked Adam.

The man shook his head. "No, afraid not. I have something wrong with my leg, can't get in."

Adam nodded, satisfied with Jake's answer.

"Did you girls come from the motorway?" he asked.

"How do you know?" asked Harriet.

"I've been watching the street and field from the attic. With my binoculars. It's a mess." The kettle clicked off, and he prepared the teas. "I've been on the radio, you know, the CB. Truckers and that. The traffic is blocked all around London, and the military has put a barricade in place, around the M25."

"A barricade?" said June.

"Yeah, no-one in, no-one out. We're on the inside." He put the teas on a tray. "Let's have these in the lounge."

They walked through, and Harriet moved a hoody off the couch. She sat down next to a cat.

"How can they put up a barricade?" said Harriet. "I need to get to Manchester. They can't just stop us from going anywhere."

Jake shrugged his shoulders. "National emergency. You must have heard the radio announcements. Full zombie apocalypse by the sound of it."

"You see!" shouted Adam.

Jake smiled at Adam. "First stage is they try and lock everything down," said Jake. "That won't work of course. By now the virus will be spreading quickly throughout the country, and there'll be outbreaks everywhere."

"You're an expert are you?" said June.

Adam chipped in, "Everyone knows this mum. It's what happens in a zombie apocalypse."

Jake nodded. "Bright, aren't you?"

June shook her head. "For God's sake, sorry, but this is ridiculous."

"Is that what the policewoman was, a zombie?" said Harriet.

"You've seen one?" asked Jake.

Harriet told them what had happened on the motorway.

Jake sighed. "Blimey. Sounds like a typical zombie attack. They're merciless, with only one aim. To destroy and to eat flesh."

"Look," sad June, "thank you for taking us in, but please, we need to stop talking like this, you're frightening my son. Besides, it's all just ridiculous. This will all be sorted out in a few days."

No one said anything, and June's words fell flat into the silence.

Harriet said, "What do we do?"

"We lock-down here," said Jake. "I've enough supplies for months, and we can make this place safe."

"What do you mean by lock-down?" said Harriet.

"Put blackouts over the window, nail the doors closed, nail the windows closed. Sit tight until the initial die-off is over. People will be most dangerous in the first few weeks, so we just lock-down and wait it out."

June put her cup down. "That's it, come on Adam, we have to go. This man is nuts."

Adam didn't move.

"Adam! Come here now," she stood up and jutted her hand out.

Adam still didn't move. "But mummy, maybe the man is right."

"Wait a minute, June, let's just think about this," said Harriet. "Maybe we should just stay here tonight and talk about it in the morning?"

June looked around the room, all eyes on her.

Jake said, "I didn't mean to scare you, June, I'm sorry. Look, just stay here tonight. It's not safe out there now. I'll give you some food to take with you tomorrow."

June sat back down and threw her arms up. "Fine."

Chapter 2

Jake showed them upstairs. There was his bedroom, two spare bedrooms, and a bathroom. Pretty standard for a suburban new build.

Harriet was to sleep in one of the spare rooms, which Jake had turned into a study/storage room.

"This airbed should be fine," said Jake, giving a few finishing squeezes on the foot pump.

At least he's eager to please, thought Harriet. But then he probably didn't get to speak to a lot of women his age; too many survival magazines, ninja weapons, and camo gear.

"I'll be in there," said Jake to his guests, pointing to the room next to Harriet's. "I'll probably be up late, and you might hear some power tools." He handed everyone some ear plugs. "You can use these."

"Power tools?" said June.

Jake nodded. "I'm going to to get to work on securing the place." June gave him a sharp look, he smiled back at her. "Just the windows."

"Ok, thanks, Jake," said Harriet. "Thank you very much for being so generous. You're very kind."

Jake blushed. "That's ok," he quickly started back down the stairs. "I'll see you both tomorrow."

Once he was downstairs, June whispered, "This guy's a bit weird, are you sure about staying here?"

"I think he's mainly harmless, and besides, I don't see we have any other options, do you? We can get out of here first thing."

June shrugged, "Do you want to sleep in with us?"

"Thanks, but I think I'll be ok."

June didn't look convinced, "If you're sure. We'll see you tomorrow. Nice and early."

"Ok, night June." She waved at Adam, "Night Adam."

"Night Harriet," said Adam.

Harriet closed the bedroom door behind her. The desk and a few boxes took up most of the floor space. There was just enough room for her airbed. The desk housed a PC, many game boxes, manga magazines, and novels about war, soldiers, space, etc.

Harriet looked out the window; the lights were still on in the street, and a murky orange watched over the stillness. No houses had any lights on that she could see, and only one house had a car in its drive. It seemed most had ignored the emergency broadcast to stay home.

She gasped as she saw movement outside; a figure emerging from the darkness. She ducked down and peered over the window sill, watching as the figure shuffled, not walked, along the middle of the empty street. It was difficult to make out details in the low lights, but it looked like a man, maybe in his fifties, fat, wearing a shirt and tie. He dragged his left leg behind him, and as he got closer, Harriet noted his shirt was covered in blood. The skin on one side of the man's head hung off; it rested on his shoulder, flapping gently as he walked.

Harriet pulled her hand over her mouth and ducked out of sight, breathing heavily. She fought the rising panic; breathe deep, breathe slow, one, two, three, close your eyes…

She found the courage to look again. The man was disappearing into the darkness. She quickly closed the curtains and climbed into bed.

She started to cry. She didn't want to, but she couldn't help herself. It was all she could do to stop her panic from engulfing her. She allowed herself the luxury of crying.

Harriet woke in the darkness, and for a moment she was back in bed in her Camden flat. She reached over to look at the clock on her bedside table, but instead, she found the chair leg of Jake's desk.

She sat up on her elbows, remembering where she was.

A strange sound from downstairs sent a shiver down her spine, the sound of an electric motor, muffled through her earplugs.

Power tools. Jake said they would hear power tools.

She wondered if the sounds would attract zombies, and struggled to get back to sleep. Eventually, tiredness won out, and the hypnotic rhythm of the tools lulled her to a shallow slumber.

Harriet woke early - it was six o'clock according to her watch. An immediate nervousness set upon her stomach, as the memories of yesterday flooded into her mind.

She sat up and carefully pulled back one of the curtains a little, peering out to the street.

Empty.

She had expected to see a crowd of zombies outside the house, baying to get in.

She pulled out her earplugs and got dressed. She went to the bathroom.

The house was silent - she was the first to wake. She wondered how late Jake had stayed up last night, 'securing' the house.

Although feeling a little rude going downstairs while Jake was still asleep, she needed a drink of water. And a coffee. She was sure Jake wouldn't mind.

Harriet padded down the stairs, wincing at the few creaks on the stairs.

The house was dark.

She paused at the bottom of the stairs and stared at the front door. Wooden slats had been screwed across the full length of the door - there was no way to open or close it.

That's why it was dark - the door window and the porch glass had been covered with large wooden boards.

Walking quickly around the ground floor, treading carefully in the darkness, she found that all the windows had been covered. The back door in the kitchen was also sealed shut.

She was trapped in darkness. This is what Jake meant by securing the house - no one in, no one out.

Including her.

Scared, she crept upstairs and gently opened the door to June's room. She was asleep, but Adam was awake, his eyes looking up at her from the darkness. He waved and said "Morning, Harriet."

Harriet rushed her finger to her lips and hushed him. She leaned down next to June and shook her gently awake.

June stretched and opened her mouth to speak, but Harriet, and also Adam, hushed her.

"What is it?" whispered June, a frown on her forehead. "What time is it?"

"It's just past six in the morning. We're in trouble."

June sat up quickly and grabbed her jumper. "What do you mean?" she quickly glanced at Adam to check he was ok.

"I've just been downstairs - he's screwed wooden planks across all the windows and doors. We can't get out."

"What?" She got out of bed and pulled her clothes on. "Get dressed, Adam. Tell me exactly what's happened."

Harriet shrugged, "That's it. Every door and window have a load of planks over them - he's trapped us, we can't get out."

June shook her head angrily. "I knew that little bastard was bad news. Come on, we have to get out of here." June put her hand on the bedroom door handle.

"Wait," said Harriet, "just wait a minute. Let's think about this."

"What is there to think about? The man's a bloody nutter."

"I know, that's what I mean. Last night, he never mentioned anything about this - he knew we didn't want to be locked in and he was all smiles and promises we could leave today."

"What's your point, Harriet?"

"If he catches us trying to 'escape,' how do we know what he's going to do? He could be dangerous."

"Are we in trouble, Mummy?" said Adam.

June crouched down beside her son. "No, don't you worry, darling. We're ok." She hugged him and said to Harriet, "Well, we have to do something. I want to see."

The three sneaked down the stairs and June held in a gasp as she saw the planks nailed across the front door. They went into the kitchen, the room in darkness with only slight slivers of light able to pierce the gaps in the planks.

June held her hands to her face. "Dammit. Dammit! How could I be so stupid," she whispered.

Adam took a closer look at the planks on the kitchen door.

"Mummy, these are screwed in."

"Come here Adam," she held out her hand.

"But mummy, we can try and unscrew them, we could do it quietly."

"He's onto something, June," said Harriet. "I'll bet there's a screwdriver around here somewhere. Either in this kitchen or in that spare room I was sleeping in."

"Soldiers always have tools around," said Adam.

"He's not a soldier," said June. "I'll look down here. Do you want to check your room?"

Harriet nodded and looked at her watch. "It's six thirty. Let's hope he was working late on this."

Harriet crept up the stairs, again wincing at the creaking staircase. She went back into the spare room and searched for a screwdriver. Her hands were shaking.

"Calm down, come on."

She slowly pulled out drawers and looked through boxes. It didn't take long to find an old tool box under a pile of tired army clothes. She grabbed a few screwdrivers and took them to the kitchen.

"Found some," she said, holding them up.

"So did we. And that's not all, look at this." June eased open a drawer to reveal many large and deadly looking knives.

"Wow. They look pretty serious," said Harriet.

"They are." June took out two large knives, both with thick handles and double blades, one smooth and the other serrated. She passed one of the knives to Harriet.

"What? I don't want one."

"Take it, we're not in Kansas anymore."

Harriet took the knife. June passed her a sheath, and Harriet put the knife in it, tucking the ensemble in the back of her jeans.

"Come on, we don't know how much time we have," said June.

They each took a screwdriver and started to work on the planks. Adam was tasked with standing at the bottom of the stairs to listen for any sounds of waking.

Unscrewing the screws was much harder work than Harriet had thought. The drill Jake used had done an excellent job.

"This isn't going to work," said Harriet after five minutes had only yielded three screws. "There are hundreds of them."

June looked over the boards. "Not hundreds, but definitely a lot. If he comes down when we're halfway through…"

As if on cue, Adam came back into the kitchen and pointed upstairs. "He's awake," he whispered.

Harriet looked at the boards and the screws on the floor. She remembered the knife in her back pocket. She stood up, about to put the knife away, then thought the screws on the floor were more obvious; she kneeled down to pick them up.

June grabbed her wrist, "What are you doing? Calm down."

Harriet took a few deep breaths.

The sound of footsteps came from above them.

June picked up the three screws from the floor. "Keep hold of your knife, but put the back of your shirt over it, tuck it well down in your jeans. You may need it."

Harriet nodded and stood up, doing as June had said.

Adam tiptoed out of the kitchen.

Harriet looked at the board they had been working on. Although dark, the missing screws shone out to her like a beacon.

"What do we do now?" she said.

"What people always do in the morning, make a cup of tea," said June, smiling.

She opened and closed cupboards, not trying to be quiet.

"I think we should be listening to the radio today," said June in a normal voice, making Harriet jump.

Harriet mouthed, "What are you doing?"

June whispered, "Everything is normal, we are good with this, ok? If he catches us, I don't know what he'll do."

Harriet's eyes lit up in realisation. "Oh," she mouthed, then louder, "Yeah, I'm sure the police will have everything under control in a day or two."

Adam walked into the kitchen, looking confused.

"Everything's ok, isn't it Adam?" said June, winking at him.

Adam smiled, "Sure, mum," he said, catching onto the facade straight away.

Bright kid, thought Harriet, I needed it spelled out to me.

The sound of footsteps came from the stairs.

June turned the kitchen light on.

"Where do you think the sugar is?" she said in a bright voice.

Jake appeared at the door, he stopped still and surveyed the kitchen, looking at each person in turn. "Everyone alright?"

Harriet held her breath, unable to speak.

June smiled, "Sure we are. Just trying to rustle up a cup of tea. You don't mind, do you? I can make you one?"

Jake stared at June for a moment, then his face relaxed, and he smiled. "Course I don't mind. I'd love a cuppa. I don't have any sugar though. It's not good for you."

"Oh, that's ok. I could do with cutting down myself."

Jake looked at Harriet. "How are you Harriet, did you sleep ok?"

Harriet forced herself to smile and look Jake in the eye. "Yes, great thanks."

Jake held her eye for a moment, then turned back to June. "The cups are in there." He pointed to a cupboard above the kettle. "And how are you, young man?"

"Tip top, reporting for duty sir!" Adam mocked a salute.

Jake laughed, "Good lad."

Harriet felt the knife pressing against her lower back. It felt like it was jutting out from her shirt.

June filled the kettle with water and flicked it on.

"You sure you girls ok?" said Jake.

June faced Jake, a broad smile on her face. "Of course, why wouldn't we be?"

Jake held out his hands and looked around the room. "Uh, why do you think?"

"You mean the boards?" said June.

Jake nodded.

"I think it's great. It's safe."

Jake looked at Harriet, his face expressionless.

Harriet nodded and managed to say, "I saw one of them in the street last night. I was worried they might get in, but not now."

June moved closer to Jake and put her hand on his shoulder. "Look, Jake, I know I might have been a bit rude last night."

Jake glanced at the hand on his shoulder and barely hid a smile. He shrugged.

"But, last night, when I got to thinking, in the dark, just how dangerous things are now." She pointed to the boarded window. "This is the best thing you could've done."

She's good, thought Harriet.

Jake blushed a little. "I thought you'd be angry, and want me to take them down."

"And let those things in? No way. We need to keep Adam safe. And you can keep us safe, can't you Jake?"

Jake let out a small laugh. "You know, I thought you'd go all crazy."

June joined in the laughter, "Oh no, not at all!"

"I thought that I'd have trouble with you both! But you understand, I have to keep you here, we have to stay together if we want to be safe."

June nodded. "Absolutely Jake, absolutely. What do you think Harriet?"

Jake turned to Harriet, and she opened her mouth to speak, but she didn't have the chance.

June pulled the kettle out of the wall and swung it hard at Jake's head, striking him hard. The metal chimed with a loud bong like a bad cartoon joke.

Jake stumbled forward his eyes locked on Harriet, a dumb look of surprise on his face. He reached out to grab the sink, and June hit him again.

He fell like a sack of potatoes to the floor. He lay motionless.

Adam stared at his mum, "Wow…"

Harriet, her heart racing, also stared, unable to speak.

June put the kettle down. "What are you both looking at? Come on, we have to be quick." She ran over to the boards and took out the screwdriver from her pocket, making a start on the screws. "Adam, find something to tie him with. Harriet, you look like a goldfish. Come on, let's get these boards off."

Harriet was smiling, and enjoying the adrenalin rush she felt. "That was amazing, no way I could've done that."

June just smiled and motioned at the boards.

"Oh, of course." Harriet kneeled down and started unscrewing.

Thirty minutes later and they were nearly done. Both Harriet's hands hurt badly. Blisters had formed on her fingers and palms. But she didn't give up.

One more board to go and they could reach the door handle and hopefully get out. The sunlight shining in through the gap left by the removed boards was enough motivation to keep them working double fast.

"How's he doing?" said June.

Adam looked at Jake. "Still out."

Jake's hands had been tied with the kettle cord - they couldn't find anything else.

"So, where's Adam's dad?" asked Harriet, feeling close enough to safety to make small talk. "Or is that a sore subject?"

June let out a small snort. "Long enough ago now not to matter. A good man, don't get me wrong, but just never there for us. He's army through and through."

"I guess it must be tough, with him not being around. Was he away a lot?"

June nodded. "I thought I'd handle being an army wife, but… I got lonely, you know?"

Harriet noticed Adam watching them both, and decided not to press any further.

"Got ya!" shouted June in triumph.

June's last screw popped onto the floor. The board hung now on one screw. They both pulled on it, and with a few tugs, it was out, falling to the floor with a bang.

The two women cheered and hugged each other. Harriet felt tears on her cheeks.

"Sorry," she said wiping them away. "I guess I didn't know how scared I was."

"Don't be daft love," said June, giving Harriet another hug. Adam ran over and joined the group hug, his little arms reaching only half way around Harriet's back. Then Adam let out a cry, and his arms were gone.

Harriet looked up and gasped; she stepped back towards the door in shock, unable to catch a breath, her heart banging against her ribcage.

"Let him go!" shouted June.

Jake, the kettle cord around one of his wrists, stood by the sink, his arm tight around Adam's neck.

"You stupid bitches!" Spittle spat out of his mouth as he spoke, hanging down in thin white strands towards Adam's head. "Stupid, stupid, stupid!"

"Mummy," Adam started to cry, his face red, his eyes wide open in fear.

Harriet couldn't move, she had pushed herself up tight against the kitchen door, frozen in fear.

June started to walk towards Jake, "Come on now, Jake, let's not be silly. He's only a boy."

Jake shook his head. "Oh no, I'm not falling for that again. You aren't nice, you're horrible, and you cheated me! You stupid fucking cow, I'm in charge. Get it? I'm in CHARGE."

He moved backward, tightening his grip on Adam's throat, causing him to scream in pain.

"I'll break his neck!"

June suddenly jumped forward, pulling the knife out of her back pocket. She plunged it into Jake's shoulder.

Jake yelled out in pain and let go of Adam, who ran towards Harriet and wrapped his arms around her. Adam turned his head around, watching his mum fight with Jake.

Jake grabbed June around the head and pulled her towards his knife drawer. June writhed under his grip, trying to pull herself and her knife free.

"Do something!" shouted Adam, looking up at Harriet.

Harriet only looked at him, her body unable to move. She heard herself let out a small whimper.

Jake grabbed the knife drawer and pulled it open. A muffled cry escaped from June as Jake squeezed his arm harder around her head. He pulled out a knife from the drawer with his free hand and plunged it into June's back.

She screamed, a loud blood-curdling scream, echoed by her son who watched his mummy slump under Jake's grip.

Jake looked at Harriet, spit dripping from his mouth, his eyes wide open and crazed, and he laughed.

It was his last mistake.

His attention wandered for a second, enough for his grip on June to weaken. She pulled out the knife from Jake's shoulder. He cried in pain, his head snapping around in a fury, but it was too late. June dug the knife into his side, once, twice, three times.

Jake's cry's turned into murmured gurgles, as blood pumped out of his mouth. His eyes glazed over, and the two of them slid to the floor.

Harriet screamed and held her head in her hands.

Adam ran to his mum and hugged her. "Mummy, mummy, don't die!"

A wave of nausea rushed over Harriet. She felt light, her vision went dark, and she passed out.

Chapter 3

Harriet opened her eyes. Her head was sore. Black holes swam in and out of her vision, but she saw Adam clearly enough.

The young boy was sitting beside his mum, holding her hand, his body jumping with small sobs. His face was forlorn, staring dead ahead with empty eyes, red through crying.

A pool of blood covered the kitchen floor, Jake's body lying next to June's, a knife stuck in his side. His eyes were wide open, looking into space.

Harriet took a few moments to calm herself, to stop from vomiting. The kitchen door was right next to her.

"I have to get out of here," she said and scrambled to the door, pulling at the handle.

Adam started to cry behind her. She paused and turned to him.

"You can't go," said Adam between sobs.

"I can't stay here!" she said, almost shouting. Adam stared at her, his eyes and cheeks red with tears. "We can't stay here," she corrected herself.

Adam shook his head. "What about my mum?"

Harriet felt panic rise in her stomach. She had never seen a dead body before, never mind two. Never mind two murders.

"We need the police," she fumbled in her pocket for her mobile phone and pulled it out. Her hands shook violently. There was no signal. "Shit!" she shouted and threw her phone across the kitchen.

"What about my mum?" shouted Adam.

"I don't know," Harriet put her head in her hands.

"We can't leave her. We need to bury her."

Harriet thought about being outside, digging a hole, those things walking the streets.

She moved closer to Adam and took his free hand. "Adam, I'm really sorry what happened to your mum. She was a lovely woman, and what she did was very brave, but we have to go."

"Where?"

"I don't know. Somewhere else. We can't stay here, in this house." She wondered if the smell of the dead bodies would attract the things.

"We can't leave my mum. I'm not leaving her like this."

Adam held a defiant look on his face, he stared straight at Harriet and pulled his hand out of hers.

Harriet took a deep breath. "Ok, wait here. I'll go and find a spade."

The day was hot, and Harriet's sweat-soaked clothes clung to her skin. No one had ever told her how hard digging was. She had been at it for an hour, and the hole was still only a shallow foot deep. Would that be enough to bury June?

The garden had a high fence and a solid gate. There had been no sign of any zombies.

Adam had spent his time between being in the kitchen with his mum's body, and out in the garden watching Harriet. It made her feel uncomfortable, the small boy staring at her.

He brought her drinks of water and pieces of toast and fruit.

The Dead Lands

It was early evening before the hole was finished.

Harriet lay out the sheet on the floor of the kitchen. It immediately turned red as it soaked up the blood. Harriet tried not to gag.

She rolled June's body onto the sheet, puffing and letting out small moans as she struggled with the weight. Something else she had learned today - dead bodies were really heavy. She would need Adam's help to get the body into the back garden.

"Ok Adam, if you can push, and I'll pull. That's right," said Harriet as they moved the body into the back garden. Tears flowed freely down Adam's cheeks.

The grave was shallow, only a few feet, but Harriet didn't have the energy to dig more. They rolled the body into the grave, and it fell in with a dull thump. The sheet fell from June's face, and her eyes stared up from her grave.

Adam's legs gave way, and he fell to the floor, crying. "Mummy," he said under his breath, over and over.

Harriet filled in the grave, now crying herself.

The next day it rained.

Harriet and Adam had both slept in the spare room. She was grateful for the physical exertion of digging the grave - she didn't think she would have been able to sleep otherwise.

They sat in the lounge, Harriet's stomach turning at the smell coming from the kitchen. She would be glad to leave, even if it meant going outside where the zombies were.

"Ok, Adam, we have to try and find some help. I think we should go into town and see if we can find a police station."

Adam shook his head. "We have to find my Dad."

Harriet sighed, "Look, Adam, I think that finding the police will be easier. Don't you?"

He shook his head, refusing to look at Harriet.

"Adam, I think we have to do what I say now. I have to look after you until we find someone."

Adam turned round to face her, his face screwed up in anger. "You can't even look after yourself. You let my mum die, you didn't do anything! I want to find my dad!"

Harriet stared at the boy, his words having the same effect as if he had hit her in the stomach. "I'm sorry Adam. I didn't know what to do." She felt tears trickling down her cheeks.

Adam turned away from her, folding his arms. "I know where my dad's base is. We have to go there."

Harriet nodded. "Ok. Ok, Adam, we can do that, if that's what you want to do, then we can do that." She wiped away her tears. "Where's his base?"

"We get to the M25, then we can follow the M4. I'll know the junction."

Harriet thought to herself, the M25 was the motorway she had escaped from a few nights ago. She didn't want to go back there. "Adam, I'm not sure if we can-"

"You can't help me! The police can't help! We have to find my dad. Only the army can help against the zombies."

Harriet sat back against the couch, feeling defeated, feeling empty. She was out of fight. Besides, maybe he was right. "Ok, Adam. Let's go to your dad's base."

"I was going anyway. You're not in charge of me." He left the room, pausing to say, "I'm going to find some survival gear."

Harriet sat in the lounge for twenty minutes or so, unable to move. She couldn't describe how she felt, beyond simply scared to be alive.

The sounds of Adam moving about upstairs broke the silence, and she listened as if hypnotised.

He appeared at the lounge door with a small backpack on. He had a hunting knife tucked into his belt. "Coming?"

Harriet nodded and stood up.

"That's your bag," said Adam pointing to a larger backpack on the floor.

Harriet picked it up and followed Adam. They stepped out of the house, and Harriet looked nervously up and down the empty street. No zombies.

The rain fell hard, the skies dark with clouds. Harriet pulled up the hood of her waterproof, and they walked towards the fields, back towards the motorway.

After ten minutes of trudging through the thick mud of the saturated fields, they heard gunfire. Adam visibly brightened.

"It's the army - maybe Dad's there, come on!"

He walked ahead of Harriet as she struggled in the muck and driving rain.

Crossing a country path into another field, a motorway bridge became visible. Although difficult to see in the dull light, it was apparent many green trucks lined the motorway exit.

A large crowd of people congregated in this lower portion of the field, near the motorway exit.

Adam charged toward the motorway, the gunfire becoming louder the closer they got.

"Wait!" Harriet quickened her pace to catch up with Adam.

Another sound mixed with the gunshots - shouts and high pitched screams.

Adam heard them too and stopped running. He turned and allowed Harriet to catch up.

"Who's screaming?" he said.

"I don't know, stay with me. Ok?" She held out her hand. Adam looked at it for a moment, then took it. "I imagine your dad wouldn't rush into something, would he?"

Adam shook his head. "No, he'd want to do a recon."

"Ok, well, let's walk slowly and do a, erm, recon."

Adam seemed satisfied, and they kept a gentle pace as they neared the bridge.

They started to mix with the edge of the crowd. People ran in all directions. No one seemed to know where they were going. The field and the embankment leading down to the motorway teemed with a confusion of bodies, the air thick with shouts and screams.

A middle-aged woman stood near Harriet, tears streaming down her eyes. "Millie, Millie! Where are you?" shouted the woman.

A man in a mud-covered suit ran past pulling a young boy by the hand, an even younger girl on his shoulders. The girl held onto a teddy bear.

No one paid any attention to Harriet or Adam.

Gunshots, screams, shouting, engines. All these sounds melded to make an ominous cacophony that sent a chill up Harriet's spine.

A young woman, running past Harriet, tripped and fell. Harriet rushed forward and helped her up.

The woman, her face pale, her eyes open wide, stared at Harriet, then at Adam. She grabbed Harriet by the shoulders. "Get out of here, get him out of here, they're shooting at everything!"

"What, who's shooting? The Army?"

The woman let go of Harriet and continued running, "They're shooting anyone, they shot my husband." She disappeared into the crowd of people.

Adam tugged on Harriet's arm. "What does she mean?"

"I don't know Adam, she's probably confused."

"We need to find the army."

Harriet looked around her. The field was churned to mud. Gunshots, loud and close continued to crack in the air. Hundreds of people running in all directions.

"No one knows what to do…" she said.

There was a high scream from close by. Harriet turned to the sound and saw a young man falling, an old woman seemingly attached to his neck. The two landed on the floor, and the woman lifted her head, peeling a large flap of skin from the man's neck in her teeth. Blood spurted high into the air, and the man let out a brief yell before his head slumped forward.

Adam screamed, and Harriet pulled him in close. No one helped the man.

"Come on, we have to go." They changed direction and headed back the way they had come, away from the motorway.

Adam didn't offer any resistance, but sprinted after her, holding tight onto her hand. He let out small cries of panic as they ran.

Harriet pulled left and right, avoiding the randomness of the crowd. Adrenalin kept her moving.

She spotted a rising path that led from the edge of the field.

"Up this way, Adam."

Another scream. A woman fell with two zombies pulling at her stomach. They fought over the woman's entrails as they unwrapped from her gut. Harriet covered Adam's eyes and yanked him forward, hard. "Come on Adam, don't look."

They reached the path, which was busy with other people trying to escape the field. It inclined steeply, and Harriet pushed her legs hard up the trail. She gasped as a view of the motorway below opened up.

A maze of hundreds of cars blocked the road on both sides. Fire's burnt freely, and hordes of people moved in-between the charred and empty vehicles. A military fence ran across the motorway and up the embankment, against which multitudes of bodies pushed and swelled. Soldiers were crouched on the other side, firing into the people.

"What are they doing?" shouted Adam.

"Shooting at the zombies, come on," she pulled on Adam's arm again, a little too hard, but she needed to get him away.

They reached the top of the incline and kept running, the thick mud making speed difficult. Harriet pushed against her fatigue, against the pain in her legs, and took one step after the other, fear driving her on.

To their left was a wood, thick with undergrowth, dark and foreboding.

Gunshots rang out from further up the path. Harriet stopped and stared into the distance. Adam tugged on her hand, "Let's go."

Fifty yards or so ahead, some figures crouched on the path, emitting brief bursts of light, accompanied with staccato cracks of sound. They were soldiers, firing at the people on the track. Screams echoed with each shot.

"This way!" she pulled Adam to the left, and they ran into the woods. They were not the only ones; many people were taking the same escape route, a panicked run of prey.

Shot's followed them, and Harriet gasped as a couple to her right fell as they ran, eruptions of red around each.

She ran. She held tight onto Adam's hand, and he ran with her. The sound of her breath and the sound of Adam's cries drowned out the screaming and gunfire.

People around her fell.

Branches and bark exploded as shots went wide.

They ran further into the wood, jumping over branches, tramping through thorns. Harriet felt a pain in her ankle, but she kept going.

Soon the sound of gunfire became distant. The crowd around her thinned. She had no idea how much time had passed.

"Keep running, Adam."

"I can't!"

"Keep running soldier."

Soon, there was no sound but their running and the rain falling through the trees above. Passing a ditch, Harriet led Adam into it.

"We can rest here, just for a few minutes."

They crouched deep in the undergrowth. Harriet pulled Adam close, and he hugged her, burying his head into her shoulder.

Chapter 4

It was dark when Harriet woke. She didn't remember falling asleep, and couldn't imagine how she had. The down after the adrenaline high, she guessed.

She glanced at her watch, it was ten at night. Insects chirped in unison, and the odd owl hoot broke what was otherwise a deathly silence after the noise and panic of the afternoon.

Her first thought was Adam - he was no longer in her arms.

"Adam," she whispered in the darkness. There was a mumble of a response from beside her. She felt around and found him sleeping a few feet away from her.

She shook him gently, and he stirred awake. His eyes stared at her from the darkness.

"Are you ok?"

Adam didn't answer. He turned away.

"Adam?" She put her hand on his shoulder. He shrugged her off quickly and with force.

"Get off."

Harriet pulled her hand back and held it in mid-air, not sure what to do with it.

"What is it, Adam?"

"My mum's dead because of you," he hissed back at her.

Guilt rushed over her. Adam was right, wasn't he?

"You did nothing," said Adam. "You just stood there. You're useless. And then you took us to the bad soldiers with the virus instead of the good ones."

"Adam, I don't think the soldiers had the virus, I think…" she caught herself and stopped speaking.

"My mum would've known what to do," said Adam. "But she can't now because she's dead."

Adam began to cry again, his body shaking with sobs, getting louder.

Harriet slowly moved towards Adam. "I'm sorry, Adam, I really am. I know, I'm not very good at things like this." She put her arm on Adam's shoulder again, gently. He tried to shake her away again, but it was without commitment.

"I'd do anything to change what happened, but I can't." She put her arm around the young boy. "But what I can promise is that I'll do everything I can from now, to keep you safe, and to find your Dad."

"How will we find him?"

"I don't know," said Harriet. "But we will."

An hour later they hitched up their backpacks.

"We need to bury these," said Adam, pointing at the wrappers of the protein bars they had eaten. "We have to cover our tracks."

"Ok," said Harriet, bending down to help Adam bury the plastic wrappers. She smiled as Adam earnestly dug in the ground. She had a rush of feeling for the boy, realising she meant every word earlier - she had to keep him safe.

"So which way?" said Harriet after they finished with the wrappers.

Adam took out a luminous compass from his pocket and studied it for a minute. "This way," he said with confidence. "North West. My Dad's army base is north of the M4. It's this way."

"Yes sir," said Harriet, saluting and smiling.

Adam looked at her and shook his head, but she saw a small smile in the darkness.

They walked in silence for a good while, the odd crack of branch underfoot punctuating the rustle of leaves on the wood's floor.

There were no lights in sight, which Harriet found comforting after what had happened at the motorway. She didn't want to see people for a while. What would happen when they reached the military base, what would they do?

But how else could they find Adam's Dad?

"Why don't you have any children?" said Adam, his surprise question making Harriet jump.

"I don't have a boyfriend."

"Why not?" said Adam as he threaded through some low bushes that lay over their path.

"I'm too young, and I haven't found anyone I like enough yet."

"Ok."

They walked in silence for another five minutes, then Adam started his interrogation again. Harriet couldn't help but smile.

"What do you do?"

"I'm a recruitment agent."

Adam stopped and looked at her. "What's that?"

"I help people find jobs."

"Ah ok. Sounds boring. Jobs are boring, so finding them for other people must be even more boring."

Harriet laughed. "You know what, I think you might be right."

"Why do you do it then?"

"It just sort of happened, I guess. I needed a job when I finished university, and that's what I got."

"You're one of the bovines."

"What do you mean?" said Harriet.

"My Dad says that most people are bovines - they never think about what they want to do, and they just end up doing stuff that bores them. He says most civilians are bovines."

Harriet had no answer.

"I bet you go out getting drunk every weekend."

"Well, yes, but that's just having fun."

"Dad says bovines need to get drunk to forget how boring their lives are."

"Well, maybe your Dad doesn't know everything." To her surprise, she felt a bit offended, or maybe she was annoyed because a ten-year-old seemed to have summed up her life.

Adam stopped and held his hand up. Harriet froze. "What is it?" she whispered.

"I heard something," he said.

There was a click, and a powerful light shone from the darkness ahead of them. Harriet held her hands up to cover her eyes.

"Halt! Put your hands up," shouted a disembodied voice from beyond the light.

Harriet obeyed and glanced at Adam. She was relieved to see he had his hands up, too.

"Who are you? Tell us your names."

"Adam."

"Harriet."

The light switched off, and a few figures became visible in the darkness - soldiers.

"Sorry, ma'am. We have to check you are not infected. The zeds can't speak."

Harriet's heart was beating fast against her chest. She moved forward slowly and put her hands protectively around Adam's shoulders.

"Zeds?" said Harriet.

"Zombies."

"Told you…" whispered Adam to Harriet. Then to the soldier, he said, "We're looking for my Dad, he's a soldier."

The soldier at the front of the group, a tall man, crouched down in front of him. He lifted the intricate looking goggles from his face and said, "Is he now? What's his name?"

"He's a sergeant. Donald Allen."

The soldier glanced behind, at the other soldiers. "Ok, son, ma'am, you should come with us. It's not safe out here."

"Do you know my Dad?"

"I've heard the name. You need to come back with us to our base."

Harriet gently squeezed Adam's shoulders. "Let's go, Adam, they can help us." He looked up at her, and she smiled and took his hand. "Come on."

They followed the soldiers into the darkness. Harriet felt her heart relax, her breathing slowing down. Even given what had happened by the bridge, she felt safe - the need for order and authority outweighing her fears.

They were to be taken to a military camp.

They joined a troop carrier full of a ragtag collection of civilians in various stages of shock, distress, and numbness.

The only person who seemed excited was Adam. Harriet held him close as the truck rumbled through the woods and over dirt tracks, and she felt his heart thumping fast. The few glances she caught from him showed an excited face full of anticipation.

"Do you think Dad will be there to meet us?"

"I don't know, Adam. He might not be, so let's just wait and see."

The truck stopped in a busy and vast courtyard. The tarpaulin was pulled back by two soldiers, and a third hustled them out onto the wet concrete. A grand four-story building surrounded the yard on three sides, the fourth side being the entrance: a road, lined with trucks, leading out into the woods.

Soldiers ran through the courtyard, the air rang with shouts and engines and boots sloshing through the puddles left by the recent downpour. Groups of civilians were being moved from trucks into buildings, into tents pitched in the courtyard, and into other vehicles.

Powerful floodlights sat high on metal struts, shining bright white beams across the throng of the courtyard.

Harriet jumped as shots cracked in the air. Tall sentinel towers surrounded the base. A marksman fired into the woods beyond the fence, most probably at approaching zeds. Harriet took Adam's hand and crouched down next to him.

"Stay close to me, ok?"

Adam, his eyes wide, looking around in fascination, nodded.

"This way," shouted a soldier. He led them and the other people from their truck through a door into the large building. They were taken through a few corridors into a plain, empty, beige room with a solitary desk, behind which sat a smart looking young soldier.

"Well done, you are the last lot we can take in. Our patrols are over, we're full. I'm Lieutenant Byrd." He stood up, his arms behind his back. "You should be quite safe here for now, as you can imagine. I understand the events of the last few days have probably been quite terrifying for most of you, and that you may have lost much."

His face glowed softly with a kind and sad smile.

"You can be assured that this is the best place for you all now. Her Majesty's finest are here to protect you."

Harriet squeezed Adam's hand.

"Where's my Dad?" he whispered to her.

"Shhh. We'll find out soon."

Lieutenant Byrd walked to the near side of the desk as three other men in uniform entered the room.

"These men will take you to your rooms."

The group started to shuffle out after the soldiers. Harriet felt a hand on her shoulder, it was Byrd.

"Ma'am. Would you and your son follow me please."

Harriet shook his head, "Oh, he's not my son, he's-"

"That's quite alright ma'am, this way." He led her away from the group, through a door on the other side of the room. They walked down a yellow painted corridor and stopped outside a door. Byrd opened it, motioning Harriet and Adam inside.

The room was a medium-sized office with a desk and some filing cabinets lining one of the gray walls. A large map of the UK covered the wall behind the desk.

An attractive officer with short blond hair and sharp blue eyes sat behind the desk. He stood up as Harriet and Adam entered and reached his hand forward, which Harriet took, surprised at how flustered she was feeling.

"Please, sit down." He motioned to two chairs. Adam and Harriet sat on them.

The man smiled and said, "I'm Lieutenant Dalby, very pleased to meet you. I believe you are Harriet, and, Adam?" He smiled at Adam.

"Do you know my dad?" he said.

Dalby nodded. "That's why we brought you here."

Adam's face lit up, a beaming smile, "I told you," he said to Harriet, "I told you he was here."

Looking at the happiness in Adam's eyes, Harriet felt a warm glow again. She reached over and hugged him.

As she held the boy, she turned to look at Dalby. Dalby was no longer smiling. He shook his head slowly.

Harriet pulled herself away from Adam, feeling the colour drain from her face.

"Adam," said Dalby.

"Are we going to see him?"

Harriet held Adam's hand tightly.

"Adam," Dalby paused. He leaned forward and spoke in a soft voice. "Yesterday morning, I was with your dad."

"Where is he now?" Adam looked from Harriet to Dalby, sensing the change in the room's atmosphere.

"He was a courageous man, Adam, your dad."

"Can I see him?" said Adam, his voice quiet, pleading. Harriet felt tears well in her eyes.

"He saved a lot of men. Without him, many brave soldiers would not be alive, but I'm sorry Adam. He didn't make it himself." Dalby shook his head, his brow furrowed with sadness.

Silence sat in the room, heavy and numb.

Adam stared at Dalby. "No," he said, quietly. Adam turned to face Harriet, "He's not right, is he? He's lying, isn't he? My dad can't be dead."

Harriet felt a tear trickle down her cheek as she looked at the life drain from Adam's eyes. She turned to Dalby. "Are you sure, his name is Sergeant Donald Allen, there's no mistake?"

Dalby shook his head slowly. "No mistake, I'm sorry. Sergeant Allen died yesterday afternoon in the execution of his duties. Such a brave man, Adam, a brave man."

Adam started to shake. He rocked back and forward. Harriet grabbed onto him and held him tight. He pushed against her and yelled. He screamed, his mouth wide open, letting out long and mournful cries, the like of which should never be heard from a young boy. Harriet felt the pain and wished she could take it from him.

Chapter 5

The night was long. They were put up in barracks with other 'refugees.' She had to accept that's what she was now - a refugee. She and Adam had no home, no place to go, no means to support themselves.

Life as they knew it was gone.

About thirty other people were sleeping in the room - a mix of all society. The zombie apocalypse made no distinctions or judgments - all would suffer.

Adam had somehow fallen asleep. He and Harriet had small camp beds beside each other. Cheap blankets and thin mattresses, but what more could refugees expect? Harriet lay still in the dim light from the overhead lamps - turned down for night time, but not entirely out. Probably so the two soldiers standing by the door, 'for their own safety,' would be able to quickly dispatch of anyone displaying zombie tendencies.

At least she was safe, thought Harriet. The last few days had been so non-stop, so base, so just-staying-alive, that she hadn't had time to think beyond anything but getting her and Adam to somewhere safe.

But what now?

She tucked herself into the small bed and turned over, the light frame of the bed creaking as she shifted her weight. She tuned out the mumbles of conversation, the sobs from the dark bunks, and tried to sleep.

The hardest part to tune out was her own mind.

She reached over and kissed Adam gently on the forehead, and rested her hand on his shoulder. How had she ended up looking after this boy, this orphan? Now her responsibility.

She would have to step up.

A shrill alarm broke her nightmares apart, and Harriet sat up sharply. The lights were on full, and the soldiers were loudly ordering the occupants of the barracks to get up and get dressed.

"Adam!" shouted Harriet grabbing his arm.

The boy sat up, dazed, his eyes red from his earlier crying.

"We have to get dressed."

The siren continued to blare above all other noise, a shrill repeating klaxon that hurt Harriet's ears.

One of the soldiers held his hand to his ear and was talking quickly - must be some sort of in-ear radio, thought Harriet. The second soldier watched the increasingly panicked members of the barracks, glancing at his partner.

Harriet helped Adam on with his coat and handed him his rucksack.

The soldier on the radio nodded to the other, who on receiving the subtle notification jumped into life.

"Ok people, move now, we need to move, move, move!" His voice boomed above the siren, and he motioned urgently with his gun.

Everyone sprung into action, quickly scrambling over each other to get to the door and out. Harriet imagined this is what it felt like in a real fire evacuation, not the practice drills they used to repeat every month in her office. Now for real, all order and consideration forgot, just get me out.

She grabbed Adam's hand and pulled, "Come on, we have to be quick."

She ran forward, and Adam tripped, catching his foot on the corner of the bed. She tried to turn against the tide of people to go back for him but was pushed over herself. She fell down between two beds.

A hand grabbed onto her and pulled her up. A tall, dark, broad man with a shaved head said in a strong African accent, "Are you ok?"

She nodded, "Yes, but my boy," she pointed back to the cots.

The man nodded and pushed his way quickly through the people to grab Adam. He hoisted him up and held him close to his chest.

"Let's go," he said.

Harriet followed the man out the door.

Once outside, the noise of the sirens lessened, but the chaos increased; shouting, engines, gunshots, explosions.

Harriet was pushed into a flow of people. She looked for Adam and saw him and the man now a few people behind her. The man's eyes locked onto hers and he pushed forward, trying to reach her.

A second stream of people joined from the left, and Harriet was buffeted amongst the throng, becoming disoriented in the panicked crowd. Within moments she lost sight of Adam and the man.

"Adam!" she shouted. Her voice drowned in the chaos.

She shouted his name again, and again, trying to fight the flow and stay in one place, but being dragged in a predetermined direction, like in a river, like a fish being funnelled to the sea.

Her only thought was to find Adam; to do that she needed to get out and above the crowd.

She pushed her way sideways against the flow and struggled to keep her footing as the now terrified people pushed against her. A man shoulder barged her and, in a fury, she shoulder barged him back, thrusting harder and faster. She squeezed past him and, with her new found boldness, began to make progress against the sea of panic.

She reached a truck and pulled herself up onto its roof. The frightened faces of the people glowed under the harsh glare of the floodlights. The crowd was being funnelled towards a group of waiting trucks by the fences of the base.

A fire burnt in the third floor of the main building. A man in flames hung from one of the windows. His body jerked and his arms swung wildly. His flesh was black.

At the edges of the crowd, soldiers fired at what she assumed were zeds. Their efforts were in vain. The zeds had infiltrated the crowd. A man grabbed a passing woman and sunk his teeth into her neck. People nearby screamed as they were bathed in blood, and a hasty space formed around the unfortunate woman. The man, his face and hands dripping with blood, turned again to the crowd, looking for new flesh.

Dragging her eyes away from the horror, she scanned the chaos.

She saw Adam.

The large man was free from the crowd, still holding Adam and running back towards the building. They disappeared into a doorway off the courtyard.

"Adam!" she yelled uselessly against the wall of noise around her. She had to get into the building, but if she jumped back into the crowd, she would be rushed away. There had to be another way.

The truck she stood on was parked against a high concrete wall. She managed to pull herself up onto the wall. On the other side, she saw a door into the building, about fifty yards away. More importantly, there was no crazed mob of people.

A flake of concrete next to her chipped off and hit her on the leg, hard, stinging painfully. Then another. She was being shot at.

She jumped off the wall onto the other side. Something burnt in her shoulder. She landed hard on the ground and let out a gasp of pain. She grabbed her shoulder trying to squeeze the pain away. It felt wet. She looked at her hand, it was covered in blood. I've been shot, she thought.

She pulled her top back to assess the wound - a large graze on the top side of her arm. The bullet had only skimmed her flesh.

A wave of nausea passed through her.

Harriet pushed her fear to the back of her mind and ran towards the doorway. Some soldiers ran past her, ignoring her.

She reached the doorway, but it was locked shut. There was a window next to it. She quickly scanned around her and near the bottom of the wall sat a pile of bricks.

She grabbed one and threw it at the nearest window.

The brick bounced off.

She cursed and picked up the brick again, and moved closer to the window. Shielding her eyes, she hit the window with the brick; once, twice, then harder, and harder again, and then it smashed. Shards of glass bounced off her face and neck.

She used the brick to remove the glass from the edge of the pane and started to climb through.

A hand grabbed her on the shoulder. She turned around to look into the eyes of a young soldier.

"What are you doing?" he said.

"My boy, the boy I am looking after, he's in here, I have to find him."

The soldier looked nervously behind him. He was a young man with a shaved head and acne. "You know what, fuck it. Do what you like." He ran off towards the fence to join a group of other soldiers.

Harriet pulled herself through the window and was in a medium-sized dark room. It looked like some sort of classroom - she could make out desks in the darkness.

She ran to the door and paused. How was she going to find Adam? Think, where would they go, why had he gone back in the building?

She had to assume the man's intentions were good, to keep Adam safe. So if he wanted to help Adam, wouldn't he want to find her? There could only be one place he would go, back to the barracks, back to their room.

She opened the door into a low lit corridor, the blasting volume of the siren again cutting up the air with its incessant wailing. The hallway was empty and long, with many doors along its length.

Thinking back to their hasty evacuation from the barracks, they had exited the middle of the building. Harriet had just entered the right wing, so if she headed left… Seemed easy enough. Harriet set off running along the corridor.

She reached a T-junction. Some soldiers were down the far end of the corridor to her left, so she ran right.

She heard a shout and the sound of running.

She ran faster.

She turned into a long corridor. The sounds of footsteps came closer, and she realised she couldn't reach the end of the hallway before the soldiers caught her. She tried the nearest door.

Locked.

She ran a few yards and tried the next.

Locked.

Panic enveloped her, and she heard herself pleading under her breath, "Open, open, open."

The next was also locked.

She glanced at the corner of the corridor, still no soldiers, but their footsteps echoed loudly.

She tried the next door. Her last chance.

It opened.

She burst into the room and slammed the door. She was in a small office containing a desk and a wardrobe. She climbed into the wardrobe.

Standing as still as she could, not daring to breathe, she listened for the soldiers. All she heard was her heartbeat - surely they could hear it, too?

Then the sound of several people running past the room.

She paused for a moment, then got out of the wardrobe and opened the door to the corridor slowly. She peered down it to see three soldiers at the far end. She ran out of the room in the opposite direction.

Turning a corridor, she collided with a body coming the other way. Harriet fell back and held her breath, ready to fight, but relaxed when she saw an old woman in front of her.

The old woman was wearing the white overalls of a cleaner, her face was pale with fear and her eyes wide open. She breathed fast and held her hand to her chest.

"Where're the barracks?" shouted Harriet.

"What?"

"The barracks?" Harriet grabbed the woman's shoulders.

The woman recoiled and pointed behind her - "Back that way, take your first left, then straight down that corridor."

"Thanks," said Harriet. She bolted past the bemused old woman, her footsteps echoing in the empty corridor.

She followed the cleaner's directions. Twice soldiers ran past her, but they ignored her. It seemed that some cared, and others didn't. Or maybe the situation was just getting worse by the second.

She reached the barracks.

She opened the door and went in.

The room was empty.

Even though the siren was still blaring its incessant alarm, the room felt silent, and still. Her heart sank, and Harriet dropped onto the nearest bunk. Where could she start looking for Adam now?

Chapter 6

Above the siren emerged a sharp scraping sound, the noise of metal against the laminate flooring. Harriet looked up to see a moving bed in the far corner of the room. A large hand appeared from below and grabbed the top of the bed, pulling up the huge body of the man. Adam jumped up beside him, a wide smile on his face.

"Harriet!"

Harriet and Adam ran towards each other and hugged, Harriet again surprised how strong her feelings were for Adam - how strong her relief, her warmth.

"Sorry," said the man, his voice low and sonorous. He was well over six foot, and maybe a few years older than Harriet. He wore a white t-shirt that clung to a well built upper body. His face was downcast, sad almost. "I tried to keep up with you, but I wasn't able, not while keeping hold of Adam."

Harriet smiled. "It's ok, thank you."

Adam said, "His name is Arthur."

Arthur nodded to Harriet.
"Thanks, Arthur."
"It's no problem."
"I'm Harriet."
"Hello, Harriet."
Adam pulled on Harriet's hand. "We need to go."
"Where to? There are soldiers everywhere. And zombies."
The siren stopped, and the air suddenly felt empty, Harriet's ears searching for sound.
Then the lights went out.
"The power," said Arthur.
Adam squeezed Harriet's hand. "I have a torch." Adam rustled through his backpack.
A click, and then the thin faint yellow beam of a low powered torch.
The beam first shone at Harriet, then at Arthur, then at the door.
"So where to?" said Harriet.
"I saw a garage when they brought me in here, maybe we can get a vehicle, " said Arthur.
"Where was it, can you remember?" said Harriet.
"I think so. We need to go out the back of the building."
They set off into the maze of corridors, turning left and right, heading further into the heart of the base with no real idea where they were headed. Faint shots and distant screams were now the ambient sound. Every now and again Harriet felt her heart jump as a yell or the rapport of gunfire sounded too close for comfort. But they saw no-one. It seemed the building was empty.
They reached a door that led outside. They stepped into the darkness and relative silence. Sounds of chaos echoed from the other side of the building but seemed distant.
A road led to the left and right, both directions to darkness - the floodlights had also died with the power outage.
"I think I came in on this road," said Arthur.
"Which way for the garage?" said Harriet

Arthur paused and looked up and down the road. He shrugged. "Let's try this way." He beamed a wide grin.

They turned right and ran down the road. To their left was a wide grass field, contained by a large fence, the glint of its metal just visible. The buildings of the base stood to their right.

They ran past a small alleyway. The sound of fast footsteps. A scream.

A soldier ran out of the alleyway, his arm raised, a knife in his hand. He was upon Harriet as soon as she had seen him. The blade came down, and she dodged to the left, tripping and falling as she did so.

She landed on her injured arm and cried out in pain.

Arthur body-checked the soldier, sending him flying. The soldier scrambled to get up, and Arthur swung his fist hard. It connected with the soldier's face, a heavy crack sounded in the air as his nose splintered. The soldier fell with a heavy thump, out cold.

Harriet got up and stared at the man on the floor. His face was smeared with blood. There were no visible cuts - it looked like he had smeared his entire face with blood himself.

Harriet's shoulder stung. She rubbed it.

"What's wrong with your shoulder?" said Arthur.

Harriet shrugged. "It's ok. I got shot."

Arthur smiled. "Tough lady."

"Come on," said Adam, staring wildly around him, as if expecting another attack from any direction, any second.

They continued down the road until they reached a turn off to the left.

"Down here, I think," said Arthur.

They headed down a tree-lined and thin road for a few hundred feet. A low, wide, gray building emerged from the darkness, plain concrete walls and corrugated iron roof. A single small door.

Harriet got there first and put her hand on the door. "You think this is the garage?"

"Try it…" said Arthur.

Harriet turned the handle, it wasn't locked. She opened the door.

A dark room, its far walls not visible. Gray shapes lined the sides, maybe cabinets, tables, other furniture. Two large forms in the darkness. What little light there was glinted off their metal bodies - vehicles of some sort, jeeps.

Also, sounds. The shuffling of feet; bodies bumping into inanimate objects knocking them over, falling over them; moans; hisses; painful calls of despair.

Zombies.

It was impossible to tell how many, or where they were.

The sounds were coming closer - it seemed they didn't need light to find the living.

Harriet fought the urge to run from the room. "This place is full of those things, can you hear them?" she whispered.

Arthur turned to Adam. "Give me your torch."

Adam handed it to Arthur, who turned it on.

"Are you sure we-" Harriet gasped.

The light revealed a writhing mass of the living dead, their faces frozen in bloody and mindless desire. The moans of the zombies doubled.

This time, Harriet did run from the room, dragging Adam with her. Arthur slammed the door behind them.

"How many are in there?" she said.

"Too many," said Arthur. "We need another plan."

"But we need the vehicles, we have to get out of here."

Adam pulled on Harriet's sleeve.

"What is it?" she said.

"We don't have much time," said Adam.

"What do you mean?"

"All those people back at the base, there's a good chance they're all going to be zombies soon," said Adam, speaking quickly. "The soldiers don't seem to be able to do anything. We have to get out of here, or we'll be surrounded."

Harriet felt fear at the boy's words. She looked at Arthur. "We need those vehicles."

"We can't kill all those things. We have no weapons," said Arthur.

The door banged causing all of them to jump. The zombies had reached the door and were no doubt piling against it, hearing and sensing the live flesh on the other side.

"We'll let them out," said Harriet. "Lure them away."

"That would work," said Arthur nodding thoughtfully. "If we can open the door to the front of the garage, one of us can…"

"Act as bait," said Harriet.

The three looked at each other.

"I'll do it," said Harriet, taking a deep breath.

"No!" Adam grabbed hold of her leg.

"The boy is right, I should do it," said Arthur. "The boy needs you."

Harriet shook her head. "Nothing going's to happen me, you're talking as if it's a suicide mission."

Arthur took Harriet's arm and whispered to her, "He cannot lose anyone else. Please, let me do it."

Adam squeezed her leg, "I want to stay with you."

Looking at Adam, she knew Arthur was right.

"Ok. I'll stay with you Adam, Arthur can be the distraction."

Adam smiled.

"So, Arthur, you get the garage door open, lure them out," said Harriet. "Me and Adam come in the back way, get one of those vehicles started and come find you?" said Harriet.

"That sounds about good to me," said Arthur.

"What happens if we can't get them started?"

Arthur thought for a moment. "I'll run in a circle through the woods for about five minutes. I'll end up back here, you guys wait for me. If we have the jeep started, great, we go. If not, then we run, together."

"What do you think Adam?" said Harriet.

"Ten-four," he said.

Harriet smiled. "Ok, let's do it."

The door rattled again, and the sound of moaning from the other side echoed into the night, chilling Harriet to the core. The sound of the dead should never be heard by the living.

"I'll be shouting to get them to follow me," said Arthur.

"Ok, be quick, and Arthur…"

"Yes?"

"Good luck."

The giant man smiled. "No problem."

Chapter 7

Arthur disappeared around the side of the building, and a few moments later Harriet heard a distant clunk and a few bangs - Arthur opening the garage door.

Silence, and then a loud shout broke into the night, the deep voice of Arthur booming through the woods and clear air.

The effect was immediate. The back door stopped rattling and the moaning faded. Shuffling feet could be heard moving away from the door.

Adam mouthed to Harriet, "It's working," and reached for the back door.

Harriet placed her hand on his, "Wait a minute…"

They stood in absolute silence, Harriet's ear against the door, listening.

Arthur's shouts faded.

"Ok, now, let's go," said Harriet.

She pushed the door open slowly, peering into the dark through a small gap. She heard no movement, saw no shuffling shadows. No moaning. No hissing. No despair.

"Pass me your torch."

Adam gave Harriet the torch. She held her breath and switched it on, pointing it into the room.

Nothing.

She swept the beam around the room - no zombies.

Two army jeeps sat in the middle of the garage. There was another door in the left wall.

"Come on."

They walked carefully into the garage, taking the left side. Adam held on tightly to Harriet's hand. Harriet swept the torch beam from left to right, her eyes primed for any movement, her ears sharp for any sound apart from their footsteps against the concrete floor.

The garage door was open, a gentle breeze blowing in. The road ahead was empty - Arthur must have led them into the woods. He would be back soon, hoped Harriet.

Adam pulled on her hand.

"What is it?"

He pointed to the table that lined the wall next to them. Harriet aimed the beam.

"Weapons," said Adam.

Hammers, crowbars, knives.

"Good spot."

She reached forward and took a crowbar. She passed a hammer to Adam.

"You be ok with that?" said Harriet.

Adam sighed and nodded his head, "Of course I will."

"Sorry, of course, you will. Let's checks these cars."

"Jeeps," said Adam.

"Ok, Jeeps."

Each jeep was locked.

"Great. Now what?" said Harriet.

"It's an army garage. The keys will be in here somewhere. What about in there?" Adam pointed to the closed door to the left of the garage.

"Ok, stay behind me, Adam."

She opened the door slowly. It led into a small dark room containing a desk and filing cabinet. She crept in.

She moved the torchlight around the room slowly. Before she had made a full sweep, the beam highlighted a panel on the wall, upon which hung some keys.

"You're a genius, Adam. How did you know?"

"It's army. My Dad was Army."

She reached down and kissed him on the forehead. "He'd be proud of you."

Harriet covered the few steps from the door to the panel and shone her light on the keys.

"Adam, it looks like these are license plates. Can you read out the number on the- Adam!"

A movement to her left, shuffling, a loud moan.

Adam let out a cry.

Harriet spun around, and her torchlight showed a body in army greens, darkened with blood stains, bearing down upon Adam, its arms outstretched.

Adam fell.

The zombie soldier hissed as it went for Adam.

"No you fucking don't." Harriet raised her crowbar and brought it down hard on the back of the zombie's skull.

There was a horrifying, and at the same time satisfying, crack as the hard metal of the crowbar met the solid bone of the dead man's skull.

She brought up the crowbar and smashed it down once more.

She felt liquid - blood - splatter over her skin. The crowbar sunk through the skull and into soft tissue below, like she had stuck her finger through an eggshell.

Adam cried out.

"Hold on Adam, hold on."

The zombie was motionless. Harriet grabbed it by the shoulders and pulled the dead weight off Adam with a struggle.

She pulled up Adam and hugged him. "Are you ok? Did he bite you? Are you bit?"

"No, he didn't get me."

She held Adam at arm's length and shone her torch over him. He had blood on his face. She felt a moment of panic. She wiped it away with her hand - no cuts, no bite underneath.

"I'm ok, Harriet. It's ok."

"Good." Harriet realised she was shaking. Her fear wasn't for herself, but for Adam. "I should have checked the room, I'm sorry Adam."

"It doesn't matter. Let's just get in the jeep before any more turn up."

"Good thinking."

She found the right key and put it in the door of the jeep.

"Look," said Adam.

"What?"

"The road."

Adam pointed out of the garage.

Shapes. Lumbering shapes out of the darkness, slow but purposeful - heading for the garage. Groaning, the new sound of the night.

"Get in the car Adam," said Harriet softly as she opened the door.

"What about Arthur, he's still-"

"Adam, get in the car."

Adam got into the passenger seat.

The zombies were close, they would be in the garage within a minute.

Harriet ran around the side of the Jeep and got in the driver's seat. She locked the door - Adam had already locked his. He was pale, staring ahead, breathing fast.

"It's a swarm. I told you we didn't have time - I told you we had to go quick."

"It's ok Adam. We're safe in here - nothing can get us here." She didn't know whether that was true.

They watched the approaching horde, low moaning vibrating through the air and deep into Harriet's bones. It wasn't just a sound though, it was a telegraph, a broadcast of the desperation of the trapped beings inside their dead bodies.

Adam held Harriet's hand, and he breathed fast and deep. Harriet's own breathing had increased, and sweat was forming on her back. She worked hard to stop a panic attack. She looked at her watch - how long would Arthur be and what could he do once he was here?

The first of the zombies walked into the garage, and straight towards the jeep. They had the knowledge it seemed, of exactly where their prey was.

The zombie walked directly into the bonnet, and shuffled to the side, its eyes staring straight ahead, vacant and dead. No iris, all pupil. It had been a young woman. It was wearing a white sweater now splashed with blood. Its jaw was hanging loose, and it gnashed uselessly against the air, seemingly frustrated at the smell of flesh it couldn't reach. It had a massive gash in its neck, out of which a thick red tube hung - it was an artery. Harriet felt sick.

So engrossed had Harriet been in studying the first zombie to reach the Jeep, that she hadn't noticed the others. Slow, lumbering bodies encircled them, the air vibrating to their groaning lament.

Adam started to shake and whimper. He buried himself in Harriet's arms, and she held him tight. The dark cadavers now surrounded the vehicle, their damaged and bloody figures pushing against the windows. Some tried to bite at the glass, others simply pushed their faces up against it, their dumb animal intelligence unable to produce any more productive actions.

Harriet felt a scream build in her stomach, and she fought to push it down. It was the fear of being surrounded by dead humans, by zombies, trying to get into a car to eat her; it was the exhaustion of the past few days and the fight from one place of survival to another; it was the unrecognised loss of everything her life was and would probably never be again; it was the pain of watching Adam go through the death of both of his parents; it was her fear that her failings had allowed the death of Adam's mother; it was the loss of hope.

Two quick rapports of gunfire.

Two zombie heads on the driver side of the vehicle burst in red blood and flesh.

More gunfire, more course and fleshy thumping sounds, like a melon being hit with a sledgehammer.

Adam sat up, his eyes wide. "Who is it? Is it Arthur?"

"It must be," said Harriet.

More gunfire, short bursts this time, and the heads of zombies at the front of the vehicle exploded in red tissue mists.

The driver's door opened quickly and Harriet, expecting to see the large dark form of Arthur, was instead shocked to see a smaller man, a shock of blond hair and pale white skin.

It was the good-looking lieutenant she had met yesterday evening - Dalby.

She smiled at him, "Oh, thank you, thank god, we thought we were finished!" Relief flooded over her.

Dalby didn't smile. He climbed into the vehicle. "Where are the keys?"

"We can't go yet," said Adam. "We have to wait for Arthur."

"Who the fuck is Arthur?"

Harriet's brow furrowed but put his rudeness down to circumstance. "He is our friend, we had a plan to get these vehicles and get out of here. He should be here in a minute - he led all the zombies away."

"He didn't do a very good job, did he? Give me the keys."

Harriet had the keys in her left hand. She slipped them into her jacket pocket, feeling uneasy in the Lieutenant's company, his manner setting off an internal alarm. Simply put, he scared her. "We have to wait for Arthur."

Very quickly her relief had turned to fear.

Dalby looked to the ceiling, an exasperated sigh. "We don't have time, now give me the fucking keys!"

Harriet sat between Adam and Dalby. She moved a little away from Dalby, squeezing up next to Adam, shielding him.

"No," she said.

A thump from somewhere. Spinning blackness and white stars in her vision. The taste of blood and throbbing pain in her jaw, her head back against the seat. Adam yelling.

Dalby had hit her.

She shook her head and straightened up, focusing on Dalby. She felt warm blood trickle down the side of her chin. Her jaw was throbbing.

Dalby was pointing a handgun at her. "I won't ask again. We can all get out of here alive, or you can decide to wait for your boyfriend, and only I get out of here alive."

Chapter 8

Arthur breathed quickly, pushing his way through the undergrowth. The darkness in the woods was complete, and he struggled to keep upright as he fought through branch and bush to stay ahead of the pursuing zombie mob. The sound of their moans floated in the darkness, surrounding him, an unearthly sound that pushed right into his soul. It was impossible to tell how close or far they were, but the cracking of undergrowth from behind him let him know they weren't giving up.

Arthur cursed as a branch scraped his head, drawing blood. He pushed on, hoping that Harriet and Adam would drive on without him. He had lost any idea of where he was, never mind the garage.

A hiss caught him off guard, it was loud, close, in his left ear. He felt a warmth on his neck, or did his imagination and fear put it there? Adrenaline spiked in his veins, and he ran faster, his feet feeling for safe ground.

But his extra drive and speed brought carelessness, and he fell forward. He tumbled and rolled down a steep incline. Soil and dried leaves filled his mouth and eyes. Tiny thorns and branches pierced his skin.

Arthur scrambled up, seeing nothing, the sounds of his hunters ever present.

A loud crack of wood above, and suddenly a weight was upon him. Fingers dug into his shoulders, and the snap-snap of jaws threatened death inches from his face.

He swung with his fist, following the sound of the jaws and he connected with flesh and bone. The weight fell off him.

He scrambled up and ran, not caring what direction. A hand grabbed his leg, he shook it off.

His lungs screamed - he was a big man, not used to this much running. His heart beat viciously, trying to get blood through the miles of arteries.

How long could he continue? If he could keep going until sunrise at least, he might have a chance.

Gunfire.

In the darkness, not far away, the sound of gunfire.

A salvo of single shots.

Arthur ran towards the sound.

Adam was crying again, curled up in the corner, hiding from Dalby. Harriet's was sick of seeing Adam crying - all she wanted was a place where he wouldn't cry anymore.

And another of her life's new maxims was she couldn't let anyone else die. It didn't matter that a soldier was pointing a handgun at her, asking her for the key in her pocket. The key she could just give to him. She wouldn't leave Arthur behind.

The zombies had surrounded the Jeep again and were shaking the vehicle, pushing against the window.

"I've had enough of this," said Dalby.

He hit Harriet around the head with the butt of his gun. Her head bounced against the back of the seat, and she saw stars.

The Dead Lands

Her vision doubled, and she saw two hands rising to strike her again.

The gunshots led Arthur straight to the garage. He pulled open the back door. Zombies crowded the jeep, but they were in a line. He could manage them - he had too.

They still hadn't seen him. He sneaked over to the workbench on the right of the garage and picked up a hammer.

Then he let rip.

"Party time guys!"

He ran into the zombies, striking each one hard on the head, using all of his considerable strength. The skulls caved and shattered like thin glass. One by one Arthur crushed their heads, brains and blood and flesh squirting and spraying across the garage, slopping onto the far walls - the force of Arthur's strikes not just killing the zombies, but obliterating them.

He pulled open the driver's door of the Jeep and for a moment was stunned to see a soldier in the driver's seat, a gun in his right hand, raised.

Harriet was in the passenger seat, blood dripping from her forehead and mouth, her eyes dazed.

The soldier turned to face Arthur.

The soldier didn't stand a chance.

Arthur grabbed the man's arm and pulled it towards him, hard. The unnatural angle of the pull yanked the man's shoulder out of his socket with an audible crack.

The soldier yelled in pain as Arthur flung him to the floor. Arthur leaned down and punched the soldier once. Twice. That would do.

Arthur jumped in the jeep and pulled the door closed.

"Are you ok?"

Harriet nodded, her head bobbing gently from side to side. She was concussed. He could look at that later.

"The keys, where are the keys?"

A zombie appeared at the driver's window.

Adam pulled the keys out of Harriet's pocket. "Here," he said.

Arthur took the keys and started the vehicle.

He rammed his foot on the accelerator and the Jeep shunted forward with a loud roar.

They got onto the road, collecting a few zombies on the bonnet. Arthur hit the breaks, and the zombies flew backward onto the tarmac.

He accelerated, running over them, the Jeep bouncing up and down on its loose suspension.

Within a minute or two, the road was clear of bodies.

Ahead, nothing but the night.

When Harriet awoke, she had a hell of a headache. She also had a bandage around her head.

She was sitting in the passenger seat. Outside, it was light. Arthur and Adam sat by a small campfire, with a little animal roasting on the end of a stick. The smell was, and Harriet's stomach rumbled, reminding her it had been a long time since she had eaten.

She got out of the car and immediately had to steady herself on the door frame. She was overcome with a sudden wave of nausea and dizziness.

A hand took her arm and led her gently beside the fire. "Careful," said Arthur. "You have suffered a serious concussion. That soldier guy got you pretty good."

Harriet eased herself down onto the floor. Adam smiled at her, she smiled back.

"What are we cooking?" she said.

Adam's smile grew wider. "Squirrel!"

She must have pulled a hell of a face, for Arthur and Adam both let out full belly laughs.

"I built the traps with Arthur's help," said Adam. "And the fire."

"He is a real boy scout," said Arthur ruffling the young man's hair. "I think we will be ok with this one."

Adam turned the squirrel spit, looking pleased with himself.

"My head hurts like hell," said Harriet. "Did you put on the bandage?"

Arthur nodded. "You have a very deep gash in your forehead, I stitched it up the best I could with the medikit in the Jeep. You also have pretty bad bruising in your jaw. Sorry, but I could not find any painkillers."

"Arthur's a nurse," said Adam.

Harriet smiled, "Thanks, Arthur. Not just for patching me up, but for helping us back there."

"It is no problem." He sniffed the charred squirrel carcass. "What do you think Adam? Good to eat yet?"

"Yeah, I think so."

They took the small mammal off the spit, and Adam carved it up using his knife.

"What time is it?" asked Harriet, realising she had no idea how long she had been out for. "Or even, what day is it?"

"It is about five o'clock in the evening after last night." Arthur smiled. "We are probably about ten miles from that place now, east."

"Where are we going?" said Harriet

"Adam has some ideas…" Arthur turned to Adam.

"Remember Harriet," said Adam, "a few days ago I told you that in an apocalypse the people would be the most dangerous thing?"

Harriet nodded, vaguely remembering.

"Well, my Dad says that in a crisis you should get away from most people and hide out until things settle down."

"You have a plan?"

"My Dad would always take me to Cornwall. There's a place there, but I forget its name, something bay. But I think we should go there. I know how to get there."

"What do you think, Harriet?" said Arthur. "Sounds good to me."

Harriet nodded her agreement. "Let's go. Let's go to the beach."

They slept in the back of the Jeep that night. It wasn't too tight a fit as either Harriet or Arthur would be taking turns to keep watch, listening for zombies, or people. Luckily, neither came their way.
Adam slept soundly through the night, although his body jerked and he moaned quietly, nightmares obviously stalking his slumber.
Harriet hoped that in a day or two, they would reach a small town and the people there would tell them that the army had fixed whatever the problem was, and the virus had been cured. They would say to them that everything was going to go back to normal and that they should come in for a hot bath and a nice meal before heading back to their proper homes.
But she didn't think that would happen. She felt that this was how it would be from now.
Adam let out another small cry and waved his arm around in his sleep.
"Shhh," said Harriet as she put her arm around him and cuddled him gently. "Shhh, it's ok. I'm here, I'll look after you."
Adam settled back into sleep, and Harriet dozed off herself a few minutes later, while Arthur sat in the driver's seat, watching, waiting, hoping.

The Dead Lands

Train to Hell

Chapter 1

Two hundred and fifty feet of wet clay above, and ten miles of darkness ahead and behind. The 1503 Eurostar train from Paris to London sat still in the black of the tunnel.

Thirty minutes of no movement.

No announcements.

Sarah was going to miss her meeting in London, which meant she would have to arrange another meeting, which meant she would have to work late, which meant she wouldn't be able to pick up Clarissa from the nursery.

She tried to call her husband again. A busy signal. No internet connection either. She closed her laptop.

There was a hum of electricity and the sound of engines starting.

"Finally," said Sarah to no-one in particular.

The train shunted forward slowly for a minute or so, and then stopped.

The electrical hum died, as did the lights.

"Oh, for fuck's sake," she said under her breath.

A few lonely gasps echoed through the pitch black carriage. Someone let out a small murmur.

Under-lighting from below the luggage rack flickered into life with a momentary buzz, bathing the carriage in a soft yellow glow, like the nighttime incandescence on an overnight flight.

"This is ridiculous." Sarah stood up and marched down the carriage towards the front of the train. She was going to find someone who knew what was going on.

The train was more quiet than usual with many seats unoccupied. She guessed it was the virus keeping people from traveling. It had been all over the news for the past few days; the usual sensationalist fear mongering.

She reached the dining car and found her first Eurostar employee in the canteen.

"What the hell is happening?" said Sarah. "We've been sat here now for over thirty minutes."

The young man behind the desk opened his mouth to speak but closed it again as Sarah showed no sign of letting him.

"We should be in London by now. Instead, I'm stuck here in the darkness like some mole, with no phone signal, no wifi. I can't even let the office know what's happening, I'm the Chief Finance Officer, and I'm going to miss the finance meeting and who the hell's going to pick up my daughter from nursery?"

The young man tried his best to smile, "I'm afraid I don't know, I've only been told-"

"What have you been told?"

"- I've been told that we're held up, for reasons unknown."

"Reasons unknown? Bullshit. Someone always knows, just not you. Who the hell can tell me what's going on?"

The man pointed further up the carriage. "The conductor may be able to tell you, madam," he said.

"Right."

Sarah turned on her heel and stomped through the next two carriages, looking for the conductor.

"Anyone seen the conductor? Is there a conductor around here?" said Sarah as she walked through the carriage. Most people ignored her, but one old man sheepishly pointed towards the front of the train. She half waved thanks as she walked past.

The conductor was at the very front of the train. He was stood in a compartment separating the front carriage and the driver's cab. The driver's cab was open, and the conductor was talking to the driver. They spoke in low voices, but animated. The driver's face was red, and he looked angry. The conductor, a fat man with a small hat, held up his hand to silence the driver when he noticed Sarah enter the compartment.

"Yes madam, can I help you?"

"I hope you can," she peered at his name badge, "Abdul. Are you able to tell me why we've been standing still for the last thirty minutes, Abdul, and why we're now in near darkness?"

The conductor didn't look happy with the questions.

"I'm sorry, madam, but we are experiencing a few engineering difficulties at the moment. Once we have them resolved an announcement will be made."

Sarah shook her head, tired of the rote excuses.

Abdul continued, "If you could return to your seat please, madam."

Sarah pointed her finger at him. "I'm sorry, but I'm not going to accept that. I want more detail as to why this train has been sitting here for the past thirty minutes, why the power is gone, why no announcements have been made, and what you are going to do about it?"

Abdul didn't look concerned with Sarah's demands. "I'm sorry, madam, but I am going to have to ask that you return to your seat and-"

"Now listen to me," interrupted Sarah. Abdul raised one eyebrow but made no effort to interrupt her back. "I am on the board of a very large and powerful multinational chemical company. We conduct much of our business on the European mainland and as such a large portion of our extensive travel budget is taken up with our employees using the Eurostar. I've met with the Eurostar board many times and am on first name terms with many of your top bosses." Her voice was raised, and people in the compartment behind were craning their necks to listen in.

The conductor straightened his collar. His calm demeanour seemed to be slipping.

"It only takes one phone call to find out what's going on and to report obstructive personnel. I can't make that call at this precise moment, of course, because the network is down, but networks won't be down forever." She paused for a moment, using her well-practiced boardroom power-speak to let her last comment and its implications sink in. "Now, I would like to know what is going on."

There was a small chuckle from the compartment behind. Someone was enjoying the show.

The driver, who had been watching Sarah's outburst with interest, said, "She may be able to help. If she has these connections, like."

Abdul nodded. "What is your name, madam?

"Sarah. Sarah Beauchamp."

"Good to meet you, Sarah. This is Alan, our driver. Please, this way."

She followed Abdul and Alan into the cramped driver's compartment. A futuristic dashboard with many flashing lights, most of them red, took up most of the small room. A sizeable slanted window offered a view of the tunnel outside. The powerful lights of the train illuminated the tunnel for a good hundred meters or so ahead. Track, gravel, dirt, brick walls. The track sat on a rise which dipped either side to meet the tunnel walls. Imposing solid dark brick repeated forward into the black.

Sarah felt a twinge of vulnerability, their isolation starkly illustrated by the silent tunnel, threatening to engulf the train...

"Right," said Sarah, crossing her arms, but softening her tone. "What's happening, Abdul?"

It was Alan who answered. "They've shut the bloody power off!" His eyes were wide open, and scared thought Sarah.

"What do you mean?" she said.

Abdul motioned for Alan to be quiet. "About thirty minutes ago we were told to hold our position. Which we did, as you know. They gave us no reason as to why. We tried to contact control, but were told simply to hold."

"Those bastards," mumbled Alan. Sarah began to feel the same fear that had apparently taken hold of the driver.

"We tried to find out why," said Abdul, "but got nothing. Until about five minutes ago."

Alan interrupted, "They told us they won't let us in the station! Borders have been shut."

"What?" said Sarah.

Abdul continued, "While we've been under the channel, the government have shut the country's borders. No one in, on account of the virus."

"They can't do that!" said Sarah.

"That's what I bloody thought," said Alan, "They can't keep us out of our own country. So I got us moving again."

"And that's when they cut the power," said Abdul. "We're running on battery power now - we can keep the air con on and some lights, but it won't last long, and it's not enough to get us moving."

"They can't do this," said Sarah, anger rising in her. She pulled out her phone, still no signal. "Fuck!" she threw the phone onto the floor. It clattered into the corner of the room. Her cheeks flushed red. She picked up the phone.

Regaining her composure, she said, "They can't trap us like this."

"They have," said Abdul. "It seems things have… evolved… since we left Paris. We can't go to the UK, and we can't get to France. No one wants us, we are trapped."

Alan sat in his now useless driver's chair and flicked a few switches. "They shut the power off as soon as we started moving.

Can't believe it. I know some of the fellas in control, they wouldn't do this. Must be the bloody government."

"I believe the directive has come from the top, Sarah," said Abdul.

"Ok," said Sarah, "Can you get me an outside line? There must be a way to contact someone in London? I wasn't bluffing about my contacts."

"That's what I was hoping." He picked up a phone from the dashboard and passed it to Sarah. "This is the only line we have out of here, listen for yourself."

She put the phone to her ear. It was ringing. She held it for a few more minutes, the three people standing in silence. It kept ringing.

Sarah turned to Abdul. "What if no-one answers? What are the protocols for evacuating the train?"

Abdul shrugged. "We can leave the train and walk up the service tunnel. There are entries every few hundred yards."

"Well, we can't just sit here. I think we should evacuate," said Sarah.

Abdul looked thoughtful for a moment, then slowly nodded his head.

"You may be right," said Abdul, "but we will have to be careful how we go about it. If we incite panic in the passengers, then, well, it could be very dangerous."

"How many people are on the train?" said Sarah.

"Not many," replied Abdul, "I think the manifest was around a hundred."

Sarah winced, she had hoped for less.

"That's not too bad," said Abdul. "Normally we would have a few hundred. This virus has really given people the frights."

The virus. If it was serious, did that mean her family was in danger? She could count on Ian to go and get their daughter, but what if they catch it? How do people even catch it? She hadn't paid much attention to the news over the past few days. She had been too busy.

Abdul was talking, but she only caught the end of his sentence, "… in one place, and that will be the easiest to manage."

"What?"

"We need to get everyone in one place. We can put out a message for everyone to come to the front of the train."

"Even then," said Sarah, "we can't be sure things won't go bad."

Abdul nodded. "Let's just do it. The sooner, the better."

Chapter 2

David listened carefully to the message over the loudspeaker. Finally, some official recognition they'd been sitting in a dark tunnel for nearly an hour.

"If all passengers can move to the front of the train, we have an important announcement. I repeat, all passengers please move to the front of the train."

David got up and put on his suit jacket. He took his overnight bag and walked down the carriage, being joined by other passengers. The queue shuffled forward uncertainly, people looking around for reassurance they were doing the right thing.

After traversing a few carriages, David noticed a small commotion in the middle of the current carriage. An old couple and young man were sat around a table. The old couple was asking the other passengers for help, and mostly being ignored.

David stopped by the table. The young man was in a corner seat by the window. The old couple was on the opposite side of the table.

"Everything ok?" asked David.

"Are you able to help?" said the old man. "This young man doesn't seem very well. I think he's French."

The young man was pale and sweating. His breathing was fast, his chest moving up and down at speed. He looked at David with pleading red eyes. He tried to hold up his hand but didn't seem to have the strength as his arm flopped onto the table. He whispered something in French.

"I'm a doctor," said David.

"Oh thank goodness," said the old woman.

"Can I examine you?" said David.

The man nodded.

David squeezed in next to the man and began a rudimentary examination. The man's heartbeat was fast and irregular. His temperature was raging. His skin was clammy. He was fighting for breath. He was weak. His eyes were bloodshot.

He needed immediate medical attention.

The old man was saying something, but David didn't hear. He was looking at his phone in dismay, seeing no network signal.

"Can either of you get a signal on your phone?" he asked the couple.

They looked at their mobiles, and both shook their head.

"Dammit," said David. "We need to find the conductor and get this train moving - this man's in urgent need of help."

The queue filed passed, many anonymous pairs of eyes looking with interest at the table.

"Are you able to find a conductor?" said David to the old man.

He nodded, "I'll go now." The old man joined the slow crawl of the queue.

"Be quick…" said David. As quick as you can, thought David. For a nagging thought had taken hold of him. The virus.

The young man let out a tight cry, his face spasming in pain. He began to shout in French. His arms swung wildly.

"He's having a fit," said David, trying to hold down the man's flailing arms.

But David was worried it wasn't a fit. The man's eyes were wide open, his eyeballs pushing against his eyelids as if straining to escape. The man grabbed the side of the table and let out a high yell. He banged his head against the window, repeatedly, the hollow bang echoing around the carriage. Blood stains appeared on the glass.

The queue had stopped and was staring at the man. The old woman sitting opposite screamed David felt himself edging away. This was like nothing he'd ever seen.

The man froze, his body rigid, his face contorted in pain, his mouth in an evil grimace. Spittle spat through his clenched teeth onto the table.

His head flung forward, and he hit the table with a thump. A few passengers let out a loud gasp. Another scream.

David's lizard brain was telling him to run, but his mind was telling him he had a duty of care. He had to help. He reached over and felt the man's pulse.

The young Frenchman had no pulse.

The queue stood still, watching in horror, but fascinated as if the events unfolding were a live drama for their entertainment. Eventually, some people tried to push past the stationary members of the queue, having decided the show was over. The man was dead. Nothing more to see.

David looked up and around at the expectant faces. He needed to find someone with authority on the train. He had to report the death.

He stood up.

The old woman, now also standing a safe distance from the table, asked David, "Is he ok?"

David shook his head. "No, I'm sorry. He's dead."

Sympathetic 'oh dears' were muttered.

"Please," said David loudly, "I have to get to the front of the carriage and report this. Please, no-one touch or go near the body, he may be infectious."

A few gasps sounded throughout the carriage at the word 'infectious.' People nearby shifted away from the table.

David took advantage of his promotion to a position of authority and squeezed through the queue. People moved aside to let him pass.

He was almost at the door of the carriage when someone shouted, "Doctor, are you sure he's dead?"

"What?" said David, turning to try and find the source of the voice.

A middle-aged man in a suit, standing near the table where the body sat, said, "Doctor, I'm sure I just saw him move."

Muscles in a dead body could spasm, giving the appearance of life. It was a rare phenomenon. The last electric throes of existence. "Yes, I am quite sure that-"

A horrible scream pierced the carriage. The people around the table reeled back as the dead man leaped forward and grabbed the businessman.

The dead man opened his mouth wide and threw his head forward, biting deep into the businessman's neck.

The businessman released a gurgling cry. Blood spurted from his neck and hit the roof of the carriage with force, making a sick splattering sound.

The dead man shifted his position, taking a deeper bite into the neck and tendons of the flailing businessman. The blood fountain changed direction, spraying laterally, dousing the nearest passengers.

Within seconds, the carriage was in chaos.

People tried to flee from the two men and spurting blood.

The cramped conditions of the carriage added to the panic. People pushed. Screams filled the air. Punches were thrown. David fell back into the nearest bank of seats. Someone tried to climb over him.

Shouts, pushing, shoving, violence.

David was pinned into a bank of two seats. He heard two men shouting at each other, and the muffled crunch of fist against bone. More shouts, people crying.

David curled in the corner of the seats, keeping away from the fighting and the panicked exodus.

Eventually, the aisle cleared as the crowd managed to spread itself into the two adjoining carriages. With the screams dissipating, David became aware of a different sound.

Muffled moaning. Snuffling, like a pig searching for truffles. Crunching. Wet sloppy sounds.

David peered around the side of the seat. Halfway down the aisle, the businessman's body lay still. The not-so-dead young man leaned over him, his hands deep in the corpse's torso, pulling out a string of intestines, biting into the red flesh, squirting blood and part digested foodstuff onto the nearby seats.

The young man looked up.

David ducked back in behind the seat, not sure if he had been seen. He thought quickly and dug up all the snippets of news on the virus he had heard: infections passed by bites; incubation times vary from minutes to days; reanimation.

Reanimation. David had been cautious in fully believing the stories he'd heard. Like most of the scientific community, the anecdotal stories of the virus and its effects seemed too fantastic to be accepted without proper validation and review.

It all seemed pretty damned real to David now though. 'Zombies' was the word he had been fighting. but was now ready to accept.

The eating sounds stopped. A loud moan echoed through the carriage.

David felt a cold hammer of fear hit him.

He peered around the corner of his seat again.

The zombie stood upright, dripping in dark brownish-red blood. It breathed heavily, the face of the young man it used to be unrecognisable. Its pupils were stone black, its mouth pulled back in a powerful snarl, its teeth snapping open and closed with a chilling click.

It saw David and shuffled forward, almost tripping over the body of the dead businessman, but somehow kept balance. It raised its arms, its hands opening and closing in time with the snapping of its jaws.

David threw himself out of the bank of seats, falling face forward into the opposite seats. He pushed himself up and scrambled to his feet.

The zombie was only a few yards away, its moaning reaching a frenzied crescendo, as if excited.

David ran to the carriage door, an automatic sliding door with no handles. It moved painfully slowly. David cast a panicked glance behind him, the zombie was almost on him.

The door gave way a few feet, David pushed through, feeling the zombie's hand grasp for his shoulder. He ran into the next carriage, where a group of people was pushing against the far door, trying to escape further up the train.

He glanced behind him.

The automatic door had opened, and the zombie was slithering into the carriage.

Chapter 3

Sarah and Abdul stood at the head of the carriage. Alan was in the driver's cab, listening to the still unanswered phone. The passengers were beginning to file into the front carriage.

Sarah leaned over and whispered to Abdul, "I think it's best if you give the news. It will look better coming from someone in a uniform."

Abdul nodded, "I was planning to."

Some of the passengers were taking seats. Many inquiring glances were cast in Sarah and Abdul's direction.

"You going to tell us what's going on then?" shouted one man.

This question acted as a catalyst for the more timid passengers, and a barrage of questions was fired at the conductor.

Abdul raised his hands in a conciliatory gesture. "If everyone would please just sit down, I have an important announcement to make, when everyone is here."

This satisfied some, but not all, and the questions kept coming. Abdul did his professional best to deflect them.

Sarah noticed a commotion towards the bottom of the carriage. She tapped Abdul on the arm.

"Something's happening…" said Sarah.

"I think you're right," said Abdul. "Let's have a look." They threaded through the crowded aisle, the passengers craning their necks to see the cause of the commotion.

Suddenly, screams.

"Zombie!" shouted one passenger.

Panic engulfed the carriage. The seated passengers jumped up. Everyone at once tried to get away from the far end of the carriage.

A middle-aged man took a hard case from the roof rack. He banged the case against the window, over and over again, but it wouldn't break.

Sarah and Abdul were pushed into a bank of four seats. Sarah fell onto the table. Abdul pulled her on to a seat.

"We have to get back to the front of the train," shouted Abdul.

They climbed over the backs of the seats, Abdul struggling to pull his hefty frame up and over.

From on top of the seats, Sarah could see the fight at the far end of the carriage. Passengers were trying to get in from the adjoining carriage, but others in this one were fighting hard to keep them out. A standing battle; fists flew, kicks. A large man received a fist from a woman passenger trying to get into the carriage. He responded by banging her head against the open door, knocking her out cold. She was trampled underfoot as more passengers lined up to try and fight their way through.

Another group of passengers had joined the man with the case trying to break the windows. They flung cases, kicks, fists, and themselves at the windows.

Three men were running towards the driver's cab, pushing people out of their way.

Some cowered in their seats, huddling together, terrified.

"Christ, what now?" said Sarah.

"We have to get out of here," said Abdul. "We can open the train's door. We have to get out, now."

They climbed over the seats to the front of the carriage.

Sarah shouted to the passengers, "This way, we need to get out, this way!"

Her voice was lost in the chaos, but a few people in the seats nearby heard and got up to join her and Abdul.

Alan emerged from the driver's cab, ruffled, shaken. A group of passengers was in the cab.

"They just burst in," said Alan, "trying to get the train started. I tried to tell them."

"Don't worry about it," said Abdul quickly. "We're getting out of here."

Abdul worked a key from his belt into the slot by the door. He turned it and then pulled the door open, stiff without the hydraulics.

"Alan, you go first and help the people down."

Alan nodded dropping the six feet or so into the dark tunnel. Abdul leaned through the doorway "Ok?"

"Ok," shouted Alan in reply.

Sarah helped two women, maybe mother and daughter, towards the door. "Wait for us outside." They nodded and climbed out with Abdul's help.

Then a man in his thirties. No one else paid any attention to them, too involved in their own little pockets of chaos.

"Ok," said Abdul to Sarah, "your turn."

Sarah moved to the doorway, but then stopped. The screams from the bottom of the carriage had taken on a new violence.

Two men at the doorway to the carriage were wrestling, but one of the men wasn't fighting fair. He was impervious to blows. He didn't stop, he didn't fall. His mouth hung open, his face was covered in blood with what appeared to be strings of flesh hanging from his jaw.

Zombie.

The man fighting it tried to backtrack but was trapped against the weight of bodies behind him. He fell into the seats. The zombie let out a deep moan and dived into his flesh feast.

Sarah turned to Abdul, "We have to move, now."

Chapter 4

David stood behind the group of people trying to push their way forward into the next carriage. The door was only wide enough to allow one, maybe two people through at once.

As soon as the zombie chasing David announced its presence with a loud moan, panic gripped the twenty odd people in the carriage. They scrambled for the door, pushing, hitting, kicking, shouting, screaming.

David saw a pair of legs on the floor, the body disappearing into a crowd of people. He saw a man grabbing another young man by the neck, shouting at the stranger, swearing, his face contorted in rage and fear. He saw the old woman from before pushed back against a table at an unnatural angle, her back bent out of shape, her mouth open wide, screaming, tears pouring down her face. The old man was nowhere to be seen.

David felt a second's despair, then shook himself into action. The zombie was only twenty feet away, it would be on him in a matter of seconds.

He quickly scanned the windows - four seat-bays ahead, to his right, next to the throng of passengers at the front of the carriage, he saw a red knob affixed to the top right corner of the window. There was a chance that could be his out.

He jumped into the bank of seats and climbed towards the window.

A hand grabbed his leg and tried to pull him back. He shook his leg free.

He passed the table where the old woman lay, he quelled the dark feeling in his stomach, the feeling he was leaving her to die, and pushed on to the next seat bank. This was the one with the red knob on the window.

He had been right - it was an emergency window break. If he pulled it, it should shatter the window.

Something hit his face, and he fell towards the window. His vision spun in white stars for a millisecond. Pain throbbed through his jaw.

Someone had hit him.

He tried to reach for the red knob, but a hand grabbed his leg and pulled. The man doing the pulling snarled at David, "Where do you think you're going, wait your turn!"

David kicked out with the other foot and connected with the man's jaw. This put the man off balance enough to give David the seconds he needed.

He hit hard against the red knob, and immediately the window shattered. A million spider web cracks spread through the window in an instant, accompanied by a satisfying crunch.

David elbowed the window, and the shards of glass fell like a sheet of crystal dust, leaving behind an empty hole in the side of the train.

A scream from the aisle.

The zombie had reached the passengers and had wasted no time in getting its bite of flesh. The neck of a teenage girl was pulled apart, the skin tearing with a hideous squelching ripping sound as flesh and muscle were drawn back to reveal tendon and bone. Blood spurted out at velocity, pumping from the torn arteries in the girl's neck.

"Hey!" shouted David, "This way."

A few heads turned in his direction. David jumped through the window.

The jump was at least ten feet high. He landed on the hard ground, jarring his legs. He stood up quickly and backed away from the window, looking up to see if anyone would follow.

Someone leaped through the window, landing hard on the compacted ground, moaning in pain.

Another person followed.

Satisfied others had found the escape route, David turned and ran the length of the train, guided only by the low light of the orange glow from the train's windows. Carriages stretched far down the tunnel, their dark hulks hanging in the darkness like a line of sleeping whales.

The sound of regular thumps followed him as one person after another jumped through the window. Screams echoed past him, filtering out of the open window and bouncing through the tunnel, taking on a nightmarish quality.

David stopped running. He thought of the businessman having his guts torn out. The young woman having her throat pulled open.

He fell to his knees and held his head in his hands.

He yelled into the darkness of the tunnel.

A man ran past him, glancing at David, giving him a wide berth.

David stood up and looked back to the window; one dark shape after another leaped from the dull light of the train into the promising darkness of the tunnel.

The image of the old woman, bent over backward across the table flashed through his mind. The woman he had left lying there.

What can I do, he thought. I've done enough.

More people ran past him.

He joined them.

Chapter 5

Sarah and Abdul jumped out of the door, followed by Alan. The man in his thirties and the mother and daughter were waiting for them.

The air in the tunnel was damp and cold. It hung on Sarah like a blanket; oppressive and silent, like it was watching her.

"Where now?" said the man in his thirties.

Sarah turned to Abdul, who turned to Alan.

Alan opened his mouth to speak but was pushed forward by a man jumping out of the carriage. The man looked at the group standing by the train, terror in his eyes, blood splattered across his face. He ran into the darkness.

Two more people jumped out of the train and ran.

"Come on," shouted Abdul, "let's just get away from here." He pointed up the tunnel.

Shouts and screams followed them as they ran. A sound that struck them still with dread reverberated through the empty black.

A moan, loud and deep, filled the tunnel.

"Where are the service tunnels Alan?" she said.

"They run parallel to the main tunnel, entrances every hundred yards or so."

"They have doors?"

"Aye."

"Let's find the next one then."

The sound of feet scraping against stone and earth echoed strongly down the tunnel.

"The service tunnels - what do they look like?" said Sarah.

Alan shrugged. "I've never been in one. A door, I imagine."

Sarah used her phone to shine against the walls of the tunnel. The others did the same, walking quickly, looking for the door.

As they walked, others ran past. Some slowed to see what Sarah's group were doing, but they didn't stay for long.

"Here it is," said Alan, pointing his light at a small door in the tunnel wall.

He pulled the handle, it was open.

"Come on." He motioned urgently.

The man in his thirties shone his phone light into the doorway. A small room was beyond containing a set of old drawers and a metal filing cabinet. A door in the far wall.

"Ok, looks good," he said.

They piled into the room and closed the door behind them. Their phone's lights danced around the walls, looking for a light switch. Sarah found one and flicked it. Dull yellow light filled the room.

No one spoke. They breathed deeply, allowing themselves time to rest. A feeling of safety, of escape, permeated the room and the group shared a few smiles, seeing each other properly for the first time.

"I'm Jason," said the man in his thirties.

Sarah, Abdul, and Alan introduced themselves. The two women were mother and daughter; Cynthia, the mother, and Mary, the daughter.

"So what now?" said Jason, "you guys got a plan?"

"Sort of," said Sarah. "First, you need to know something."

Sarah told them the reason the train had stopped - that their government had closed the borders, and they'd been left, abandoned in the tunnels beneath the sea.

Jason looked shocked for a moment, Cynthia put her hand to her mouth, "My goodness. Are you sure?"

"Absolutely, miss," said Alan, shaking his head. "Never would've thought it. The buggers."

The group stood in silence for a moment, absorbing the news that their government had left them to die.

A scream from outside broke the silence. Everyone jumped.

"We need to get out of here," said Sarah. She turned to Alan. "So does this door lead to the service tunnels?"

Alan nodded. "I guess so. And they should go all the way to the mainland."

"Ok, so we walk back to England."

"How far is it?" said Mary.

"From here," said Alan, "about five miles. Not too bad."

The group nodded in agreement. Not ideal, but better than being stuck on the train.

"Hold on a minute," said Jason. "If the government has closed the borders, what's to say they haven't closed these service tunnels too?"

Alan shook his head, "I guess no reason. How'd they close it though? Don't think they have big doors at either end."

"There must be some way to shut the tunnels," said Abdul. "I guess there'd be some safeguards, security I suppose."

"And if not," said Sarah, "what's to stop them putting a few soldiers with guns at the end."

The last comment from Sarah struck a chord of doubt into the room, their temporary relative safety forgotten.

"We can guess all day long," said Abdul. "I vote we just walk, and see what happens." He half raised his hand.

The rest of the group did likewise.

"Good, let's do it then," said Sarah. She put her hand on the doorway leading from the small room. "Let's stick together. Keep our mobile lights on."

A considerable bang shook the room. Cynthia let out a small scream and grabbed her daughter.

Another bang - the door into the central tunnel shook. Someone was on the other side, pushing against it, rattling it, trying to get it open.

A muffled voice shouted from the other side, "Hey, let me in! Open the door, please!"

One, two, three kicks against the door.

"What do we do?" said Alan.

Chapter 6

David reached the front carriage of the train. A dull thud from above made him jump. He looked up to see a man banging his hands against the window.

A moan echoed throughout the tunnel. David turned, looking into the darkness. The low light from the train windows cast distorted squares of yellow upon the floor of the tunnel, revealing dark earth and stone.

Three people emerged from the shadows and ran past David, not giving him a second look.

He had to find a way out of the tunnel - it wouldn't be long before more people were infected. Maybe that businessman had turned already. David had read there was no definite incubation period. Could be minutes, could be days.

David felt panic setting in. He turned and set into a run. After a few steps, he tripped, stepping on a loose rock. His foot caught under one of the sleepers. His momentum yanked his leg to a stop, and he twisted his ankle hard. Something tore.

It took a few seconds for the shock to pass and for the pain to take hold. A sharp, direct pain, stabbed into his ankle. He rammed the side of his forearm into his mouth to stop from yelling.

He grabbed his ankle and squeezed hard. He guessed that he'd torn a tendon in the fall.

His foot hung limp.

Another moan sounded in the tunnel, the tall walls amplifying the sound into something primal, terrifying.

"Shit," said David. He breathed deeply to dispel the panic pooling in the bottom of his stomach.

The sound of the moan died away and was replaced by a sound even more terrifying - the shuffling of feet, and of earth moving under the uncertain steps of something not entirely in control of its limbs.

Getting closer.

David peered into the shadows. The nature of the light didn't reveal anything more than movement, but David had no doubt what was coming.

"Shit," he said again.

He pulled himself along the ground until he was by the side of the train. He got on all fours, and cried out as the movement in his ankle caused a sharp jut of pain.

He used the train to give himself leverage and pulled himself up onto one leg. He grimaced.

If he could get through the next few minutes he should be okay - he would get used to the pain. It was shock and blacking out that was his enemy now.

He breathed fast, forcing air in and out of his lungs.

The shuffling. Closer.

A figure was now visible, two carriages down, moving slowly towards him.

David hopped away from the approaching zombie, supporting himself against the cold metal of the carriage.

He reached the front of the train and hopped out into the powerful light beams; two dazzling eyes staring into the dark secrets of the tunnel.

There was a heavy thud from the other side of the train, like feet landing on crushed rocks and earth. He guessed the carriage door had opened and people were jumping out.

David needed help - he might never get out of this tunnel without it - especially if being hunted by zombies.

He pulled himself forward, too fast. He banged his foot on the floor and a white-hot pain seared through his body. He fell forward, flat on his face. His mouth hit the hard metal track and filled with fragments of broken teeth.

More pain.

He pulled himself forward.

"Hey, hey!" he shouted, spitting out blood and teeth.

No one paid any attention. A group ran past, lighting the way with their phones.

Another dreadful moan filled the tunnel. Cold and deep. The sound reverberated into David's very bones, into his soul even.

He glanced behind him, a shape appeared at the corner of the train.

Panic was now David's friend - adrenalin shot through his body and numbed the pain in his leg. He pulled himself along, digging into the earth to get the grip needed, peeling back the nails on his fingers as he did so.

The shuffling followed him, always there, always present.

David didn't dare turn round - he couldn't afford the milliseconds it'd take.

It seemed he crawled along the floor forever. Minutes disappeared into a gray passing of time, where there was only one painful dig into the ground, followed by another. His ankle dragging in agony, his brain flooded with adrenaline. He fought to stay conscious.

And still, the shuffling followed.

Up ahead a light appeared on the side wall of the tunnel. A dull orange spilled into the black, like a lighthouse. A door had been opened. A group of people disappeared into the door, then closed it behind them.

The light, so brief, so promising, disappeared.

"Hey! Help!" David croaked. He realised he was crying.

He pulled himself towards the door. He gasped for oxygen. Every cell of his body hurt. His fingers felt as if they'd been clawed raw to the bone.

But he carried on. He didn't stop, every movement of his arms against the earth kept him alive for another few seconds, bought him a few more feet.

And neither did the shuffling stop. It became more desperate, more certain.

Soon it was all he heard.

The shuffling, nothing but the shuffling and its echo.

David reached the door.

He hit it with his fist.

He pushed against it with whatever energy he had left.

"Hey, let me in! Open the door, please!"

A hand grabbed his leg.

Chapter 7

The door rattled with another bang and an accompanying shout, more panicked than the first.

"We open it," said Sarah.

She reached for the door handle.

"Hang on," said Alan. Standing closer, he got his hand on the door first.

Sarah paused and stared at him. "Open the door - whoever it is, needs help."

Jason stepped forward, "Maybe this guy is right, we don't know what's out there."

"I'm not listening to this," Sarah reached forward and tried to open the door. Alan pushed her away.

"Stop it!" said Cynthia, standing at the back of the room.

A muffled cry came from the other side of the door.

The grip on David's ankle was firm, like a cold vice.

He spun onto his back. A torn and broken body covered in blood leaned over him. It was wearing the uniform of a Eurostar employee, a young man. Its white shirt was now scarlet and ripped open, its guts hanging down like red jungle vines onto the floor.

Its mouth opened slowly, then snapped shut quickly. It fell towards David.

David managed to roll fast to the left; once, twice. There was a thump as the zombie landed on the dirt beside him.

David pulled himself away. It followed, also dragging itself along the floor. Reaching his leg just as David pulled it away.

He shouted again, aiming his shout at the door.

Sarah, nearly pushed off balance by Alan, recovered. Her heart was racing, and she felt many nerves in her face twitching. Blood rushed to head. Her body tensed. She was used to fighting in the boardroom, but physical altercations were foreign to her.

She was surprised to see how little control she had over her physical reactions, due to a simple push.

She fought hard to stand up straight. "Open the door, Alan."

Alan shook his head. His eyes darted around the room.

Abdul stepped forward and grabbed Alan's hand.

Alan stared at Abdul for a second, then stepped back.

Sarah reached forward and opened the door.

Abdul grabbed the fire extinguisher.

A pillbox of dull orange-yellow light spilled into the tunnel.

It gave David a moment's hope, and he kicked with his bad ankle at the zombie. David cried out in pain but managed to dislodge the hand from his leg.

Two people ran from the doorway.

A large man in a uniform raised a fire extinguisher high above his head and dropped it hard on the zombie's head. There was a dull clang combined with a wet cracking sound.

The zombie let out a final hiss, then lay still.

David let out a sigh of relief. "Thank you!" he shouted as he lay back, closing his eyes. Exhaustion hit him, as did pain. He grimaced his teeth and breathed hard.

"Are you ok?" It was a woman's voice.

"Has he passed out?" said a man's voice

David shook his head slowly, "I'm still here… my ankle."

"Let's get him out of here."

David heard other voices.

Strong hands grabbed his armpits. Someone grabbed his feet, and he cried out in pain. They let go.

"Which ankle is it?" said the woman's voice.

"Right," he whispered.

Gentle hands lifted his injured leg by the knee. He was pulled along the floor for a few yards, his ankle kept clear of the ground.

Light shone through his eyelids; the texture of the floor changed from earth to cold concrete; sounds took on a closer echo. He opened his eyes a little, but the light hurt. He closed them again.

Pain washed over him.

He felt his consciousness wavering. He was happy to let it go.

Darkness.

"So what do we do now?" said Alan, motioning towards the man on the floor.

The man was passed out, lying flat on his back. Sarah had rolled up the bottom of his jeans to reveal a swollen and angry looking ankle, large purple bruises. His hands were a red and bloody mess - his fingers being the source of the blood. Some of his nails were missing. His mouth had dried blood around it.

The man was well dressed, somewhere in his early thirties.

"I guess you would have left him?" said Sarah, casting an angry glance at Alan. She wouldn't forgive him for what he had done. It would achieve nothing to ferment a fight, but she wouldn't let him off lightly.

Alan snorted and folded his arms. "We can't save everyone."

Abdul patted the air, a calming motion. "It is what it is. Let's think now what to do. The plan hasn't changed."

"He's safe now," said Jason. "So you're right, the plan hasn't changed."

"What do you mean?" said Sarah.

"I mean that he's safe. We can go on," said Jason.

Alan nodded. "This fella's right. We've saved him now, so we don't have to wait around. Ain't none of them things getting in here."

Sarah shook her head. "He's passed out, we don't know that he's ok."

"What about all the other people on the train?" said Jason in a soft voice. "I don't see you worrying about saving them. The ones that were running down the tunnel, the ones that were attacked in the carriage."

Sarah shot him an angry glance but had no answer.

"It wouldn't seem right," said Mary in a quiet voice. Sarah smiled at her unexpected ally. "He's here with us now. It wouldn't seem right to just leave him."

"Mary," said her mum, "this man is right. He's safe now. We can't be expected to save everyone."

"We're not trying to save everyone, mum, just this one man."

Cynthia looked at her daughter for a minute, not finding anything to say, then looked away, towards Alan and Jason.

"I think we go, now," said Alan. "Before things get worse."

Jason nodded. "Agreed."

Sarah felt the man's pulse. It was strong. He was breathing normally. He had probably passed out from shock, fear, exhaustion.

Jason and Alan were right - if they left him he wouldn't die.

"So let's get out of here," said Alan.

Jason opened the door that led out into the service tunnel.

Abdul's eyes met Sarah's.

It wasn't right.

"No. I'm staying," said Sarah.

"What?" said Alan.

"Why?" said Cynthia.

Sarah wondered why herself. "It just doesn't feel right."

"I'm going to stay too," said Abdul.

Alan shook his head, "What is wrong with you two? We need-"

Jason interrupted - "It doesn't matter, let them stay, we go."

Alan shrugged, then nodded.

"What about you two?" said Jason, turning to Cynthia and Mary.

"We're coming," said Cynthia.

"Mum…" said Mary.

"Don't start Mary, we're going."

Sarah tried to make eye contact with Mary, but she kept her head down.

"Ok, good luck," said Jason. "And thanks for getting us out of the train."

"No problem," said Sarah. "And good luck to you as well."

Jason, Alan, Cynthia, and Mary left. Mary raised her head as she left the room. She mouthed "sorry" to Sarah.

They closed the door after them. It echoed with a metallic clang.

Chapter 8

The room felt very quiet. The door back into the tunnel shook gently. A scratching sound. More zombies.

"What do we do now?" asked Sarah.

Abdul shrugged. "How is he?"

"I think he's ok. No idea how long it'll be before he comes round through."

"I guess we wait then." Abdul sat on the floor beside the man, easing his large girth down with a tired sigh. "I could do with a rest anyway. As you may have guessed, I don't get a lot of exercise."

Sarah smiled and sat down next to Abdul.

"A rest may be a good idea."

She took out her phone. No signal.

Now, with time to think, she found herself scared. Scared of her thoughts; of what may have happened, or was happening, to her husband and daughter.

"Are you ok?" said Abdul.

She realised a tear was running down her cheek. She wiped it away, embarrassed. "I'm ok."

"You have people you're worried about?" said Abdul.

She nodded but didn't say anything. She was worried that if she spoke, she would start to cry like a child.

"I have too." Abdul pulled his wallet out of his dusty jacket. He opened it and removed a picture that he passed to Sarah.

Abdul was in the middle of the picture, surrounded by four children, ranging from young to teen. Two boys and two girls.

"It's ok to be scared," said Abdul. "We aren't in a boardroom anymore."

Sarah passed the photo back to Abdul, and she let herself go. She let the tears flow. "God, what is happening," she managed to say through loud sobs.

"I don't know," said Abdul. "But we have to try and stay alive, for the people who we care about."

Sarah wiped the tears away from her cheeks. "Do you really think they'll be ok? Our families?"

Abdul shook his head. "I have no idea. Who knows what it's like up there now."

"If those things have got into the city…"

They sat in silence for a few minutes. The only sounds were the occasional scratching on the other side of the door, and the rasping breathing of the young man they had rescued.

"You look like you have a lovely family, Abdul."

Abdul smiled, his large jowls creasing into a well-practiced position. "Oh yes. I am a fortunate man. I have a good job, I work good hours. I spend a lot of time with them. Very lucky man."

Sarah smiled back, finding it hard not to. "I have one daughter, Clarissa, and my husband, Ian. My daughter is three. I don't see her very often."

Abdul sighed. "Well, we can change that, once we get out of here, can't we?"

She said nothing in return but pulled out her phone. She scrolled through to her favourite photo; her, Ian, and Clarissa at the beach.

The man coughed. Sarah quickly put her phone away and leaned forward.

His eyes opened, and he squinted against the light. "Where am I?" he said softly.

"You're safe," said Sarah.

He made to sit up.

"Careful," said Abdul, helping him up.

"You got me in from the tunnel?"

Sarah nodded. "One of the zombies nearly got you. You passed out." There was a clang and a scratch on the tunnel door.

"That him?" said the man.

"No, we killed your one. Must be others," said Sarah.

"I saw one turning," said the man. "They change quickly."

"How are you?" said Sarah.

"I'm ok. I think." He leaned forward and inspected his ankle. It was swollen, covered in wonderfully coloured bruises. "I think I've torn my perineal tendon."

"Your what?" said Abdul.

"Sorry, my ankle. I'm David. I'm a doctor." He held out his hand to offer a shake, then noticed his fingers. "Ah yes… That was me crawling across the floor."

Sarah and Abdul introduced themselves.

"Well, thank you for saving me. Sorry for passing out - damned embarrassing. I don't know what happened - the pain, I guess, and the shock, fear."

"How's your ankle now?" said Sarah.

"Bad. I don't think I can walk on it."

Sarah felt a twinge of disappointment in her. "That's ok. We can work something out."

David looked around the small room. "I thought I saw more of you, what happened?"

Sarah glanced at Abdul, and the look must have said enough as David turned red.

"Ah, I see. Well, thank you, I guess I owe you both my life and possibly my continued existence, thanks to your kindness."

"We're going to get us all out of here," said Sarah, anticipating David's next comment.

David shook his head. "Look, I couldn't possibly ask you to sacrifice your safety-"

Abdul stood up and smiled. "Listen, there is no choice. If I have to, I will knock you out and carry you myself." Abdul paused before smiling at David.

David returned the smile. "Ok, it seems my mind is made up. Well, thank you. Thank you very much." He looked around the room. "I will need a stick, something to support myself on. Either that or you'll both have to support me. This ankle is going to be shot for a good while."

There was only one piece of furniture in the room that would help - a metal frame filing cabinet.

"Maybe we can take that apart," said Sarah.

Abdul examined it. "Yes, I think we can use the support posts."

They spent the next thirty minutes pulling at the filing cabinet. Abdul using his Allen key set, the one he carried at all times due to the many quick fixes he attended to during his working day.

David took off his coat and use this to cushion the top of one of the support posts. A fully functioning walking stick.

"How is it?" asked Sarah.

"A little too high, but it will be fine."

By now the scratching at the door of the little room had graduated to a continuous banging and rattling. News was out about the fresh meat inside.

They opened the other door into the support tunnel. A cold draft blew into the room. The darkness was uninviting, foreboding.

Abdul went first, using his phone as the group's torch.

He performed a cursory investigation of the tunnel. It was about fifteen feet across, ten feet high, and with a flat concrete floor. The tunnel wall was constructed of bricks that had turned a dirty black, covered with moisture, the air damp and cold.

"Feels like the sea is about to come in," said David.

Abdul shone the phone light ahead of them, illuminating twenty feet or so. "Not a lot of warning if something comes at us," he said.

"Well let's hope they haven't got in here," said Sarah. She felt a chill, and not just from the cold air of the tunnel. The thought that they could be blind prey, like moles, hunted by living dead creatures was hard to believe, but terrifying all the same. She wondered how terrifying it would be once she fully accepted what was happening. Abdul was right - they weren't in the boardroom anymore.

They set off along the tunnel. Their footsteps echoed with a strange shuffle, the sound bouncing off one wall to another, ironically making their steps sound like a train. It was too loud, thought Sarah. Too loud for this darkness.

Progress was slow, David only able to hop along. Every now and then he let out small murmurs of pain.

"Are you ok?" said Sarah.

"I am. My ankle likes to remind me it's still there every now and again."

Sarah couldn't see his face clearly in the shadows, but she sensed his smile.

"Let us know if it get's too much."

They walked in silence. Although longing for the warmth of conversation and contact, their fear of what may lie ahead muted any thought of talking.

All the better to hear what may be coming.

The walk was uneventful for the first hour or so. Sarah had no idea how much ground they covered, it was impossible to tell in the pitch black. One step after another, the same as the last, the tunnel unchanging. Maybe they had stepped on a giant treadmill and would walk forever in this purgatory, not getting anywhere, just step by step closer to death.

Then came the explosion.

Chapter 9

First a white wall of light far up the tunnel. A flash that momentarily blinded Sarah. She instinctively held up her hand to protect her eyes. Next was the rush of warm air, and then came the sound. She wasn't sure if the sound was the air or the air was the sound. It was all one. Warm, then hot. Loud, then incredibly loud, a sound she had never heard before. A star-crushing bang, an earth-moving rumble, an atmosphere-splitting crack, all at once. It filled the tunnel, and her ears, and then her head and whole body. As if every cell was displaced and replaced with sound.

She fell.

The echo of the explosion bounced around the tunnel like waves caught in a harbour. From the front, to the side, to the back. The air stilled and cooled, but not quite to the chill of before, a background warmth left hanging.

Her face felt hot.

"Is everyone ok?" she shouted into the darkness.

"I am ok," said Abdul. His phone light came on again. He shone it around.

"I'm good," said David, his voice strained. "If someone could help me up please."

Abdul shone his light at David. Sarah used it to find him and help him up.

"What the hell was that?" asked Sarah. "An explosion?"

"I think so," said Abdul, "What else could it be?"

"I guess we are lucky we weren't closer - it must have been right up at the top of the tunnel," said David.

Sarah had a terrible realisation. "What about the others?"

"The others?" said David.

"The people that left ahead of us."

"They might be ok," said Abdul. "Maybe a bit more burnt, but ok, hopefully."

Sarah didn't feel so sure. They would have been walking much faster than them. How much tunnel could there be?

Brick dust fell from the ceiling.

"What do you think, Abdul, a gas explosion?" said David, steadying himself on his crutches.

Abdul stared into the dark of the tunnel, breathing heavily, his lungs struggling with the dust-laden air. "I'm not so sure."

Sarah realised what Abdul was thinking. They shared a glance.

"It may not have been an accident," she said.

"What do you mean?" said David

Sarah quickly explained the reason the train had stopped - that they had been forced to stop, that the county didn't want them anymore.

David let out a heavy sigh. "Persona non grata, eh? Well, I guess they were right to stop the train. Thinking about it objectively. It was carrying infected."

"What happened on the train, David? Where did the zombies come from?" said Sarah.

"A young French man. He changed in front of my eyes. It wasn't pretty." David joined Abdul in staring into the depth of the tunnel, towards England. "And I guess what you're thinking now is that if that explosion wasn't an accident…"

"It was set off purposefully," said Abdul. "To block the tunnel."

"And stop anyone getting through."

The group stood in silence for a moment, the full implications of their situation taking nest. Sarah's stomach turned, and she fought a wave of nausea. She was experiencing something she had never felt - true fear for her life.

No use standing around doing nothing.

"Come on, we have to move," she said. "The sooner we find out what the situation is, the better." She wiped her forehead, and her hand came away a mucky brown, covered in a film of dust and sweat.

"Ok, let's go then," David limped forward in earnest, "I'll try my best not to hold you up."

For another thirty minutes, they walked carefully along the tunnel, the air becoming hotter as they got closer to England. There was still no sound other than their strangely echoing footsteps, punctuated with the metallic tip tap of David's makeshift crutch.

Belying his bulky frame, Abdul cut ahead, marching forward with purpose, his light searching out the end of the tunnel, or the blockage.

"So you're a doctor?" asked Sarah.

"Time enough for small talk now?" smiled David. "Yes, I am. A junior doctor at the children's." David let out a small murmur of pain and readjusted himself on his crutches. "What do you do?"

"Oh, nothing important. I'm a mum. I have a young girl and a husband."

"Being a mum's very important."

"I'm not very good at it," she said.

"I'm sure that's not true," said David.

She didn't answer, because it was true, thought Sarah. Clarissa had cried at her last birthday - Sarah had been called into a last minute conference in Manchester and missed the party. The latest in a litany of missed appointments, missed days out, missed birthdays.

They walked.

The heat became uncomfortable, and Sarah regularly wiped her brow as dusty sweat trickled into her eyes.

"Whatever exploded, must still be burning..." said David.

Abdul raised his hand and shouted them to a stop. "Look!"

He held his light up high, and the weak beam illuminated a pile of rubble. Rocks; metal girders; earth in dark mounds; steel panels.

A body. Half a torso protruded from the bottom of the pile.

Sarah ran forward. She heard the accelerated tip tap of David's crutch behind her.

"Careful, he may be infected," said Abdul.

They stood around the body carefully. It was wearing a uniform, the head covered in dust and earth. Sarah recognised the uniform.

"Alan? Can you hear me?"

She leaned down, out of reach of his mouth, just in case he had turned.

David reached forward and carefully felt for a pulse.

"Don't get too close," said Abdul.

"He's alive," said David.

Alan's eyes opened, and he coughed violently. Blood spat out of his mouth.

Sarah and David pulled back.

"Hot, it's too hot," whispered Alan.

Abdul took off his jacket and pushed it under Alan's head.

Sarah automatically went to try and move a rock sitting on Alan's chest. The stone was hot to the touch, she snapped her hand away.

"We'll get you out of here, Alan, don't worry," she said.

He shook his head, earth falling off, revealing his face, burnt beyond recognition. "I'm finished. Should have stayed with you lot. That'll teach me."

"Don't be stupid," said Abdul. "We can move these rocks and-" Abdul put his hand on a rock and pulled it away quickly, just as Sarah had done. "Red hot."

Alan spoke again, more quiet, more laboured. "My legs, crushed. I think everything else too." He was only visible from his chest up. The rocks on his body were smeared with thick blood, and what looked like chunks of flesh. Sarah turned away, nausea revisiting her.

"Listen," he whispered. "Back about fifty yards, ladders, to vents. We're under land now." He coughed loudly, rasping. More blood spat out of his mouth. "Maybe they haven't sealed the vents yet."

He closed his eyes. His breath rattled. Phlegm.

Sarah felt tears in her eyes. She had never watched anyone die before.

David reached forward and felt his pulse again. "It's very weak."

Abdul shook his head. "There's no way we can get him out, and who knows what mess is under those rocks."

"We have to sit with him," said Sarah. "We can't just leave him."

She sat down and took his hand. Alan opened his eyes slightly and looked at her. He smiled.

"I'll look for the ladder," said Abdul. He walked down the tunnel.

David took out his phone and turned on its light. He shone it up around the rubble. In the top left corner of the tunnel was another body.

It was Mary.

"What about the others?" said David.

Alan just shook his head.

A few minutes later and he stopped breathing. His hand went limp in Sarah's. She wiped tears from her eyes.

"Ok, let's go."

Chapter 10

Abdul's light explored the tunnel wall.

"I've found it," he shouted.

Sarah and David joined Abdul at the bottom of a rusty ladder. It reached twenty feet up to the roof of the tunnel, where it disappeared into a hole in the ceiling.

Sarah went first and climbed the ladder to the top, through the hole and up into the black.

Her heart raced. The darkness had taken on the same fear that it had as a child - the unknown, the monster in the closet, except now the monsters weren't in the closet anymore, they were walking around, looking for live flesh.

Flesh like hers.

She put up her hand to grab the next rung - but it wasn't there, the ladder had ended. She blindly explored with her hand and found nothing around her.

"I'm at the top," she called down, wishing she hadn't as her voice echoed loudly.

"What do you see?" said Abdul.

"Wait," she replied.

Holding on carefully with one hand, she took out her phone and turned on its torch. She was in a small concrete room. The ladder had protruded out of the floor and finished five feet up. She simply stepped to the left onto the floor.

A closed heavy metal door was the only other feature.

She leaned over the hole and whisper-shouted to the others in the tunnel below.

"It's ok. Looks like a door out of here."

"Does it open?" asked David.

"Hang on."

She tried the door. It moved slowly, stiffly and with a loud creak, but it opened. The loud creak took on the attribute of every other sound in this strange hollow world, and bounced vigorously in the empty concrete space, taking minutes to die. Fear gripped her at the thought of what might be listening.

"It opens, come up."

David came next, moving slowly to protect his ankle from hitting any of the rungs.

Abdul was last, carrying David's crutch.

"So that's the door," said David, repositioning himself on his crutch. "Shall we see where it goes?"

"Alan mentioned vents," said Abdul.

"I don't really care where it leads as long as it leads out," said Sarah.

Abdul shone his phone light out of the room. A thin dark tunnel, only four feet wide, led into the darkness and inclined steeply. A dull blue glow lay an indeterminate distance ahead.

"Looks like daylight," said Sarah.

Abdul took the lead, David next and Sarah at the rear.

Their footsteps didn't echo here - maybe the tunnel was too thin, the concrete thicker - but Sarah found the silence unsettling.

"How are you doing David?" asked Sarah.

He let out a heavy puff of air. "Hard work." He turned and gave her a smile, "But up is good as far as I'm concerned."

The glow ahead got closer slowly, but it was still impossible to judge the distance. A sound was now penetrating the silence, a rhythmical thud, deep and distant.

The glow in the corridor became a light shining out of the side of the wall. It was a junction in the tunnel. They soon reached it, and Abdul turned off his phone, it now being light enough for them to see without it.

The noise had got louder, a mechanical thump with the background hum of powerful electricity.

They turned into the new corridor.

A loud, excited moan filled the air.

Sarah gasped.

"It's ok, it's ok," said Abdul. He stood to the side to allow David and Sarah enter the room.

Sarah shielded her eyes against the sudden brightness.

They were in a huge circular room, in the middle of which was a large piece of machinery, the source of the thumping sound. It was a huge fan, directing air through a large hole in the ceiling. The promising blue light of day beamed in from above.

The paddles of the fan turned fast and vigorously within a mesh cage. Inside the cage, was a zombie, pressed up against the mesh.

The zombie's back was sheared off to the spine.

Every time the fan turned, it sliced off another millimetre of flesh, bone, and organs, spreading the mess across the inside of the cage.

The zombie seemed unconcerned that it was only a half-man. Its jaw clicked angrily, moans and grunts of frustration piercing the regular clunk of the fan.

"My God," said David. "How does it even move, its nervous function must be completely shredded." He hobbled over for a closer look.

"Careful," said Sarah.

The zombie became excited as David approached, and it bit into the mesh of the cage, cutting its lips and gums, leaving thin tendrils of pink flesh behind.

"Ah, I see," said David. "its spine is still intact, so I guess that's how it's moving. They must be completely imperceptible to pain though." He carefully dodged a thick puddle of blood on the floor. "I guess they don't need blood either."

"It's not natural," said Abdul. "If I were a religious man I'd say they were devils."

"Are you a religious man?" asked Sarah.

"Of course," said Abdul.

David leaned in for a close look at the zombie's face. It pushed forward with a surprising lurch, its teeth gnashing viciously. David jumped back and fell, his crutch clattering on the floor.

"Christ!" he said.

"I told you to be careful," said Sarah. She helped him up.

"Look, here," said Abdul.

A spiral staircase followed the wall of the room, leading up, towards the light and presumably outside.

Sarah took one last look at the forlorn figure behind the bloodied cage, its existence being shaved away slowly by the powerful paddles of the fan.

They climbed the spiral staircase, with Sarah at the front, David in the middle, and Abdul at the rear, their pace slow.

As they got closer to the top, Sarah's anxiety grew. Assuming there was a way out, she wondered what was waiting for them outside. The world she had been buried under for the past few hours, which had seemed so far away, was about to become real again. Would it be the world she remembered?

The staircase eventually stopped by a doorway.

"Fingers crossed," she said.

She turned the handle. The door opened easily.

The group let out a nervous laugh, smiling, breathing sighs of relief.

Sarah stepped out into the day. She breathed in the warm wet air - it looked like it had rained recently. The clouds were clearing, and the sun felt warm on her skin. She realised how relieved she was as tears fell down her cheeks. Free again. In the world again. She kneeled down and ran her hands through the wet grass.

They were in a large farm field, flat and stretching up a gentle hill, closed by hedges. A small wood in the distance.

The structure they had left was a squat featureless grey building sitting in a dip in the field. Its function would never be guessed by the casual observer.

"What now?" said David.

Sarah shrugged, "I don't know. We walk I guess."

"Shall we head for that wood?" said David. "I like the idea of cover."

They set off towards the wood.

Chapter 11

They were halfway to the woods.

Sarah became aware of movement from the top of the field. Two vehicles were approaching. Dark green by the looks of them. Jeeps.

Army.

"Guys," she said, pointing to the approaching vehicles, "Look."

Abdul and David fell silent. The buzz of the jeeps carried well in the still country air.

"Friend or Foe?" said David.

"No idea," said Abdul. "But what can we do? There's nowhere to run."

Although only a few hundred yards away, it seemed to take forever for the jeeps to reach them. Sarah's body tensed, every muscle tightened.

Waiting for the shot.

The jeeps skidded to a halt twenty yards away, and four soldiers jumped out.

"Down, get down, get down on the ground, now!"

Sarah got onto the ground immediately.

"Hands on your head! Now!"

She heard David's voice, "We are not infected, I'm a doctor, none of us are infected."

There was no response from the approaching soldiers.

Sarah raised her head. She saw boots about ten feet away.

"Where have you come from?"

"We were in the-" began David.

"The farm," interrupted Sarah. "We've come from the farm, we were staying there last night."

"Which farm?" said the disembodied voice from above her.

"Cherry Farm." She had taken her daughter to a city farm a few years ago. Cherry City Farm.

Mumbled conversation between two of the soldiers.

"You all look very smart for farmers?"

Sarah's brain had stopped. She was out of ideas.

"We work for Clarissa's Farm Feed, meat suppliers," said Abdul. Sarah smiled inwardly at Abdul's use of her daughter's name. "We were discussing terms this morning when they came."

"Who came?" barked a soldier.

"The things," shouted Sarah. She worked the words into a terrible cry, and she forced tears. It wasn't hard. "They came, and they ate the farmer, we had to run, we had to leave him. It wasn't us! I promise." She let out another cry, ramping up the hysteria.

More mumbled conversation between the soldiers.

"Ok, stand up."

Sarah stood up, her face red with crying and tears. Still waiting for the shot.

Four soldiers, all young, all looking scared and uncertain. Their eyes pierced through each member of the group, examining their physical state, their clothes. Sarah whispered an inward prayer of thanks that Abdul had used his conductor's jacket to rest Alan's head.

"You're going to come with us. You may be infected, so we'll need to restrain you."

"I can assure you, we're not infected," said David, his gentle tones couldn't be more out of place in the current situation.

The soldier ignored him. "Get us three restraint kits, Crowe."

One of the soldiers ran back to the jeep, rummaged in the back seat for a minute and returned with three yellow bags. Handcuffs and what looked like dog muzzles were pulled out of the bags.

"Now, hang on a minute," said David.

"It's ok," said Sarah, casting a warning look at David. "We understand."

"Good," said the soldier who seemed to be in charge. He was tall, dark hair, well built. But still didn't look old enough to shave, thought Sarah.

Two other soldiers approached and tightened the muzzles on first. It bit into her cheek.

They took David to the jeep to sit him down before fitting his restraints, as once restrained he couldn't use his crutch.

"Get them back to the station," said the soldier in charge. "We'll sort the vent."

They were squeezed into the back of one of the jeeps, and two soldiers got in the front.

"Where are we going?" asked Abdul, his voice muffled due to the muzzle.

"Holding. You need to be put in holding and examined," said Crowe.

The other soldier turned to face them. "I'm private Dutton. Are you guys ok? You look a little beaten up?"

Crowe started the engine, and the jeep bumped along the field back the way it had come.

Sarah nodded. "We're ok."

"Sorry about all this," said Dutton, indicating the restraints. "Things have gone a bit wild."

Crowe cursed as the Jeep went through a large dip in the field, causing the engine to rev hard and for the passengers to be thrown about roughly.

"What is holding anyway?" said David. "You say we are being examined - I'm a doctor, I may be able to help."

Dutton glanced at Crowe before replying. "It's a quarry, about four miles from here."

Crowe shook his head. "Can it, Dutton. They don't need to know any of this."

Dutton looked like he wished he could say more, but instead lowered his head and turned away.

The handcuffs were biting into Sarah's wrists, especially given the rough nature of the ride so far. She was glad when the jeep left the fields and turned onto a road.

Crowe accelerated, and they raced along the thin country lanes.

Abdul leaned close to Sarah. "I'm not sure I have a good feeling about this."

"I agree. But what can we do?"

Abdul shook his head and leaned away.

Sarah knew what it was like to deal with bureaucracy and people who followed the rules. Painful at the best of times, and impossible at others. This, she felt, was one of the impossible times.

The Jeep pulled sharply around a corner, the back skidding out a little.

"Take it easy, Crowe," said Dutton from the front of the jeep.

"I don't want to be out on these roads too long," said Crowe, accelerating out of another corner. Sarah was pulled from left to right as Crowe sped along the roads.

Sarah leaned forward to be better heard by the soldiers. She decided to aim her questions to Dutton - he seemed the most amiable.

"I have a husband and a young daughter. In London."

Dutton glanced back at her, not seeming to want to take his eyes off the road. "Ok, I think you should probably ask the officer in charge of holding about them."

"Do you have a phone that works? Surely the army has communications."

The engine revved loudly as Crowe accelerated onto a straight section of road.

"What?" shouted Dutton.

"Bloody mouthpiece," said Sarah, "Can you take this mouthpiece off, I feel like some sort of animal!"

"You know I can't do that," said Dutton.

Sarah closed her eyes and counted slowly. She felt a hand on her shoulder.

"Look, I just need someone to try and contact my husband. I can give you his name, email address, phone number, Skype address, anything. I just need to-"

Crowe turned to face her, "Look, don't you fucking get it? There are no comms. Do you think you're the only person with fucking kids? Now shut up."

"Crowe!" shouted Dutton.

There was only a millisecond before the crash, but it was enough for Sarah to see the stationary red van sitting on the wrong side of the road, tight round the bend. The next sensation she had was one of motion, incredible motion, like a fairground ride without the restraints.

A sharp pain in her head.

Squashed against the sizeable soft body of Abdul, but her arm at a strange angle then pushed against something hard and cold.

Noise all around her, like a racetrack, a revving engine.

Bone-jarring motion, incredible pain in her lower back.

Head thrown forward, neck strained.

Silence.

Darkness.

Chapter 12

Sarah opened her eyes.

She was lying on her right side. The taste of blood was in her mouth.

Then the pain hit.

Pain from everywhere. Her cheeks felt torn, she guessed the mouthpiece had cut through her flesh. Most of her muscles ached, but especially her left arm. It felt turned through an unnatural angle, pain throbbing in her shoulder like a sledgehammer.

She knew panic was coming, but there was nothing she could do to stop it. A low guttural cry built in her chest and erupted through her mouth. She wasn't able to help herself. She tried to move, to struggle. She was still in the jeep, against something soft.

Ahead she saw foliage, dirt, branches.

A still body hanging from a seat belt.

The jeep was lying on its right side.

"Stop moving," shouted a disembodied voice. Sarah frantically moved her eyes, looking for the voice, but her head wouldn't move. "Stop bloody moving."

"I can't move," she managed to say.

"Good. I'm going to try and get you out."

She recognised the voice. It was Crowe.

There was a groan from her right side, through the soft warmth she was lying on.

"Abdul?"

"Yes… I'm here."

"Everyone stay still," repeated Crowe.

"Are you ok?" said Abdul.

"I think so, but I hurt everywhere," said Sarah.

"David? Can you hear me David?" said Abdul.

There was no response.

If Crowe was outside, it meant that the body hanging off the seat belt in front of her was Dutton.

A wrenching metallic sound vibrated through the jeep. Sunlight beamed in where the door had been.

Sarah turned her head slowly to the left, fighting the pain and stiffness. She was rewarded with a vision of a deep blue sky, cloudless.

Crowe's head appeared in the gap left by the door.

"Ok, I need to get you both out of here," said Crowe.

"Both?" said Sarah.

"You and Abdul."

"What about David?" said Abdul.

"He's dead, so is Dutton."

"What? David," Sarah shouted, turning her head again. She couldn't see beyond Abdul.

Abdul let out a strange moan, "Have I killed him? Is it me?"

"I don't think so," said Crowe. "He was thrown out about 30 feet back. Skewered on a broken branch."

"My god," said Sarah, "No!" She had only known the man for a few hours, but he had been a part of her life that, although short, would be indelibly inked on her mind forever. Survival from the dark. The three of them, small sources of light that had emerged from the tunnel. And now one of those lights had gone out. Extinguished. Snuffed out in a second of carelessness.

Sarah was suddenly angry. "What the hell is wrong with you? You killed him! Your stupid fucking driving killed him!"

"We don't have time for this," said Crowe. "Trust me, we really don't have time for this. Just count yourself lucky I wasn't skewered too when I was thrown out."

Sarah grimaced. He was right. No one could help her now, except Crowe.

Crowe looked to his right for a moment, then back down to Sarah. "Listen carefully, I have to get you both out of here."

"Shouldn't we wait for help? You have called for help haven't you?" said Sarah.

"Like I said, we don't have time. Now shut up. I've got to work out how to do this."

He disappeared.

"Hey, hey!" shouted Sarah, but there was no answer.

"It's ok, he'll be back," said Abdul.

Sarah tried to push herself up towards the doorway of the overturned Jeep. It was impossible with her hands cuffed behind her back.

"Save your strength," said Abdul. "We will need it once we get out of here."

"We can't just lie here," she said.

"He'll be back."

Sarah closed her eyes. Images of her daughter flashed before her. She pushed them away.

A noise from the top of the jeep. Crowe was back.

"Ok, I found the keys to your handcuffs." He leaned down through the door and reached in behind Sarah. He moved her arms to get at the cuffs.

"Christ!" she called out involuntarily as pain shot up her arms.

"Ok, done," said Crowe.

Sarah moved her right arm out from behind her, grimacing every inch of the way. She looked at her hand and forearm, both heavily bruised.

"What about the other one?" said Crowe.

"I can't," said Sarah.

"You have to."

"I can't," she shouted this time.

"Fucking hell," Crowe reached down and grabbed her arm, and pulled.

Sarah yelled in pain as Crowe pulled her up out of the vehicle by both her arms. She swore and kicked with her feet.

Crowe let out a shout of exertion and pulled her up and out of the vehicle. He was standing on the side of the jeep, which was now the top. He laid Sarah down next to the open door.

"That fucking hurt," she spat through gritted teeth.

He undid the muzzle. "Don't sweat it. Look."

Sarah looked at where Crowe was pointing.

The jeep had come to rest on the side of a field after plowing through a hedge. About fifteen feet from the vehicle a thick crop of tall wheat began. At the far end of the field, deep amongst the crop, Sarah focused on what at first was only a blur of movement. Then the blur became figures, then the figures became twisted, shuffling, deformed beings. Their moans carried across the still county air, mixing with the birdsong and cricket sound to make a strange and despairing country melody of doom.

Hundreds of them.

She pulled off her muzzle and winced hard at a sharp pain in her cheek.

"Suck up the pain love," said Crowe. "Things will hurt a lot more if we don't get out of here soon."

"What's going on?" said Abdul, blind to the advancing zombie army.

Sarah pushed herself up on her aching arms. Fear, in the form of adrenaline, was pulsing through her veins. It was amazing what fear could do, how the human body could mask pain. Her left arm hung uselessly by her side, but her right moved painfully with persuasion.

"Let's get big man out," said Crowe. "Got a feeling he won't be as easy as you." He leaned over the door of the jeep, "Hey, big man, can you move?"

"My side hurts," said Abdul, "but I think I can move if you can get me upright."

"That's the fucking magic ticket though, isn't it," said Crowe under his breath.

"How will we move him?" said Sarah.

"We can't. He'll have to move." Crowe jumped off the jeep. He went to the back of the vehicle and, taking his handgun from his belt, smashed the back window with the butt of the gun.

The group of zombies moved at the same steady pace towards the jeep wreck. Maddeningly slow, but with a controlled certainty, as if they knew they could take their time. Moan and step, moan and step.

We'll get there.

We'll get them.

Crowe rustled in the back of the jeep and threw out a rope, a first aid kit, and a can of petrol.

He crawled back onto the top of the jeep with the rope. He put it down next to him and lowered the top half of his body, upside down, through the door.

"You need to lean forward big man," said Crowe. "Got to get to your hands."

Abdul shuffled and moved, huffing and puffing as he did so. He managed to push himself forward revealing a few inches of space that allowed Crowe to reach the restraints.

Crowe quickly undid the restraints.

"Ok, pass me the rope," he shouted up to Sarah.

Sarah got the rope and passed one end down to Crowe. The mob of undead was now worryingly close - how long did they have left, two minutes, one?

Crowe began to tie the rope around Abdul's wrists. "I'm gonna pull you up, then you're going to have to push yourself out. You manage that?"

Abdul nodded, sweating. His eyes were wide open.

The moans of the zombies now filled the air, like a telegraph of fear. The sound infected everything, Sarah felt it right into her soul, like they were speaking to her, speaking to her very life force.

They would be on them before Abdul was out...

The petrol can.

"Crowe, do you have a lighter?"

"What?" said Crowe emerging from the jeep, rope in hand.

"A lighter, do you have a lighter?"

Crowe frowned but didn't ask any more questions. He quickly took a zippo from his pocket and threw it at Sarah.

She jumped down from the jeep and grabbed the petrol can with her good hand. She limped to the edge of the wheat crop.

Moving as fast as she could, she poured petrol onto the ground, tracing out a semi-circle with the jeep at the centre.

Sarah stood back from her semi-circle and lit the zippo. She closed her eyes, prayed, opened her eyes again and threw the zippo forward.

The petrol caught light with a whoosh.

Within seconds the fire traced Sarah's semi-circle. Within a few more seconds the field behind went up. The flames raced back across the dry crop with speed, throwing thick black smoke into the sky. The fire soon caught the zombies.

The groans increased in intensity. They certainly felt the heat. But they didn't stop.

"Good work," said Crowe, panting on top of the jeep, straining with the rope.

"Have you got Abdul?" said Sarah.

Crowe gave no answer but leaned down to grab Abdul's emerging hand.

Although engulfed in flames the zombies continued to march; the same speed, the same target, like metronomes. Only twenty feet or so away.

Abdul now had a grip on the side of the jeep and was pulling himself up out of the vehicle. Crowe jumped onto the ground and pulled with the rope.

A zombie stepped through the semi-circle, flames roaring over its charred body.

It slowed. There was a popping sound, and the zombie's head exploded, sending charred flaming chunks flying through the air. Sarah gagged at the smell, like a game meat barbecue.

Another flaming zombie appeared. This one did not stop.

Sarah looked around for a weapon but saw nothing except the petrol can. She picked it up, lifting it with her good arm, ready to swing at the zombie.

She jumped at a loud sound beside her.

Crowe had shot the zombie.

Its head exploded. Sarah flinched as splatters of blood hit her face, burning. She let out a small yelp.

Crowe fired again at the next zombie to enter the semi-circle. Then again, and again.

"You'd better hurry up pal," he shouted to Abdul, "I've only got nine shots left."

Abdul answered by throwing his heavy frame off the jeep and landing on the ground with a thump.

Several zombies appeared at once from the flaming field.

"Ok, let's get the fuck out of here," shouted Crowe, firing at the two nearest zombies.

Sarah limped after Crowe as fast as she could. Abdul, likewise, hobbled beside her.

"You ok?" she said.

Abdul nodded, not speaking, out of breath.

They ran onto the road and kept running. The zombies followed but quickly fell behind.

A few minutes down the road and an explosion rattled the air.

"There goes the jeep," said Crowe. "That should get us some attention."

A billowing tower of black smoke rolled into the air.

Thirty minutes later and an army jeep pulled up beside them.

"Crowe, what the hell happened?" It was the tall soldier from before.

"Fubar sir. I crashed. We lost Dutton and one of the civilians."

The tall soldier shook his head. "Get in."

Crowe got in the front, Abdul and Sarah in the back.

Sarah sank into the seat, every muscle aching, every bone crying in pain. Her left arm pulsed in agony.

Abdul was spread out on the back seat next to her. His clothes were dirty and torn. His face was covered in sweat, dirt, and blood.

"I can't believe David is gone," he said.

"I know," said Sarah. "I know." She rested her hand on his.

She took out her phone and opened her gallery. She scrolled through recent pictures of her, Ian and their daughter.

Sarah began to cry. An emptiness had taken hold of her, and she had no way to shake it or fill it. The pain she felt in her heart was stronger than any of her physical aches.

"I'll never see them again," she sobbed through her tears.

She screamed.

No one said anything, no one stopped her.

She cried, horrible gasping cries, her body rocked in sorrow.

She caught the tall soldier's eyes in the mirror, and she saw an emptiness there, too.

Abdul squeezed her hand.

"You'll be safe in the base, ma'am," said the tall soldier.

"You not taking them to holding?" said Crowe.

"You can vouch for them, Crowe? Am I right?"

"Yeah, I guess. These two are good."

"That's settled." The tall soldier looked at Sarah in the rearview mirror again. "We'll have you in a warm bed tonight, receiving medical attention. You'll have food and protection. That's the most anyone can hope for today. It may be all anyone can hope for, for a while. You understand?"

Sarah nodded, but she didn't know if it was enough.

But it had to be if she ever wanted to see her family again

Tower Block of the Dead

Chapter 1

A crow circled and drifted towards the window. It landed on the ledge, balancing precariously. Its dark eyes stared at Chris.

Crows shouldn't be up this high, thought Chris.

He sat on a couch by the window, on the nineteenth floor. He could see all the way to Liverpool city centre. Simeon sat on the couch opposite, a thin man with dark hair and dark eyes. Darker than the crow's, thought Chris.

A large man sat next to Simeon. He had a game console controller in his hand and was staring into a 76-inch flat screen that hung on the wall. Chris bet that no-one else in the tower block had a 76-inch screen.

The crow took off into the blue sky. Chris watched it turn into a speck in the distance.

"Have a cigarette mate," said Simeon pointing to the packet of Benson and Hedges on the coffee table.

Chris shrugged, "I'm trying to give up mate."

"Don't be soft lad. Have a smoke," Simeon again motioned to

the cigarettes.

Chris picked up the packet and took one out. He lit it with the zippo that sat next to the pack. He inhaled. It felt good. It helped him relax.

"That's better," said Simeon.

Another large man appeared at the doorway with a cup of coffee. He was older. He had greying hair. He wore a white T-shirt tucked into black jeans. He fixed his eyes on Chris and sipped from his coffee.

"Why you giving up the smokes?" asked Simeon.

"Me Nan's going on about it."

Simeon let out a small laugh. "Good that. You hear that fellas? Cares what his Nan thinks. Good woman your Nan."

Simeon stood up and walked to the window. He lit his own cigarette. He stood in silence and smoked.

Chris took some long drags on his cigarette, trying to push the nerves back. It was unusual for Simeon to call him when there was no deal on, even more so to be invited up to the flat.

Simeon finally spoke. "Nice when it's sunny, ain't it?"

Chris nodded, "Yeah, I reckon so."

"Yeah me too." Simeon sat again and frowned. "I've got a problem mate."

Chris felt nervous. Simeon scared him. Maybe it was the scar, the cold black eyes, the way his top lip would curl every time he smiled, like he was watching a small animal die and enjoying it.

"Oh, right," said Chris, searching for neutral words, fighting to put a neutral expression on his face. "Nothing serious I hope?"

"I'm not sure. That all depends."

"On what?" Chris put the cigarette down to stop it from revealing the obvious shaking in his fingers.

"On a few things." Simeon turned to the man standing at the doorway, who was still fixing a glare on Chris. "Tony, can you get me a cuppa?"

"Yeah, boss." Tony disappeared into the kitchen, Chris felt slight relief at not having the man staring at him anymore.

Simeon pointed at Chris with his cigarette. "You know about this business, don't you? You know that reputation is very important, don't you?"

"Yeah, defo," said Chris.

"You know what they're like out there," said Simeon, he motioned out the window. "Fucking animals the lot of them. Can't trust one fucker from the next. Kill you as soon as look at you, know what I mean mate?"

Chris nodded, his mouth dry, unable to speak.

"It's important I know who I can trust. Because if I want things to work around here, I need to know what's what and who's who, you get me?"

Simeon smiled, and Chris tried not to flinch.

"People been talking about the gear," said Simeon. He leaned forward. "Been saying that I've been cutting it. Some fucker down the dock last night was mouthing off, saying Simeon's gear was gash, saying that I was having everyone off."

Simeon leaned back, staring at Chris.

Chris had his head down. He tried to look up, but only managed a glance. "That's not right, is it, people saying that?" said Chris.

"No, it fucking ain't."

Tony brought Simeon a cup of tea.

"Cheers mate," Simeon took a sip, "Good that. Nice one." He put the cup down on the table.

Tony resumed his position at the door of the room, his glare fixated on Chris again.

"So, I told that fella to shut the fuck up, know what I mean? He won't be talking much to anyone for a good while," said Simeon. "But I have a problem."

Chris was sure that Simeon must be able to hear his heartbeat, or at maybe even see it. The sounds from the games console, some football game, played like a strange soundtrack in the background.

Simeon continued, "I checked some of the stuff. Cut to fuck."

Simeon stood up and threw his cigarette at Chris, "CUT to FUCK!" He jumped forward and rained blow after blow on Chris' head.

Chris raised his arms and tried to protect his head, but Simeon pulled his arms away.

"It wasn't me, I haven't done nothing!" Chris managed to shout before a fist hit his mouth and he felt blood and fragments of teeth in his mouth.

The man on the couch threw down the controller and pulled Chris off the sofa by his feet. He then dragged him up, so he was standing facing Simeon.

Simeon was breathing fast and deep, he sounded like a racehorse. Spittle hung out of his mouth. His black eyes bored into Chris' bruised eyes. Chris had to look away.

"Look at me, fucking look at me," shouted Simeon.

Tony grabbed Chris' head and pointed it at Simeon.

"I didn't do nothing," said Chris again, blood and fragments of teeth spitting out of his mouth. "I haven't cut nothing."

This is it, he thought, this is it. He's going to finish me. Out the window, and no one will see nothing, even if they do.

Chris' arms were pinned behind him. His legs felt weak.

Simeon motioned to Tony, "Give him a few settlers."

Without a word, Tony took a hefty swing with his right fist and connected hard with Chris' jaw. The world went black for a few moments. Then stars and dizzy vision. Shooting, throbbing pain.

Tony took another swing, with his left this time. His fists like bludgeons of concrete. Chris felt something tear in his neck.

Tony may have hit him again, but Chris didn't know. He passed out.

When Chris came too, he was lying on a bed. There was ice on his jaw.

"He's awake," said Tony, who was standing at the door of the room.

Chris felt the pain all at once. His head, face, cheeks, neck.

Especially his nose and jaw.

He was still alive though. Simeon hadn't killed him.

Chris allowed himself some cautious anger. He'd had enough. He was going to get out. Simeon was a fucking maniac.

Simeon appeared in the doorway. "You alright?"

Chris nodded best he could.

"No hard feelings, eh? Just business?"

Chris nodded again, struggling to see through his swelling left eye.

"I know it wasn't you, but the docks are your territory," said Simeon. "Sort your fucking crew out. This ain't going to happen again."

Chris had a good idea who had cut the gear. He was going to pay the fuckers a visit. Once he could walk.

"Ok mate, see you here next week," said Simeon. "Got another load for you. Come on then lad, on your way."

Chris got out of the bed. His head throbbed. He kept his head down. Simeon guided him out into the dark corridor. The door closed behind him.

He would have to go and see Nan.

Chapter 2

Nan lived a few floors below Simeon on the fourteenth. The lifts broke at least once a month. An old woman shouldn't have to live this high, in a shit flat with shit lifts. But the council didn't care, those fuckers didn't care about anything.

The stairwell smelled of piss and cigarettes.

Number 1434, halfway along a paint peeled corridor. He knocked on Nan's door.

"What the bloody hell has happened to you lad?" said Nan when she opened the door.

"Got mugged didn't I."

"Get in here you silly bugger." She hustled him into her flat and into the lounge. The sun beamed in the window, and he had to squint after the darkness of the corridor. "Sit down, I'll get you a cuppa."

He eased himself onto the couch, his head throbbing.

His Nan went into the kitchen and set the kettle boiling. Chris heard her mumbling.

He noticed blood spots on his white Adidas trainers. "Bollocks," he said. He'd only got them last week.

The lounge was decorated with trinkets. His Nan loved to go to Stanley Dock market. She went nearly every Sunday and always came home with a new ornament, picture, plant or some other crap. It then joined the rest of the crap in the small lounge.

The TV was on full blast, as usual. The news. Something about riots in London, and a virus. Who gave a fuck about London? Telly was always going on about bloody London.

His Nan came back in carrying two cups of tea, walking slowly, shaking her head. "I don't know, always bloody trouble. Look at the state of you, we need to get you to hospital my boy."

"No hospitals, Nan, don't worry about it, I'm alright."

She sat down beside him, looked at him again, and pulled her hands to her mouth with a big intake of breath. "Oh, look at my boy." She started to cry.

"Aw, don't cry Nan, I'm ok," he hugged her. "I'm alright Nan, I promise."

"I know you are this time, but what about next time? You're only nineteen, you shouldn't be getting this trouble."

He held on to his Nan. It felt nice. He knew it was stupid, but he felt sort of safe when he hugged her.

Soft lad. He pulled away from the embrace.

"There won't be a next time Nan, just some kids messing about."

She gently touched his swollen left eye. He flinched.

"You don't look alright." She went to the kitchen again and returned with her medicine box. She'd had that little metal tin for years, ever since he could remember.

"Have two of these," she passed him two ibuprofen. She took out a TCP bottle and sprinkled it liberally over a cotton ball. "This is going to sting."

She rubbed it around his face, and she was right, it did sting.

"Nan, bloody hell!"

"Who's the tough lad now then eh?" she said, laughing.

After a few minutes of tidying him up, she rested her hands on his. "Now then, Chris. You going to tell me what really happened?"

"Nan, I told you, I was mugged, a few lads down by the chippy this morning."

Nan's eyes narrowed. "It wasn't that Simeon was it? He's bad news him."

"No it wasn't, I told you, why don't you believe me?"

"Because I know what you're like! You forget, I'm your Nan, I brought you up my boy. That Simeon, his whole family, a lot of badduns."

"Look, Nan, I told you I'm not hanging around with him anymore. Learned me lesson last time didn't I?"

His Nan shook her head. "I just worry about you, you know I do. After what happened to your mum…" Nan's eyes teared up.

She always cried when she talked about mum. Couldn't blame her. He missed Mum too.

He gave his Nan another big hug.

"It's alright Nan. I'll be ok."

"Oh, I hope so. I really hope so."

They finished their embrace, and Nan wiped away the mascara from her eyes. She stood up, straightening her dress.

"Now, how about a nice big dinner tonight? I was saving that chicken for Sunday, but I reckon you could do it with tonight. Will need your strength up."

Chris smiled, his Nan was great.

"Now, you want to watch one of your films?"

"Nah, I've got to go out for a bit."

"You should be resting," said Nan.

"I know, but I've got to sign on, haven't I? Or they'll sanction me."

"Won't they let you off, what with you getting mugged and that?"

"You're joking aren't you? Bunch of bloody fascists."

Nan shrugged, looking deflated. "Ok, off you go again I

guess."

"Don't worry, Nan, I'll be back for dinner."

Chapter 3

He didn't need to sign on, but he couldn't tell his Nan the real reason he was going out. He needed to visit the students.

Chris took the lift to the ground floor of the flats. The elevator opened into a small concrete room next to the bottom of the stairwell. Plastic bags and beer cans lay in the corner, flies buzzed.

A broken door led to the car park. He walked out, it was a sunny day.

Amy was taking her shopping out of the car. Maybe his luck was changing. His wounds should get him some sympathy.

He ran over.

"Alright Amy, how you doing? Let me help with that." He picked up a few bags.

"Hi Chris, I'm alright- what the fuck happened to you?" She stared at his face.

Chris shrugged. "Not much, just some lads by the chippy."

"Oh my god, you need to get to hospital. That looks proper

nasty. You feel alright?" She reached forward and touched his swollen eye. He didn't flinch although it hurt. He breathed in. "You need a doc to see that."

"It's nothing, I told you, doesn't even hurt. You should have seen the other guys."

Amy smiled, "Yeah, I'll bet."

"For real. Proper had 'em."

"Is that why there's no marks on your knuckles then?"

"I used a bat."

Amy shook her head.

"You want a hand up with that shopping?" said Chris.

"Yeah, that'd be nice."

He picked up two of her bags and carried them through the car park towards the tower block.

He glanced sideways at Amy. She was wearing the white top he liked - she looked proper fit.

"So Amy, did you think about coming down to that gig with me? It's at the Royal Court, proper good night I reckon."

Amy laughed. "I don't think you should be going anywhere looking like that. Maybe when you feel a bit better?"

"I told you, I feel fine, I-"

Any wasn't listening anymore. Her sister, Cheryl, was running out of the apartment block, wearing curlers and a yellow dressing gown covered in ducks. Cheryl's slippers slapped against the ground, echoing like someone flicking a pack of cards.

Cheryl was a pain in the arse.

"What's up Chez?" said Amy.

"Bloody hell, girl, where you been?"

"I've just been doing the shopping, you know I have."

Cheryl took a few deep breaths, her skin was red. It was the first time Chris had ever seen her move anywhere faster than a gentle walk.

"It's going off," said Cheryl.

"What is?" said Amy.

"Yeah, what is?" said Chris.

Cheryl looked at Chris for the first time. "What the fuck happened to your face?"

Chris opened his mouth to reply, but Cheryl had already forgotten about him and turned back to Amy.

"London is proper fucked, it's all on the news. That virus is all over the place."

"What virus?" said Chris.

"I thought the army had sorted that?" said Amy,

"Whatever, it's a right fuckin' mess. TV is going off and on, and a lot of internet is down."

"What virus?" repeated Chris.

"The fucking virus that's been all over the news you idiot." Cheryl shook her head.

"Yeah, I don't watch TV, do I," said Chris quietly.

"Come on," said Cheryl, grabbing Amy's hand. "We're going."

"Where are we going?" said Amy.

"Ma reckons we should go to Uncle Tim's caravan in Formby."

"Won't he be using it?"

"Who fucking cares! Better than getting the virus. He's not going to kick us out, is he?"

Cheryl pulled her sister towards the tower block. "Chris, put that shopping under the car will you. We'll need that," she shouted over her shoulder.

"See you, Chris," said Amy, disappearing back into the building.

"What about the gig?" shouted Chris. But she was gone.

He stood still, two bags of shopping in his hands, staring at the door of the tower block.

"Bollocks," he said.

Chapter 4

So far it had been a bad day. A beating followed by being ignored by Amy. Chris knew exactly who was going to feel the full force of his wrath.

Those fucking students.

It had to be them that cut the stuff.

They lived in some fancy apartment down by the docks, no doubt paid for by their rich mummy and daddy. One of them was doing chemistry or something so probably thought he was being Billy Big Bollocks by cutting the gear and making extra cash.

Posh twats.

You don't come up here and mess me about, thought Chris.

He caught the train from Oriel station and fumed for the fifteen-minute journey into the centre of town.

He fidgeted with the knife in his pocket.

He got off at Central station and made his way through the town centre towards the waterfront.

Town had a funny atmosphere. Seemed to be a lot of aggro

about - even more than usual for a Saturday afternoon with the footy on.

Two fellas rolled out of a nearby pub, yelling and shouting. Another fella jumped out after them, covered in blood, and grabbed the other two.

Normally Chris would have stopped to watch, but not today. He had a mission.

He dodged a few more fights and reached the Docks. He made his way up to the student's apartment and knocked.

He waited.

He knocked again.

"Fuck's sake," said Chris. He was too riled up to leave. He needed to use his anger.

He tried the door. It was locked.

He shoved at it and shoulder barged it, but the door didn't budge. All he did was hurt his shoulder.

He kicked it, and it jarred his leg.

"Fuck!" he yelled.

There was a fire extinguisher at the end of the corridor. He took it and used it as a battering ram against the door, just above the handle.

Loud bangs accompanied with chipping wood. At last, some satisfaction.

A doorway opened further down the corridor, and a young woman popped her head out.

Chris snarled at her and shouted, "Fuck off if you know what's good for you."

She immediately disappeared back into her apartment.

Holding the extinguisher high, ready to take another swing, the door opened.

"Ok! Ok!" A man opened the door, his hands held up.

Chris pulled back his blow just in time to avoid connecting with the young man's nether regions.

"What do you want?" said the man with a wavering voice.

"James, you prick, have you been cutting my stuff?"

"What?" said James, "Who the… Chris?"

"Yeah, it's Chris."

"What the fuck happened to your face?"

"Shut it!"

Chris barged in through the door and pushed James backward. James back peddled, trying to keep his footing. Chris pushed him all the way to the couch, which he fell onto.

"Whoa, Chris, what's going on?"

"You know what's been going on. One of you posh twats has been cutting my stuff, and I want it sorted."

James held up his arms. His initial fear seemed to have passed. "Chris, you know us, we would never cut the stuff. We know never to mess with you."

"Bollocks. Had to be one of you two. I don't sell to no-one else on the docks."

James shook his head and smiled, "Chris, why would we ever cross you. We're not stupid enough to get on your bad side. We know how dangerous that would be."

Chris was unsure how to proceed. James seemed to be telling the truth. He didn't look scared. Surely if he had cut the stuff, he would have been scared.

"Well, someone's been cutting my stuff, and I want to know who. Where's Jules?"

James motioned back down the hallway, "He's in bed, not feeling well. Someone bloody idiot bit him last night, can you believe that?"

"Bit him? Did he have fucking rabies or something?"

"I don't know. But he's been feeling pretty bad this morning."

"You ought to get him to a hospital."

James shrugged. "What can you do, stubborn bugger. Look, Chris, how about I make a cup of tea, and we see what we can do about your drugs?"

A cup of tea did sound nice. He was gasping.

"Yeah, alright. I'll sit myself down here eh?"

Chris eased himself into the seat by the TV and James went

into the kitchen.

"Jules," shouted James. "Jules, would you like a cuppa?"

A strange guttural sound, like a moan, came from Jules's room.

"Fuck me," said Chris to himself, "sounds like the bugger's dying."

"Jules?" said James. He left the kitchen and went to James's room.

Then all hell broke loose.

A terrifying scream filled the apartment. Chris jumped up and pulled his knife out.

Another scream, accompanied by a loud moan.

"Jesus…" said Chris, unable to move. He wanted to get away, but he didn't want to get any closer to those sounds.

James appeared in the doorway, blood streaming down his face. It looked like there was a large gash around his eyeball.

"Help!" his voice was high pitched, like a little girl's, thought Chris. James stumbled into the lounge and grabbed Chris, trying to hide behind him.

"What are you doing? Get off!" shouted Chris. The two men span in a circle as James struggled to cower behind Chris.

A hideous moan from the doorway stopped their dance.

"Fuckin' hell," said Chris.

Jules, or at least something that looked like Jules, stood in the doorway. Its skin was pale and mottled, like damp paper, looking ready to drop off his skull at the lightest touch. Blood covered his mouth and neck. His eyes were solid black.

His mouth opened and closed rapidly, clicking and gnashing like comedy wind up teeth.

James let out another scream, even louder and more girly than the last.

Chris grabbed James and pushed him towards the Jules thing.

The Jules thing grabbed James and used his chattering gnashes to make quick work of James' neck. Blood squirted like a fountain across the walls, deep red and thick. Bits of flesh flew into the air, little pink globules of nerves, skin, and tendons

James' screams turned into gurgling bird calls.

"Bollocks to this," said Chris. He quickly ducked the two students and ran from the apartment, grabbing the fire extinguisher as he left.

Chapter 5

Standing at the door to James' apartment block, looking out over the pedestrianised area of the Dock's shopping precinct, things had apparently taken a turn for the worse.

Chris was glad he had the fire extinguisher.

A woman ran past him, screaming, blood pouring from a large gash on her shoulder. Three things that looked like the Jules-thing, all covered in blood with entrails hanging from various parts of their bodies, shuffled after the woman, moaning loudly.

A man in a tracksuit was trying to get into a white car, but a small child gnawed at his knee, squirting the vehicle with blood. The man screamed, trying to shake off the kid thing, who was impervious to his blows.

Only ten feet away, an old woman lay face down. An old man pulled her spine out of her back, blood and small pieces of flesh spraying into the air as each vertebra popped with a horrible splat sound.

"Fuck me…" said Chris. He knew what this was.

It was the zombie apocalypse.

Surprisingly, he wasn't scared. He had only one thought - Nan.

He ducked back into the doorway of the apartments, took out his phone and dialled. The call dropped straight away. He tried a few more times and finally connected.

"Nan, stay in the flat, whatever you do don't go out."

"What are you talking about Chris? I need to go and get some veg for our roast tonight."

"Nan! Listen to me, just this once, trust me, do not leave the fucking flat."

"Language, Chris, were you born in-"

"NAN, sorry, listen to me, don't leave the flat. Sorry for swearing."

Silence for a minute, then she said, "What's going on?" her voice sounded different. He realised he'd never heard Nan scared before.

"Things are... happening outside. Don't worry, I'll be home soon. Just lock the door and don't let anyone in but me, got it?"

"Is it this virus?"

"Yes Nan, it's the zombie apocalypse."

Silence on the line for a moment, then, "Bloody hell. Like that film the other night?"

"Exactly."

"Bloody hell," she said again. "Hurry up and get home, lad. And be careful."

"Will do, Nan. Love ya."

He hung off the call. Now to get back.

The trains would be off, the busses would be engulfed. He would have to run all the way.

Or steal a car.

The man in the tracksuit had lost his fight with the kid and was lying on the floor in a pool of blood and organs. The kid zombie was munching away happily on what looked like a lung.

"Right," said Chris. He took a deep breath and charged towards the kid.

The kid zombie looked up at the last moment and snarled.

Chris brought down the fire extinguisher hard on its head. The small skull caved in, fragments of white bone sinking deep into the pink brain matter.

The zombie kid fell forward, dead for the second time.

Chris then caved in the head of the man in the tracksuit. He was taking no chances. The dull clang of the fire extinguisher against concrete signalled Chris had pounded right through the man's head.

That should do it.

Luckily, the car keys were in the door. Chris hadn't fancied searching the man's pockets - he was a bloody mess, his skin ripped back to reveal an almost empty ribcage, bits of organs half hanging out amongst torn tissue and bones.

"What a stink," said Chris.

He got in the car and stowed his fire extinguisher beside him. He pulled out of the car park quickly, running over one of the zombies chasing the woman. It bounced off the bonnet with a thump.

Joining the main road, Chris had to swerve hard as a car came straight at him from the opposite direction. He avoided it, just, and glancing in the rearview mirror, he saw the car smash into a lamppost.

Rogue cars were not the only hazard. Panicked people and hungry zombies ran across the road at random. Chris did his best to avoid the people and hit the zombies.

He raced past an office building to his right, flames bursting out of its windows. A person jumped from the eighth floor and hit the ground with a nasty splat. Three zombies immediately fell onto the free feed.

Fires, screams, crashing cars, blood.

It was getting hard to tell who was who. Chris took a simple approach - if it runs, it's human, if it walks, it's zombie.

He left the centre of the city and got onto the dock road heading back towards Bootle.

He didn't get far.

A red car in the corner of his vision was all he saw. There was a loud crash and then the front of his stolen vehicle span to the right. Chris held on tight to the steering wheel as the car spun in two wide circles, before mounting the pavement and hitting a warehouse on the side of the road.

Chris took a deep breath, the pain of bruised ribs, thanks to the seatbelt, adding to his physical ailments.

The red car that hit him was twenty feet away, crashed into the same warehouse. An angry looking zombie was battering at the window, banging its head and fists against the glass.

Smoke poured out of Chris' car's bonnet. The engine had stopped.

Chris turned the ignition. Nothing.

"Bollocks," he said. He was still a good few miles from home.

A van raced past, flames pouring out of the bonnet and windows, a charred figure hanging out from the passenger side. It hit a police car on the other side of the road and the two vehicles flipped through the air, flying in opposing directions. The police car exploded.

Chris would have to leg it back home. No way he was getting in another car.

He opened the door, grabbed his extinguisher, and took a quick look up and down the road. Zombies shuffled towards him from a side road about thirty yards away.

He turned off the main road. He was going to take a route home through the housing estates and high streets. There might be more zombies that way, but he fancied his chances against them more than the crazy traffic on the main road.

If he was going to die in the zombie apocalypse, it was going to be because of a zombie and not some skidding fucking Prius.

He turned down a residential street of red-bricked terraced houses. It was full of zombies and running people. Families mainly, couples with kids. Groups of kids.

One fella with a baseball bat was making quick work of any

zombies that came close.

A woman was swinging an ironing board at the head of one unfortunate zombie.

Some kids were using small cricket bats to attack what Chris thought at first was a zombie, but one that seemed to be shouting out for help.

Chris ran down the street, dodging the undead, the living, and the fighting.

Something grabbed his shoulder, but he shook it off and ran faster.

He quickly stepped over a figure that fell onto the ground in front of him.

He jumped to the left to avoid a crazy kid wielding a bloodied cricket bat.

He was breathless by the time he got to the end of the road. How could he keep this up all the way home?

Chapter 6

After the call from Chris, Nan sat on the couch in silence. He was prone to flights of fancy, that was for sure. Not the brightest lad, but something about his voice on the phone had sounded different.

Different in a good way. None of the big talk, the pretending to be someone he wasn't. She realised what it was - he had sounded like a man. Like her Gerry, may he rest in peace, used to sound.

Even so. Zombie apocalypse? They had watched some film the other week about zombies. All blood and gore and guts. Not really her cup of tea, but Chris seemed so keen, and she would have watched anything if it had meant he was in the flat with her, and not out getting into trouble.

The film had been pretty daft. People coming back to life after being chewed to bits. Daft.

She put on the BBC news. Riots in London, like it had been for the past few days, and a virus. But no one said anything about people coming back from the dead.

Nan stood up, letting out a long sigh as her knees reacted painfully. She walked to the window and looked out across the city. From her high vantage point on the fourteenth floor, she could see right to the new skyscrapers around the docks.

Three columns of smoke were rising from the city centre. That wasn't normal, thought Nan.

She took her binoculars from the sideboard. They had belonged to Gerry - he had been an avid bird watcher and had saved up for months to get these 'bins,' as he called them. She aimed the bins to the streets surrounding the high rise.

She took in a deep breath. Bodies lay on the floor of the car park - she counted seven. But even more alarming was that some of the bodies had a person crouched over them, seemingly feeding on the carcasses.

She focused on the nearest body. A traffic warden was pulling out the body's intestines, and eating them.

Nan dropped the bins and ran to the kitchen. She threw up in the sink.

"Bloody hell," she said. "I need a cuppa."

She put on the kettle and paced the kitchen. It looked like Chris was right. It was the bloody zombie apocalypse.

Chris ran down a second street full of people, zombies, and feral kids swinging cricket bats, baseball bats, tennis rackets, and kitchen knives.

He hefted his extinguisher high and brought it down on the head of a zombie that had got too close. "Bollocks to you mate!" he shouted as he repeatedly pummelled the head of the zombie, who looked like it used to be a milkman. Blood and pieces of skull flew out from under the red extinguisher.

"Hey, watch what you're doing, nobhead," shouted a high pitched voice from near Chris.

Chris looked up and saw a kid in a tracksuit with a baseball bat, wiping a pink chunk of brain off his white tracksuit.

"Shut it," said Chris.

"Fuck off," said the kid.

Chris had an idea.

He threw the extinguisher at the kid, aiming to miss, but it was enough to make him flinch.

Chris jumped forward and grabbed the baseball bat.

"Get off!" shouted the kid.

"Give me the bat you little prick."

They wrestled for a few seconds, and Chris managed to prise the bat away from the kid.

"Do one!" shouted Chris.

The kid stuck his finger up, aimed a well-placed kick on Chris' shins, and ran off.

Chris let out a small cry and was about to run after the kid, but then remembered where he was, and what was happening.

He began running again, feeling safer with the weight and flexibility of the baseball bat in his hands. He took a swing at a passing zombie, the connection ringing with a hollow metal clang. The zombie wobbled, and Chris hit him again, caving the left of its skull. It fell to the ground.

"Nice one," said Chris eyeing the blood on the end of the bat.

He ran again.

His lungs struggled with the pace. He couldn't keep it up all the way back home.

First, get off the street, then think.

He ran down a small alley in-between two houses into the small backyard of a house. Tall brick walls surrounded the yard. A battered wooden shed sat in the corner.

He looked in the back window, into a kitchen. He saw an old woman, her eyes wide with fear, holding a kitchen knife. She was waving it and shouting at him.

Chris smiled and shouted, "It's ok lady, I'm just getting me breath."

She ran out of the kitchen.

Chris took out his phone. He didn't want Nan to get worried - it was going to be a few hours before he was home. No signal though.

But he had a plan now.

He opened the door of the yard that led into the back alley that ran between the rows of tenement houses. He stepped out into a thin, brick floored lane, bordered by the houses.

He ran to the house opposite and looked over the wall. An empty backyard. He went to the next, looked over that wall. Not what he was looking for. He went to the next, and the next, and the next.

Nan sat in the lounge with her cup of tea, changing channels, looking for news. It was mostly the same story, seemed to be on repeat. Riots in London, a virus and the newsman telling everyone to stay in their homes.

Some channels were gone completely.

She turned off the TV.

The picture turned to black, and there was a small hum as the set powered down. Once that was gone, there was no sound in the apartment save the ticking of her wall clock. It was an hour since Chris had called. She pushed down the fear that something had happened to him.

She sat in the relative silence. She took a picture of Gerry from the table beside her couch and looked at it. Tall, strong, worked hard at the docks all his life. He had been her rock, until their daughter, Kerry, died. When Kerry died, Gerry had fallen apart. He had doted on her like crazy, did anything for her.

When she went, it was like she took Gerry's heart with her. He had become a shell of a man.

He died a few months later.

"Oh Gerry," she said. "You'd know what to do. I hope you're watching over Chris. Help him, Gerry."

A scream from the corridor outside the flat. She dropped the picture, and it landed hard on the floor, the glass frame cracking.

Another scream.

Nan's heart beat fast. She held her chest.

A loud bang on the door.

Nan shuffled back on her seat and let out a small cry, "Oh, God save me."

Another loud bang, "Mrs. Benson! Mrs. Benson, help, help me!"

It was a woman's voice. One that Nan recognised. It was Amy, that girl that Chris was soft on.

"Mrs. Benson!" The girl's cry was loud, desperate, "Help!"

Chris had told her not to let anyone in. But how could she ignore someone shouting like that?

She looked at the photo of Gerry on the floor. She knew what he would have done.

She got up and went to the door as quick as she could. She looked through the eyehole. It was Amy alright, her face covered in tears, mascara running down her cheeks. She was banging on the door, panicked glances to her left.

Nan opened the door.

Amy looked shocked as if she hadn't expected the door to open.

Nan grabbed her arm, "Get in here girl."

Nan stuck her head into the corridor and looked where Amy had been looking.

Only six feet away, Mrs. Williamson from down the corridor was in her dressing gown, covered in blood. Her chest was pulled open and her heart was hanging free, blood spurting, rhythmically decorating the corridor wall red. Her jaws clicked up and down, her hands reached out for Nan.

"Bloody hell," Nan ducked back in her flat and pulled the door shut. She locked it.

Chris was halfway down the alley, and still no joy. The noises from the adjoining streets were getting louder and more violent. More screams, more yells, more bangs, breaking glass, revving engines. There had been an explosion, and in the near distance, a few rapports of gunfire could be heard. He wished he had a gun.

He fancied poppin' some zombie's heads.

He pulled himself over the wall again to check the next house. Bingo.

A powerful Kawasaki 250cc Ninja sat in the yard. Pristine. With a great big bastard chain locking it to the ground. As he would have expected in this neighbourhood.

He threw the bat over the wall then climbed over himself.

He tested the lock on the bike, just in case. Solid.

The house was a typical two-bed terrace, like the one he used to live in with his Mum. White paint peeled off the brickwork.

Next to the motorbike was a kid's trike.

The top half of the back door was a glass screen.

He used his bat to shatter it.

"Daddy!" It was a young lad's voice.

He quickly reached through the broken window and opened the door.

A shout came from upstairs, a man's voice, "You'd better be fucking gone by the time I get down mate!"

Bollocks, thought Chris. This was going to be trickier than he thought.

Chris ran into the kitchen and quickly looked around, hoping to see the keys hanging on the wall, but he saw nothing. Heavy steps stomped down the stairs.

Chris tucked in behind the kitchen door, and held the bat high, ready to swing.

Footsteps in the lounge, then towards the kitchen.

A man appeared. A big man. Shaved head, white t-shirt.

Chris brought the bat down hard.

There was a heavy clunk, and the man fell to his knees, holding his head, red appearing between his fingers and running down his arm.

"Ya bastard," shouted the man through gritted teeth. He turned his head to face Chris. "What the fuck are you doing?"

Chris raised the bat again and pretended to swing. The man flinched. Good, he was scared.

"Sorry, mate, I need your bike. Just give me the bike, and I'll be gone."

The man frowned. "Me fucking head you prick. What am I supposed to do about me head?"

"Look, I just need your bike. I need to get home."

The man supported himself with one hand, the other holding his head and let out a moan. "Think you've cracked me skull."

"You'll survive mate." Chris looked around the lounge. Some keys were sitting on the coffee table. "Is that them? Is that the keys?"

"Fuckin' take them, you dickhead."

A little boy appeared at the bottom of the stairs. He saw the man on the floor and burst into tears, "What have you done to me Dad?"

Chris grabbed the keys. "I'm sorry, alright? I just need the bike."

"You've killed me dad!"

"He's not dead," said Chris.

"I'm not dead, lad," said the man.

"You're not going to die too, dad?"

"No, I'm alright lad, I'll be ok." The man looked at Chris again, "Just take the fucking keys you bastard, and get out of here. Leave us alone."

Chris looked at the young lad, could only be about nine or ten. The same age he was when his mum died.

"What does he mean 'are you going to die too'?" said Chris.

"His mum died two years ago," said the man. "Now he thinks I'm dying as well. Just get the fuck out of here."

Chris grabbed the keys.

"I'm sorry." He ran out into the yard. He unlocked the heavy padlock and sat on the bike. He started it. It gave a healthy throaty purr and revved into life.

Chris sat on the bike for a few seconds. There was the sound of an explosion, followed by a few screams, from the nearby street.

Chris jumped off the bike and ran back into the house.

The man was sitting on the couch, his T-shirt covered in blood. The young lad was mopping it up the best he could with towels, crying.

They both looked at Chris.

"What the fuck do you want? I told you to go," said the man.

"It's not safe here. Come with me," said Chris.

"What?"

"Come with me, I gotta get me Nan, then I'm gonna get her out of the city. Get to the beach or something."

"You fuckin crazy?"

"It's the zombie apocalypse mate! Can't stay in the city."

The man shook his head. "You come in here, brain me, rob me bike, and now you want to go on fuckin holiday together?"

"I'm sorry about your head. I didn't mean to hit you that bad. I've had a bad day."

The man studied Chris's face. "I guess you have. What the fuck happened to your face anyhow?"

"Don't worry about it." Chris ran over to the window and peered out through the net curtains. A zombie stood still by the window, half of its brain and one eyeball hanging on its shoulder. Its head exploded as a woman with a spade cleaved its skull in half. Blood splattered on the window.

"I have to get out of here, get back to me Nan. I reckon we can all go. I'll ride, you get on the back, and the lad can go in-between."

The man shook his head. "We're not going anywhere." He went to stand up but wobbled and fell back again onto the couch.

"Maybe he's right dad, even if he is a prick," said the lad. His face was red from crying, but he'd finished with the tears now. He had a shaved head too, and a white T-shirt. Looked like a mini version of his dad.

"You can't look after him, with your head like that," said Chris. "What happens if the next person to come in here isn't as nice as me?"

The man let out a snort. "This is a fucking joke."

"Dad?"

The man shook his head and hugged his son. "Go up and grab your bag, Nate. Put your coat on and pack your warm things. Not too much though."

The lad ran upstairs.

Chris smiled and held out his hand, "I'm Chris."

The man took it. With a firm grip. He was a big bastard alright. He squeezed hard, and Chris felt his knuckles rub against each other.

"I ought to fuckin brain you." The man shook his head, "and I will do when I'm better. But you're right, we have to get out of here."

"That's right," said Chris grimacing through the pain in his squeezed hand. "Maybe it's one of them things, you know, twist of fate and that."

The man gave one final squeeze, "I'm Terry." He let go of Chris's hand. "Now help me get me stuff."

Chris helped Terry up the stairs and stood by the door while Terry packed a small rucksack.

They went downstairs, and Terry locked up the house. They got on the bike.

Chris revved it hard. The engine sang in high pitched complaint.

"Careful, dickhead!" shouted Terry.

"Sorry mate," said Chris. He eased the engine gently, and they rode out into the alleyway.

Chapter 7

"Come on girl, sit yourself down here."

Nan motioned for Amy to sit on the couch. Amy was shaking, her skin pale. Her eyes wide open.

She looked at Nan, "What's going on?" Her voice shook. She was on the brink of tears.

Nan rested her hand on Amy's. "It's the zombie apocalypse, dear. I'd best go get you a cup of tea."

Nan went into the kitchen and began making the cuppa for Amy. Poor girl, obviously terrified.

Amy shouted in from the lounge, "What do you mean, zombie apocalypse?"

"It's the virus, it's everywhere now. My Chris tells me it's zombies. You know, like on the films. Do you take sugar dear?"

"Erm, one, please. Chris told you? Where is Chris? Is he ok? I saw him this morning."

"He doesn't look too good does he?" Nan brought in the cuppa and placed it on the table in front of Amy. "He told me he was mugged. I don't believe him though. I think he's been messing around with that Simeon again."

"He told me he was mugged too. Is he ok?"

"I hope so. He went out. I got a call from him an hour or so ago, said he was on his way home and I that wasn't to open the door to anyone. Glad I made an exception for you though." She smiled at Amy as she eased herself onto the couch.

"Now, what happened to you then?"

Amy held her head in her hands. "We were going to go to Formby, our uncle has a caravan there."

"Oh, very nice."

"Yeah, my sister thought it'd be safe there, and we wouldn't get this virus." Amy shook her head as if fighting with her thoughts. "I thought this virus was like a bad flu or something? Zombies aren't real are they?"

"I'm not really sure dear. It seems that everything is possible these days, what with these i-computers and phone-pads." She took a sip of her tea. It was a good brew. "So what happened then? How come you aren't on your way to Formby?"

"Cheryl went out to get some stuff, food and that, about an hour and a half ago. I got worried, shop is only round the corner. So I went out to see if I could find her. Phones had stopped working." The cup in Amy's hand started to shake.

Nan guided the cup onto the table. "And then what happened?"

"I had just left the flat. That's when I saw Mrs. Williamson. She was moaning, covered in blood, I thought she was ill, but when I tried to help her, she tried to bite me." Amy burst into tears. "Does that mean she's a zombie?"

Nan hugged Amy, "There, there, dear, there, there."

Amy spoke into Nan's neck, her voice muffled, "So I ran away, I couldn't get back to my flat without having to go past Mrs. Williamson, so I thought I'd try Chris', I mean, your flat."

Nan continued to hug Amy. Poor girl.

Chris raced the bike down the alley. If there was one thing he could do, he could ride. He'd never been able to own a bike as fast as this, of course, but he'd stolen a few.

Nate sat squashed in between Chris and his dad. Both Nate and Terry held tight around Chris' waist. Terry had a strong grip. Chris hoped he'd forgive him for hitting him on the head. He was a big bastard alright.

"Turn left here mate," shouted Terry, "You'll get to the alley behind Smithston Street. Long one that, takes us onto the main A-road. Short ride to Bootle from there."

Chris nodded and took a tight right.

"Careful nobhead! You trying to shake us off?" shouted Terry.

"Sorry mate. Just trying to be quick."

Chris turned onto the next alley and revved hard, the motorcycle took off under them.

A man emerged from a backyard just ahead. Chris swerved delicately as the man tried to grab them.

Buggers are everywhere, thought Chris. But a hell of a lot less than on the main road.

Which was where they turned to next.

The A-road was a trunk road that would lead directly to Bootle. He knew it well.

He stopped at a junction.

"Last main road I was on was the dock," said Chris. "Nightmare mate. Cars crashing everywhere, zombies all over the place."

"So?" said Terry.

"Just warning you," said Chris. "Hold on tight. Things may get a bit mad, like."

As if on cue, an explosion rocked the air, and a thick plume of smoke rose a hundred yards down the road.

"See what you mean," said Terry. "Hold on Nate, you got that? Hold on tight."

"Yeah don't worry Dad."

"Everyone ready?" said Chris.

He revved the bike, hit the clutch and speeded onto the road.

Thirty miles an hour, forty, fifty, sixty miles an hour in seconds. Chris expertly banked the bike left and right to avoid traffic, panicked people, burning cars, stumbling zombies. Nate and Terry tightened their grip around his waist.

He kicked down through the gears as they approached traffic lights at a crossroads. Even though the lights were green, Chris didn't trust that anyone would be paying attention to the lights, so he pulled to a stop.

Just as well.

A fire engine zoomed across their road. It was on fire, screams coming from the cab. A few seconds, a rush of speed, a red blur, heat. The truck's horn honked, its siren fired intermittently.

It ignored a curve in the road and plowed straight into a shop front at full speed.

It exploded.

"Cool," said Nate.

"It's not cool," said Terry. "People died there lad."

"Sorry, dad."

Chris kicked the bike into gear, and they were on their way again.

He took a turn off the main road into smaller and smaller branch roads until he was on the street leading to his tower block.

He pulled into the car park. Two cars were on fire. Several zombies wandered around the car park, bumping into vehicles, moaning.

One looked at Chris and let out a moan. It walked directly towards them. The others followed suit.

"Wait til they get a bit closer," said Chris. "Then we'll leg it round them. They're slow as fuck. We should be alright."

They got off the bike and waited. When the now grouped zombies were about ten yards away, Chris, Terry, and Nate ran in a wide circle round the zombies towards the high rise.

A group of lads ran out of the high rise. They wore tracksuits, baseball caps, balaclavas. Two had motorcycle helmets on. They carried various weapons; bats, knives, spades. They stopped.

"Are youse zombies?" shouted the one at the front with a balaclava on.

Terry grabbed Nate and pulled him close.

Chris held up his hands, "No mate, it's me, Chris, from the fourteenth floor, you alright Benno?"

Benno pulled up his balaclava. "It's just Chris."

The gang, satisfied, ran into the car park. They shouted immediately on seeing the zombies following Chris, and they dived into them, swinging their weapons.

"Not bad for a bunch of scallies," said Terry.

They got to the lifts. "Hope the power is still on."

It was. The lift opened, and a young couple froze, fear on their faces on seeing Chris and the others.

"It's alright," said Chris, "We're not zombies."

They said nothing. The man put a protective arm around the woman, and they squeezed past Chris, Terry, and Nate, keeping their distance. Once a few feet away, they burst into a run.

The three got in the lift and went to the fourteenth floor.

The door opened. A zombie was halfway down the corridor, an old woman in a white dress, splattered with blood. It limped towards the lift, moaning softly, its breathing rasping and laboured. It had a large hole in its chest.

Chris ran forward and struck the zombie on the head with his baseball bat. It fell, its blood decorating the wall. Chris hit it again, and a third time. The skull shattered and brain tissue hung out, stuck with chips of bone. It was dead, again.

"See where you get your practice for hitting people on the head," said Terry.

"Told you I was sorry mate." He motioned for them to follow. "Here's me Nan's."

Chapter 8

"Here he is!" Nan held out her arms and embraced Chris. "Where have you been, I've been so worried."

"Sorry Nan, it's a bit mad out there."

"Can we get in out of this corridor?" said Terry.

Nan and Chris moved to the side to let Terry and Nate in.

"Who's this?" said Nan, looking wary.

"This is Terry, and his son Nate. Helped me get back. Let me, erm, borrow his bike."

Terry gave Chris a sharp look. "Hello," he said to Nan, "Thanks for letting us in."

"Don't you worry," said Nan.

She led everyone into the lounge.

"Amy!" said Chris.

"Hello Chris," said Amy, with a sheepish smile.

"What are you doing here?"

"Long story."

Terry came into the room and smiled at Amy. "Hello," he said.

Amy smiled back, "Hi."

Nan took centre stage as everyone settled themselves on the couch and dining table chairs. "Who wants a cup of tea then?" She stared at the blood on Terry's T-shirt, and the dried blood on his shaved head. "What the bloody hell happened to you lad?"

"You alright?" said Amy, jumping up, "That looks nasty."

"It is. Ask laughing boy here about it," he motioned to Chris.

All eyes turned to Chris. He felt himself going red.

"He hit me dad on the head with a baseball bat," said Nate.

"You did what?" said Nan.

"Chris!" said Amy.

Chris shrugged, not sure what to say or do. No matter how he played the excuses in his head, they didn't sound right.

He sat on a dining chair in the corner of the room as Nan and Amy crowded round Terry, tending to his wound, cleaning him up.

It was early evening. Chris took out a cigarette, he'd been holding off all day, but he thought he deserved one now.

He wondered if Nan was still going to make that roast.

She did.

They sat around the table and ate Nan's delicious roast.

Chris told the story of how they had got here, trying his best to underplay how he had got the bike. But Nate made sure everyone knew what had happened.

"Well," said Nan, "I'm just glad you are all here in one piece, and Chris didn't do you any proper harm."

Terry's skull wasn't fractured. He had a massive bump though, and a raging headache. He had gratefully taken Nan's heavy painkillers she got for her hip operation. They had dulled the pain a little.

"You can't half be a bloody idiot at times, Chris," said Amy.

"I've said I'm sorry! You don't know what it's like out there."

Terry said, "Don't worry. We're ok with it. He just owes me big time. Don't you mate?"

Chris smiled at Terry. No one seemed bothered about his injuries anymore, it was all about Terry's head.

"Well as long as everything is ok." said Nan "Don't need any more nonsense going on, what with what's going on out there."

Mention of outside and everyone stopped talking. Up until then, they'd been having a nice bit of scran, chatting like friends. Everything had seemed alright. But they were far from alright.

"What're we going to do?" said Amy.

"Why don't we stay here?" said Nan.

Chris shook his head. "Don't think that's a good idea."

"Why not?" said Amy.

"Yeah, why not?" said Terry.

"You saw Benno and his bunch of scrots downstairs, running round kitted up like a bunch of assassins or something."

"He's a baddun that Benno," said Nan, shaking her head.

"There's plenty of badduns round here. That's what I mean. Think about it, no bizzies, no nothing. You think the zombies are bad? Wait til the scallies work out they can do what they like."

They exchanged nervous glances amongst themselves.

"What do you reckon then?" said Terry.

"I reckon we get out of here. Go to the beach," said Chris.

"Formby?" said Amy.

"No, further. Reckon we go to Wales. Away from people."

"Sounds like a nice idea," said Terry, "but how do we get there? You said it yourself, the roads are proper dangerous. We can't all get on my bike."

Chris smiled. All eyes were on him, and he had the answers. "We don't need to get on your bike, I know something better."

They spent the night at Nan's.

Chris offered to give up his room for Terry and Nate, secretly hoping that he would be able to sleep in the lounge with Amy, but they declined.

Instead, he listened to Amy and Terry talking and laughing in the lounge, into the early hours.

Chris couldn't sleep. He was far too wired. What a day. A beating in the morning, a zombie apocalypse by evening.

What the hell would tomorrow bring?

Especially given his plan for getting everyone out of here.

Chapter 9

It was an early rise for everyone. It seemed Chris hadn't been the only one who didn't sleep well. Everyone sat around the table, bleary-eyed, as Nan served up the last of her eggs, some toast, and a good supply of tea.

It was a grey day; a thick heavy coating of cloud covered the sky all the way to the city. Numerous columns of smoke rose like fluffy cotton wool pillars.

"How we all doing?" said Chris.

Amy smiled, "I'm ok, how are you, feeling any better?"

"A little bit." He had a booming headache, his jaw was stiff as a board, and his eye felt puffier than a pack of Wotsits.

He nodded sheepishly to Terry, "How's your head mate?"

"I'll survive."

"Put the telly on Nan," said Chris.

"Where's your Ps and Qs? Bloody hell," said Nan as she flicked on the TV with the remote.

Silence fell over everyone as Nan flicked through the channels.

Every channel, one after another, showed a still dark green screen with white writing:

Please be informed that the country is currently in a state of emergency. Citizens are ordered to stay indoors until notified by official channels that it is safe to return outside. This is a national security directive and will be enforced in the strongest possible terms, with no prejudice.

"What the bloody hell does that mean?" said Nan.
"It means," said Terry, "that if we go outside, you get shot."
"Dad?" said Nate his little face screwed up in worry.
"Don't worry son. I won't let anything happen to you," he hugged Nate.
"Sounds like a load of bollocks to me," said Chris. "They have to catch you first."
"But we can't stay in, can we?" said Amy, "After what you said yesterday about having to get away from the city?"
"No we can't," said Terry, "Look, they just want an excuse to shoot anyone, so once all this is sorted out they don't have to fight a load of cases of murder."
"Typical bizzies, bunch of twats," said Chris.
"Language," said Nan, nodding towards Nate.
"Sorry Nan," said Chris.
"Is it dangerous to leave then?" said Amy.
Terry rested his hand on Amy's arm. Chris pretended not to notice. "Don't worry. I think we ignore it. What do you reckon Chris?"
Chris nodded. "They'll be too busy with the zombies to bother about us. I reckon we still get out of here."
Nan cleared away the empty plates. "Well, that's decided then," she said.
"You said you had a plan," said Amy.
"Yeah, let's hear it," said Terry.
Chris settled into place, all eyes on him. "Right, I've been out

on the roads, pretty dangerous out there," he glanced at Amy, "cars are all over the place, zombies everywhere. Reckon it will be a bit better today. Most people won't be driving I reckon."

"Why not?"

"They'll be dead, they'll be zombies, or they'll be hiding out," Chris counted of his reasons matter-of-factly on his fingers.

"Oh, God save us," said Nan.

"So we want to get somewhere safe," continued Chris, "out of the city, before people come out of hiding and all the gangs get going."

"How do you know so much about this?" said Amy.

"It's in all the films. Standard survival stuff," said Chris.

"You watch all them Bear Grylls things too, don't you?" said Nan.

"Yeah, he's pretty good. Ex SAS and that."

"So, about the roads?" said Terry, getting impatient.

"Yeah, right," said Chris, " So we need something pretty hefty-like to get us to Wales - something we can all fit in, we can all get our stuff in, something that can handle messed up roads…"

He paused for effect. Everyone was waiting on his word.

"How about a Hummer?" he said.

"A what?" said Nan.

"Hummer," said Terry, "it's an American military vehicle, except some people have them as cars."

"Arnie has one," said Nate.

"Does he?" said Chris "Didn't know that."

"Yeah, he got one years ago."

Chris nodded, it seemed like the sort of car Arnie should have.

"Hummer would be nice," said Terry, "but don't reckon they'd have many round here." Terry held up his arms. "Hardly LA hills is it?"

Chris took a sip of tea. "I know exactly where there's one."

He paused again for more effect.

"Bloody hell Chris," said Amy, "will you just tell us?"

"Ok, sorry. Simeon has one in his lock up."

Nan threw up her hands. "Oh, I should have known he'd have something to do with this. Thought you didn't hang about with him anymore?"

"I don't!" said Chris. "I just saw it a few weeks ago. Big bloody thing. We'd all get in that."

"So we steal it? From Simeon?" said Amy. "You're off your head, you."

"Good at stealing, aren't you Chris?" said Terry. "Maybe we bang him on the head with a bat."

"He'd deserve it though," said Nan. "Nasty piece of work."

"Drug dealer," said Amy. "Messes up all the kids around here. Thinks he's some sort of drug lord. Right nobhead."

"Ok," said Terry. "So let's say this Simeon fella hasn't already done a runner, how do you reckon we get this Hummer?"

"I told you, I know where it is. We can rob it," said Chris.

"Guess you don't need the keys, do you?" said Terry.

"Reckon we might do with a Hummer. Has microchips and all that."

"So we'll have to do the same you did with me? Get the keys of Simeon?" said Terry.

Nan shook her head. "Don't like the sound of this, he's mad that Simeon fella, a proper baddun."

"Don't worry Nan," said Chris. "I reckon me and Terry can handle it."

"Do you now, soft lad?" said Terry.

"I do," said Chris.

Chapter 10

Simeon's apartment was on the top floor. He had a network of scallie spies dotted around the high rise estate, ready to let Simeon know if the bizzies were coming. Being on the top floor meant he had plenty of time to prepare.

That's what Chris used to do, be one of Simeon's spies. It had given him some status and stopped others from messing with him. Of course, it didn't stop Simeon from messing with him, but that would have happened whether Chris worked for him or not, so it had been a no-brainer.

After keeping dixie for a few years he started doing little drug runs round around the estate, then robberies, then beatings, then moved onto having his own territory, down by the docks.

And then the zombie apocalypse.

Chris and Terry stood by the door of Simeon's flat. Music blared out from further up the hall. Some RnB shit. Chris preferred his music sixties and seventies, proper Rolling Stones and Led Zepplin. Dylan too, of course.

Chris held his hand up to signal Terry to stay still. He pressed his ear against Simeon's door and listened.

He heard nothing.

That didn't mean anything of course.

Anxiety built up in Chris's stomach. The next move would be declaring war on Simeon, and there would be no turning back.

Of course, Simeon might not be in the flat, he may have done a runner. Or turned into a zombie. Chris hoped he'd turned into a zombie.

"I can't hear anything," said Chris. "Reckon we check it out."

Terry nodded and motioned for Chris to stand clear.

Terry took a deep breath, raised his leg and kicked against the door.

It shuddered violently in the frame, made a huge banging noise, but didn't give.

"Keep going Terry, these doors are shit. Cheap crap."

Terry nodded and kicked again.

A door opened further up the hall, and a teenager with a shaved head popped his head out. His eye's opened wide.

"What the fuck are you doing? Simeon's going to kill you!"

There were no phones, no internet. No-one could get hold of Simeon to tell him.

"Wind your fucking head in or you're next."

The teenager held up his hands and retreated back to his flat.

"One more," said Terry. He kicked hard and the wood around the lock splintered. Another kick and the door flung open.

Terry ran in first, the baseball bat held high in his hands. Chris followed.

They ran into the lounge, where Chris had received his beating the previous morning. It seemed like a world away.

Terry whistled, impressed, as he looked around the room. Brand new stereo system. Massive flat screen that took up half the front wall. Smooth leather couches. An intricate eastern rug. Beautiful glass tables. Modern art.

But no Simeon.

"What now?" said Terry.

"Keys, look for keys. Could be anywhere."

They started to tear the place apart. Terry went to work in the kitchen, pulling open drawers, cupboards, looking in all the appliances.

Chris went into the bedroom and pulled the black silk sheets off the bed. Pulled all Simeon's expensive clothes off the rack. Emptied all the drawers.

He found the trashing of Simeon's apartment deeply satisfying. He ripped some of Simeon's expensive shirts. He ripped the silk sheets. He pulled the pillows off the bed and- he paused.

"Terry, check this out!"

Chris picked up the gun that had been under the pillow and ran into the kitchen. He held up the weapon, a wide grin on his face.

"Bloody hell," said Terry. "You know how to use that?"

"Course I do," said Chris, checking to see if the gun was loaded. It was. "Loaded n'all. Nice."

"Be careful though eh?"

Chris dismissed him, put on the safety, and tucked the gun in the back of his belt. "Those keys must be here somewhere."

Chris looked in the lounge. He pulled the cushions out of the couch, turned over the glass coffee table. He pulled the large flatscreen off the wall, which fell to the floor with a massive crash.

Chris surveyed the destruction of Simeon's flat, and he was pleased. He just hoped Simeon would come back to find it.

"Bingo!" shouted Terry.

"You found them?" said Chris.

"I have! In the bloody Rice Krispies." He pointed to the emptied cereal box on the kitchen table.

"Nice," said Chris.

Movement in the corner of Chris's eye. It was a split second, but enough to save his life. He dived to the left, away from the corridor. A gunshot sounded, and the lounge window shattered.

He landed on the floor but scrambled up and ran into the

kitchen. Terry jumped back out of his way and grabbed the baseball bat, holding it high in the air, ready to strike.

Chris aimed the gun at the wall that separated the kitchen and the corridor. The sound of heavy footsteps, running.

Chris let off a volley of shots into the wall. Plaster sprayed into the air.

A yell of pain and a thumping sound.

Chris darted out of the kitchen and ran to the corridor. It was Tony, the man who had beaten him yesterday. He was on the floor, holding his neck, blood was pumping out over his fingers and onto his white shirt.

Chris raised the gun and fired three more times, the bullets hitting Tony in the chest, and one in his head. Tony slumped back.

Terry appeared.

"Bloody hell," he said. "That one of Simeon's guys?"

"Yeah. He's a nobhead. Was a nobhead, I mean."

Chris was shaking, he could hardly hold the gun. He tucked it back into his belt. He rubbed his face and ran his hands through his hair. He breathed fast and panicked, like a rabbit who had just escaped from the hounds.

Terry put his hand on his shoulder. "That the first time you shot someone?"

Chris nodded.

"Alright lad. Let's get out of here. We've got what we need."

Terry leaned down to the body and took Tony's gun. He searched the pockets and found a knife and another magazine for the gun.

"You'll have to show me how to use this," said Terry.

Chris nodded. "I will do. Hey Terry?"

"Yeah?"

"Don't tell me, Nan, ok?"

"No worries. Won't say nothing."

"Ta, lad."

Chapter 11

The lockup was a good ten minutes walk from the high rise.

"We'll go get the Hummer first, then come back and get the others," said Chris. They set off from the apartment, quickly but cautiously.

Not trusting the lifts, they took the stairs.

"The power will go any minute," said Chris. "Sure of it. Don't want to be in a lift when it does."

When they got to the entrance of the high rise, the gang of lads from before were there.

"Alright," said Benno.

"Yeah, sound," said Chris.

A few eyes were on Terry. Looking at his size. His head.

"What happened to your head mate?" said one of the lads.

"Banged it," said Terry.

The lad said nothing but continued to look at Terry.

"Where you off?" said Benno.

"Going for a walk," said Chris. He motioned to Terry to follow them.

"Dangerous going for a walk at the moment. Them zombies are everywhere."

Chris shrugged. "We can handle it."

"Need anyone to look after your Nan while you're gone?"

Chris stopped walking. He turned to face Benno.

"Why, what do you think's going to happen to her?"

Benno shrugged. "Don't know mate. Anything could happen with these zombies around. Thought you might want us to keep an eye out."

Chris shook his head slowly but was careful to try and not let his anger show. "Nah, reckon she'll be alright. We'll only be gone ten minutes."

"Whatever you reckon mate."

Chris and Terry walked away.

When out of earshot of the gang, Terry said, "I see what you mean. They'll be feral by the end of the day. Soon as they realise the bizzies won't be round... Jesus."

"That's why we need to get out of here. Bad enough fighting zombies, never mind them little pricks n'all. They're like terriers, bloody hundreds of them. Let's hurry up and get this done."

They broke into a jog and ran through the car park, into the back alleys of the estate.

They met their first zombie within a minute, round the corner.

Terry shouted in surprise and swung his bat, almost a reflex action. It connected with the zombie, a clean strike. The zombie shook its head and stood stunned. Terry took another swing, and it fell to the floor, blood spurting over the fence of the small alley they were in.

They moved quickly, meeting a few more zombies, but luckily no more than two at a time.

They arrived at a large yard, lines of garages.

"This where you saw it?" said Terry.

"Aye, that one there, number 40."

"Think he'd put a Hummer somewhere a bit more secure."

"Everyone know's it's his lock up. You'd have to be a fucking nutter to break in."

Four zombies shuffled in at the far end of the yard. Looked like a group of nurses, blue uniforms covered in blood. Skin and unidentified organs hanging randomly from their bodies. Large rips in the flesh on their faces, arms, legs.

All moaning, excited.

"Here," said Terry handing the lockup keys to Chris. "I'll sort this lot out. Best keep the numbers down while we can."

Chris took the key and ran to the garage door. He held his breath and tried the key. It turned and clicked.

He let out a sigh of relief.

A quick glance to check that Terry was handling the zombies; he was, his bat swinging hard to the left and right. Dull clanging thuds and flying brain matter. Bodies falling to the ground, dead for the second time.

Chris opened the lockup door, it moved with a loud metal screech.

The Hummer.

It sat in the darkness, black and gleaming. He had seen it driving around the estate many times, as out of place as a priest at a disco. Simeon had always driven slow, made sure everyone saw him in his black killer whale of a car, made sure everyone knew the power, the money he had at his disposal.

Well, it's mine now nobhead, thought Chris

He pressed the button on the key, and the Hummer's lights flashed, and a few beeps sounded. Open. Chris smiled.

"Come on Terry, we got it," shouted Chris.

He squeezed down the side of the lockup, opened the door and got in. Leather upholstery, shining, gleaming, brand new. Looked after.

The engine started cleanly and at once - a far cry from Chris's old Vauxhall that chugged and rattled for a good few minutes before the engine held. Chris laughed. "Nice."

Terry opened the passenger's door and climbed in. His massive frame easily accommodated in the ample space of the Hummer.

"It's alight this," said Terry looking around the interior. "Nice find," he smiled at Chris.

A zombie appeared at the front of the lockup. It was an old man in a well turned out suit, probably a dapper chap a few days ago. Now, a shuffling bloody mess. It held up a bony hand at the Hummer, clicked its teeth in that weird way they did, and walked towards them.

"Let's try it out then," Chris revved the engine, put the Hummer into drive and put his foot on the accelerator.

The Hummer took off, fast, the wheels screeching loudly in the confines of the lockup. The zombie received all two and a half tonnes of vehicle square in its chest. It flew back across the yard, and hit the opposite lockup, leaving a bloody mark on the door.

Chris hit the brakes hard to stop them from hitting the same door.

"Easy lad!" shouted Terry.

"Don't worry about it."

The zombie they had just hit crawled along the floor towards them. Chris drove slowly over its head, a satisfying crunch sound under the vehicle as the zombie's skull was crushed.

He turned the wheel and drove out of the yard at speed, bumping over the zombie bodies that Terry had left.

When they got back to the high rise, Benno's gang of scallies where nowhere to be seen.

"Glad them numb nuts have gone," said Chris. "Reckon they would have given us all sorts of grief with this Hummer."

They had left their mark though. A car was on fire in the far corner of the car park. It burned brightly. The fire sounded a low rumble, occasionally popping as car parts burst and exploded. It was the only sound in the otherwise silence. None of the usual shouting, music, kids playing, traffic noise.

"Weird isn't it?" said Chris.

"No people," said Terry. "That's the worst of it. You reckon everyone is a zombie?"

"That, or dead."

"Or hiding out I guess."

"We should get a move on," said Chris, feeling afraid. The atmosphere was taking on a malevolent feel, something he couldn't explain.

"I'll go up and get the others, reckon you stay here and look after the Hummer," said Chris.

Terry shook his head. "No way mate. If we're getting my son down from up there, I'll be going up. You stay here."

Chris was about to protest, but when he turned to look at Terry, he saw in his eyes it was useless to argue. Chris had only seen eyes like that once before; some Mum with her son was in a newsagent Chris had been robbing. He reckoned she would have killed him if he'd gone anywhere near the boy.

"Ok," said Chris. "You want me to show you how to use the gun?"

"Yeah, but be quick."

Chris went through loading the weapon, taking off the safety, how to aim, fire, and explained the kick he was going to get.

"Most people shit themselves when they see a gun, so if it's people, you probably won't have to worry," said Chris.

Terry nodded, leaving the vehicle, tucking the gun into his belt. "Prefer this anyhow," he held the baseball bat sternly in both hands.

Chris watched Terry run into the stairwell of the flats - they had parked right outside. Terry disappeared up the stairs. Fourteen floors, it would take him a while to get there, but Terry looked fit. Chris was sure he could handle it.

Terry took the stairs at a steady pace. He was used to stairs, he had run up thousands and thousands in his time, usually with his fire kit on his back, so this was nothing. He was careful though, he wanted to preserve his energy - he wasn't going to fight fires this time, he didn't know what he might have to fight.

His footsteps echoed eerily against the bare concrete of the stairwell. He peered around every corner carefully and looked up ahead. His ears strained for sound, but nothing except his footsteps.

On the seventh floor, however, he heard a scream. It was low pitched, maybe a man. Terry was satisfied it was from the floor he was on, so it wasn't Nate.

He kept going up, one careful step after another.

Chris was nervous. His eyes darted around the car park like a cat stealing food.

Movement to the right, his head snapped around. A small black shape took off into the air; it let out a loud caw sound. A crow.

Chris' heart raced. A fucking crow and he nearly filled his pants.

It was the sitting still, the waiting, the not moving that was giving him the fear. He needed to be doing something.

He took out the gun and counted his bullets. He took the safety off.

He gripped the gun handle, holding it up, moving it in whatever direction he looked, ready to fire.

Hurry up, Terry.

Terry reached the fourteenth floor with no incident.

He hoped that Nate and the others had got all the stuff packed as he had told them. Essentials only, tinned foodstuff, blankets. They would have to pick up any other stuff they needed on the move. Nan didn't seem to have much in her apartment they could use. Just full of useless trinkets.

He knocked on the door. "It's me, Terry, we're back."

The door opened cautiously, and Nan peered through the gap.

"Oh thank God, youse alright? Where's Chris?"

"He's down with the Hummer"

The door opened fully. Terry walked in, and Nate ran towards him, jumping up into his arms. "Dad!"

"You alright big man? You been looking after this lot?"

"He's done a great job," said Amy smiling. "I'm glad you're alright."

"So you got this car then?" said Nan.

"We do. And we need to go. You got everything packed?"

Nan pointed to some bags on the couch. "That's everything."

They each grabbed a bag.

Terry noticed that Nan was crying.

"Are you ok?"

Nan nodded. "I'll be alright, just a silly old woman. I'll never be coming back here, will I?"

"You never know," said Amy. "Once everything is sorted out, you can come back."

Nan wiped her eyes. "I'm sure you're right. I'm just being daft."

Terry felt sorry for the old woman. He didn't know how long she had lived there, but it looked like leaving was difficult for her. He didn't think she would be coming back to the flat, ever.

Nan picked up the binoculars and the picture of Gerry. She put them in the bag she was carrying.

"Ok, I'm ready. Let's go."

Chapter 12

Chris eyed the growing group of zombies on the far side of the car park. They had arrived a few minutes ago. First one, then another, then another.

Luckily they didn't seem interested in coming towards the high rise - the belching grey smoke and roaring flames of the car held their attention well.

Even so, Chris kept his head down and tried to stay still. How did they find people, he wondered. Smell? Vision? Movement?

Chris still gripped the gun in his right hand. The baseball bat was sitting on the passenger seat.

No sign of movement yet from the apartment block.

Come on Terry.

Apart from the zombies, everything was still, horribly still. Something in the atmosphere just felt wrong. Towers of smoke in the distance indicated tens of fires in the city and beyond.

Chris' heart missed a beat.

The other side of the car park - figures approaching. About ten.

Fast, not shuffling, not zombies.

Tracksuits, hoodies, balaclavas. They carried weapons. One of them raised what looked like a baseball bat and pointed it towards the Hummer.

The group parted, and a person that Chris recognised came to the front.

Simeon.

He was wearing jeans and a white t-shirt. It was covered in blood. There were no obvious cuts on him. Must be someone else's.

Still no sign of Terry and the others. Chris felt panic grip him. Simeon would be on him in seconds.

"Hey Chris," shouted Simeon. "Game over lad!"

Chris would probably be safe in the Hummer. He made sure the doors were locked.

But what about when Terry and the others got here? Simeon and his group would make mincemeat of them, even if Terry did have a gun. Maybe Simeon had one too.

No, he would have it out already.

Chris had an idea.

He wound the window down an inch. He pushed the barrel of the gun out the gap, pointed it towards the approaching gang. He pulled the trigger.

The effect was immediate.

Simeon's crew dived in behind cars.

The zombies let out a loud moan and turned towards the bang. They saw the hiding scallies and began their lumbering walk towards them, their groans taking on a feverish pitch.

They could definitely tell the difference between a burning car and living flesh, that's for sure.

Terry, Nan, Nate, and Amy paused on the stairs.

It was hard to tell where the gunshot had come from, its sound ricocheting around the concrete stairwell made it directionless.

"Was that a gun?" said Nan.

"I reckon," said Terry. He took out his gun and held it uncertainly. He didn't feel comfortable, or powerful, with a gun. He felt like a kid who didn't know what he was doing.

"What do we do?" said Amy. Their voices echoed loudly in the relative silence after the gunshot.

"The same as before, just a bit more slowly. Let's be careful." Terry motioned for them to continue down the stairs.

Simeon shouted from behind a car. "You can't hide in there forever Chris, what happens when Nan gets down here then?"

A few of the scallies ran from behind the cars and towards the zombies. They started to plow through them with their baseball bats, axes, and spades. Blood and fragments of bone scattered into the air.

But more zombies, a lot more, were arriving from different sides of the car park.

Chris let go another shot.

Simeon made a dash from behind one car to another. Chris fired a few times but missed.

Benno darted in behind the same car as Simeon. Chris fired again.

The shots were attracting a lot of attention. It must have been the only sound for miles. The sound cracked through the air. Zombies were now arriving in their tens, squeezing into the car park, in between the cars.

Simeon's gang had their work cut out for them, but they were smashing and slashing their way through the crowd of undead with relish. They looked like they were enjoying it. Violence and death with no consequences.

A blur of movement as Simeon darted from one car to another, closer. He was now only about ten yards away.

Chris let out a volley of shots. The bullets splintered the car's frame and shattered the windows.

Benno and another scallie joined Simeon. Chris fired twice, and then the gun clicked.

Bollocks. Out of ammo.

"You bloody idiot," said Chris to himself.

"You never were the brightest," said Simeon, standing up, a triumphant grin on his face. "Let's be having you."

He ran towards the Hummer, holding his baseball bat high.

Chris quickly fumbled the window up. Just in time. Simeon smashed his bat against the glass.

The window vibrated, but it held, no problem. The bat bounced off harmlessly.

Simeon slapped his palm onto the window and brought his face close up to the glass. He pointed at Chris.

"Best go have a word with your Nan then," said Simeon.

Benno appeared next to Chris, "Gonna get you, ya nobhead! And your Nan!"

They ran into the high rise.

Chris gripped the steering wheel. He squeezed tight, his knuckles going white.

He yelled.

Terry and the others ran down the stairs, ignoring the gunshots from below. They reached the third floor and stopped. They heard shouting.

Terry held the gun out in front of him as he had seen cops do in American TV shows.

"Nate, stay behind me, got that?"

The young boy nodded, his eyes wide with fear and excitement.

They reached the landing of the second floor, and there was the sound of a door banging shut from below.

Terry held up his hand to stop the others and then held his finger to his mouth to indicate silence.

Footsteps running up the stairs. Echoing rudely in the silence.

Terry held the gun up and pointed it at the top of the stairwell.

A shaved head appeared.

"Benno?" said Amy.

Another head appeared; swarthy, dark hair, small eyes.

"Simeon!" shouted Nan.

Terry let off a shot, he didn't even think. The word, the name, had been like an ignitor switch.

The bullet ricocheted off the wall, missing Simeon's head by a few feet.

Benno and Simeon retreated back down the stairs.

Chris heard a shot from inside the high rise.

That must have been Terry.

Chris surveyed the car park. The zombies were filling the far edges, moving in like a wall. The scallies were doing their best to keep at bay, but were slowly being overrun.

One of them, in a green Adidas t-shirt, was up against a white van, three zombies surrounding him. He swung wildly with his ax and cleaved the top of one head, but the other heads locked onto his shoulders. Bright red blood spurted across the van, like some abstract painting they'd have in some art gallery.

The zombies were keeping the scallies at bay, but not for long.

Chris had to move.

He slid over to the passenger side which was nearest the entrance to the high raise. He grabbed the baseball bat, took a deep breath and opened the Hummer door.

He jumped out and ran into the high rise. Shouts and moans from the scallies vs. zombie battle behind him followed him into the high rise, then took on a tinny quality as he ran up the stairs.

He heard another shot.

Terry ran to the top of the stairwell and fired again at the retreating figures. Simeon disappeared around the corner.

"Wait there," shouted Terry to those behind him.

"Dad!" shouted Nate, his face taking on a forlorn look. Amy put her arm around him.

"It's alright Nate, wait there."

Terry walked cautiously down the stairs, his gun out in front of him, his nerves causing his finger to twitch at the slightest sound or movement.

"Take it easy lad…" he whispered to himself as he approached the corner.

Chris accelerated up the stairs.

He bumped into someone coming down. He tried to keep his balance, but lost it and slipped forward, landing on his face. His bat bounced out of his hand.

He felt a quick sharp pain to the side of his cheek. He'd been kicked hard. Stars zoomed around his vision.

There was a loud bang, and he felt another pain, this one in his shoulder, hot and biting. He let out a loud cry and rolled to the left, trying to get away from whatever was attacking him.

Terry saw a melee of figures on the landing.

The one on the floor was Chris, and the two standing were Benno and Simeon.

Terry pulled the trigger.

Chris let out a cry, grabbed his shoulder and rolled to his left.

"Shit," said Terry.

He fired again, and blood burst from Benno's chest.

Simeon jumped over Chris and ran down the stairs before Terry could get another shot off.

Chris got up. He took his hand away from his shoulder, it was covered in blood. The bullet had glanced off his shoulder. It wasn't deep. Even though, it hurt.

"You shot me you dickhead!" he said to Terry.

"Now we're even," said Terry.

The sound of a door slamming from below.

Simeon.

"Shit, the keys to the Hummer," said Chris, "Still in there."

Terry and Chris leaped down the stairs.

They got to the bottom and ran out of the high rise, Simeon

was in the Hummer and was starting up the engine.

Terry raised his gun and fired at the Hummer as it pulled away into the car park.

"Don't bother," said Chris, "Proper bulletproof."

Chris ran after the Hummer. Terry followed.

The Hummer pulled to the left and right. It ran over zombies and crashed into stationary cars sending them sliding to the left and right.

"Hey!" shouted one of the scallies, seeing Simeon making his escape. He joined the chase.

The Hummer ran into a thick bunch of zombies, and its bonnet rose into the sky as it rolled over the bodies. Simeon lost control, and the vehicle spun to the right, crashing into a parked white van.

Before he could reverse, the chasing scallie pulled open the door.

"Where you going nobhead?"

He grabbed Simeon by the shoulders and yanked at him, trying to dislodge him from the Hummer.

In turn, a zombie grabbed the lad from behind sank its teeth into the back of his head. Blood spurted with a nasty squelch.

Simeon tried to pull the door closed, but the zombie fell into the Hummer, blocking the door.

Chris and Terry held their distance as many zombies congregated on the vehicle.

Rotten and bloody hands pulled at Simeon and yanked him out of the driver's seat. He let out a yell as teeth sunk into his flesh, ripping and tearing at his muscle and skin. Blood fountained into the air as an artery was pierced. Pink tubes of intestines were fought over, and a dripping juicy heart was held high by one zombie as the others struggled to grab it.

"Fuckin' hell," said Terry.

Chris smiled, "Couldn't happen to a nicer bloke."

Moans from behind. Zombies were approaching.

A scallie lay dead a few feet away. A large ax was in his hand.

Terry picked it up.

"We need that Hummer," said Terry, feeling the weight of the ax.

By now, at least ten zombies stood around the Hummer, picking apart the remains of Simeon and the scallie.

"You ready?" said Chris, holding his baseball high.

"Let's do it," said Terry.

Chris ran forward. "Come on then you undead nobheads!"

Chapter 13

Nan, Amy, and Nate stood on the stairs. Shots.
Terry said something to Chris, their voices floating up the stairs. Then the sound of their footsteps as they ran away.
"Where's me dad going?" said Nate.
"Don't you worry son," said Nan, resting her hands on Nate's shoulders, squeezing gently. "Your dad'll be back."
Amy walked slowly to the edge of the stair-well and peered around the corner.
She put her hand to her mouth and gasped.
"What is it?" said Nan.
"It's Benno, he's dead."
"Oh God save us," said Nan as she pulled Nate closer.
"What do we do Nan?" said Amy.
They couldn't stand here, on this stairwell. It was cold, it smelled, and it was terrifying to be surrounded by concrete with the world falling apart outside.
"Let's get downstairs, and get these bags down." Nan gently

pushed Nate towards the pile of bags. "We gonna have to get out of here quickly."

Between them, they picked up the bags and lugged them down the stairs onto the ground floor.

Nan realised they had made a mistake.

Outside was teeming with the zombies. Loads of the young scallies from the estate were running around with makeshift weapons, fighting them, and getting killed by them.

A fire burnt in the corner of the car park. It belched thick black smoke into the sky, its burning roar the background to the shouts, moans, and screams that filled the air.

Chris and Terry were nowhere to be seen. Nan felt panic spread through her. She squeezed her hand to her chest as a tight pain reminded her she was no longer young.

Nate ran to the door of the high rise. He pointed to the far end of the car park, "Look! It's me dad!"

"Wait, Nate, wait!" shouted Nan.

"Stop," shouted Amy.

But Nate didn't listen. He charged out into the standing battle in the car park.

"You bloody idiot," said Nan, under her breath, to herself. They should have stayed put.

"Stay here Nan," said Amy, "I'll go get him."

"No you won't, girl," said Nan, gripping Amy's hand. "You stay here with the stuff."

"But Nan, I'll-"

"Listen to me girl. This ain't a place for young'uns, you understand?"

Nan took her frying pan out of one of the bags. "You stay here, got it?"

Amy nodded.

Nan walked quickly, almost jogged, out into the car park, trying to ignore the pain in her dodgy hip.

A zombie appeared to her left. It was Mr. Kapoor from the Chemist's. His white coat was covered in patches of blood, and one of his eyes was hanging out, like them joke glasses you could get in Southport.

He reached a bloodied hand towards Nan.

She swung the frying pan hard, connecting with Mr. Kapoor's skull with a dull clang. He tottered, and Nan hit him again. His head cracked, and he fell.

"Sorry, Mr. Kapoor," said Nan.

There was a high cry from ahead. Nate was on the floor, two zombies were closing in on him. He must have fallen.

"Hey!" shouted Nan, "Leave him alone, you pair of nobheads!"

She broke into a run. Her hips, and now her knees too, cried out in pain. She swung the frying pan and connected with another zombie, Mrs. Grantham from the church group. She always was a stuck-up bint, always going on about her Jack going to Uni. Nan felt satisfaction as Mrs. Grantham's skull cracked.

A third zombie lurched for Nan, but she managed to get out of the way and swing the frying pan again to hit this zombie, who she didn't recognise, hard on the back of the head. It lost balance and fell onto the bonnet of a white Subaru. She swung again, and again. The skull cracked, and a portion of brain spilled out onto the hood of the car.

She lent over and helped Nate up.

Nate was unable to speak, his face white with fear. He pointed to the other side of the car park.

The Hummer. Surrounded by zombies. Chris and Terry were running towards the group.

Nate tugged on Nan's hand, but she couldn't move. He tugged harder. "Come on Nan!"

Her left hip had stopped. It was frozen, she couldn't move her leg. Excruciating pain tore up the side of her body.

She grimaced through the pain. "You go and stay with Amy."

"But me dad?"

Nan shook her head. "Your dad can manage himself. You go look after Amy."

"What about you?"

"I'll be alright son."

Nate looked at Nan, he looked at her hand on her hip, and he looked carefully at her face. She tried to hide her pain.

"I'm staying with you," said the boy.

Nan opened her mouth to speak, but the air was sucked from her throat. A bang, louder than anything Nan had ever heard, surrounded her. Then she flew through the air.

Nate's hand slipped from hers.

Chris raised and hammered down his baseball bat with one fluid motion, landing on the nearest zombie's skull with an audible and jarring crack. The zombie dropped to the ground like a lead weight, its brains spilling out of its shattered skull.

To his right, Terry did the same with his ax, hewing to the left and right, his muscular arms and shoulders having no trouble smashing to pieces the frail remains of humans in front of them.

It was easy, thought Chris. They were too busy eating Simeon and Benno to realise that a second death was upon them. The only danger, thought Chris, was getting tired with all the baseball bat swinging. Terry didn't seem to have any trouble, but then he was one of them muscle men.

The moans diminished as the number of zombies fell. Terry and Chris soon cleared the ten or so zombies that had crowded in around the Hummer.

Simeon's body lay at the centre of the scrum. His torso had been shredded, all soft tissue and organs ripped from his insides. His ribs lay exposed, decorated with threads of guts and sinews of flesh like a macabre Christmas tree.

"What a fucking mess," said Terry, turning his nose up at the sight.

"Couldn't have happened to a nicer bloke," said Chris.

More moans from behind them.

"Come on, we've got to get out of here," said Terry. "Give me the keys."

"What? No fucking way."

"We haven't got time for this. You ever driven anything this big?"

"No. Have you?"

"How about a fucking fire engine," said Terry.

"You a fireman?"

"Yes, nobhead."

Chris begrudgingly held out the keys.

He crawled across to the passenger side.

Terry got in next to him and closed the door.

Just in time.

The sky lit up in a fierce yellow. A huge boom sounded, followed by a loud ringing, Chris not sure if it was his ears or the world. The Hummer shook violently to the left and right. A deep vibration drilled through Chris's body.

Pieces of metal and wood rained down on the windscreen.

"What the fuck?" shouted Chris, instinctively shielding his face, even though everything bounced harmlessly of the strengthened glass.

"Something's exploded - look!" Terry pointed to the corner of the car park.

Where one car had been burning, there was now four cars and a van burning.

"Fucking hell…" said Chris.

Deep red flames licked high from the vehicles, black smoke tumbled skyward, blacking out the sun.

"Heat must have set off the petrol in the others," said Terry. "We got to get out of here. Whole car park could go up."

"Let's go then nobhead!"

Terry put the Hummer into reverse, and the powerful engine rolled over the many zombie bodies and pushed the cars behind out of the way.

He quickly drove the fifty or so yards back to the apartment. The car park was scattered with burning pieces of debris. Zombies, some on fire, shuffled through the wreckage. A few dazed scallies were running away. Some were being eaten.

They pulled up outside the high rise. Chris wound down the window, there was Amy.

"Come on," he shouted, banging on the side of the door.

Amy shook her head, "Where's Nan and Nate?"

"What?" shouted Terry leaning over, "He's not with you?"

"He ran to try and find you," said Amy, standing at the side of the Hummer. "Nan legged after him."

"Fuck!" shouted Chris. He jumped out the Hummer. "Get in here, and close the door."

Terry jumped out the other side. He shouted across the bonnet to Chris, "Let's split up, you take the left, I'll go right."

Chris charged into the burning landscape of twisted metal, smoking carcasses, and hungry zombies. His body was charged with fear and anger. Mainly anger. Everything in him always turned into anger at the end. His love for Nan was now anger. He raged through the car park, swinging his bat to the left and right, hard, infused with an energy that came from right inside him.

A scallie ran out from behind a van. He held up his hands, "Chris, it's me, Davo!"

Too late. Chris swung his bat and cracked Davo's skull into pieces. It shattered apart into a bloody red mess.

He ran past a blue Merc into an area of six empty parking spaces. There was Nan.

She was on the floor, next to a white BMW. A piece of large metal stuck out of the boot of the BMW, burnt black and smoking.

It had missed Nan by a few feet.

She was awake, but he could tell she was in pain.

A zombie was behind her, only a few feet away. It had seen her, and Nan had seen it, but she wasn't running. Why wasn't she running?

"Nan! Fucking move will ya!" Chris ran towards her.

"Me hip's gone," she shouted.

Another shout, this one high pitched, a young boy. Nate.

Chris, only yards away from Nan looked to his left. Nate was on the floor. Two zombies held onto a leg each, pulling themselves to Nate. They would be on him in seconds. They would be chewing on his leg in seconds.

Nate's eyes locked with Chris, wide with terror, tears flowing from his young face. He held his arms to Chris. He screamed.

Chris looked at Nan. She shook her head and pointed at Nate, "Get him, lad, don't be a bloody idiot!"

Chris listened to Nan, he couldn't allow himself to think. He had to shut his mind off. Just like when he was a young boy, do what Nan tells you to do.

He ran towards Nate and brought his bat down hard on the zombies. Smash, smash. Blood squirted onto the wheel of the nearby car and all over his face.

Nate was screaming.

Someone else was screaming.

Nan.

The zombie had reached her and was biting into her neck. Blood covered its face. Nan's arms and legs shook uncontrollably like an out of control doll. She let out a warbling gurgling scream. The zombie pulled away, ripping out a tendon, then peeled back the skin all the way down Nan's arm.

Chris picked up Nate and ran towards Nan. He used his free arm to hit the zombie on the head, the power coming from his one arm enough to shatter the skull of the fucker.

A few seconds. That was all. A few seconds too late. He'd fucked up again.

Nan shook like she was having a fit. Chris kneeled beside her and let Nate down. Tears poured from his eyes. He started to shake, too. He felt as if his heart had been ripped out.

"Nan! Don't die, I'm sorry, come on Nan, I need you."

Nan tried to speak, but her voice came out as a bloody gurgle. She held up her arm slowly and rested it on Chris's cheek.

"No," said Chris. Then he shouted it. He embraced Nan.

Someone pulled on his shoulder, a steady hand.

"Dad!" shouted Nate.
"Come on, we have to go!" It was Terry.
Chris fought against the hand, he didn't want to let Nan go, but there wasn't any fight left. He let himself be dragged away.

Chapter 14

Chris was in the backseat. He didn't remember much of the escape from Liverpool.

Terry drove the Hummer through the city, pushing vehicles out of the way, avoiding and running over zombies, outrunning people trying to stop them. Outrunning the fires.

It had taken a good few hours to get out of the city. They headed south and east, back inland so they could cross the Mersey at the Runcorn bridge. Using the tunnel didn't seem like a good idea.

They didn't see too many other cars. But plenty of zombies, and plenty of people. Gangs of people, running, fighting. Families together. People on their own, young children on their own. Amy wanted them to stop and help, but Terry said no. He said that it would be too dangerous.

"Remember the Titanic? When the rescue boats went back, they were swamped. They sank. That would be us. You don't think people will fight and kill to get this Hummer?"

Terry tried to keep them on the smallest roads, the little country roads that threaded through the Cheshire fields. Sometimes they had to hit the main roads, but when they did, Terry would use the road as a guide and drive the Hummer in fields next to the road. The Hummer seemed to be able to go anywhere. It had been a hell of an idea.

They headed towards Wales and the mountains. It was early evening before they passed the border.

Chris spent most of the journey in silence. The others had left him alone. They felt their own sorrow for Nan, but they didn't dare guess how it had affected Chris.

Chris was trying to find the anger that had helped when his mum died, but it was wasn't there.

All he found was nothing, a blank. He was a blank. No emotion left.

Amy had put her arm around him and whispered soothing words through her own tears, but he felt none of that.

He had never built up a wall around Nan. He never thought Nan would let him down, would leave, at least not without warning.

Zombies. Fucking zombies.

There it was. The anger, a hint of it, at least.

He looked out the window, they were driving across a field, slowly. A main road was beside them, but it was full of traffic and fires.

Figures wandered along the road, despondent, lost, stumbling. Dead.

And beyond the main road were the futuristic towers of an industrial park by the sea. All the lights from the factories, which had once made it look like a set from a sci-fi film, were gone. Out of control fires raged instead, hundreds of fires. Huge fires. The sky was burnt yellow and orange and dirtied with smoke and floating black debris. It looked like the end of the world.

Chris sat up.

"We need to turn inland."

Terry glanced at him. "You alright mate?"

Chris nodded. "We need to turn inland. Get away from the sea. There're no people inland."

Terry looked around the field they were on. No shuffling figures, no marauding gangs. Just sheep.

He slowed the Hummer down and turned round to face Chris.

"Hey Chris, thanks. For saving Nate," said Terry.

Chris shrugged. "It's ok. No problem."

"But it was a problem. You did something for... I can't guess how hard it was." Terry was talking quietly. "I'll never forget what you did."

Nate turned around and smiled at Chris.

Chris felt something inside. Warmth. He pushed it away.

Amy held his hand, but he didn't really feel it.

Nate spoke to his dad, pointing out something on the map. Terry nodded and started up the Hummer again, turning left, south, away from the sea and towards the middle of Wales and the mountains, and no people.

Chris looked at the picture of Granddad that Nan had rescued from the flat. He didn't have a picture of Nan. He held the binoculars that she had also saved. He kept them close to his chest. He tried to fight the tears, but he couldn't.

No one had ever loved him like Nan. No one ever would. He was alone now.

Just him and the zombies. All the undead together.

Tower Block of the Dead

Plane Dead

Chapter 1

"That's strange."
"What is?"
"Still no response. Let's do another diagnostic. Make sure our radio isn't out of action."
"Ok, running diagnostics."
"I'll try the Tower again... This is flight WA-1254, Captain Andrew Bracknell to Tower. Acknowledge please."
No response. Just static.
"Diagnostics all look green, Andy,' said Peter, the co-pilot.
Andy keyed the transmitter again. "This is Captain Andrew Bracknell, WebAir flight WA-1254, Airbus A319-100 from Malaga, requesting acknowledgment from Manchester Tower."
Nothing.
"We've been in holding now for an hour, Andy," said Peter.
"We're still good for fuel."
Andy glanced at the fuel gauge, just to be sure. He had checked the indicator five times in the past ten minutes.

The plane shuddered for a few seconds. Turbulence. The holding pattern had them at cloud level. Grey, repeating, incessant cloud.

"When did we last hear from the Tower?" said Peter, looking over the instrumentation panel, a green and red glow from the numerous diodes and switches reflecting off his skin.

"About twenty minutes ago. Something must be wrong. How busy is the airspace?"

Peter looked over the radar. "They're stacking high."

"Not just us then, must be something wrong. Who's that?" He pointed at a small blip on the radar.

"That's WA-4657. Stewart and Mark."

"See if you can get them on the radio."

Peter turned a dial on his transmitter. "WA-4657, this is WA-1254. Stewart? Mark?"

There was a short pause, then a voice, grainy and slightly distorted. "Hi, it's Stewart. I guess you having trouble talking to ATC?"

"Hi Stewart," said Andy. "You think we have a situation?"

"Possibly," said Stewart. "Have you tried anyone else? We seem to be getting quite a stack here."

"Not yet. How's your fuel?" said Andy.

"Good. A few hours. You?"

He looked at Peter who mouthed a number to him, "We got another fifty-three minutes. We'll have to start approach somewhere, soon."

There was loud knocking on the cockpit door, and a voice from the other side, "Captain, it's me."

Andy glanced to the CCTV screen that linked to the cameras in the cabin. It was Jenny, the head stewardess. Andy had flown with her before, a good woman who had been flying for a good twenty years. Very capable.

Andy nodded to Peter who got up and opened the door.

Jenny looked flustered. "Captain, I think we have an issue."

"Ok, give me a minute." He spoke into the radio again.

"Stewart, I have to deal with something here. But see if you can start talking to any other planes - we're going to have to start landing, or spreading to other airports. Going to have to get some order sorted."

"Sure thing, Andy. I'll be back in touch."

Andy turned to Jenny. "What's up?"

"The passengers are getting very restless Captain, angry even. We're running out of excuses." She glanced at the radio. "Is something wrong?"

"There could be. We have no contact with the Tower. We lost it about twenty minutes ago."

Jenny's face scrunched into a worried expression.

"It's ok," said Andy. "We're going to sort out an approach pattern." He smiled.

"Ok, Captain," said Jenny, but she didn't look convinced. "What shall I tell the passengers?"

"I'll speak to them."

She looked relieved. "Another thing, we have an ill passenger."

"How ill?"

"Very. The other passengers don't want to sit next to him. They've been mentioning the virus."

"What symptoms is he showing?" said Andy.

"Sweating, fever, coughing, floating in and out of consciousness. The passengers nearby are demanding that we move him."

"Ok." Andy stared at the grey beyond the window, thinking. "We got any spare seats?"

Jenny shook her head.

"They'll have to stay put. Can we move the ill passenger to the back? Put them in the galley?"

Jenny paused. She looked scared herself. But she said, "Ok. I'll do that. How long is it until we land?"

"It'll be within the next fifty minutes. One way or another."

Peter let out a small laugh.

"Sorry?" said Jenny.

"Nothing, don't worry about it. You'd best get back to it Jenny, let me know if anything changes."

She nodded and left the cockpit. When she opened the door, Andy could hear raised voices. Anger. Fear.

"I'd best chat to the passengers," said Andy. He picked up the intercom. "This is your Captain speaking, ladies and gentlemen. I would like to apologise for the delay. We have been in a holding pattern around Manchester for the last hour due to adverse weather conditions on the ground. We've had some pretty thick fog, making landing difficult. The weather has lifted, so we are now in a queue and will be making our approach soon. I would like to apologise again and thank you for your patience in this matter. If there are any changes, I will let you know. We should be landing in the next forty minutes or so."

Andy put down the radio.

"You think that will do it?" said Peter.

"Let's hope so."

Chapter 2

Jenny waited until the Captain began his announcement before making her way to the back of the plane. Passengers listening to the Captain were less likely to bombard her with the same questions about landing, the hold-up, or the sick passenger.

Her plan worked until she got near the back of the plane where the sick passenger was sitting. His name was Frank. He was a man in his sixties, traveling with his wife, Tracy.

Tracy was arguing with a passenger next to her, a young man with a neat haircut, white T-shirt, and numerous tattoos.

"I understand what you're saying," said the man, "but we can't really risk it, can we? There's nothing to say he hasn't got the virus."

Those seated nearby sounded their agreement, their voices edged with an undercurrent of anger. Jenny looked over the surrounding passengers. Ordinary people, the people she saw every day in her job. Probably saw most of them two weeks ago, happy, chirpy, excited about their holiday. Now angry, full of blame. Scared.

"Where have you lot been?" A red-faced man pointed at Jenny. His eyes were wide open.

Jenny ignored him and leaned over to speak to Tracy and Frank.

Tracy was close to tears. She held her husband's hand tightly, her face screwed up in worry. Her breathing shallow.

Frank himself was struggling to breathe. Sharp, hard gasps. His eyes half open. Small dribbles of drool pooling on his chin.

"Tracy, can you and your husband come with me please, we're going to try and find him somewhere more comfortable."

Tracy nodded, looking relieved, her eyes full of hope.

The man next to the couple slid out into the aisle. "Well, I think it's for the best. Obviously sitting here isn't going to be good for him. He needs more space."

The nearby passengers again confirmed what the man was saying.

"He needs medical attention."

"It's best that he gets somewhere to lie down."

"It's too cramped and hot for him here."

Jenny nodded to Carl, another steward, to come and help.

"Come on then," Carl said to Tracy, helping her out of her seat. "Let's get you into the back."

Jenny helped Frank up. It took a few nudges to get him to move, "Come on Frank, we're going to get you somewhere more comfortable."

Frank looked at her with glazed eyes, seemed to realise that he was expected to move, and shuffled along the three empty seats into the aisle.

The plane shook.

More low cloud turbulence.

Frank fell forward and landed on a woman in the seat opposite.

She cried out, pulling back, trying to get away from Frank. She pushed him.

"Get him off me!" her voice was tinged with panic.

The woman's husband gasped and pushed at Frank. Jenny caught Frank as reeled back into the aisle. Carl helped to steady Frank.

Jenny gave a stern look at the two passengers, and then with Carl, walked Frank down the aisle the few yards to the galley section at the back of the small plane. Passengers edged away as they passed.

Tracy stood in the galley, her hand on her mouth, watching her husband.

Jenny and Carl manoeuvred Frank onto one of the steward's seats and strapped him in. His head lolled from left to right. Jenny pulled the galley curtains closed.

"When are we landing?" said Tracy. "We have to be landing soon, he needs a doctor."

"Would you like a drink?" said Carl.

Tracy looked confused for a moment, then said, "Yes, a coffee, please. No, a gin. Gin and tonic."

"Coming up."

Jenny rested her hand on Tracy's shoulder. "We should be landing soon, ok? I've just spoken to the Captain, and we will be approaching in the next thirty minutes or so."

Carl passed the drink to Tracy. She took it with shaking hands. "Do you think he has this virus?" she said in a hushed voice, her eyes glancing towards the curtains separating the galley from the rest of the plane. "I'm sure it can't be that serious. Probably something he picked up in Spain. He was fine only a few hours ago. We wouldn't have got on the plane otherwise. We haven't been eating anything funny either."

"Has he been-" began Carl, then he stopped himself. "Has he been in any fights?"

"You want to know if he's been bitten, don't you?" said Tracy. "That's what they say isn't it, that people who are bitten get it?"

Carl put on his most placating voice, the one Jenny usually heard him use with screaming toddlers, "It's important that we know exactly what's happened so we can get him the right treatment as quickly as possible when we land."

Jenny glanced uneasily at Carl. Earlier that morning in a pre-flight briefing they had been told to look out for passengers with bite marks, flesh wounds, or any sort of skin trauma. These passengers would not be allowed to fly. They had also had to ask all the passengers if they had been bitten or attacked in the previous week.

"It's ok, Tracy, you won't get in any trouble," said Jenny. "Sometimes we forget things, and only remember them later on. What's most important is that we find out what's happening."

Tracy downed the rest of her gin. She looked at the thin curtain separating the galley from the cabin. She turned her back on it, drawing Carl and Jenny in closer.

"He had an argument, last night, at a restaurant," she said quietly.

"Go on," said Carl.

"It was a Spanish man, he was rude to people, pushing and shoving. Shouting. Frank is usually very placid, he's not an angry person, but this man, he pushed me over." She fought back the tears. "And Frank grabbed him and pushed him away. They had a bit of a scuffle."

Tracy folded her arms and let out a small cry.

"Come on Tracy, almost there," said Jenny.

"It's on his shoulder. I think the man scratched him maybe, or something, it's on his shoulder."

Tracy couldn't stop the tears anymore. She sucked air in and out, trying not to cry out loud.

Jenny hugged her and looked over her shoulder, nodding to Carl.

Carl leaned over to Frank and pulled his T-shirt to the side to reveal a ringed bite mark at the base of his neck. Red and swollen. White pus crusted around the bite.

"Shit," said Carl.

Jenny had once been in an emergency landing, a few years ago. The plane had lost an engine. Emergency oxygen masks, fire engines on the runway, passengers in tears, panic.

She had felt sacred then, but that fear was nothing to the cold anxiety that gripped her on seeing the bite.

"Carl, do you want to look after Tracy? I'll just go and see the Captain."

Tracy leaned down to hug Frank, crying.

Jenny rushed down the aisle, ignoring the shouts of the passengers.

Chapter 3

Andy clicked on the responder. "Hey, Stewart."
"Andy, You sort out the passenger issues?"
"Let's hope so."
The plane shuddered. Andy glanced out the window, but of course, saw nothing but water droplets on the windscreen and the monotonous thick nothing of the clouds. It was a habit though, looking out. Human's couldn't seem to get entirely used to switching their perception over wholly to machines and dials.
"Got some bad news, Andy."
"Shoot."
"It seems no airports are answering anyone."
Andy paused, looked at Peter. Concern.
"Say again, Stewart."
"No airports are talking. Everything is dark. We've been trying everywhere nearby. Liverpool, Doncaster, Rotherham, Leeds, East Midlands. Nothing. And now we have a jumbo jet joining us from down south. London has gone dark, and they have headed

up here hoping for somewhere to land."

"Jesus Christ," said Peter, running his hands through his thinning hair.

"Ok Stewart, I guess we need to get some sort of approach in order," said Andy.

"We're working on it. Give us your fuel times, and we'll put you in the queue."

"Forty-seven minutes."

There was a moment's silence, presumably as Stewart made a note.

"Ok, you're fourth down. We've got the most fuel, so we'll be acting as traffic control. Any questions, come through us, save the airwaves going crazy."

"Sounds like you got a good handle on this Stewart."

"We try our best," said Stewart, the smile apparent in his voice. "Ok, you should be starting your decent in about fifteen."

"Got it. Just give me the shout."

"Will do. Good luck."

"You too. Don't hang on too long. Out."

"Out."

Peter shook his head slowly. "What the hell is going on down there?"

"You think it's the virus?" said Andy.

"I don't know. Surely it can't be that serious?"

"I guess it may be. Anyway, let's not worry about it for now. We have to think about landing. We don't have much time. Let's go through the checks."

"Sure."

Peter leaned forward to adjust a dial, and then there was a knock on the door.

"Captain, it's Jenny."

She sounded even more harassed than she was five minutes ago. Scared even.

Andy got up and opened the door. The noise from the cabin was much louder.

Jenny rushed in, her face flushed.

"What is it?" said Andy, closing the door.

"The ill passenger, I think they have the virus."

Peter swung round, "What? Oh shit."

"Hang on," said Andy, "let's calm down. Tell me what you know."

Jenny took a few deep breaths, fanned the air around her face. "Frank, he's called, we moved him to the galley, the other passengers were getting angry. After talking to his wife, she admitted he had been bitten by someone last night."

"My God," said Peter, "and they still got on the plane, even with all the warnings?"

"Where are they now?" said Andy.

"Still in the galley, with Carl. We've got the curtains drawn."

"Did any of the other passengers hear you?"

Jenny shook her head. "No, they were too busy moaning."

"Good. Ok, well done Jenny. We're going to be landing in fifteen minutes, so we just have to hold on that long. You think you can manage that?"

Jenny nodded.

"I'll put on the seat belts sign, you make an announcement, let them know we are landing."

"Ok, leave it to me."

Chapter 4

Carl poured himself a drink of water. He was hot, he was feeling anxious. It was a stressful flight, and he would be glad when they were on the ground again.

Tracy kneeled next to her husband.

The loudspeaker beeped into life.

"Ladies and Gentlemen, this is your chief steward Jenny speaking. The Captain has turned on the seatbelt sign. If I could ask all passengers to return to their seats and store away all hand luggage in preparation for landing. We are about to make our descent into Manchester very shortly. Thank you once again for your patience."

Carl heard the unified sighs of relief from the passengers beyond the curtain. Tracy looked up at Carl. "What do I do?"

"Here, have my seat." He and Jenny could take Frank and Tracy's seats.

"Are we landing now, really?" said Tracy.

"That's what the Captain said." He knelt down next to Tracy.

"You sit yourself down, and I'll buckle Frank in."

Tracy sheepishly sat down in Carl's fold-down seat and took her place.

Carl reached for the buckle behind Frank. Frank lolled to the left, then to the right.

"Come on know, Frank, let's stay still."

"Is he all right?" said Tracy.

Carl didn't respond, he was having trouble keeping Frank on the small seat. Frank was unresponsive, his eyes closed.

The plane shuddered, and Frank fell forward, on top of Carl. Carl lost his footing and fell back, hitting his head on the metal food drawers behind him. Frank's heavy body pinned him to the floor, his face inches from Carl's.

Frank opened his eyes.

Jenny replaced the loudspeaker phone. The passengers seemed to have taken the news well and were buckling in. A multitude of clicks rang out throughout the cabin.

She should go down and join Carl, but her feet wouldn't move. For some reason she was scared. She was scared of the virus.

She stared at the curtain at the far end of the cabin. The plane shuddered. The garish green and orange curtains swung from left to right.

She heard a scream. Numerous heads turned to the back of the plane, where the cry had come from. Some turned back to Jenny, their eye's questioning.

And then another scream, this one louder, more terrible. A gurgling yell, like someone being murdered. The passengers joined in, and a chorus of cries echoed around the plane, traveling from the back to the front like a macabre Mexican wave.

The curtain shook, then fell from its rungs, pulled by a bloody hand. Tracy stood there, her mouth contorted in agony. Frank appeared behind her and sunk his teeth into the back of her head and pulled, ripping her scalp clean off, stretching the skin on her face until it ripped apart, revealing a gleaming and bloody white skull.

Jenny screamed, too.

Carl stood in the corner of the galley, his mouth hanging open, unable to make a sound as he watched Frank gnawing into the neck of his wife.

Although shocked when Frank had opened his eyes, he had managed to push him off. Only he had pushed him directly towards Tracy. Frank had reached out his arms and grabbed his wife, who made the fatal mistake of pulling him towards her. Her husband repaid her love by sinking his teeth into Tracy's neck.

Blood spurted like a fountain from her neck, covering Frank's face, and dripping onto the floor as Frank gnawed into the flesh of his wife's throat. There was a ripping sound, and Frank turned to look at Carl, half of Tracy's scalp and face hanging from his mouth, her hair forming a grotesque and bloody beard.

Carl found his voice. He screamed. Loudly.

Frank threw Tracy's body onto the floor.

This is it, thought Carl. He closed his eyes, waiting for the inevitable pain as his skin was torn from his muscles. He hoped he would pass out from the shock.

He let out a few small murmurs.

A few seconds passed, and nothing happened. Carl opened his eyes, Frank was gone.

Carl felt relief wash over him. Then he remembered he was on a plane, thousands of feet in the air, with what appeared to be a zombie. Relief disappeared and was replaced with panic.

No need to ask where Frank had gone - the terrified shrieks from the cabin told him Frank found the varied menu there more appealing than Carl's skinny frame.

He peered around the corner of the galley, keeping a careful eye on Tracy's body. She was lying face first, her head in the cabin, her legs in the kitchen. Blood pooled around her head turning the carpet a sticky red.

Carl gasped, but the sound was swallowed by the sounds of

sheer terror in the cabin. It seemed everyone was screaming, yelling, shouting, crying.

The aisle was full of people as mindless terror forced the passengers to flee from the back of the cabin, and from Frank. They climbed over the seats and each other to escape the hideous form of the bloodied Frank as he moaned and hissed his way down the aisle. He eventually caught an old man, who had fallen under the feeling mass of those younger and stronger than him.

Frank bit into the old man's leg and pulled his head back, bringing a sizeable chunk of flesh and a trouser leg with him.

Carl knew what he had to do.

Hide.

He fumbled with the toilet door, pulled it open and ducked in. He slammed the door behind him and locked it.

"Worst flight ever," he said, before leaning over the small sink and throwing up.

Jenny stood frozen in fear as a wall of terrified and desperate passengers began a slow build in momentum, spilling through the aisles and over the seats, heading towards the front of the plane.

The people at the front, not having witnessed what Jenny had seen, stood up and looked behind them in bemused panic, which quickly turned to pure terror as they realised the wave of passengers wasn't stopping. They were going to be engulfed, and there was nowhere for them to go - no plane left.

A few held their ground, pushing back against the fleeing passengers. Fists began to fly.

One middle-aged man, his face white, his eyes so wide they looked as if they were about to pop from their skull, ran for the cabin door. Jabbering mindlessly, he pulled and wrenched at the handle, trying to open it.

If he succeeded, thought Jenny, they would all be dead. "Stop, you'll kill everyone," she shouted, but the man paid no attention. Her words were lost in the chaos. She found herself too terrified to move.

Another passenger, a young man, saw the door opening attempt and leaped forward, hitting the older man around the back of the head. The older man turned, a look of shock on his face. The younger man punched him again, and then, seemingly overcome with some sort of bloodlust, continued to reign blows on the older man, beating him again and again, until his face disintegrated into a bloody tangle of bone and cut flesh.

A woman then hit the younger man on the head with a fire extinguisher, and continued the blows with the same frenzy, the young man's skull caving in within seconds.

Jenny screamed again.

Hands grabbed her around the shoulder.

"Jenny, get in here, now."

Before she was able to turn, her body was jerked backward, through the cockpit's door.

Andy closed the cockpit door and the screams, so visceral, so penetrating just a second ago, suddenly took on a muffled and otherworldly sound, as if the hell she had just been in was now only a distant dream.

Andy locked the door.

"Are you ok?"

She managed to nod. Her breathing was fast and out of control. She was taking in huge gulps of air, shaking.

Andy sat her down on the fold-down seat at the back of the cockpit.

"Relax, breathe softly. You're ok now. You're safe."

She pointed at the door, "What if they-"

Andy shook his head. "No chance. Since 9-11, you need a fucking battering ram to get through those doors."

Her breath was coming back under her control. Her panic subsided to a manageable level.

"What the hell happened out there?" said Andy

"Frank, he was ill. I thought he was asleep, but I don't know, I made the announcement, and next thing, I saw Tracy at the back of the plane, and… oh God"

"It's ok, take your time."

"And, Frank, he appeared and bit her, bit right into her!"

"He bit her?" said Peter "Fuck. It's true then."

"True?" said Andy.

"What they've been saying on the internet forums, about the biting with the virus. It's a zombie virus."

"Zombies?" said Andy. "Like Night of the Living Dead?"

"Has to be."

"Well, whatever is happening, we need to get this plane down. Get Stewart on the com, we need to land now."

Chapter 5

"Stewart, we've got trouble, big trouble. We need to land now."

"Ok... can you wait 5 minutes?"

"No. This isn't a request, it's a courtesy call. We're landing."

There was a moment's silence. Andy checked the cabin camera. There were three active zombies now - Tracy had turned, as had an old man. The fights near the plane door were intensifying, a standing battle of around eight people.

A young girl sat huddled in the corner at the front of the plane, hugging her knees up to her body, tears pouring from her face. She could only be about six. The cameras had no sound, but Andy could read her lips well enough, Mummy, Mummy, Mummy, over and again.

"Stewart, we have infected on board."

"Infected? With this virus? Ok, but surely 5 minutes won't make any difference."

"Stewart, listen carefully, and trust me, remember who you are talking to." He took a breath. He didn't even believe himself. "The virus, it's like a… A zombie virus."

There was a pause. Then, "What?"

"A zombie virus, like the films. I have people on my plane eating each other. I'm looking at my cabin camera now, and the fear, the panic has reached a point where we have a group of passengers trying to open the cabin doors, and another group fighting them off, and down the bottom of the cabin, we have three, so far, zombies, making their way through the passengers. We need to land now. And I'm going down, whether anyone is in our way or not."

Peter smiled. Andy nodded at Jenny. She looked relieved but too shaken to get anywhere near smiling.

"Ok," said Stewart, his voice quiet. "Make your approach, I'll redirect anyone in your way."

"Thanks, Stewart."

Andy took a second to look at the picture of his pregnant wife tucked in the right side of the instrument panel. He didn't look for long, he couldn't afford to have his attention drawn from the task at hand.

"Peter, prepare for landing. Let's go."

"Sure thing Captain."

"Hey, I'm home." Andy put his bag down in the hallway.

His wife, Mary, ran down the stairs, her face open with anticipation. "Well?" she said.

He had planned to pretend that it had all gone wrong, but he couldn't help but burst into a huge smile.

"I got it. You can call me Captain from now on."

"Yey!" Mary ran down the rest of the stairs and hugged Andy. "Well done! That's amazing."

"Well, you know, wasn't too hard, really."

She laughed and hit him playfully on the arm. "Don't say that. You've worked so hard. You deserve it."

She was right.

"So what now?"
"Well, I'm going to be switched to long haul. My first routes will be in the middle east. Dubai, Abu Dhabi."
"But we can stay in Knutsford?"
"Course we can. Or we can move to the Middle East. No tax... Think how much we could put away in a few years."
"Well, let's think about it. First, we have to celebrate tonight. I've booked us a table at that new Italian."
"Ah, so you did have faith then?" said Andy
"I figured that whether you got the Captaincy or not, you'd want to go out." Mary smiled.
Andy held her by the shoulders. "Bloody hell, a Captain."
They shared a laugh and a long kiss.

Andy pushed the nose of the plane down, it would be a quick descent. Noises of muffled chaos still filtered in from the cabin. He glanced in the camera - the little girl was gone. There were five zombies now. They changed fast. Why hadn't Frank changed fast though?
"Keep Stewart on my headset," said Andy.
"Done," said Peter.
The sound of the engines increased in pitch, and the plane rattled noisily as they dropped.
He had practiced emergency landings, water landings, lost engine landings, and many other disaster scenarios in the simulator many times. But he'd never practiced a Plane Full of Zombies landing. He tried to block out the noises from the cabin. The screams, the cries for help, the sounds of misery and despair.
"Shit!" shouted Peter.
Andy had already seen it. As they dropped out from cloud cover, a white and red plane appeared in front of them. Too close. Looked like it was following the same route to the runway.
"Who the hell is that Stewart?"
"Hang on," said the bodiless voice, followed by a few moments pause. "No idea, they're silent."

"Christ, we're going to be going down right on top of them."
The other aircraft was about 300 meters away.
"Shall we abort?" said Peter.
"No, we'll land behind them."
Andy slowed the plane, bringing it as slow as he dared without stalling the aircraft.
"Everyone ok?" He turned to look at Peter and Jenny. They both nodded.
The airport was only a few miles away, they would be landing within minutes.
"What's that?" said Peter, squinting through the windscreen, looking ahead, towards the airport.
Andy focused ahead. "It looks like smoke."
"Lot's of it," said Peter.
Four or five tall, thin columns of grey and black rose into the air like woolly pillars.
"Jesus. The airport looks like a war-zone," said Peter.
"What's wrong?" said Jenny.
"Nothing, I hope," said Andy. "There are several fires at the airport. Don't worry we're still landing."
Andy concentrated on keeping the plane headed towards the runway, he had practiced landing without guidance from Air Traffic Control many times.
The door to the cockpit shook with a loud bang. Jenny let out a small shout, her seat was right next to the door.
Another bang, and then another. They came fast and hard.
"Don't worry," said Peter. "No-one is getting through those doors."
Andy ignored the knocking, the desperate and terrified people trying to get into the cockpit. He ignored the fact that some of his passengers had been infected with a virus that brought them back from the dead and impelled them to eat other people. He ignored all of it. The best he could do now to help anyone was to get the plane down. It was his responsibility.
"What the hell is that?" Peter was staring at the radar. Two

blips moved quickly across the green screen, heading towards the cluster of planes, the other blips, that were circling the airport.

"Hey Stewart," said Andy. "You picking that up on your radar?"

"We got them," said Stewart over the transmitter. "Looks like two aircraft approaching fast."

"What do you think, can you get a visual?" said Andy, still doing his best to concentrate on keeping the large plane as slow as possible while not dropping out of the sky.

"Hold on, hold on…" said Stewart.

The blips melded with the cluster of planes.

"Christ!" shouted Stewart, his voice filled with surprise. "Two Tornados, really kicking it. Just flew across our nose."

"Air Force? What the hell are they doing here?" said Andy, now watching the blips closely. They had shot past the circling planes and seemed to be turning for another pass.

"I don't know," said Stewart, "Maybe here to help? Hang on, they're coming back."

Andy felt anxious, he didn't know why.

"Here they come," said Stewart, "Hold on, what the hell is- Jesus Christ! Fuck!"

There was a blur of static.

"Stewart?" said Andy. "Stewart? Come in, come in Stewart?"

"Andy!" shouted Peter, pointing out the windscreen of the plane.

Jenny screamed.

Ahead, a blue and white plane dived from the bottom of the clouds, its left wing missing, the stump belching thick plumes of black smoke. The markings on the tail were those of Stewart's airline. The plane began to spiral and pirouette in a tight spin like a ballet dancer. Andy suddenly had a vision of the paper airplanes he used to throw over the bridge near his house when he was a young boy. They would float for a few seconds, then plunge to the earth, caught in a hopeless spin.

"They're gonna hit," screamed Jenny.

Stewart's plane smashed into the Boeing ahead.

"Pull up!" said Peter.

But Andy held fast. They didn't have enough fuel for another pass.

There was a huge flash of white and yellow and then a mighty sound like the crashing of mountains. Both planes dropped from the sky like burning stones. A black cloud erupted in front of them. Andy held on tight to the control stick as turbulence rocked the plane.

The windscreen cracked, hit by a piece of flying debris.

The plane leaned sharply to the right. The wing must have been clipped. Andy struggled to keep the aircraft straight.

Warning beeps and buzzers sounded in the cockpit. Flashing red lights lit up.

"We gotta fuel leak," said Peter, "the left flap is stuck, we're losing cabin pressure, looks like we've caught some debris."

The sky cleared again as the plane passed quickly through the debris and smoke of the explosion. Andy kept fixated on the runway. They were only a few hundred feet up.

From the corner of his eye, he saw the base of one of the columns of smoke that surrounded the airport. It was another plane.

The airport was littered with downed planes. The Air Force was shooting them down.

"What the hell, Andy? What the hell is going on?" said Peter, his voice overcome with panic.

"The radar, Peter, where the hell are those jets?"

Peter stared at the radar screen.

The engines whined as Andy kicked a bit of extra thrust as they dropped altitude.

"Coming round for another pass."

"Shit," said Andy.

They were only a few hundred feet off the ground, falling quickly. It was a much steeper descent than Andy was used to, but he could handle it. He had to. He glanced at the picture of his wife.

The plane passed through a plume of smoke from a burning 737 on the ground, its fuselage cracked in two, the wings nowhere to be seen.

Alarms continued their atonal chorus.

"Ok, everyone ready?" said Andy

"Shall we tell the passengers to buckle up?" said Peter, a wry smile on his face.

Andy glanced at the cabin cam. The same chaos, no idea they were about to land.

"There!" Peter pointed to the left, over the control tower of the airport. Two jets could be seen approaching. Tiny specks, quickly increasing in size.

He had to hope they had another target, for if they fired now, no way he could outmanoeuvre any incoming.

"Ok, we're coming in hard."

Andy pulled up on the stick, trying to keep the nose high. The concrete of the runway approached rapidly.

The cockpit collectively held their breath as the grey of ground raced towards them. There seemed to be a few seconds of painful silence and then…

The plane hit the ground hard with a screech and a bounce. Andy jerked out of his seat. A new wave of screams sounded from the cabin.

Peter engaged the reverse thrusters.

The two air force jets passed low over the plane, their sound huge.

Andy pulled the stick to his left, the plane swung hard, still going fast. It ran off the runway, across the grass onto the next feeder lane.

"Where the hell are you going?"

"We need to disembark immediately." Andy pointed to the departure gates, a few hundred yards ahead. The glass windows were level with the height of the cockpit.

"Christ," said Peter.

"Get ready with the reverse thrusters again," said Andy.
"Ready."
The gates approached quickly.
Andy held the plane steady as it raced past a baggage truck on fire. There was a lurching screech of metal, and the plane was dragged to the right as its wing clipped the nose of another stationary aircraft. He wrestled with the stick as they veered from left to right.
"Ok, Peter... Ready... Ready..."
The glass of the departure gates took up the whole of the windscreen.
"Now!"
Peter pulled the thrusters on full. The engine roared.
Glass shattered as the nose of the plane smashed into the departure gate. The whole plane shuddered, and there was the piercing sound of ripping metal. Andy expected the plane to stop when the undercarriage hit the building, but the noise and the fact they were still sliding into the gate suggested the undercarriage had been sheered off.
Seats, a vending machine, a small coffee stall scattered as they were hit by the full weight of the plane.
They slowed, the friction and the thrusters doing their trick, the bottom of the plane screeching against the polished departure gate floor.
Andy was flung forward in his seat, the seatbelt biting hard as they came to a sudden stop. The rear undercarriage must have hit the building. Screams and yells from the cabin rang out loudly.
A new salvo of alarms rang out in the cockpit.
"Everyone ok?" said Andy.
Peter wiped some glass fragments out of his hair, "I think so."
"Jenny?"
She nodded, taking deep breaths. "Yes, I'm ok."
"Good," said Andy. "Now let's get the hell out of here."

Chapter 6

Carl pulled himself up and clutched his head. He felt a trickle of something warm down his forehead - blood. He must have banged his head in the crash. Had it been a crash? Surely if they had crashed, he wouldn't be alive?

Must have just been a very bad landing, then.

He turned on the cramped toilet's tap, it was still working. He wiped away the blood from his head. He heard the cries and screams from the cabin.

Zombies. He hadn't signed up for that. His girlfriend had thought it would be the perfect job for him. Get to see the world, get to travel, get to meet lots of new people, and, oh plenty of time for her to get with that mechanic, Dave.

Dave, what a prick.

What a job it had turned out to be. Lost his missus and now surrounded by zombies. Should have stayed at the call centre.

Calm yourself, thought Carl. No time to go over lousy life choices.

He pushed his ear up against the door of the toilet. Sounded like a bloody free for all out there.

He took a deep breath, realised his hands were shaking. He tried to hold them still. No good, he would have to do this with shaking hands. He opened the door slowly, just an inch and peered out He half expected a zombie hand to push through and rip his throat out. But that didn't happen.

The back half of the cabin was empty, it looked like everyone had run from the zombies, and then the zombies had run after the people, and now everyone was crushed in the top half of the plane.

The noise was unbearable - a mixture of crying, of shouting, the sound of violent scuffles, and worst of all, the sound of moaning. It was a deep resonating sound that filled him with dread.

A body was on the floor of the cabin. What looked like Frank was leaning over it, getting his fill.

Carl eyed the fire extinguisher on the other side of the galley. He could take Frank out with that. Straight on the head, like in the films. But did he have the guts?

Anxiety rolled in his stomach, his hands were still shaking, his head pounded, and his mouth was dry. But he could do this. Dammit, he could do it.

He sneaked out of the toilet, wincing as the toilet door creaked, but he needn't have worried, the noise from the front of the cabin was overplaying any of his sneaking sounds.

He took one last glance at the Frank zombie and ran to the other side of the galley, where he grabbed the fire extinguisher.

Carl stood at the top of the aisle, extinguisher in hand - it was one of the small ones that should only be used for electrical fires. I guess they were the most common fires on planes. Either way, he reckoned it would do some damage to a skull.

He felt nauseous.

He imagined that Frank was wearing a blue mechanics uniform and that his name was Dave. He took one last deep breath and ran down the aisle, shouting as he did.

A few yards away and Frank-zombie turned and stared straight at him.

Not only blood around its mouth, but long thick pink tendrils of flesh hung from its teeth, wobbling like a bad joke.

Carl brought the small electrical-fires-only extinguisher down on Frank's head, and there was a dull clang.

Frank wobbled and fell forward. Carl hammered down again, just to be sure. Then again, just to be extra sure. The zombie's skull crushed flat in the middle, pink brain bursting out the sides of the white cracked bone.

Blood pulsed through Carl's head, and he felt wobbly, his vision dazed and sound muffled. He thought he heard the Captain's voice.

There was a sudden surge of noise. The crowd of passengers in front of Carl began to push forward. Carl watched as the movement of people revealed a group of four or five zombies, munching on passengers, oblivious to the forward surge.

If the passengers were moving forward, it meant they must be getting out of the plane.

And Carl was the only one behind the zombies. He would have to take them all out if he wanted to get out.

The first would be Frank's victim, a teenage boy ironically wearing a zombie T-shirt - "Day of the Dead" it said in bold red letters covered in blood.

The lower portion of the boy had been torn open, and his intestines decorated the floor like bad-taste-bunting.

This one was harder. Without seeing the bottom half of the boy, it looked like he was just asleep.

But Carl knew he wasn't.

He brought down his weapon hard on the boy's head, smashing his skull with the first crack, obliterating it with the second and third. Three seemed to be the optimal skull destroying number.

The crowd moved forward a few more feet.

The next zombie was a few feet ahead, on its knees, feasting on a broad middle-aged woman in a yellow flowery dress, now drenched with a vibrant contrasting red.

Carl repeated his zombie death method on both the zombie and the dead passenger, 1-2-3, dead again.

Eight more to go.

Chapter 7

Andy adjusted his new Captain's hat in the mirror and looked at himself for a moment, pleased with what he saw. Not in a conceited type of way, but pleased with what his clothes represented.

His Captaincy.

His years of struggle. Living in a trailer at the end of a godforsaken Arizona airport so he could fly parachuters for free, just to get his hours up.

Month after month of rejections and having to work for cut-price airlines on call 24-7, just for the chance to earn a few pounds.

Pulling the worst hours at the worst airlines, hardly ever seeing his wife. Living in a godforsaken town in Latvia near some stag-do destination, only getting home one week out of seven.

And now, a transcontinental pilot with a prestigious Middle East airline.

He'd done it.

Mary came into the bedroom.
"What do you think?" asked Andy, straightening his hat.
Mary smiled. "You look great. Daddy."
Andy's hand's dropped to his sides, and he spun round to face Mary. "What?"
She held up a pregnancy test pen. He stared at it for a minute before the thin blue line came into focus.
He smiled, then he grinned, then he laughed. He picked up Mary and spun her around, his hat falling off.

Andy looked in the monitor that piped through to the cabin cameras. The passengers were getting over the shock of the landing. They pulled themselves up from the floor and slowly, in small pockets, continued their confused melee. The ones at the back, closest to the line of zombies began to scramble away in panic. The ones near the cabin door started up their fight again; those trying to open it against those trying to stop them opening it. And the pounding on the cockpit door began again in earnest.

"What the hell are they doing," said Peter, taking a second out from shutting down the plane's engines. "Why don't they open the door? Someone just needs to look out the window."

"They must all be terrified," said Jenny.

"The madness of crowds," whispered Andy.

"What?" said Jenny.

"Nothing, we need to get the cabin door open."

"Can you not open it from here?" asked Jenny.

"No. It needs to be done manually. Safety mechanism to stop any accidental openings at 30,000 feet," said Andy. "I'll see if anyone is listening."

Andy picked up the intercom. "This is your Captain speaking. We have landed, you may open the cabin door, I repeat, you may open the cabin door."

A few people started to point at the intercom and at the cockpit. They began shouting at those trying to keep the door closed.

"Keep going Andy, it looks like they are listening."

Andy repeated the message a few times, and it eventually filtered through. Those trying to keep the door closed stopped and stood bewildered for a few seconds, before being hustled out of the way, mostly with punches, kicks, and shoves. A scramble of hands grabbed the door, and within seconds the cabin door was open.

The crowd pushed, and the first few people by the door fell twenty feet onto the hard floor below.

"Quick!" Jenny leaped forward and grabbed the transmitter from Andy. She shouted into the mouthpiece, "Pull the orange lever on the right, pull the lever." She repeated her shout over and over and again, her voice becoming more frantic as she watched more people being pushed to nasty injuries on the floor below.

Eventually, someone pulled the lever, and the emergency slide burst out from the side of the plane, inflating quickly, like a time-lapse video of a bright orange plant growing to the ground.

There was a collective sigh of relief in the cockpit.

The crowd surged forward and jumped onto the slide, emptying into the departure lounge.

Andy, Peter, and Jenny watched the passengers spill into the dusty, glass covered floor from the safety and silence of the cockpit.

The passengers didn't run, though. They pooled around the plane, seemingly scared to move away from its protective hulk. The reason quickly became apparent.

The floor of the lounge was littered with bodies, and teeming with zombies. Mutilated former humans dragged broken and sliced limbs behind them as they crawled through the lounge, searching for fresh meat.

Bodies of all ages, colours, and sizes lay around the floor, spread over seats, in broken windows. Not only people in civilian clothes but also military uniform.

It looked like a battlefield.

A man with a checked shirt, his body bent awkwardly over a

bank of seats, slowly came to life. He struggled to sit up straight in the chair, a large bullet wound in his chest, his shirt stained different shades of red. A large gash in his leg hampered his attempts to stand up, his suit trouser torn and bloody with a hunk of charred flesh peeking through.

The man eventually got to his feet and hobbled towards the crowd of people waiting around the plane. He let out a large moan.

A couple broke from the crowd and ran.

This acted as a catalyst, and the rest of the passengers followed, running in all directions from the plane, screaming.

The old hobbled, quickly, gasping for breath. The young sprinted through the dead zone, easily avoiding the slow grasping zombies. Children screamed and cried and followed their parents.

"Shall we go?" said Jenny.

Peter got up.

Andy held up his hand, "Wait, look, over there." He pointed to the far end of the departure gate, where the corridor thinned and led back to security and check-in. A fast and fluid movement, a scurry of figures in the dark, caught everyone's attention.

"What is it?" said Peter.

His answer came in the form of a few brief flashes of light, followed a split second later by the loud and unmistakable sound of rapid gunfire.

The young couples and families at the head of the escape fell immediately.

The people following stopped dead, frozen in fear. Another volley of gunfire and they fell.

A group of soldiers moved quickly into the departure lounge, firing as they came. The passengers fell like skittles, most of them too stunned and overcome to respond to the lightning attack from their own army.

"Jesus Christ," said Peter.

"Oh my…" said Jenny.

"Look," said Andy.

A soldier was pointing at the plane. He motioned to a group of nearby troops, and four of them broke from the central assault team and made their way towards the aircraft.

"Ok, we have to go, now!" Andy jumped up and opened the door of the cockpit.

He fell back in surprise. Peter caught him.

By the door of the cockpit stood a young man, covered in blood, a small fire extinguisher in his hand. Around him, on the seats and on the floor, lay the bodies of some passengers, their skulls caved in.

"Captain?" said the man.

"Carl!" shouted Jenny. "I thought you were dead."

"Almost," said Carl. He smiled at Jenny. He looked at the bodies surrounding him. "They were zombies, I swear!"

"Well then, good work, I guess," said Andy.

"I heard gunfire," said Carl, "what's going on?"

"We need to hide," said Jenny.

Sounds of shouting from outside. Loud voices, barking commands. A ripping sound came from the cabin door. The slide disappeared. More shouts, asking for ladders.

"Who the hell is that?" said Carl.

"The army," said Andy.

There as a metal clang as the top of a ladder hit the bottom of the cabin door.

Andy held his finger up to his mouth and motioned them down the aisle.

The clang of boots on the ladder became louder. Andy realised they wouldn't make it to the back of the plane.

He stopped. He kneeled down and rubbed his hands over the nearest corpse, covering them in blood. He rubbed the blood over his face, his hair and his white Captain's shirt.

The others copied him immediately.

Carl waved his arms around, and everyone looked at him, "It won't be enough," he whispered. He stuck his hand deep into a stomach wound of an old man and pulled out a long chain of intestines.

Andy nodded and motioned to the others to do the same.

Peter stuck his hands into a nearby carcass and pulled out a series of unidentifiable entrails. He gagged.

Jenny lay down and put some of Carl's stolen intestines over her back and down her shirt.

They all lay still, covered in blood and pieces of the dead passengers.

Andy was on an aisle seat with his head back. He opened his eyes a tiny amount and spied on the cabin door.

A soldier clambered into the cabin. Just a young boy. Couldn't even be twenty. He had a gun hoisted over his back. He quickly jumped up and scanned the cabin, his gun held up, ready to fire.

He looked behind him, into the cockpit. Did a quick sweep.

"Anything, private?" said a voice from outside the plane.

"Can't see anyone, sir, looks dead. Loads of bodies, sir."

"Bodies?"

"Yes, sir. Zeds, I guess." The young man had gone pale. He stared at the body of a young girl in a seat next to him, her neck pulled open to reveal her spinal column and tendons.

"Do a full sweep, private. A bullet in the head of every corpse. Could be zeds in waiting."

The private sighed to himself. "Ok, sir."

Andy observed as the private walked up to the first corpse. He raised his gun and fired once. There was a bang, loud in the confined cabin, accompanied by a damp thumping sound as the bullet lodged in the corpse's skull.

There were maybe twenty bodies between the private and the group. They only had a minute or so left.

The private took his second shot. Another bang, another wet thump.

Andy felt something tugging on his leg. He carefully eased his head down, satisfied the private's attention was on his somber task.

Jenny was tugging on his trouser leg, she was lying on the

floor next to him. Her eyes peered through a ring of an intestine, open and scared, her pupils huge.

Bang, thump.

Bang, thump.

They could jump the private when he got near, thought Andy. But what of the rest of the soldiers? They wouldn't stand a chance.

Bang, thump.

Maybe he could tell the private the truth, appeal to his better nature. Andy laughed inwardly. The best they could hope for would be to be taken to the private's CO, and then no doubt they would be shot. Just like all the other passengers.

Bang, thump.

Jenny grabbed his trouser leg and pulled hard.

He shrugged. He was out of ideas.

Chapter 8

It had been a good day. Andy had completed his first flight from Manchester to Dubai.
He relaxed in the luxurious lounge of the Hotel Jamerah, taking another sip of his beer. He had two days respite before his next flight back to Manchester. He had it all planned - take it easy tonight, grab a fine meal and a few drinks. Get up tomorrow and spend the day by the beach, followed by a swim in the crystal clear waters of the Arabian Gulf and maybe a visit to Dubai old town.
He nodded to the waiter, "Thanks, can you charge it to my room please?"
"Of course sir," said the smiling young waiter. Andy left him a handsome tip, then went back up to his room on the twenty-seventh floor.
His room looked inland, and in most places that would have been inferior to a beach view, but not in Dubai. Andy went straight to the balcony and looked out across the impressive

skyline, dominated by the Burj Dubai, the world's tallest building. It stood like a tower of rock, a bony finger reaching to the clouds, a myriad of lights dancing around its frame like a million fireflies.

He added a new item to his itinerary. The view from the top must be fantastic.

There was a knock on his door. Maybe it was his pilot, James.

It wasn't James, it was a man in a suit.

He held out his hand. "Hello Captain Bracknell, I'm Simon Calder, the Middle East Airlines representative in Dubai."

Andy took his hand and shook it. "Hello, pleased to meet you, please come in."

The two men made their way into the spacious hotel room. Andy motioned towards the balcony. "Please, take a seat. Would you like a drink?"

"No, it's ok Captain."

"I must say, this is very nice of the airline. Is this a sort of hello, a meet and greet type thing?"

Calder looked uncomfortable. "I'm afraid not, Captain. This isn't a social call. Please, take a seat."

Andy continued to pour himself a drink. He poured himself an extra measure. The man's demeanour was quickly making him nervous. Had something happened on the flight? Had he done something wrong? Maybe his co-pilot had reported him for something.

Andy sat down at one of the room's small tables.

Calder took a deep breath and spoke. "During your flight, we received notification from Manchester, while you were in the air that..." he faltered.

Andy looked into the man's eyes. "What? What are you here to tell me?"

"I'm very sorry to tell you, Captain, that there was a car accident early this morning in the UK involving your wife."

The sounds of the words echoed with a tinny resonance and time itself seemed to slow down.

"Your wife was pronounced dead at the scene. I'm very sorry

Captain, you have my full sympathies."

Calder continued to talk, but Andy didn't hear much of what was said. The room took on a strange cotton wool consistency, and Andy felt himself sink into the white, into the nothing. He looked at Calder, whose lips moved, but with no accompanying sound. Andy felt nauseous, and there was a ringing sound in his ears.

"Captain, can you hear me? Are you ok?"

Some words, a question, he was expected to answer. He was fine, wasn't he? Was he ok?

"Yes, I'm fine, thank you."

"I know this must be devastating news, and the airline will do anything we can to help you. If you would like I can stay with you now and-"

"No," said Andy. "No, it's fine. Thank you, but please leave."

"Of course." The man reached over and left a card on the table. "If you need to contact me. You are of course excused from flying detail. I'll be in touch tomorrow."

Calder walked out of the room.

Andy called after him, "There's no mistake is there? I mean, no chance of there being a mistake?"

Calder shook his head. "No mistake. I'm very sorry."

He left the room and closed the door behind him.

Andy sat in the silence. The most profound, most terrifying silence he had ever known.

Mary. The baby. Gone.

He grabbed his head in his hands and cried, his body shaking violently.

What now?

Bang, thump.

Bang, thump.

"This is fuckin' disgusting," said the soldier to himself, now only a few aisles away.

Andy felt the tension building around him. He could feel Peter,

Jenny, and Carl waiting, looking to him to make a move. It was funny how they still looked to him for an answer, for a decision to do something, even when it was their lives on the line. Was it because he was the Captain, and there was some strange institutional hierarchy implanted in their minds? They already handed their lives over to his decisions when they got on the plane - was it just a simple continuance of the same pattern? The plane may have crashed, but he was still the Captain.

The Crash.

Andy thought about the crash, the awkward landing into the departure lounge.

The plane was sticking out of the building, a significant portion of it still outside. Maybe there were no soldiers outside.

Now he had a plan. He just needed the order of command and trust to hold when facing death.

The soldier would reach Peter first, who was lying in the aisle with his face covered in human giblets and warm blood.

Andy watched the soldier carefully - the young man moved slowly but carelessly. He wasn't expecting anything to happen. As far as he was concerned, he was in a plane full of dead people, a metal tube of dead and stinking corpses, the pungent iron smell of blood and innards making the plane feel like an infected abattoir. Dirty, rotten, death.

Andy stretched his hand forward slowly and eased out the in-flight magazine from the rack in front of him. The duty-free one, the thicker one. He rolled it up carefully in his hands into a tight cylinder.

Bang, thump.

The soldier was only a few feet away, he raised his gun and pointed it at Peter's head.

Peter's eyes sprung open, "No, wait!" he shouted.

"What the?" said the soldier, he paused.

Andy jumped up and let out a loud yell. He pushed the rolled up end of the magazine into the soldier's eye.

At the same time, Peter grabbed the soldier's legs and pulled.

The soldier fell, his helmeted head landing in the emptied torso of a corpse.

Andy moved quickly. He leaped into the aisle and fell on the soldier. He looked into the man's eyes, they were wide open with fear and surprise.

Andy raised his fist and hit the young man once, twice, there times, each punch ringing through his knuckles and jarring his arm, a sickening thump underlining each strike.

The soldier tried to buck his torso to get Andy off, but it was too late. Andy threw a few more punches, and the soldier's nose exploded. His eyes closed over. Andy continued to punch the soldier. He felt teeth smash under his fist.

Someone grabbed him from behind.

"It's ok, Captain, we got him. We got him." It was Carl. He eased Andy back, away from the soldier.

Andy shook his head and looked at the young man lying on the ground. His face was a bloody pulped mess, his nose flat, his teeth shattered. Andy felt sick.

Jenny jumped up and manically brushed of the entrails from around her like she was brushing off a nest of ants. Peter did the same.

"Now what?" said Jenny. She looked nervously at the front of the cabin.

"We go out the back," said Andy. "We can get onto the runway, and figure it out from there," said Andy.

"Good plan," said Carl.

They ran to the back of the plane where Jenny and Carl set about opening the back door. Jenny activated the emergency slide. It dropped to the side of the plane and inflated noisily with a burst of high air compression.

"Ok, let's go," said Andy.

Peter jumped down first; he flew down the slide and hit the ground hard.

Jenny followed.

Carl went next. Gunshots followed Carl as he raced down the

orange inflatable, the soldiers having noticed the escape attempt. Carl put his arms up to shield his head.

The sound of boots on metal rang through the cabin. Soldiers coming up the ladder.

Andy jumped on the slide and lifted his legs, allowing himself to slide with no control. The ground raced towards him. He heard shots. He saw the others on the runway running towards a maintenance truck, shots following them.

Andy glanced towards the departure lounge and saw flashes of muzzle fire dance behind the broken windows.

Then he hit the ground hard. The momentum carried him forward, and he rolled on to the concrete. He jumped up and ran.

Bullets bounced around him.

Peter waved from inside the truck, "Come on Andy!"

Andy ran from side to side. He didn't know if it helped, but it was what they always did in the films. He jumped into the maintenance truck and slammed the door. Bullets rattled over the truck.

Peter let out a cry and blood splashed across the dashboard.

"You're hit," shouted Andy.

"My arm," said Peter, grimacing. "I'm ok, only grazed, I think." He grabbed his shoulder and squeezed tight. Blood oozed from between his fingers.

"Let me drive," said Andy.

"No, we haven't got time to swap. I'm ok."

Peter hit the accelerator. The truck pulled off with a squeal.

The passenger window shattered. Carl and Jenny ducked in the back seat.

Peter raced towards the runways, the gunfire faded.

Chapter 9

The truck bounced over the runway, pitted with holes and ruptured slabs of concrete, pierced with fragments and chunks of steel. The remains of airplanes. Some still smoked, only just crashed from their fiery end. How many planes had they shot down? wondered Andy.

As if in cruel answer, a loud explosion rocked the air. All eyes in the truck looked skyward. A bulbous cancerous lump of smoke spread across the sky, a few hundred feet up. Small black fragments escaped from the burst, and then, like a dying whale, the carcass of a plane fell from the cloud. White and blue, in half. A wing followed. A tail wing. The second half of the aircraft. Bodies.

"Christ, those bastards. How can they?" said Peter.

"Their own people," said Jenny. "It's horrible."

The two jets responsible for the carnage were visible flitting in and out of the cloud line. They dropped and turned in a wide circle, heading towards the airport.

"Peter," said Andy.

"Yeah?"

"Those planes. They're coming back. We need to get off the runway."

Silence as Peter looked into the sky, watching the planes coming towards them.

He hit the brakes and turned the truck sharply.

"Go round, get to Terminal 1," said Andy. "We can get into the car park through the maintenance tunnel."

Peter hit the accelerator of the truck, and the engine whined. Faster. They needed to go faster, they were up against supersonic jets.

Andy stared out behind the truck. There was a flash underneath one of the planes.

"Shit," he said.

"What?" said Carl.

"Drive Peter, fucking drive!" shouted Andy.

"What do you think I'm doing?"

A white tube of smoke in the air betrayed the missiles journey, it would be on them in seconds.

"There!" Andy pointed to under a plane access tunnel.

Peter pulled the truck hard to the left. The two left wheels lifted and the right wheels squealed.

The missile changed trajectory to follow.

The truck drove under the access tunnel.

The explosion.

Surrounded by white light. Thumps of metal on the roof of the truck. A spike of metal pierced the roof, missing Jenny's head by inches. She screamed.

The truck burst through the smoke back onto the open runway.

"Hug the building," said Andy.

Peter drove the truck yards away from the side of the airport building, passing one gate after another, racing under the many access ramps and planes sat waiting for passengers that would never arrive.

Windows shattered as the two planes passed over, a few hundred feet.

"Fuck this," said Andy, "we won't make it."

"Let's ditch," said Peter.

He brought the truck to a screeching halt as near to the gate as possible.

They jumped out of the truck. The air was damp and heavy, ominous somehow as if the world had suddenly turned against all life.

The sound of the two jets filled the air.

They ran into the building, into the empty staircase that went up one flight to the departure gate.

"What about soldiers?" said Jenny.

"More chance against them than those jets. Let's just be careful, come on," said Andy motioning for everyone to follow him.

The building shook as the jets passed low overhead. They screeched into the distance.

The group climbed the stairs which led to the gate's waiting area. Andy looked through the glass walls.

No people. No soldiers. No zombies.

They moved carefully into the lounge. Rows of empty chairs. A vending machine with flashing lights. An arcade game sang out twee songs over racing car noises. Beyond these low electronic sounds was a deep silence. Andy had never been in an airport this silent.

"What now?" said Carl.

"Anyone got a car parked here?" said Andy.

"I do," said Jenny. "It's only small. A Peugeot."

"If it goes, it'll do. Where are you parked? Staff parking?"

She nodded.

Andy looked down the length of the silent departure gates. A few hundred yards of nothing. And then would be baggage reclaim and the arrivals lounge. There must be people, soldiers, somewhere. Zombies.

"Let's stick together, keep your eyes open," said Andy. "How's your arm, Peter?"

The left arm of Peter's shirt was stained a dark red. He was holding his shoulder tightly.

"It's ok. Stings like hell though."

They set off at a jog through the departure gates. Soldiers would be looking for them. Andy wondered how long before they were found.

Not too long.

"Freeze, don't fucking move!"

The voice came from behind.

The group stopped running. No-one turned.

Andy's heart raced, thumping hard against his chest. Adrenaline pumped through his body.

"Hands up, and turn around, very slowly."

The four obliged.

Two soldiers stood a few yards away. Machine guns raised, pointing at them. It was the first time Andy had had a gun pointed at him. It felt strange, to be just a trigger pulling decision away from death. To be so utterly dependant on the whims of the men in front of him.

"Where have you come from? You come from that plane?"

"We're not infected," said Andy, slowly, measured.

"Are you from the plane?" repeated the soldier, also speaking slowly.

Andy felt all eyes on him. For a moment, he wished he wasn't the Captain. He wished they weren't all relying on him to make the decisions, to answer for them. He toyed with the idea of running at the soldiers, getting himself shot, relieving himself of the pressure, of the pain he felt every day.

But he didn't. Instead, he said, "No, we aren't from the plane. We are crew of flight GH-5673. Due to take off thirty minutes ago. Before, all this. We've been hiding in the toilets. We were scared, didn't know what was happening."

The soldier eyed Andy carefully. The other, a young man with bright red hair cut close to his head, pointed at Peter and said, "What happened to your arm?"

"I got shot."

The soldier stared at Peter. "Do you need medical assistance?"

Peter shrugged.

The first solider, a sergeant, going by his stripes, said, "You need to come with us. I think you are from a plane that recently landed. If so, you need to be quarantined."

A loud moan echoed in the empty air.

"What was that?" said Jenny.

"Zeds," said the Sergeant.

He motioned them along with his weapon. They walked down the corridor, heading back the way they had come. Every now and then a shot, or a moan, broke the silence.

"What's happening?" said Andy. "Where is everyone?"

"Not sure myself," said the Sergeant. "We have orders to keep the infection out."

"So you are shooting innocent people then?" said Jenny, her voice wobbling.

The Sergeant gave her a sharp look.

"Easy," whispered Carl, and he put his hand on her arm. She shrugged it off.

"How can you do this? How can you kill all those innocent people, innocent children, you're monsters!" she shouted.

The Sergeant spun round. "They were infected! We have to contain the infected."

"They weren't infected, not all of them. You must know that. Monsters." Jenny hissed the last word. "You're even worse than the zombies. You make me sick." She spat towards the soldiers.

The Sergeant's face flushed. Whether it was anger or shame, Andy couldn't tell. "Listen, you have no idea what's going on out there, you have no idea!"

"So you think the answer is just to kill everyone," said Jenny. "Fucking hero's, the lot of you."

"We're following orders," said the Sergeant.

"That's what they said in Nuremberg," said Jenny.

"She's right," said Andy. "If you know what you're doing is wrong, then you can't hide behind orders."

The group stood in silence. The Sergeant looked from Andy, to Carl, to Peter, and then to Jenny. He was in his early twenties. Tough looking, strong. Typical jarhead army haircut.

The other soldier, the one with the red hair, had been quiet for most of the exchange, just watching his Sergeant. But now he spoke.

"They told us that they were all infected. But I know they weren't. We knew that, Sarge, it's obvious," he said. "These people are right, we're monsters." He had tears in his eyes. He sniffed loudly and looked to the side, out the window of Gate 23, trying to hide his tears.

The Sergeant opened his mouth to speak but didn't. He stood still, his mouth hanging open. He closed it. He looked up and down the corridor. It was empty for as far as they could see. More moans rang out, closer, this time.

"You were on the plane that crashed into the departure lounge, weren't you?" said the Sergeant.

Andy nodded.

"How many were infected on the flight?"

"We had three hundred and seventy-two passengers," said Andy. "Before we got off the plane, I counted about twenty dead. Maybe a handful escaped that had been bitten. But I would say that the rest were ok. Just trying to stay alive."

The two soldiers looked at each other, the math firing between them in silent blinks and stares. Over three hundred innocents, dead.

The Sergeant took a deep breath and exhaled loudly. He looked on the brink of tears of himself. He cleared his throat.

"I'm Sergeant Chimer. This is Private Hutchinson."

Andy and the others introduced themselves.

"Where are you going?" said Sergeant Chimer.

"We're trying to get to the car park," said Carl. "We have a car, we want to get out of here. We have families."

Andy felt a brief stab in his heart. His only family was a photo in his trouser pocket.

"Ok," said Chimer. He looked at Hutchinson and held his radio up to his mouth. "Runway Base, this is Chimer, Runway Base, this is Chimer, come in. Over"

"Sergeant Chimer," came the muffled reply, "this is Runway Base. Over"

"We've spotted them. Looks like they are heading towards the arrival's lounge, they've doubled back on us. Hutchinson and I will give chase. Over."

"Roger Chimer. Do you need assistance? Over."

"Negative Runway Base, we got this one, Over. Out."

"Out."

Hutchinson smiled at Chimer.

"Let's get you out of here then. Come on, we have to be quick."

Andy felt relief flood into his veins and his heart. He didn't realise how tense he had been until the feeling had passed. He didn't know how much faith he had lost in humanity until these two soldiers had suddenly restored it.

Chapter 10

The group ran through the airport unassailed, with the two soldiers as their escorts. Chimer ran at the head of the group, Hutchinson following behind.

As they reached the shopping area, the airport took on the look of the aftermath of a riot.

The shop windows were shattered, glass fragments dripping with blood, hanging with ripped clothes, and most gruesome of all, with chunks of flesh. Alarms rang out with a shrill narcissism, all the different tones, and intervals melding into one constant cacophony like terrible insects from an alien world. Bags, suitcases, and holdalls lay open and abandoned, their contents spread like laundry confetti.

But what Carl found the worst was the bodies. Men, women, children, all lying in various states of disfiguration. Some looked like they were just sleeping, resting up against the chairs, slouched across doorways. Like well dressed drunks. Others had been ripped to shreds, bright red gashes in their flesh, their midriffs spilling intestines and other unnamed organs across their laps. Blood oozed from some corpses like thick red jelly.

And some had gunshot wounds.

The soldiers guided the group carefully around the corpses. Chimer moved with practiced caution, quickly assessing the terrain with a keen eye, whether it be corridor, lounge, or shopping area

His radio buzzed every now and again, and he would fire a quick two-word response - maybe a check-in.

"Come on," said Carl to Peter, who was running at the rear of the group. Hutchinson stood behind him, impassive, but watchful.

"I'm ok," said Peter, holding his shoulder.

"Are you?"

"Just feeling a bit faint. The sooner we get to the car park, the better."

Peter was pale. His shirt was dripping red blood.

"Do you have any first aid gear?" Carl said to Hutchinson.

Hutchinson shook his head, "All back at Runway Base."

"Come on," Carl put his arm around Peter.

A small gap had opened up between them and Andy, Jenny and Chimer.

Carl jumped at the sound of a gunshot.

Chimer was crouched on one knee, his gun up by his shoulder. He fired again and a zombie, walking out of the toilets, fell with a clean headshot.

"Come on, move it!" shouted Chimer. He increased his pace.

They reached the lifts. The huge elevators that went to the car parks, designed to hold twenty people and all their luggage.

"You trust these?" said Andy as they congregated by the lift.

"You mean power?" said Chimer.

Andy nodded.

"No problem, we've seen to that." He pressed the button, and the lights indicated the lift coming down from the fifth floor. "Which floor is your car on?"

"The third," said Jenny.

"Sarge," Hutchinson pointed to four zombies shuffling towards them from the far corridor. He crouched onto his knee and fired four shots, each one hitting its mark. The shots echoed almost painfully in the confined space of the lift lobby. Each zombie fell with a thud.

"Stand back," said Chimer. He held his gun up as the lift reached their floor with a ding.

The doors opened.

Empty.

"Ok, let's go!" said Chimer, hustling the group in. They couldn't move quick enough to satisfy him. "Go, go, go!" Carl helped Peter in. Peter seemed heavier. He let out a small groan.

Chimer and Hutchinson took one last look around the empty lift lobby, guns raised, before pressing the button for the third floor.

They stood in silence as the lift climbed slowly. The sound of alarms from the shops faded and the whine of the elevator hummed in the enclosed metal space.

We should just stay here, thought Carl. I don't want to see what the world is like.

Chimer and Hutchinson crouched by the doors and raised their guns. They motioned for the others to crouch.

The doors opened slowly, and the two soldiers moved out slowly in unison, each scanning one side of the car park.

Car alarms replaced the shop alarms with an equal yearning urgency. The dark shell of the large car park stretched for hundreds of meters. Flashing yellow, orange, red and white lights from the many car alarms made Carl feel like he had stepped into a cheap nightclub.

"Where are you parked?" said Chimer above the sounds of the alarms.

"This way," Jenny pointed and made to get up and run in that direction, towards the far end of the car park. Chimer grabbed her shoulder, roughly, pressing her down, keeping her crouched.

"Tell me where, stay behind me," he said.

Jenny shook off Chimer's hand. "There, in the middle, at the far end."

Chimer raised his hand, "Listen," he said.

They listened. Nothing but the manic car alarms. Then Carl heard it. Quiet at first, but once the sound registered, he couldn't un-hear it. It got louder in his mind and seemed to burrow straight into his brain.

The moaning. Like a profound shift in the very earth, but one that reached into his soul.

"There's hundred's down here. Let's stay tight. Wait here," said Chimer. He fell onto his stomach and crawled from the lift across the empty lane to the first column of parked cars, taking up position on the left side of the column. He peered around the end car and shook his head. He made a hand signal to Hutchinson.

"What is it?" said Andy to the Private.

"Aisle is full of zeds."

Chimer pointed to the opposite aisle. Hutchinson crawled to it and peered around the side of the bonnet. He whistled quietly.

The two soldiers made a series of hand signals to each other, then Hutchinson motioned for the group to crawl to the middle of the column of cars, in between the soldiers. They did so.

"Zeds everywhere," whispered Chimer. "We need a new plan."

Hutchinson crawled over to Chimer, and they began to talk in hushed tones.

Peter, sitting up against a car, let out a small moan. He looked bad. He needed help, thought Carl.

Carl peeked over the top of the bonnet. How many zombies could there be?

About twenty feet away, a thick crowd of figures milled in the semi-darkness. They bounced off each other and the cars mindlessly, their hundreds of feet shuffling against the dry concrete to create a strange white noise almost like waves on a beach.

"Shit!" said Carl, his nerves and fear getting the better of him. He had spoken louder than he meant to. He immediately pulled his hand to his mouth, but it was too late.

A few of the nearest zombies snapped their heads in Carl's direction. They saw him and let out a huge moan, sounding almost excited.

The effect was terrible and hypnotic.

The reaction spread through the crowd of undead and one by one, they turned and moaned, their mindless shuffling becoming a guided desire for warm flesh.

Hutchinson stared at Carl, hard, then looked past him to Chimer. "Compromised sir, many hostiles."

"Shit," said Chimer. "Ok, this way!" He ran across the aisle to the next column of cars.

Hutchinson grabbed Carl, "Come on, and don't fucking move without me telling you to."

Peter held out his arm, "Carl, can you help?"

Carl shouldered Peter, and they hobbled after Chimer, Andy and Jenny. Hutchinson stood behind Carl and Peter, his gun tracking the first zombies that exited the aisle and shuffled towards them. He fired three times. Three zombies fell.

The next aisle was full of zombies, as was the next. Chimer led them across one aisle to the next. Carl and Peter limped after them, falling behind.

Chimer stopped running at the fifth aisle.

"This one," shouted Chimer. He crouched on his knee and fired slowly, methodically.

"Hurry up!" shouted Hutchinson, still with Carl and Peter. Peter was pale, hardly able to support himself.

"We need to stop this blood," said Carl. "He's going to pass out." Although Carl's real worry was that Peter was going to die.

"We can't stop here," said Hutchinson

Zombies poured out of the aisles behind them and filled the road. The shuffling and moaning echoed upon itself to create a thick wall of terrible sound, just as terrifying as the sight of the creatures making slow movement towards them.

Peter stumbled over his feet and fell. His eyes were closed.

Carl tried to rouse him, but there was no response.

"Shit," said Hutchinson.

The group from the second and third aisles were only feet behind them.

A zombie from the fourth aisle, only the distance of one car away, appeared - a man in a T-shirt and khaki shorts, his left leg only a stump from the ankle. It somehow managed to keep its balance and raised its arms, moaning at the sight of Carl, Peter, and Hutchinson. It was quickly followed by others.

Carl panicked. They were surrounded. Boxed in by cars, two walls of zombies, and the brick wall of the car park across the road.

"What do we do?" he shouted, looking at Hutchinson.

Hutchinson let off a few shots. "We go over the cars."

"What about Peter?" said Carl looking at the unconscious figure on the floor, covered in blood, pale, breathing heavily, clammy white skin.

"We have to leave him," said Hutchinson. "He's dead anyway, we have no medical equipment, and he needs a blood transfusion." Hutchinson grabbed Carl's arm and pulled him towards the column of cars.

"We can't!"

"You want to live?"

"Sorry," Carl said quietly to Peter.

Carl followed Hutchinson as he climbed up onto the nearest car, a black BMW.

He glanced back at Peter. His eyes had half opened. He raised his arm and let out a small whimper, reaching for Carl.

The wall of zombies fell on him.

Carl climbed up on the car, over the bonnet and into the gap before the next. Screams followed him, Peter's screams. Moans hummed like an excited theatre crowd, and thick squelching sounds and the cracks of breaking bones rose into the car park.

Carl bent over, sudden cramps attacking his stomach. He threw up. Tears flowed from his eyes. He wanted to curl up and let the zombies get him.

Two zombies tried to squeeze into the gap that Hutchinson and Carl stood in.

"Come on," said Hutchinson, grabbing Carl. "We have to go."

Carl felt himself climb over the next car, drop into the gap, then climb the next, and again and again. He wasn't really doing it. Everything felt like a nightmare. All he could see was Peter holding out his hand, one human to another, asking to be saved.

Chapter 11

Andy watched in dismay as a wave of zombies filtered out of the last aisle, blocking his view of Peter and Carl. It hadn't looked good. Peter had fallen.

"Move!" Chimer jumped up from his knees, the zombies in the aisle having been cleared.

They ran fast past the cars, the sounds of frenzied shuffling and rasping exhalation never far away.

Andy dared to glance behind him. Two things; a group of zombies following them down the aisle; two figures climbing over the central column of cars, two rows back. It looked like Carl and the other soldier.

No Peter.

Andy swallowed hard. He knew what that must mean, but he couldn't let it register, not yet.

"Where's your car?" said Chimer as they reached the end of the car park.

"Back this way," said Jenny. "It's a red Peugeot."

"Chimer," shouted Andy, "we need to wait for these two."

Chimer nodded and raised his hand, they came to a stop by the column of cars that Carl and Hutchinson were climbing over. Eventually, they jumped down from the last vehicle to join Andy and the others.

"What happened to Peter?" said Andy.

Carl, his eyes red, just looked at Andy and shook his head.

"Come on, let's find this car," said Chimer.

They ran past many aisles, Jenny finally slowing. "There!"

The wall of undead was half an aisle away, moving with uncertain dedication towards the group.

Jenny pulled out her keys and climbed in the driver's seat. Andy got in the passenger seat, Carl in the back.

"You coming?" said Andy.

Chimer looked uncertainly at the approaching group of undead.

"We'll never get through them, sir," said Hutchinson.

"We could do with your help," said Andy. "God know's what it's like out there."

Chimer took his radio, "Chimer to base. Chimer to base."

"Chimer, where the hell are you?" came the static bathed reply.

"We've encountered some difficulties. We are forced to abandon the airport."

"What? What's going on sir?"

Chimer looked at Hutchinson, who shrugged.

"Look, I'm speaking to Corporal Ford, right?" aid Chimer. "Some serious shit is going down. We have to bug out. If you've got any sense, you'll do the same yourself."

"Sir, what-"

Chimer turned off the radio

Andy smiled. "Thanks. Now let's get out of here."

Chimer got in the back of the car, and Hutchinson got in the other side so that Carl was in the middle.

Jenny pulled out of her parking spot. An old woman with half her scalp hanging off lurched onto the bonnet of the car, spreading blood across the windscreen.

Jenny accelerated hard. The wheels of the little Peugeot spun loudly and then caught. The car catapulted forward, and the old woman flew off the side, leaving behind her scalp, stuck to the radio antenna.

Jenny drove the car quickly through the car park, following the exit sign. She pulled sharply to the left and right, avoiding stumbling, reaching zombies.

The exit sign pointed to the left. She turned and slammed on the brakes. A thick bunch of dead blocked their road to the exit ramp.

"What now?" said Jenny.

"Hold here for a minute," said Chimer. He wound down his window and sat out on the door frame. Hutchinson copied him, on the other side.

They both opened fire. The gunshots echoed loudly in the concrete enclosed car park. Blood sprayed from the heads of the numerous figures blocking their path, and they fell, one by one.

"Let's go," shouted Chimer from outside the car. "We can-," he let out a sharp yell.

Andy heard Hutchinson shout an exclamation. There was the sound of gunfire. Andy spun round to try and see what was happening.

Chimer fell back into the car, holding his right arm.

Hutchinson retook his seat. "Shit! Fuck! Those fucking zombies! Fuck!" he banged his gun against the back of Andy's seat.

"What happened?" said Andy.

"Just drive, there's more coming," said Chimer calmly. He stared hard at Andy.

"Ok, Jenny let's go."

Jenny put her foot down, and the car accelerated towards the group of dead zombies. Andy braced as the car bounced over the two-time dead bodies. A number of sickening thud sounds came from under the car.

A few seconds later they were on smooth tarmac again.

"We need to cut your arm off," said Hutchinson.

"You got bit?" said Andy, turning around again.

"Don't stop, keep going. We can't risk getting swamped."

"Sir, if we cut the arm off, then maybe-"

Carl let out a yell.

"What's happening?" said Jenny, glancing furtively in the rearview mirror, fright apparent in her voice.

"Keep driving," said Andy.

Chimer's eye's had closed, and his body was convulsing.

"He's turning into one of them!" shouted Carl, trying to get as far away from Chimer as possible, pushing up against Hutchinson.

"Ok, get him out of the car," said Andy.

Hutchinson shook his head, "No fucking way, we get him help."

Chimer let out a gurgling sound, a rattle from deep in his chest. Blood spluttered out of his mouth, through clenched teeth.

"Jenny, stop the car," shouted Andy.

Jenny hit the brakes hard, and the car screeched to a halt, halfway down the circular exit ramp.

Andy jumped out of the car and ran around the front of the bonnet to get the far passenger side.

Hutchinson also jumped out and ran around the boot.

They met by the door of the Peugeot.

"I won't let you do this," said Hutchinson.

"We can't help him," said Andy.

"We have to try."

"I've seen what happens, close up, I've just been on a plane full of these fucking things. It's too late." Andy grabbed the door handle.

Hutchinson grabbed Andy's hand.

There was no thought, Andy's free hand simply swung. It connected hard with Hutchinson on the side of the face. The Private spun against the car.

Andy punched him again, the pain of the punch jarring through his wrist, his elbow. His knuckles fizzed.

Hutchinson shook his head, steadying himself.

Carl and Jenny got out of the car.

Andy punched Hutchinson again, connecting hard with the soldier's jaw. That did it. Hutchinson fell onto the floor with a thump.

Andy pulled open the passenger door.

Chimer's body convulsed violently. His legs stuck out straight; his back pushed into the air; his head banged against the seat; his eyes bled; his cheeks pumped with air, blood spitting from his mouth with furious coughs.

Andy pulled at the Sergeant's arm.

"Help me," he said.

Jenny grabbed Chimer's other arm and pulled.

Chimer fell onto the floor, where his body, now free of any constraint convulsed furiously against the floor.

"What about him," said Jenny pointing to Hutchinson, lying cold on the floor. "We can't leave him."

Andy nodded. The three of them struggled to lift his body and get him into the car.

Chimer stopped fitting.

Andy and Jenny held up Hutchinson's body by the Peugeot's door. It was amazing what a dead weight his body was. Carl climbed in the other side of the car and pulled at Hutchinson, as Andy and Jenny fed him through.

There was a sudden gasp and moan from the ground near Andy's feet. He glanced to his left and saw Chimer - or what used to be Chimer - lying still, its eyes open, its mouth curling back in a snarl. Its head turned, and the zombie fixed its eyes on Andy. Its jaws chattered manically, and it rolled onto its side, pulling with its hands to get closer.

"Quickly!" shouted Andy.

Carl let out a puff of air and pulled hard on Hutchinson. Andy and Jenny pushed, and Hutchinson was in the car.

Andy felt a hand grab his leg. "Get in the car!"

Andy shook his leg, trying to free the hand. The zombie's head was only a foot away from his leg. It pulled hard, and the chattering jaws came within inches of Andy's calf.

He kicked his leg out and slipped free. He ran around the bonnet and got in the passenger side.

Jenny hit the accelerator, the car skidded away. In the rearview mirror. What used to be Chimer struggled to its feet and shuffled slowly and uselessly after them.

Chapter 12

They bounced out of the exit ramp, the speed causing the front of the Peugeot to hit the ground hard. Sparks flew from the front of the car.

"Where do we go Captain?" said Jenny.

Andy didn't know. There was no one at home he had to save. Twice in a year, his world had changed beyond all recognition. First, everyone he loved had been wiped out overnight. Now in the space of a short flight from Spain to Manchester, the whole world, not just his, had been ripped apart.

If he stopped to think about it, to ruminate any further, he knew he would fall apart. He had to do what he had always done. Push on, ignore his heart. Just do.

But do what?

Jenny pulled out onto the main airport road that eventually led back to the motorway. She gasped.

Smoke. Lot's of smoke. It filled the air as if they were looking through dirty grey glasses. The source of the smoke was a huge lorry on the side of the road, burning ferociously. Andy felt the heat immediately, even though they were a good few hundred feet away. The flames rose high into the air, like a primal gas beast trying to escape the Earth.

"Jesus," said Carl looking through the middle of both the front seats.

"Keep driving," said Andy.

Jenny accelerated.

They were not the only ones on the road. Military vehicles, vans, cars, motorbikes. Some moving, some wrecked. Lots were abandoned.

Jenny weaved the little Peugeot expertly, going as fast as she dared in the thick smoke.

Sounds of gunfire and explosions echoed somewhere in the abandoned world as they cut a path through the grey nothing land. No sight of when it would end, or when it would clear.

A woman, covered in blood, ran from the side of the road. Her arms waved maniacally at the car.

"Don't stop!" shouted Andy.

Jenny pulled to the right, but a little too late. The car clipped the woman, and she spun away with a thud.

"It's like some sort of hell," said Jenny.

She drilled the car forward, and eventually, the smoke thinned. The sounds of chaos dissipated behind them.

The road widened onto the motorway slip road. A line of vehicles stood stationary. Some on fire, some crashed into the backs of others. Some looked like they had people in them, but Andy tried not to look too closely.

A flash in the sky caused his eyes to veer skyward. A thick tunnel of smoke like white cotton wool followed a flaming Boeing 767 with British Airways markings as it plummeted towards the ground. A high screeching scored its descent.

Two nearby jets disappeared into the low lying cloud.

Andy felt his heart lurch, his stomach quell with nausea. All those people, families, children, just wiped out at the whim of a government who had lost control.

Was it even the government though? Who was to tell who was in control now.

"Where are we going?" said Jenny.

There was nowhere that Andy needed to go, nowhere he thought they should go. Where could be safe? Anywhere?

"What do you need to do?" he said.

"What?" said Jenny.

Andy turned to face Jenny, "What do you need to do, anyone you need to see, family?" He turned to Carl. "What about you Carl?"

"My husband," said Jenny. "And my children." Andy saw tears well in the corner of her eyes.

"My girlfriend," said Carl. "Well, my ex. But I want to see if she's ok. We live in Northwich. It's not that far."

"Where do you live Jenny?"

"Chester. We live in Chester."

Northwich and Chester were south and east of Manchester. Near each other, and more importantly, out of the city. Andy didn't know why, but he felt that it was better to head away from the city.

"Ok, let's go there then. We'll head to Northwich first, it's closest, then on to Chester. That sound good to you both?"

Carl nodded.

"What about you?" said Jenny.

Andy shook his head. "No-one. Confirmed bachelor." He smiled, throwing all the warmth behind it that he could.

So they drove, south, away from the airport, away from the city. Andy wondered how long until the traffic snarled again until they had to leave the car, but he would worry about that when it happened.

For now, they were alive.

Plane Dead

The Facility

Chapter 1

"We've got one!" Professor Lloyd stood at the door, an excited grin on his face.

Grace looked up from her computer screen. "You mean here, in the Facility?"

"Right here. The containment suite in Block C. Come on!" He waved his arm manically.

Grace locked her computer and quickly got up.

She and the Professor walked through the winding white and clinical corridors of the Facility towards Block C, five minutes away. The Professor was dictating a rapid pace that belied his sixty-something years.

"Where did it come from?" asked Grace breathlessly.

"The military dropped it off thirty minutes ago. I only just got the call. I came straight to get you."

"You haven't seen it yet yourself?"

"No, not yet."

They hurried through the busy corridors. Bright white lights buzzed above them. They passed numerous doorways, many stuck with triangular yellow hazard signs.

They reached the entrance to Block C. A wide corridor with a security desk, manned by a soldier. You needed very special permission to enter.

Grace showed her pass to the soldier. He swiped it, nodded. She then went through the battery of biometric tests: retina scan; fingerprints; breath signature.

The door to Block C opened with a mechanical swish, and she walked through. It closed behind her with the same swish, and she waited for the Professor to complete the same checks, before joining her.

"I'm always tempted to have a curry and strong whiskey before that breath test, see if that will throw it," said the Professor with an impish grin.

They walked a few more minutes. Block C was quiet compared to the rest of the Facility. Fewer people. Grace was sure the lights were a degree or two dimmer as if trying to hide something.

They reached a faceless small door in the side of the corridor. No indication of what lay beyond.

The Professor pressed his thumb against a pad by the door, and it opened. They walked into a large dark lobby, another soldier standing guard. A corporal. He nodded at Grace and Professor Lloyd. "Doctor, Professor, morning."

They went to the desk and signed in with their retina scans.

"You here to see the zed?" asked the young soldier.

"Is that what you call them?" said Lloyd.

"I guess zed for Zombie," said Grace.

The Corporal smiled, "Yep, that's what we been calling them." Grace smiled back. "Yes, we're here to see the specimen."

The Corporal laughed, "Come on Doc, 'zed' is a much better name."

"We'll see," said Grace. She waved at the Corporal as they walked off.

"You shouldn't tease him," said Lloyd.

"How do you know I don't like him?" said Grace.

"Because you forget how long we have worked together and how well I know you. He's twenty years younger than you for a start, and he's not your type."

Grace just smiled.

They entered a large darkened room, furnished with several empty chairs facing a large glass window that took up the whole of one wall - a one-way mirror that offered a silent and secret view into the containment suite. Some people stood at the window, a mix of suits and lab coats. An excited chatter bubbled in the room.

The Professor eased his way through the crowd to the front.

"Virologists coming through!" he said.

A few friendly words of banter were exchanged and eventually, Grace and the Professor stood at the window.

Grace took in a deep breath. There it was.

The containment suite was a large white room, lit with fierce fluorescents, leaving no hidden corners of shadow. Technical equipment and monitoring devices lined the room; silent flashing lights; screens with undulating sine waves; omniscient cameras on stands and around the walls.

In the corner of the room stood a soldier, a large machine gun held across his body. He yawned.

Wires from many of the devices led to a gurney in the centre of the room.

On the gurney was a body - a naked man, somewhere in his fifties. Podgy white skin with sporadic hair growth. Grace's attention was immediately drawn to the large gash in the man's neck. Inches long and an inch wide, running from the corner of his ear to the top of his shoulder. Tendrils of rough flesh, pink and unmoving like tiny stalactites protruded from the wound. No blood. It was perfectly dry.

The man's skin had a white pallor, clammy and cold, like a beached whale. Exactly how Grace expected a dead body to look.

Except the man's eyes were open, staring at the huge TV mounted on the ceiling above the gurney. His pupils followed colourful shapes on the screen as they flowed in random, dancing patterns.

The man next to Grace leaned over to her and said, "The patterns keep it occupied. Without the screen, it goes crazy trying to get anything alive. But turn on the screen, and it totally shuts down. Its brain switches to theta state."

It was Harry. He worked in the bacterial division. "It responds to visual stimulus?" said Grace, not looking at Harry.

"Auditory, visual and olfactory. Doesn't seem to feel much, and we don't know about taste yet."

"That would make sense. The virus would shut down all sensory functions unnecessary for survival. It only needs to see, hear and smell to find food. Why care what it tastes like, and what benefit would touch signals, pain, be?"

"Watch this." Harry motioned to a technician in the corner of the room. "Run the knife again."

The technician nodded and moved his mouse, clicking a few times.

A robotic arm folded at the side of the gurney came to life. Silently the thin metal arm rose and a scalpel untucked from its end. With slow, deliberate motions, the blade delicately punctured the skin in the man's bicep.

It sunk an inch into the pallid flesh.

The man made no movement, no sign that he had felt anything. He continued to stare at the wobbling liquid shapes on the screen above him.

The robot arm moved three inches to the left, cutting along the man's flesh, opening a thin black gash. No blood.

The scalpel lifted out of the arm.

The gash clashed slowly like stiff rubber until there was no sign that the scalpel had been there at all.

"You see, it feels nothing."

"We will need skin samples," said the Professor, "and we need to try and find some blood, there must be some left in that cadaver somewhere. I also need several slices of brain. But first, we'll do a complete scan and see if we can identify any areas that the virus has taken hold of."

"We're going to be busy," said Grace.

"Very," said the Professor, his eyes gleaming. "I'm particularly interested in how the virus propagates throughout the body given there is no blood flow."

"If we work on the bacteria hypothesis though," said Harry, "then we already have an answer for that. Replication throughout the internal system."

Professor Lloyd shook his head with a dismissive tut. "No bacteria could operate with the communication and synchronisation needed to maintain control of a body."

"Maybe it doesn't need to, maybe it simply locks and manipulates certain brain functions?"

Grace interrupted the two men's intellectual jousting. She raised her voice and spoke to the technician, "Let me see what happens when you turn off the screen."

The technician turned to a man at the back of the room, who stood in the shadows, barely visible. Grace squinted to see through the darkness. The hidden man wore a dark blue suit, very well fitted. He had dark grey hair plastered onto his forehead in an old-fashioned but well-kept side part.

He nodded at the technician, who then moved his mouse and clicked it twice.

The screen above the zed died, and its eyes blinked. They blinked again.

A hush fell over the collective scientists, technicians, and administrators in the viewing room.

The soldier in the lab room eyed the zed carefully and stepped back. He glanced at the mirror, then pulled his gun up, pointing it at the zed.

Its eyes moved quickly from left to right. Then its head moved. Slowly at first. Easing from side to side, its eyes scanning the room. Then the movements became more furtive.

It turned its head, sniffed. Then snapped to the right and locked eyes on the soldier.

Immediately it let out a moan. A terrible, creaking, and growing moan that filled the viewing room's speaker before getting lost in distortion.

The soldier gripped his gun tighter. His eyes opened wide, fear apparent on his face.

"Is he safe in there?" said an unnamed voice in the viewing room.

"Quite safe," said a voice from behind. Grace snapped her head around to the back of the room. It was the man in the suit with the fancy haircut. He looked at Grace.

A new sound gave her an excuse to turn away from his gaze. A clicking, a snapping. Rhythmical and fast like an out of control clock.

People gasped around her.

The dead thing snapped his jaws open and shut, staring at the soldier. It shook its head violently from side to side and pulled on its restraints.

The soldier eased back to the corner of the room. He put his finger around the trigger of his gun and again glanced through the window.

The zed continued to throw its arms and legs up, rattling its chains loudly against the metal gurney. It tugged with vicious energy against the leather, and the straps rattled in their lock holds.

The woman behind Grace let out a cry as the zed pulled hard and the skin on its wrist peeled away, revealing a layer of yellow sebaceous fat sliding over tendons and muscle.

The soldier was pale. He glanced into the viewing room, his eyes wide open.

"Enough!" said Grace. She turned and stared at the man at the back of the room.

"You've seen enough now?" he said quietly.

She nodded.

The man at the back of the room raised a hand, and the technician clicked his mouse.

The lights in the containment suite died to almost nothing, and then suddenly the screen above the man on the gurney came back into life, with its lava lamp colours and wobbling forms.

The zed's attention turned from the solider and returned to the screen above its head.

A silent monster in waiting.

Chapter 2

Grace stirred her coffee. She sat in the corner of the Facility's large canteen which was full and buzzing with excitement. News of the new arrival had spread and was the subject of all nearby conversations.

The Professor joined her, setting down a cup of tea and a large slice of carrot cake.

"Not taking part in all the fun?" he asked, a playful smile etched across his weathered features.

Grace smiled back. "It all seems like a bit of a circus, don't you think?"

"What's on your mind?" said the Professor.

"We've both worked here for, what, twenty years or so?"

The Professor nodded and took a sip of his tea.

"All this work we do," continued Grace, "All the cloak and dagger stuff, the questionable research, the military work. Does it ever bother you?"

"I would have thought that if it did, I would have left a long time ago. And I think you would have too. Are you having a crisis of conscience?"

Grace shrugged. "I don't know. It just seemed, I don't know, somewhat different today. More…"

"… Real?"

"Yes. More real. I'm used to dealing with computer simulations, rats, grown cell tissues. This is something new though, a human specimen."

"A dead one though," said the Professor wagging his finger. "It's no longer human. The body is simply a vessel for the virus now."

"We think," said Grace.

The Professor waved his hand like he was swatting a fly. "Oh, don't believe that bacteria nonsense that Harry is peddling. Just because he's tall and handsome doesn't mean he's right."

Grace laughed again. "Why do you assume I must have a crush on every man I talk to?"

"Oh come on Grace, you know I worry about you. Nearly forty, married to this place, hanging around with me. I don't like to see good things go to waste."

She smiled at the old man. The closest friend she had in the Facility, and therefore the closest friend she had.

There was a commotion from behind her. She turned around and saw a group of people crowded under the TV. Someone turned the volume up.

Pictures of flaming buildings, soldiers firing their guns, jammed motorways, and what looked like military checkpoints filled the screen. The newscaster spoke in ominous tones - London was being closed to contain the virus outbreak.

"Looks like this is the real thing," said the Professor. "They've really done it this time."

"What do you mean, 'they'?" said Grace. Then she saw the glint in his eye. "You're toying with me."

"It's what you're thinking though, isn't it?" he said. "Is this virus man-made? How ironic would that be? A virus made in a lab somewhere like this one, deep underground, safe from the hell on the surface. Imagine, maybe even this lab."

"Don't," said Grace, feeling uneasy. For some reason, the uncomfortable feeling came with an image, the image of the man in the shadows, with the expensive suit and fancy haircut. "Who was the man in the containment room this morning? The one at the back of the room?"

The Professor creased his bushy eyebrows. "He looked familiar to me, I think his name is Taylor. I've seen him mulling around in the administration section a few times in the past months. He did have an air of the unseen hand in the whole business, didn't he?"

Grace shivered. She remembered Taylor's eyes, his stare. She shook her head a little, as if shaking off a nasty smell.

"Come on Professor. Let's get to work. We should have our samples now. I want to know if this is an actual virus we are dealing with."

They both finished their drinks and left the crowded canteen, and its drama-filled news show behind.

The first run of tests suggested they were dealing with a virus, with a 98.568% probability. The negligible uncertainty was only from errors introduced by their equipment, so there was no doubt.

Grace opened up her instant messaging client and pinged Harry.

>Hey Harry guess what
>Hello Grace. I know, it's a virus. We confirmed it about thirty minutes ago
>And you didn't tell us? :0
>I didn't want to bias your results. And anyway, we have only really confirmed that it's not a bacteria. And then I had to go and have a coffee :)
>ok then, I guess I can let you off. Do you want the details?
>Please. I can't wait for the official presentation.

>it's a virulent bugger, threaded through the complete system. It seems to have replicated at an extraordinary rate. His infection was estimated twelve hours ago and from what we see the virus has a near 100% cell coverage. That is, every single cell in the host has been transmuted by the virus.
>That sounds unusual
>It is. For one thing, it gives the host absolutely no chance of fighting back as even the auto-immune system has been compromised. That's not the worst of it though.
>Go on. You have me intrigued.
>Every system in the host has been hijacked and taken over by the virus. It seems to have stopped most of what we would call the vitals - the heart, the nervous system, the lungs, and rendered them useless meat. The only activity that seems left is muscular activation and some pretty basic brain functions.
>Turned the host into an empty vehicle?
>That's a good analogy, I'll use that in my presentation.
>I would like some credit.
>We'll see. Anyway, you want to hear the rest?
>There's more?
>Indeed there is. We got some preliminary brain results through. The whole brain is dark apart from elementary sensory applications and, again, muscular activity. All it can do is move and sense. The whole human host is reduced to a device for hunting other human hosts and, well, devouring them with the end being to further its own propagation.
>A simple machine. Eating, killing. Terrifying.
> Very. It will turn you into a shell. There's nothing left of the original person.
>Nothing left, so it can't be reversed?
>No. The epilogue to this story is that while the host is busy doing its thing, there is another division of the virus busy destroying all non-necessary brain function. It's as if it wants to make sure there's nothing left of the original person. Totally destructive.

>Pretty efficient, I would say. Once it gets a host, it doesn't want to risk rebellion.
>Exactly. Evolutionary perfection.
>How does it transfer energy?
>We don't know. We're working on it.
>I'm impressed, sounds like you guys have done some pretty good stuff quickly.
>Not really. It's not a difficult virus to find. But thanks.
>I have one more question.
>Shoot.
>A million dollar question. Do you think it's man-made?
>You too
>What?
>Never mind. To answer your question, you used the word 'efficient' before. That's the scary thing - I've never seen anything so efficient. Never. Remember, it even goes to the trouble of destroying what's left behind of the person.
>That's the first time you've said person instead of host.
>Is it? I didn't notice.
>You're worried that this is man-made?
>Yes I am. I've never seen anything like this before, ANYTHING. And we work at the very edge of viral research. This would be one hell of an evolutionary leap if it were natural. There have been no in-between steps that we're aware of. Everything it does: destroying the host, shutting down specific regions of the brain, activating specific regions, has all just appeared, boom. From nowhere.
>Extra-terrestrial? Maybe our virus has floated in on a meteorite?
>That's a thought I prefer. I might go with that, for now, to keep my faith in humanity intact.
>Ok, let's go with that. We have an ET virus. Does it have a name yet?
>Yes, VST-5684.
>Catchy.

>Very. We're calling it the Zombie though.
>I can see why. What's next?
>I'm taking a break. Going to get some dinner.
>You want to grab some in the cafeteria?
>Thanks, but no thanks. I'll eat in my room, I need to make some phone calls.
>Sure, I understand. I should probably do the same.
>I'll give you a shout tonight. I might need a drink.
>Ok. Thanks for the heads up by the way.
>No problem. And remember, on the QT, please. None of this is official until I give a presentation. Probably tomorrow.
>Sure. Catch you later.
>Bye.

Chapter 3

Grace sat in her small room, on the bed. It was a functional bedroom, the same as every other professor, doctor, student and intern room in the Facility. Most lived in the Facility - the only day workers were cleaners, cooks, etc. Shifts varied from a couple of weeks up to a year. Grace was currently on a two-month stint. She wondered how anyone could handle a year. Holed up hundreds of feet underground. Enough to make anyone go crazy.

Her room was furnished with a single bed, a small bedside table, and a desk with a lamp and internal network access points.

There was no wifi. All internet connection was constrained to wires. Any communication with the outside world had to go through the main Facility switchboard. Everything was logged, and everything was monitored in real time.

She picked up the phone that hung next to her bed and waited for the dial tone.

There was a beep, and instead of the normal dial tone, a recorded female voice spoke:

"We are sorry to inform you that due to technical difficulties, all external communications have been suspended for the foreseeable future. Please refer to the communication's page on the intranet for further information."

Grace frowned. If she missed her nightly call to her eighty-year-old mum, mum would worry, she had anxiety issues.

Grace logged her laptop on to the intranet and checked the communication's page.

The same message, except this time, asking her to refer to recorded messages on the internal phone line. A Kafka-esque circle of non-communication.

She swore quietly, then got up to have a shower in her prefab plastic bubble en-suite bathroom.

Grace woke early the next day. She had decided not to go for a drink with Harry the previous night. She had wanted to avoid public places and the inevitable questions about the virus. They could wait for her presentation at lunchtime.

She had her breakfast in her room and made her way to the lab.

The Professor was already there, it was only 7:30am. He was sitting at his terminal, next to Grace's. The dull hum of machinery filled the room. Gentle lights blinked on various devices, and the faint scent of formaldehyde permeated the room. These things, which many would consider banal, soulless and empty, Grace found comforting. She had spent so many years in their presence. It was like a womb.

The Professor turned to her. His face was grim.

"What's wrong?" said Grace, not expecting the Professor to be so glum, given their achievements yesterday.

"I'm afraid I have some bad news, Grace."

"What?" she said, turning on her terminal and putting her coffee on the desk. She didn't sit down but stood with her hands on her hips.

"We've been asked to postpone the presentation, pending review."

"What do you mean, pending review?"

"I got a call last night, at around eight o'clock, I was called to the Secretary's office."

The Secretary's office was actually the Home Secretary's office. He wasn't there very often, but there would always be a representative present, usually a high up civil servant.

"Who's there at the moment?"

"Davis."

Grace let out a derisory snort. He was held in low regard in the Facility, although being mostly harmless.

"And someone else."

"Who?" said Grace, already suspecting she knew who.

"Our friend from the viewing lab yesterday. Taylor. He sat in the corner the whole time, behind me. He wasn't introduced to me, and said nothing."

Grace sat down. "What don't they like about my report? I would have thought, given our audience here, that nothing needs to be censored at this stage. It's not as if we're going public."

"I was told, with no wriggle room, that certain parts of the presentation won't stand."

"Which parts?" said Grace. She could feel her jaw tighten and her stomach tensing. Anger.

"The parts that are more speculative. Regarding the origins of the virus."

Grace sat in silence for a second, her brain firing fast to an exciting and terrifying conclusion.

"My God, Professor, don't you see, I'm right!"

The Professor made a calming motion. "We don't know that."

"Then why the hell do they want to suppress that part of the presentation? The bastards created the virus! Or at least some bastards somewhere in the world, and they know which bastards it was!"

"Or maybe they just don't want to start a lot of panic and

nonsense gossip."

Grace shook her head. "Rubbish. You think I should agree to it?"

"We don't have any choice, Grace. This is coming from the top."

She sighed and bit her lip. She used to bite her lip when she was a schoolgirl and faced with a course of action she didn't want to take. It was a habit that had followed her through her life.

"What the hell is going on Lloyd?"

"I don't know. And it looks like they don't want us to know either. Look…"

The Professor used the remote control to turn on the large HD TV on the wall. He changed it to what should have been BBC1.

"All External broadcasts are suspended for the time being. Please refer to the intranet communication's page for further details."

Grace shook her head angrily. "This isn't on. I know the secrecy involved in this place, but what the fuck do they think this is? Some sort of gulag? We are the brightest bio and viral scientists in the country, they can't treat us like this."

She stood up quickly, accidentally knocking her coffee over. It spilled onto her keyboard.

"Calm down Grace!"

"No, Professor, you should know me by now and know that this isn't a good time to ask me to calm down." She marched towards the door. "Are you coming?"

"Where are you going?"

"To find out what the hell is going on."

The Professor quickly stood up and stumbled after her as she rushed out of the room.

Chapter 4

A crowd had already gathered in the canteen. Assorted white coats, suits, and technicians stood in small groups, the general hubbub of conversation punctuated by now familiar complaints of no phone lines, no TV, no internet.

And especially, how they were all too important to be treated like plebs.

The large TVs of the canteen, which yesterday had been busy beaming the chaos taking place across the country above them, now showed only the universal nothing message:

"All External broadcasts are suspended for the time being. Please refer to the intranet communication's page for further details."

Grace and the out-of-breath Professor joined a group of bacteria scientists sat in a corner by the wall. Grace sat next to Harry.

"Bet you wish you joined me for that drink last night now?" said Harry. "Who knows what's going to happen today, the mood is ugly."

"Never mind last night, I could do with a drink now."

Harry smiled. "Do you guys know anything? It feels like we've suddenly been shut down in a hole."

The Professor and Grace both shook their heads.

"We may be about to find out," said one of Harry's colleagues, pointing to the door, where the Secretary's assistant, Davis, had just entered. It was unusual to see him in the canteen. He would usually only show himself for morale raising events. It looked like he was adding emergencies to his public appearance's list.

He was immediately subject to a barrage of questions, the interrogation firing like the opening salvo of a battle. Voices fought over each other to make sure their own particular displeasure was known.

Davis patted the air, trying to quieten the hoard of unruly scientists.

"Ok, ok, please, be quiet. I have a statement that will explain everything, please, thank you."

Harry leaned over to Grace and whispered, "Look around, amazing how quickly people will descend into a baying mob, once you sprinkle a little fear into the mix."

"Please," said Davis, "quiet, thank you."

The questions stopped, and the conversation sank to a hum, and then to nothing. An uncertain and heavy silence sat in the room. Expectant.

Ready to blow, thought Grace.

"Thank you." Davis, his blue suit perfectly creased, looked over the assembled crowd. "As you know, there has been an outbreak of some magnitude of an unknown virus on the surface. Despite our government's best efforts to contain the outbreak, which first hit our borders three days ago, it has swept across the country in an unprecedented fashion, the vector being, well, everyone."

"What percentage of coverage are we talking about sir?" asked Grace.

Davis spied out Grace. "Last estimates were 85%."

"In three days?"

"In three days."

There was a second or two of silence and then a gasp, followed by raised voices, and then more questions. The realisation of what was happening was beginning to hit.

They had a specimen of the virus in the lab, they had all seen what it was like. They all knew the virus was fatal. 85%. Do the math. Nearly the whole country wiped out in three days.

Including a lot of loved ones.

People began to cry.

"What the hell are we doing down here then? I need to get to my family!" shouted Doctor Stockbridge, a stout virologist from Sector 8. His face was flushed with anger.

Similar protests followed.

Davis took a step back. Involuntary, thought Grace, but telling. He felt the anger and fear in the room.

"Why didn't you tell us what was happening," shouted a woman's voice.

"We need to get out of here!"

"You can't keep us down here, we have to go."

Davis raised his hands again, "Please, please, I will answer your questions, but you must give me a chance to speak."

Quiet returned reluctantly to the room. The atmosphere reduced itself to a gentle simmer.

"I understand that a lot of you are afraid, and that you may feel we have kept you in the dark, and that you have been kept away from your families and loved ones."

A few rude accusations flew towards Davis. He ignored them.

"While this may be the outcome, it certainly was not the intention. I only received those numbers myself late last night. I have been kept in the dark as much as the rest of you. It seems, that, if I am to be candid, the situation above ground is now out of control."

Davis looked shaken. His face was ashen white, and Grace was sure she could see a quiver on his lip. He was scared, just like the rest of them. He had known all of this before them, had more time to process the knowledge. He most probably had his own family, that was now gone.

Cries of anguish echoed around the room as one by one, people realised what was gone. The wife, the daughter, the husband, the young son, the nagging mother. What were the chances they were in the 15% that were still alive if that number was even accurate?

Davis started talking again. "Our communication lines ceased operation this morning at 4:32am. We don't know if this is intentional or whether a catastrophic failure has occurred in the topside systems. Either way, we have no further contact with anyone above ground."

Davis took in a deep breath. Time for the finale.

"We are ordering a full and immediate evacuation of the Facility. All non-critical personnel are to report to exit stations 3, 5, and 7 immediately. Senior staff are required to report to their work's stations and securely delete all sensitive material. We have executed Protocol Icarus."

A dense and dread silence fell across the room.

"My God," whispered the Professor.

There was a sudden rush to the door, Davis was swept to the side, and he mopped his sweating brow with a handkerchief.

Chapter 5

Protocol Icarus was highlighted at the end of each new employee's induction process. Grace remembered it well, and its existence hadn't surprised her - nothing about the Facility surprised her.

Security was tantamount. Every policy, regulation, and legal construct was enshrined to maintain the security of the Facility at any cost. The overriding policy was not concerned with people breaking in, although numerous precautions were taken against unauthorised personnel, terrorist attacks, etc., but mostly involved with stopping anything from getting out. This applied to people, but mainly to the research. The only way any of the Facility's work would ever be published to the broader scientific community was through two paranoid gatekeepers; the Facility's board of directors, and an unknown governmental department that never confirmed nor denied its own existence.

The reason for this secrecy was that the research at the Facility was, as Grace heard it described in hushed terms, of an uncertain moral nature, and as such, best operated within a moral vacuum perpetrated through isolation from society.

Grace had understood the situation and indeed approved of it, as it meant she could compromise her own principles in silence, without the rest of the world, and the people she knew and loved, from being able to pass judgment. But then, after twenty years working the Facility, she didn't have many friends and loved-ones topside anymore, apart from her mother.

The Facility quickly became the life of its most valued scientists.

And so, the implementation of Protocol Icarus was like a hammer to her heart.

It was only at that second she realised how attached she was to her gargantuan underground biological research lab, how much a part of her it had become. The news that the world above was falling apart was upsetting, alarming even, but nothing compared to the cold, stark fear she suddenly felt at the removal of the Facility from her life.

For Protocol Icarus would leave nothing behind.

Slash and burn.

Strategic and Tactical Catastrophe Management.

The countdown would be over four hours. One hour for the Facility's central systems to shut down and secure themselves. The next two hours was the charging and arming of the numerous small nuclear devices dotted around the complex.

The last hour was just to be sure that everyone had a chance to get out; although, a few of the statisticians on the department had, as a playful exercise over the years, estimated how long a full evacuation of the Facility would take, and their numbers usually came in higher than the four hours given by Protocol Icarus. This disconnect became a common joke made in the same nervous way people would joke about a plane crash - an event that everyone feared, but never really expected. Still, though, that voice at the back of your mind, *what if, what if...*

And now *what if* was here.

Grace didn't want to be on the wrong side of the statistics.

A low-key siren began to hum in the background, its monotonous wail piercing enough for one to take notice, but not ear-splitting enough to instil too much urgency. Not yet. Grace suspected it would get louder as the hours ticked away.

A friendly voice announced on the loudspeaker that Protocol Icarus had been implemented, followed by a countdown.

"Three hours and fifty-five minutes."

A sick feeling in her stomach, like a hand gripping her insides and squeezing gently.

She chased after the Professor as he hurried back to the lab. He ignored her calls for him to wait. She caught up with him as he unlocked the lab doors.

"Professor, did you not hear me?"

The Professor glanced up. "I heard you, but we have no time to wait." He flicked on a few machines around him and sat down by his terminal. "What are you doing here? Go and get your things and get out. The queues at the exit stations will be huge within minutes."

He was right. But it didn't feel right to leave him here. He was Grace's friend, after all.

"Come on Professor, come with me."

He shook his head. "I have to wipe all the drives, you understand what needs to be done."

"I understand what it says in the book, but I've never understood why it's necessary, the whole place is about to be nuked!"

"If, for some reason, one of the charges failed to go off, or a single hard drive remained, a particularly industrious person, or nation, may be able to recover some of what we are doing down here. It would be disastrous."

"Disastrous? More disastrous than most of the world dying,

and you being obliterated by a nuclear explosion?!"

The Professor turned to face Grace and gave her a sly smile. "You know me, a stickler for rules."

"That's exactly not how I know you."

"Please Grace, I'll be ok. This talking is only holding me up. I will take care of everything here and see you at Exit Station 7 in an hour?"

The Professor could be a belligerent old bugger, and he had that look in his eyes. She knew, through years of experience, that it was useless arguing with him. The best she could do was let him do what he had to do quickly.

"Ok, I'd better see you there, or I'll be coming for you."

He gave her a nonchalant wave, his eyes fixated on his terminal.

She ran out of the lab.

The usual peaceful corridors of the Facility were no longer peaceful. Gone were the wandering doctors and professors, talking over reports and iPads as they walked from one lab to another. Gone were the smiles and jovial greetings of one professional to another.

Instead, they ran. Everyone ran. Panic and worry knitted on each face.

The siren had increased in volume a notch, and with it came urgency.

Grace found herself running. Her quarters were located only a few minutes from the lab. Even so, she suddenly felt the passing of time like a new sense in her body. A demanding sense that overrode all others. The ever tick-tock of the seconds took precedence over everything.

The lights suddenly switched from their bright day-like glow to a dull orange.

The Facility was conserving power, shutting down non-necessary systems as it continued its workmanlike stomp towards complete oblivion.

Chapter 6

Grace worked her way methodically through her small room, placing items of importance into her suitcase.

She didn't have much. She packed her laptop - her personal one with no work-related information. She packed her clothes and toiletries. She packed the few photos of her parents. She paused to look at the last picture she had of her mum and dad together, before dad died five years ago from pancreatic cancer. That period had been her most extended break from the Facility since she joined. Six months topside helping her mum rebuild her life without her partner of forty years. Mum nearly hadn't made it.

And for what, thought Grace? A lonely life with her daughter living in a hole in the ground doing 'important' government work.

As Grace pushed her laptop's power pack into her suitcase, she took pause. She realised she was packing for an ordinary world. For a weekend break.

Who was to know if there would be any power up above, if she would ever be able to use her laptop again. With 85% of people gone, who was keeping the lights on?

A spike of nervousness and anxiety shuddered through her being.

She continued pushing the power pack into her suitcase.

The eternal optimist.

Exit station 7 was the nearest to her quarters. It consisted of a large waiting room and gated exit, manned by a soldier, who would conduct a battery of identity and security checks on personnel before they were allowed to exit - checks hopefully dispensed with due to Protocol Icarus.

Grace was painfully disappointed to find the chain of bureaucracy still wrapped tight around the exit procedure. The lounge was full of nervous people, an angry buzz of communication and demands hanging in the air, while the flustered looking young soldier at the exit gate methodically performed his security checks.

"The whole place is going to go up in a nuclear blast in a few hours, and you want to check my fingerprints?" shouted one angry Doctor.

The soldier, with a glint of fear in his eye, said, "I'm sorry sir, but I haven't received any orders to the contrary, we all have to be checked."

"You haven't received any orders to the contrary because there are no open communication channels with the surface, you stupid fucking grunt!"

Grace looked around for the Professor, but he was nowhere to be seen. She put her case down in a corner of the packed waiting room and went to find the Professor. She bumped into Harry, who was carrying a leather holdall.

"Grace," he smiled, a pleasant window on his otherwise worried-looking face. "Where are you going? Decided against leaving?"

"Have you seen his place? They're still doing all the checks. It's going to take hours to get out of here."

"Is there any other way?"

"Not that I know of. But I have to find the Professor. He said he'd be here, and maybe he can help."

Harry looked over the restless crowd. There was an unsavoury bite to the air. "I'll come with you," he said. "I don't know what's going to happen here, but I'd rather be here after it happens, if you know what I mean."

They both rushed away from the waiting room, in the opposite direction to the crowds, back towards Grace and the Professor's lab.

It took them ten minutes or so to get there, pushing through agitated and scared flows of people heading in various directions. The loudspeaker kept countdown, every five minutes,

"Two hours and fifty minutes."

...until the end of the world, echoed Grace in her head.

They reached the lab and Grace put her hand on the closed door. Harry, who was looking through the lab's small window put his hand on hers, stopping her from going in. He motioned through the window, and Grace joined him in peering into the lab.

"It's the guy from the other morning, the government spook," said Grace. "He's called Taylor."

"I remember him," said Harry.

Taylor was talking to the obviously agitated Professor, who was waving his arms and shouting. Grace couldn't hear what was being said, the thick glass and door blocking out most of the sound.

Taylor stood calmly, regarding the Professor with what seemed to be amusement.

"Shall we go in?" said Grace.

Harry shook his head. "I don't like the look of this. Let's see what happens."

The Professor stopped talking and lowered his head. He shook it slowly and took something out of his pocket. He handed it to

Taylor.

"What's he giving him?" said Harry.

"It looks like a flash drive. He said he was wiping all the computers, all our work, so what's he doing giving a flash drive to that guy?"

"I'm not sure he wants to..." said Harry.

Taylor took the flash drive and looked at it. He smiled and put it in his suit breast pocket.

Then, in one fluid movement, too quick for anyone involved to recognise what was happening, never mind intervene, he took out a gun from his inside pocket. Surely it can't be a gun, thought Grace? Guns were never seen except on the TV, except in films. Certainly not in real life.

Taylor put the gun against the Professor's head. The Professor didn't have time to change his expression before a fountain of deep reds and purples exploded from the back of the Professor's head, accompanied by a blunt flat bang.

The Professor fell, disappearing from view.

Grace pulled her hand to her mouth to stop herself from screaming. Harry grabbed her, "Come on!" he shouted.

They ran down the corridor and into the next open lab and pulled the door shut. They pressed up against the wall and waited, keeping still. The room was dark. Grace breathed hard and fast, blood thumping in her temples, her hands shaking. The image of the Professor being shot in the head replayed in her mind as if burnt onto her retina like she had stared at the sun.

Harry grabbed her hand, and she squeezed it tight. She could hear his breathing, also loud and fast.

"We wait here," whispered Harry through laboured breaths. "Just five minutes, give him plenty of time to get far away."

"Ok," said Grace, happy to stay there in the dark, away from the now terrible world, at least for the next few minutes.

Silence, but for her heart.

Chapter 7

Grace and Harry shared a few minutes of no words in the dark lab. The siren had increased in volume.

"2 hours and 45 minutes."

The death of the Professor played over and over in her head. She had known him for over twenty years. Had seen him nearly every day. He knew her better than anyone apart from her mum.
Harry was talking.
"What?" said Grace.
"We need to leave," his voice wavered, he was finding his own troubles in processing what had happened. "We need to get the fuck out of here. There is some dark shit going on down here, and we need to get out."

"2 hours and 40 minutes."

His eyes stared at her in the low light.

Harry was right. But first, there was something she needed to do.

"I have to go back to the lab."

"Why?" said Harry. "I don't see how that can help. We just need to get out of here, sooner rather than later."

"It's ok, you go. But I have to see the Professor. I don't know why. We were close."

Harry walked over to the door of the lab and peered out the glass window up and down the corridor as far as he could. "It looks empty. Let's go, let's be quick."

"You don't have to come."

"I know, but I will."

She was glad for the company. "Thanks."

As they stepped into the corridor, the noise of the siren became louder. There was shouting somewhere in the near distance. They ran to the lab.

She opened the door and stepped in. Harry followed. The lights were off. She went to turn them on.

"Don't," said Harry.

She withdrew her hand. He was right. It wasn't completely dark anyway - the Professor's computer was on, its screensaver rolling through images of various complex DNA chains, illuminating the room with changing colourful tones.

She held her breath and looked to the floor, where the Professor's body was. At first, she saw nothing but a dark hulk, like a heavy sack. Then, as her eyes adjusted, the shape of a body revealed itself. Lying unnaturally, uncomfortably. A dark circle spread from the body's head. The Professor's blood.

She walked over slowly and leaned down beside him. She felt for this heart, just to be sure. No heartbeat, no nothing. No life. The spirit that had given him his spark was gone, evaporated in less than a second through a hole in the back of his head.

His eyes were open. Grace closed them.

"You ok?" said Harry.

She nodded and rested her hand on the Professor's. She allowed herself tears, just for a minute.

"I'm sorry Lloyd," said Grace quietly. "I'm sorry I couldn't help you. Take care, wherever you are."

The countdown rudely interrupted her.

"2 hours and 30 minutes."

"We should go," said Harry.

Grace stood up and straightened her dress. She took one last look around the lab.

"Ready?" said Harry.

"Ready," said Grace.

She turned to leave, then paused, her attention taken by a pattern on the Professor's screen she didn't recognise.

The Professor's screen saver consisted of a series of the DNA helixes of his favourite viruses. She laughed inwardly for a second at the Professor being a man with favourite viruses.

This helix she was looking at was not one of them, however.

"Hang on," said Grace. "I need to check something."

She walked over to the screen and wiggled the mouse around. The operating system came back into view.

"Wait a minute..." she said under her breath.

"What is it?" Harry joined her by the low light of the terminal.

"This is Windows."

"So?"

"The Professor hated Windows. He used Linux. Always."

"What are you thinking?"

"Why would he be on Windows? He said he was coming here to wipe everything, but he's on a different operating system."

She looked at Harry, who said, "Maybe he wasn't keen on the idea of wiping everything..."

Grace sat down by the computer hurriedly. "Ok, give me a minute. I want to restart and have a look at what's on his Linux. I think he was only pretending to clear everything down."

They waited as the computer restarted. A purple boot screen appeared, giving the user the option to start up Windows or Linux. She selected Linux. They sat for another minute or so as the operating system loaded up. Anxiety gripped Grace, but a different kind of anxiety from the one she had felt since waking up; this was an excited nervousness. The same as when she was on the brink of a new discovery.

Once it had loaded, she opened the file system.

"Let's look at recent files," she said, half to herself, half to Harry.

Some text documents had been opened within the last hour. She opened the latest one. It was a short email transcript.

```
FROM: Professor Angus Ferrera
TO:   Professor David Lloyd

TOP SECRET
```

"Ferrera, he works for Government labs in America," said Grace. "I met him a year or two ago. He was an arsehole, didn't speak a word to me."

She continued to read the transcript.

```
Well, David, it looks like the experiment
is well and truly fucked. I suggest you get
your nearest and dearest and go hide.
Forever. Adios.
```

Grace stared at the screen in silence for a minute.

She tried to open other recent documents, but they had all been deleted, and their innocuous titles, mainly dates, did little to betray their contents.

"What the hell does that mean?" said Harry.

Grace shook her head. "I don't know. But he wanted me to find it."

"The experiment, you don't think it's anything to do with

what's going on?"

"Of course not," said Grace.

"You sure? Come on. Why was Taylor here, what was on the flash drive? Why the helix clues?"

Grace turned sharply to Harry and was about to open her mouth to shout, but she stopped herself. She was feeling emotional, suggesting cognitive dissonance; the evidence was not aligning with her beliefs.

She took a few deep breaths. "I don't know, Harry. I don't know what this means. And neither do you."

"No I don't, but it doesn't look good."

"No. But we don't have all the evidence. We need to find that flash drive."

Harry sat in the chair next to Grace and let out a heavy breath. "You know what that means?"

"I do," said Grace. "We need to find Taylor."

"You think he's just going to hand it over?"

"No. But he killed the Professor remember. I would say all is fair."

"Christ," said Harry. "What a day."

Chapter 8

They ran in the low light of the corridors, the sirens now making conversation difficult. The hallways echoed with the heavy and quick steps of running employees - hurrying to collect their belongings; to clear down their confidential research; to escape.

Grace and Harry passed two exit stations as they made their way towards the administrative wing, as good a place as any to start their search for Taylor.

The exit stations were bulging to breaking point. Shouts of anger bubbled from the doors, along with crowds of people carrying holdalls, suitcases, and plastic carriers stuffed with files and clothes.

"How long until one of those soldiers gets it?" said Harry through quick breaths.

They passed into the administrative wing. It was calmer. Still the same sirens of course, but less human traffic. And those that were there moved quietly and without panic. Men and women in suits carrying briefcases and little else.

The administrative wing was a sprawling mass of around fifty or so offices. To search each one would be impossible.

"Two hours and twenty minutes."

"I know where Davis' office is, we can start there," said Grace.

She had been to the Secretary's office once, with the Professor, a few years ago. The Professor had been receiving a commendation for work on self-replicating intrusive DNA strands.

"Here it is," said Grace opening the door quietly and peering in. It was empty.

"We should be careful," said Harry.

"What is he going to do, fire us?"

"I was thinking more shoot us," said Harry looking around the empty office.

Grace paused. Harry was right. She closed the door behind them. "Let's be quick then. Now, what are we looking for?"

"Who knows. Let's just look."

It was a large room, with oak wood paneling entirely out of place in the otherwise clinical Facility. A little piece of Westminster hundreds of meters under the ground. They began digging through the various drawers and cupboards.

"I don't see any laptop, do you?" said Harry.

Grace shook her head. So far all she had found were empty drawers, stationary, photos of Davis with politicians, and in one drawer a sizeable weathered paper folder.

Grace pulled out the folder and scanned through the documents inside.

"Requisition, budgets, nothing that I can make any sense of immediately," she said.

"Put them in here," Harry passed over his backpack. Grace tucked the papers in and gave the bag back to Harry.

"There's nothing about Taylor," said Grace.

"I didn't think there would be. What now, he could be anywhere?"

Grace walked over to the window and peered through the blinds, moving them as little as she could. Two women in pencil skirts and white shirts walked passed dragging wheeled suitcases behind them. They talked nonchalantly, ambling gently as if on their way to catch a plane, not escape an underground lab about to go nuclear.

"What looks strange to you about here?" said Grace.

Harry joined her and peered out the blinds.

"Well, they all seem pretty relaxed as if…"

They looked at each other, a sudden joint realisation. Grace vocalised it. "The Admin wing has its own exit station."

"Of course," said Harry. "The government employees aren't going to mingle with us plebs when it comes to escape time."

"They've always used the normal exit station before though," said Grace. Only two months ago she had shared the elevator with Davis. A very auspicious moment.

"Of course they have, the sneaky bastards," said Harry, a smirk on his face. "They don't want to give the game away."

"Take off your lab coat," said Grace, taking her own off. Harry did so, and they stowed the white coats in one of Davis' empty wardrobes.

He was wearing a shirt, a good pair of clean Levis, and trainers.

"I guess that will do," said Grace, looking at the trainers. "I'm sure some of these guys dress down at times."

Grace herself was wearing a plain blue dress, with flat shoes. Perfectly smart.

Checking that no-one was approaching the office, they stepped out into the corridor and set off in the same direction as the two women.

They soon found themselves in a flow of administrative staff as they walked deeper into the admin wing.

Ten minutes of walking and the crowd became thicker. Not as

bad as it had been back in the labs, but enough to cause Grace to worry. She and Harry kept their heads down, not wanting to be recognised.

"Up ahead," whispered Harry, "look."

Grace craned her neck past the crowd in front of her and saw a broad set of double doors. They soon filtered through the entrance into a large cavernous room, some sort of conference hall. It was lit brightly, in contrast to the dim glow in the rest of the Facility, and buzzed with conversation and agitation.

Eight queues started halfway down the hall and led towards the end of the hall where the wall had lifted to reveal eight large elevator doors.

"One hour and fifty-five minutes."

"Plenty of time," said Grace, speaking freely. All eyes were focused on the lifts - no-one cared who she and Harry were anymore.

"What now?" said Harry.

"We have to find Taylor."

"I imagine he's long gone."

"Even so, let's look."

They walked slowly around the edge of the crowd trying to be inconspicuous in their scanning of the queues.

Harry put his hand on Grace's shoulder. "Look, over there."

In the corner a group of men stood, talking amongst themselves, looking calm, relaxed. Taylor was among them.

"We can't do anything here," said Grace. She motioned to the soldiers standing by the elevator doors. "We'll be shot within seconds."

Within seconds, however, their problem was solved. But another one began.

Chapter 9

At first, it was one scream. Ear-splitting and coarse. It took a few seconds for Grace to realise it was a man screaming. The sound was so piercing, so visceral, that it immediately struck cold fear into her.

Within seconds, more screams followed, like a wave, increasing in volume, spreading like fire through the large hall. A sudden surge of movement pushed against Grace and Harry, away from the door of the hall towards the elevators.

"What's happening?" shouted Grace.

"I don't know," said Harry, frantically looking around.

Grace grabbed Harry's hand, acutely aware she didn't want to lose sight of him.

"This way," shouted Harry. He wrapped his arms around Grace in a loose bear hug and pushed through the crowd, towards the wall, towards Taylor.

They were bumped and pushed by the mob. Harry and Grace fought hard to keep their trajectory steady, and away from the drag towards the elevators and the building sardine crush.

A momentary break in the crowd offered Grace a window of sight to the doors of the hall.

A man in a suit stood there. His shirt was covered in thick red blood, as was his face, rivulets of red dripping from his open mouth. His lips curled back, like a rabid dog. The right side of his head was missing skin. His skull was plainly visible, dabbed in globs of thick purplish material.

The man opened his mouth and let out a moan - a vast, sky-filling moan that silenced the hall for a few deathly seconds, before the screams began again, louder, more acute, more desperate.

The man, the zombie, hissed and slowly lurched towards the crowd. It latched onto a middle-aged woman and tore into the flesh at the back of her neck. Blood spurted high into the air.

Grace closed her eyes and held in a scream. Harry plowed through the crowd, eventually reaching the wall.

Grace breathed fast. She felt nauseous, and her legs shook.

"What is it, are you ok?" said Harry.

She nodded, trying to catch her breath. She managed to say, "Did you see that?"

Harry shook his head. "Saw what?"

"The man, the zombie."

"Here?"

She nodded frantically. "Here."

They were pinned against the wall, bodies and panic encasing them in a pulsating wall of flesh.

Grace looked towards the elevators. It was now the only way out.

"We have to get in the elevators," she shouted.

Harry wrapped his arms around her again and set off towards them, pushing, shouting his way through. Grace thought she even saw him snarling. She felt him breathe, felt his heart beat fast, felt his muscles strain as he fought his way through the crowd. It was a battle for life.

An old woman, Grace recognised her as one of the cleaners, fell as Harry barged passed her. She disappeared into the forest of entangled limbs below.

They reached the elevator door. It was full.

Harry and Grace pushed through, displacing some older and weaker admin staff. Harry received a punch but continued his drive through. They needed to get away from the door, or they would be caught in a continuous fight to hold their place.

They reached the middle of the elevator. Grace, who was facing over Harry's shoulder, looked back to the door. Row after row of heads trying to get in, trying to live.

The lift doors tried to close, but met resistance, and opened again.

A few feet away from Grace, just outside the lift, blood spurted high into the air. A guttural scream accompanied the sight. Panic spread through the elevator like a raucous beast, every member of the lift trapped, staring at the new arrival, a zombie, only feet away.

"Override, dammit, the door override!" shouted a lonely voice from the back of the lift.

Whoever was at the lift controls heard, for suddenly the lift doors closed, and did so with vicious authority. They stopped for nothing, but ran across feet, legs, and faces, sheering skin from those on the boundary.

They shut with a majestic clang, and accompanying yells of agony from a few by the door. The doors were covered in thick Rorschach patterns of blood.

"My hand," shouted one man, "my fucking hand!"

But no-one cared because the zombie was outside and the doors were closed.

The elevator shuddered and whining electric motors reverberated through the metal walls. An expectant silence settled on the occupants, joined in panic, fear, and anticipation.

The sound of creaking metal cables came from above, and the lift began to slowly ascend.

"There's too many of us," whispered Harry. They were still crushed together in the middle of the elevator. The breath and sweat of the crowd were raising the temperature. Perspiration broke on Grace's back and forehead.

The elevator moved, but slowly. There was a long way to go.

Grace shifted, and Harry loosened his grip on her as much as he could. She looked up at him, and him down at her. They smiled, but just for a second.

The elevator shook, and a high pitched whipping sound rattled in the shaft above. They all lurched to the left with a chorus of screams.

"There are too many people," said a deep, powerful voice from the back that brought silence to the crowd.

"There are too many people, we need to lighten the load," repeated the voice.

Grace looked for the source of the voice.

Taylor.

He was in the corner of the elevator, standing straight, his manner relaxed and calm, his expression imperceptible.

All eyes were on him.

"If we don't lighten the load, then we are all going to die, and rather soon."

Silence settled over the occupants in the elevator. As if to underline what the man, Taylor, had just said, a loud and pained creak vibrated through the elevator. It swayed gently.

"The longer we refuse to take action, the closer we all are to plunging to our deaths."

The elevator had stopped rising.

A few muffled sobs were heard. Fear spread quickly like a white flash through Grace's body. Harry's heart, pressed against hers, thumped vigorously. The elevator, a few seconds ago their sanctuary, now felt like a tomb. The bodies pushing around her felt like many flesh vices slowly squeezing the life from her.

Silence. The weighing up of the meaning of Taylor's words.

Grace looked up, trying to catch Harry's eye but instead, her attention was drawn to the ceiling.

What looked like a service hatch.

"What about that," she said, trying to point but unable to raise her arms, pinned by the weight of the crowd. "Look above, the hatch, maybe we can get out there," she shouted.

There was a gentle commotion in the elevator as the others looked up.

"She's right."

"Let's use the hatch."

Taylor interrupted the brief celebration. "And then what, we sit on the roof?"

Grace felt anger overcome her fear. It was as if he wanted to see people die.

"There should be a ladder," said Harry. "There's bound to be some sort of service ladder."

More voices joined in agreement.

Grace and Harry were below the service hatch. Harry turned to the man behind. "Climb up on my back, open the hatch."

"I don't know if I-"

"Do it," said Harry.

The man, slight and in a suit too large for him, clambered clumsily onto Harry's shoulders, helped on by many a pushing hand. The man balanced on his knees and reached up to undo the simple catch before opening the hatch. After a few tries, the trap went up and over and clanged to rest on the elevator's roof.

A draft of cool air blew in, and Grace felt immediate relief. Not only physical; a weight left her heart. The tyranny of the metal coffin had been broken.

"Can you pull yourself up," shouted Harry.

"I'll try." He pulled until his head and shoulders were through the hatch.

"What do you see," shouted Harry, "any ladders?"

"Yes, there's a ladder. It looks like it goes the whole way up."

Sighs of relief echoed throughout the elevator. A few nervous laughs.

"Thank God," said a voice from somewhere behind Grace.

The man pulled himself up onto the ceiling of the elevator. Metallic footsteps echoed from above. He called down. "The cable has snapped, only partway through though."

"Will it hold?" shouted someone behind Harry.

"I think so. I can hear engines whirring, but nothing's moving."

"One at a time everyone," said Harry, "then help the next person up before you get the ladder."

"What about you?" said Grace to Harry, quietly.

"I'm ok. You go next."

Grace shook her head. "No, I got you into this, I'm staying here to help." She looked at Harry, giving a look she hoped indicated there was to be no discussion. It worked.

"Ok, come on!" said Harry.

The crowd came alive again as people jostled for position, trying to get closer to the hatch.

"One at a time," shouted someone.

"Stop pushing."

"You're making it swing."

A woman clambered up on Harry's back, and with the help of those below and the man above, she was soon onto the roof.

Another woman followed, and then a young man in a technician's uniform. The crowd waited with nervous patience. Thank God, thought Grace.

It was after six people had got up and out that everything changed.

It started with a panicked voice from the corner of the elevator. "Oh my god, let me through, get me out of here! It's one of them!"

Chapter 10

Screams rang through the elevator and it swung from left to right as the weight shifted under the panicked stampede away from the corner.

A man on Harry's shoulders, about to pull himself through the hatch, fell as hands grabbed at him. He disappeared into the throng of legs below.

And then there was a pause in the chaos…

A terrible, deep noise. A moan that filled the air, an eruption of dread from the corner from the elevator.

Desperate cries of anguish cut the thick air in response. All semblance of order evaporated. Harry pushed himself and Grace away from the under the hatch as they suddenly found themselves under a mass of bodies trying to climb out.

"Come on Harry, to the wall," shouted Grace.

Another soul-wrenching scream and a fountain of blood spurted high. It splattered a dark red pool like squashed coral on the ceiling. It was followed by the hideous sound of bones crushing and tendons ripping.

Grace and Harry reached the wall. She could see Taylor, only four people away. So close. He stood still in his corner, placid; although a few strands of hair had escaped his lacquer's hold and hung over his face.

A man nearby pulled himself up on the lady's shoulders in front of him. She buckled under the weight, and they both fell.

"What now?" said Harry.

"I don't know," said Grace. She hugged him tighter.

She saw Taylor move from the corner of her eye.

Taylor's hand moved into his suit jacket and emerged with a gun. The gun that had killed the Professor.

He raised it into the air and fired. A deafening bang split the atmosphere of the elevator, and a sharp clang followed as the bullet passed through the metal roof.

Another second of silence, another shock.

Renewed panic.

A moan, answered by another, then the crunch of something breaking, maybe a bone. The ripping sound of flesh. Screaming again in earnest. The death throes of a crowd of people with no way to escape.

Taylor fired again, and again.

"Open the doors!" His voice boomed like that of God. It cut across all the screams, all the terror.

Eventually silence.

He levelled his gun through the crowd and pulled the trigger. The bullet hit a woman with red hair and a white suit in the head. A small hole in her forehead, but the back of her skull opened like a garish orchard.

"Open the doors, or I'll kill you all before they do."

He fired again and this time a young man, Grace recognised him from the canteen, fell back, his head dashed with thick rivulets of red.

The elevator lurched to the left as the people shifted, away from the man with the gun, away from the zombies.

One person had been paying attention though. The doors hummed into life, and they swished open, quickly. The black walls of the elevator shaft stood empty against the lights of the elevator, like the abyss. There was a gap of a few feet between the doors and the shaft wall.

"Puuuushhh!" shouted Taylor, suddenly a circus ringmaster. He was smiling. The men around him were smiling. And they pushed against those nearest to them.

Like a wave, their pushing rippled through the crowd until it reached those at the edge of the door.

The front line grabbed the side of the door, grabbed other people, knuckles white with desperation.

"Help!"

"Please, stop!"

"No!"

One by one, they slipped over the edge, some pushed by those next to them.

Screams sounded then diminished in pitch and volume as their owners fell down the shaft to the ground below. A series of sickening thuds punctuated each dying cry.

One after another. And still, the people pushed.

Grace buried her head in Harry's shoulder, and she screamed into his chest. Her heart beat viciously.

"Puuuussssshhhhh!" shouted Taylor above the pandemonium. Over and over again.

The pressure against her and Harry diminished. They had room to breathe.

Room to despair.

More screams, more thuds.

The moaning had stopped.

The was a jerk and the whine of machinery.

The lift started to move, slowly at first, then it picked up speed. A bump as it passed over the damaged part of the cable.

Grace took her head out of Harry's shoulder and pulled back. The lift was nearly empty, only ten people were left; her and

Harry, Taylor and his four friends, and two men and one woman, standing still, staring at the lift shaft, tears streaming down their faces.

One of the men was jabbering, repeating over and over again, "We had to do it, we had to do it, we had to do it."

"Well done everyone," said Taylor. He walked to the door of the elevator and looked over the edge.

She could run now, and push him, She could kill him just like that.

Taylor turned and looked Grace in the eye, holding her gaze.

She was rescued from his stare by a series of heavy thumps on the ceiling. It was the people who had made it onto the ladder.

Feet appeared in the hole, and then a woman dropped down. She landed with a bump and looked around the elevator; confusion.

"Where is everyone?"

No one spoke.

The rest of those who had climbed dropped back in, one by one. The same confusion, but they didn't ask any questions.

"It looks like we are going to make it," said Taylor.

Grace opened her mouth and moved forward. Harry put a hand on her shoulder and stopped her. He shook his head, tiny movements.

Grace stopped and stood back against the cold elevator wall, waiting for them to reach the top.

The motors whirred quietly.

There was a blood stain on the floor of the elevator door. Five longs lines, where fingers had tried to grip before their owner plunged into literal and figurative darkness.

She was aware of Taylor's presence, just behind her. She could feel it like a homing beacon in her brain. Anger seethed through her body. She clenched her teeth and gripped her hands into a tight fist. Her nails dug hard into her palms.

But Taylor was right, they would have all died if he hadn't opened the door.

Her anger grew.

Chapter 11

There as no indication of the time it took to reach the top. Minutes, hours, Grace had no idea. Her mind was blank, like the snow that used to buzz on old TV sets when the aerial was broke.

The brightness of topside caught her by surprise.

The shaft ended suddenly, and the elevator was bathed in unnatural white light, blinding her for a second.

She blinked several times and rubbed her eyes. A mumble of conversation and the clank of footsteps on the metal floor shook her from her reverie.

Harry's voice. "Come on Grace, let's go."

Taylor walked past her, and she watched him as he walked ahead.

The topside receiving room was a large hall bathed in bright white light from powerful fluorescents. In the middle of the room was a line of desks with metal detectors and X-ray machines, like an airport. Grace was used to seeing the security checks manned by blanked face soldiers.

Today, they were all empty.

The group fell mute as if scared to break the watchful and deadly silence of the receiving room. Only the distant buzz of the lights broke the absolute emptiness.

Taylor walked ahead of the group, the other men in suits following him. His footsteps clicked and echoed like a metronome.

Grace walked after him, her eyes fixed on the back of his head.

"Grace," said Harry, following her. "Hey, Grace."

She continued walking. She didn't look at the other survivors, confused and exhausted, nor at the huge hall and its gleaming white. Her gaze was fixed on Taylor.

Harry pulled her arm. She spun around, the anger inside her wanted her arm to swing, but she stopped it, just in time.

Harry looked shocked. Had he sensed the aborted swing, or was it a look in her eyes? If her eyes looked like her mind felt, then Harry must think she was crazy. She breathed slowly and tried to fix herself in the present.

Harry guided her behind one of the security gates, behind a large metal detector.

"Are you ok?" he said, his voice low, his eyes darting up and down to see where Taylor and the others were.

She nodded. Then she shook her head. "I don't know."

The sounds of screams echoed in her mind. The sound of people scrambling for freedom, for life. And then the sight of them being thrown to the bottom of a lift shaft.

So she could live.

"We should let them walk on," said Harry. "I don't want to be part of anything that happens with those guys from now."

Anger dulled the pain, stopped the voices in her head. Her thoughts suddenly became clear. She shook her head at Harry.

"We need that USB stick."

"No," said Harry. "He has a gun. He's insane."

"Yes, he is," said Grace. She walked away, dodging Harry's attempt to hold her back.

Ahead, the other survivors from the lift followed Taylor blindly. They looked like they were drunk, dazed. They exited the receiving room.

Grace knew where they were going, she had taken this journey countless times. After the receiving room was a corridor that led into a series of offices. Fake offices staffed with fake office workers. Then followed an exit into a Ministry of Defence, or MOD, owned industrial estate. No-one knew it was owned by the MOD, to any visitors it looked genuine, but every company on the estate was a MOD front.

Then would then come to the car park. And beyond, the ordinary, non-MOD world.

Except none of it was normal anymore.

Grace followed Taylor closely. She heard Harry behind her, his voice whispering for her to stop.

But she didn't stop, she couldn't. If she stopped, the horror in her mind would start again.

Taylor and the band of numb survivors left the building, entered the car park.

When thinking about the events that occurred in the next minute, Grace was hard pressed to remember the full series of events. She had only several intense frames in her mind.

The normal sky. Grace had been surprised at that. It was blue, a lovely blue.

The stone in her hand. The large grey stone she had picked up from the garden separating the building and the car park.

Running, breathing deeply.

Shouts around her. Pushing away a hand.

Taylor turning to face her, to look at her. For the first time, his calm exterior shattered. True fear in his eyes.

The feeling of the rock hitting Taylor's face would haunt her more than the sight of the people dying in the elevator. The second she felt his skull crack, she knew she had made a mistake, a dreadful and terrible mistake. The rock hitting his head jarred through her arm, right to her spine, to her soul. But she couldn't stop. The only thing that could make it better was to do it again.

She followed him to the ground and reigned blow after blow on Taylor's face. The sight of his imploded face, white and fragmented skull mixed with bright red blood and purple flesh would stay in her dreams for years.

But she still couldn't stop.

Harry saved her. He pulled her off and wrapped his arms around her again, holding her tight.

"Sorry," she whimpered, staring at the dead body on the ground.

She looked around her. The people, the other survivors, stared at her in horror, their faces twisted in fear and disgust. They backed away.

"He would have killed you too!" said Grace, her voice breaking into hysteria. "If you had been standing closer to the door, he would have killed you too…" She trailed off. Her legs felt weak. Her knees buckled, and she fell to the floor.

The cold tarmac offered no comfort. She curled up next to Taylor's dead body. His pooling blood wet her cheeks. She tried to cry, but she was empty. Her mouth opened and closed in gaping gasps, like a suffocating fish.

There was the sound of scuffling.

Some shots.

Everything went black.

Chapter 12

Like a dream, the earth rumbled below her. It moaned and lurched, buckling under some unseen force. Like mountains falling.

Was it an earthquake?

She was too empty to care. She lay in her darkness and wished for the ground to swallow her up. It was the only way to clear her mind of the images of death that replayed over and over and over.

She slept.

Eventually, Grace opened her eyes. She was in darkness.

There were a few seconds of ignorance, and then the reality of the past day hit her like a train. Her breath left her, and she leaned to the side and threw up.

Hands held her shoulders, and a voice said, "Easy, it's ok."

It was Harry.

She wiped the vomit from her mouth. Harry gently moved her away from the sick. There was plenty of space for the two of them

- they were in one of the spacious fake offices. Harry helped her up and walked her to a nearby desk. He sat her down against it. Moonlight floated in through a skylight. The empty office, quiet and calm, was almost beautiful.

She looked at him for a moment. He was a handsome man. The Professor had been right. Just an hour or two before Taylor had blown his head off.

"Why are you still here?" she said.

Harry shrugged. "Where else would I be?"

"Anywhere but here. Don't you have a home to go to?"

"I don't know. I don't really want to know. Not yet. Besides, you needed my help."

"Didn't you see what I did?"

"Yes, I did."

"So, why are you still here?" There was an angry edge to her voice, but she couldn't help it. There was so much anger in her, it had to seep out somehow, or it would eat her up.

"He deserved it," said Harry. "I don't think you did anything wrong."

"I killed a man. In cold blood."

Harry let out a small laugh. "Taylor shooting the Professor in the head, that was cold blood. Pushing all those people out of the lift... he deserved it."

"But he also saved the lives of everyone who made it."

"Maybe."

She closed her eyes again, but the image of Taylor's face, imploded like a burst football, blood and skull mixed together in a red soup, flashed in her mind.

Her eyes shot open.

Harry had a bruise on his cheek. It looked like his lip had been bleeding.

"What happened?" she said.

"When you," he paused, "took care of Taylor, a few of his cronies went for you. I pushed them off and managed to grab the gun from Taylor's jacket. I took a few hits. But I managed to let off a few warning shots. They scattered."

"Now you're alone with me. You could be with them."

Harry ignored her and rummaged in his pocket. He pulled out a small item.

"The USB stick…" she said.

"I think we'll be struggling to find a computer to use it on. The power is gone."

The power was gone… The Facility was gone.

"What happened, did the bomb go off? I can remember… Something…"

"Yes, about thirty minutes after we reached the surface. You were passed out, I couldn't wake you. I dragged you into the office here, I wanted to make sure we were hidden from Taylor's lot in case they came back." He rubbed his forehead with his hand. His face looked pained. He looked older than he did yesterday. "No other elevators made it up. We were the only ones to get out."

So many dead, thought Grace. Was this just the beginning?

She rested her head back against the desk and let out a sigh. Her body shook involuntarily. Harry sat beside her, and she moved her head onto his shoulder.

"What do we do now?" she said. She didn't want to make any decisions. The last decision she made had killed a man.

"I don't know. We will have to leave here, and see what's outside. Is there anywhere you want to go? Anyone you want to see?"

Her mum. What had happened to her mum?

"We need to go to Bristol."

The Facility was halfway between London and Bristol.

"Should we be heading to the cities? Is it safe?"

Grace turned to Harry. She had tears in her eyes. "It doesn't matter. We have to find my mum. I promised her I would call her, but I didn't."

"Ok, Grace. We'll go to Bristol. We'll leave tomorrow."

She turned her body so she was facing Harry, and she eased

herself onto his lap. She wrapped her arms around his waist. If she buried herself in his warmth, in the life of another human, one who hadn't done the things she had done, she could almost feel the good energy. She could borrow it, and find enough peace to close her eyes and sleep.

Her body vibrated softly with sobs, and Harry stroked her hair until she drifted from the waking world.

In her dreams, she reached her home and Taylor was in her kitchen, leaning over a corpse. He lifted up his head, and his mouth dripped with blood and entrails. The corpse sat up, its neck hollow, the spine visible. It was her mother.

Grace leaped up.

It was still the middle of the night.

Harry was sleeping.

Tomorrow, she would have to enter the world again and see what was left. Of both the world and of her.

THE END

Thank you for reading Surviving the Fall. I hope you enjoyed it.

Please consider leaving a review - It should only take a minute, and helps get my work out there.

The story doesn't end here.

TURN THE PAGE FOR MORE…

AFTER THE FALL
Book 2 of The Fall Series

"Once I started this collection of eight stories this weekend, I couldn't put the book down"

"I have once again been on the edge of my seat because of this author"

STEPHEN CROSS

AFTER THE FALL
The world belongs to the dead

THE FENCE WALKER
Book 3 of The Fall Series

"S. Cross has written a fantastic series for zombie apocalypse fans"

"Go ahead and read the whole series. You will love it. Great job Mr Cross!!"

"I just finished the Fence Walker and loved it"

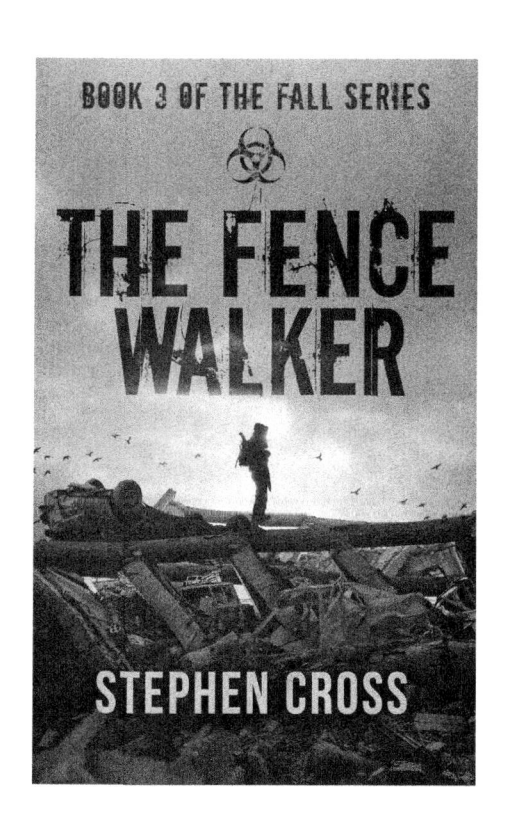

DARK ISLAND

"I don't always compare authors works… But at a certain point I kept thinking… Stephen king… That's all I'm going to say!!!"

"I cannot say enough good things about this book… I was hooked on the story from the beginning."

"I have been a fan of this authors work from the beginning… the book does not disappoint"